"*The Rakess* is a sexy, feminist, burn down the patriarchy romance with a delicious role reversal . . . Peckham lays bare all the ugliness of how women are treated from gaslighting to slut shaming to outright misogyny. And although the story is set late in the 18th century, there are elements of it you could easily see unfold today. Read it, read it, read it."

—DailyWaffle

"This fierce, feminist series debut flips the typical Regency romance script . . . Peckham strikes a perfect balance of politics, passion, and emotional vulnerability."

—*Publishers Weekly* (Summer Reads 2020)

"[T]he book that melted my ice cold heart and made me cry TWICE—Scarlett Peckham's *The Duke I Tempted*. It is BONKERS good. One of the best historicals I've ever read . . . It is devastating and emotional and a stunning book . . ."

—Sarah MacLean, *New York Times* bestselling author

The Portrait of a Duchess

BY SCARLETT PECKHAM

The Society of Sirens
THE PORTRAIT OF A DUCHESS
THE RAKESS

The Secrets of Charlotte Street
THE DUKE I TEMPTED
THE EARL I RUINED
THE LORD I LEFT

SCARLETT PECKHAM

The Portrait of a Duchess

SOCIETY OF SIRENS

AVONBOOKS

An Imprint of HarperCollinsPublishers

THE PORTRAIT OF A DUCHESS. Copyright © 2023 by Duchess of Peckham, LLC. All rights reserved. Printed in the United States of America. No part of this book may be used or reproduced in any manner whatsoever without written permission except in the case of brief quotations embodied in critical articles and reviews. For information, address HarperCollins Publishers, 195 Broadway, New York, NY 10007.

First Avon Books mass market printing: March 2023

Print Edition ISBN: 978-0-06-293563-2
Digital Edition ISBN: 978-0-06-293564-9

Cover art and design by Alan Dingman

Avon, Avon & logo, and Avon Books & logo are registered trademarks of HarperCollins Publishers in the United States of America and other countries.

HarperCollins is a registered trademark of HarperCollins Publishers in the United States of America and other countries.

FIRST EDITION

23 24 25 26 27   BVGM   10 9 8 7 6 5 4 3 2 1

For those not pictured

Author's Note

Dear Reader,

In building the world for the Society of Sirens series, I felt passionately that in portraying a group of radical women fighting for justice, it was important that they be intersectional. My characters are inspired by the racially, sexually, and economically diverse feminists, abolitionists, and reformers who have been on the front lines of the fight for equality and human rights throughout the course of history.

I want all of my Sirens to get the love stories they deserve. I have made every effort to be sensitive and authentic in my portrayal of Cornelia, Rafe, and all my characters—but I know I have my own biases and blind spots. I hope I have done Cornelia, Rafe, and their friends justice. Any mistakes I have made are my own.

Love,
Scarlett

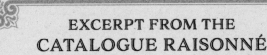

EXCERPT FROM THE CATALOGUE RAISONNÉ OF CORNELIA LUDGATE

WORK 4008:
THE BAPTISM OF THE JEZEBELS
Oil on Canvas
1797

Description: Four bare-breasted women in veils stand with linked arms in the foreground. Behind them, hundreds of aristocrats run from a stately manor wearing expressions of terror.

The women are smiling.

Commentary: The painting depicts the artist Cornelia Ludgate with three famed eighteenth-century proto-feminists: the radical author Seraphina Arden; the aristocratic matron and intellectual Lady Elinor Bell; and the infamous courtesan-for-hire Thaïs Magdalene.

Recurring figures throughout Ludgate's oeuvre, the close-knit group of women called themselves The Society of Sirens, so named for their revolutionary mission to weaponize their notorious reputations to raise interest in the cause of female rights and education.

The painting is from Ludgate's exhibition *The Jezebels*, which criticized the place of "fallen women" in society by posing them as holy figures.

The show was roundly denounced as sacrilege.

Ludgate considered it the triumph of her career.

Cornelia Ludgate tore open the wax seal on a letter and scanned the contents just long enough to see the word *regrets*.

Her stomach did an unwelcome little curtsy. This was not good news.

Another rejection. The third this week, the tenth this month.

"It's a no," she announced briskly, allowing the letter to flutter to the floor with all the other missives offering insincere excuses from her supposed allies in the cause for female rights. Her acquaintances should know she preferred to deal in cheerful, brutal frankness. Just the no's would do.

Her three best friends, scattered in poses around her painting studio in various draped costumes, groaned.

"Another?" Thaïs said with a dramatic sigh. "I've never been rejected so much in all my life."

Thaïs looked in a mirror, fluffing the red curls that fell down to her ample bottom. "At least not by anyone who's caught a look at me."

"Surely," Seraphina said, adjusting her baby daughter's head from the latch it held on her breast, "it is only a small matter of time until we receive a yes."

Cornelia did not wish to be the shatterer of hope, but there was no good news to offer—today, or in the future.

She gave her friends a rueful smile, preferring not to wear her devastation on her face. It was never good to betray such emotions, even with one's dearest friends.

"This is, in fact, the final no," she said briskly. "It seems we have run out of people to beg."

"What cowards," Cornelia's aunt, Lady Elinor, murmured.

Coward was too kind a word—*hypocrite* was more apt. Cornelia had expected some of their acquaintances to be reluctant to host her latest artistic exhibition. Wealthy liberals had once clamored for her paintings back when her work had been known for nothing more dangerous than light political subversion and a whiff of the erotic. But after this past autumn, when the four of them had torn apart the country's papers with their calls for rights for women, the name Cornelia Ludgate no longer meant mere scandal.

Now it meant sedition.

It meant danger.

It meant *no*.

"I suppose it's a measure of our success that no one will risk association with your work," Seraphina mused. "We wanted a war of shock and scandal, and we've gotten one. Now we have to fight for what we need."

And fight they had.

The battle they had waged the previous year to raise money for female rights had been an unqualified success. They were all infamous women, notorious for their liberal politics and wayward reputations. They had decided to use the public's prurient interest in their wild lives to raise money for their cause: founding an institute devoted to women's equality and education.

So far, using the sale of Seraphina's explosive memoirs, they had raised enough money to buy a handsome piece of land in northern London, where they planned to build the Institute for the Equality of Women. The trouble was, it had been *exactly* enough money for that handsome piece of land. To begin construction of the building they imagined—a place that would serve as a female sanctuary and bastion of progressive thought and education—they needed another round of funds.

But they were, once again, broke.

Which meant it was Cornelia's turn to rattle the liberal coffers of the country for coins. Her plan was to hold an exhibition of her most shocking portraits yet—a series called *The Jezebels* that depicted whores and fallen women as madonnas.

If the advance rumors already surrounding the exhibition were any indication, the series would raise enough money for them to finance the first phase of construction of the institute.

But one could not sell paintings if one could not display them. Without a space to show her work, there would be no exhibition, and no more money, and no Institute for the Equality of Women, and the cause of female rights would languish for another hundred years, and all their efforts would be wasted—

But that was desperate thinking. And if there was one quality Cornelia Ludgate did not enjoy applying to herself, it was desperation.

"We'll find a way," she said, taking care to evince a calmness she didn't quite possess. "We just have to think."

"Of course we will," Elinor said. "Perhaps we could let a venue."

"We'd need ample coin for that," said Thaïs. "And we're overspent."

Cornelia repressed the urge to slump down on the

floor and put her head between her hands. They had fought so hard to get here, risked so much. To be stymied by the nerves of people who purported to agree with them but were not brave enough to help was so dispiriting. People liked the idea of a fight. They liked to write essays in support of fine principles, to discreetly send banknotes. But they were markedly less courageous when it came to putting themselves directly in the line of fire.

A slow knock sounded at the studio door, startling all of them.

"What's that?" Thaïs hissed.

"Company," Seraphina drawled. "Just what we don't need in our hour of despair."

"Cornelia?" a man's voice called tentatively through the closed door.

Cornelia jolted up so sharply her neck cracked.

"It's Rafe Goodwood," he added, as though she would not know his voice deep down in her bones.

She gestured at her friends to cover up, smoothed her painting smock, which was sludged with oil from her palette, and rubbed the paint off her hands as best she could.

She felt her friends' eyes on her as she walked to the door, inhaled deeply, and opened it.

Rafe Goodwood stood in the doorframe, smiling at her.

She inhaled so sharply it hurt her throat.

He was more handsome than he'd been twenty years ago, when she'd last set eyes on him. Back when he'd been the most beautiful person she'd ever seen.

You hadn't seen many people yet, Cornelia.

"I'm sorry. I've surprised you," he murmured.

His voice was still the sound of oak, an appealing

well-worn timbre with a warmth that hit her like a dram of whiskey.

"I didn't think you were capable of being surprised," he added.

She rarely was. But to see him, *now*, standing a foot away from her—

She tried to find the words to greet him, but did not have a single one at her disposal.

Luckily, her aunt stepped forward. "Mr. Goodwood," she said, smiling. "Or, I should say, Your Grace. Please, come in."

He walked inside, his shoulder brushing Cornelia's as he passed. His touch made her shiver. She stepped away as subtly as she could, moving across the room to the windows as Rafe bowed to the ladies in the room.

"Please, call me Rafe," he said. "Every time I hear 'Your Grace' I think of funerals."

Elinor grimaced, shaking her head. "Ghastly. Seven, I think?"

Rafe clicked his tongue. "I hope I'm not the eighth."

Rafe had not been heir to the Rosemere dukedom when Cornelia had known him. That had been her cousin Ludo, until Ludo was killed on the way to visit a plantation in Barbados (repellent fellow, Ludo). He'd been succeeded as heir apparent by her third cousin, Peregrine, who promptly died of syphilis. (A pity; she'd liked Peregrine.) Then there'd been a curate from somewhere in Devon, who'd had a heart attack while being visited by God at a revival.

After that, she'd lost track of the parade of doomed heirs. It was too depressing.

She and Rafe would have laughed until they lost air to think that he would inherit the title back when they'd been, so briefly, confidantes. And now here he was.

A bloody duke.

She turned to face him, her composure restored by the irony of his title. "Congratulations on reaching the top of the succession," she said, for she needed to say *something* to acknowledge his presence in the room. "And be careful."

He flashed her a wry grin. "Thank you. I assure you I shall try."

She bit her lip to avoid returning his smile. It had been ages since they'd last shared a joke. And he'd changed into the kind of person she did not find amusing.

She did not consort with Tories.

A pity he'd become one. She used to like him.

Thaïs stepped forward, allowing the sheet draped over her shoulders to fall down a bit, exposing more than a hint of shapely, creamy, freckled arm.

"Who are *you*?" she asked Rafe, in a voice that implied whoever he was, she liked the looks of him.

Oh. Cornelia hadn't introduced him. How ridiculous that she was too busy trying not to stare to perform the basic courtesies she'd been trained in since her birth. She needed to collect herself.

She was a woman of poise and social graces—not a girl who froze in shock at the sight of an old acquaintance and cowered, paint-bespeckled, in the corner of the room.

She snapped up and affected the gracious smile she'd learned in aristocratic drawing rooms as a child—the one that, thankfully, was so ingrained in her manners that she could apply it even now, when she'd rather shrink from Rafe than introduce him.

"Ladies, my apologies, I'm being rude," she said in her loftiest tone. "Seraphina Arden, Thaïs Magdalene, allow me to present the Duke of Rosemere. My late uncle's heir."

Thaïs instantly fell into a low curtsy borne, Cornelia suspected, more of a desire to show off her legendary cleavage than as a gesture of respect.

Sera, who did not believe in curtsying, merely offered the same polite nod she might have afforded a beggar on the street and continued nursing her child.

"A pleasure, ladies," Rafe said. "I believe I recognize you from Cornelia's drawings."

He knew her work? That she was not expecting.

"Oh, have you seen them decried in the Tory papers?" she asked breezily. Her sketches were often reproduced in print as a symbol of dissipation threatening the stability of the country.

"I've read all about them," he said, his tone light. "I'm not a philistine, you know."

"I'm afraid I don't know *what* you are," she said.

She stared him down, watching him chew over the meaning of her words. She took care to hold herself erect, to be serene, but it was difficult as her famed composure apparently could not withstand the effect Rafe had on her. She felt as though her bones had turned to tallow, making her wobbly.

"I wondered if we could have a word in private," Rafe said, smiling at Cornelia as though there was no reason she'd say no.

As though he had not betrayed what had once been their shared beliefs.

As though he had not worked for her uncle and his foul Tory compatriots, breeding their horses, for years.

She knew by way of her wealthier friends that he'd risen to be a figure of some stature in aristocratic circles—a man sought after for his touch with magnificent steeds. The Rafe she'd known before all that—the humble horse trainer who'd lived in a cottage on her uncle's estate and been a member of the Equalist Society, espousing all sorts of liberal views—had disappeared. No one had heard from him in at least a decade.

The loss of him—the Rafe she'd thought she'd known—had always shaken her. Which was why she'd made a point not to think of him, and did not wish to see him in the tranquil sanctuary of her painting studio.

"His lordship can have more than a word from Cornelia, by the looks of him," Thaïs whispered to Sera in a much louder voice than was even remotely discreet.

Cornelia straightened, whirled around. "Ladies," she said, "why don't you go upstairs to my apartment and have some tea. Rafe and I are overdue for a conversation."

"Twenty years overdue, in fact," Rafe murmured, his eyes locked on hers.

When he stared at her like that, she couldn't move.

"Of course," Elinor said immediately. "Excuse us." She gestured for Seraphina and Thaïs to follow her. They pried their eyes away with obvious reluctance and made off toward the door.

Cornelia shut it tightly behind them, trapping herself with Rafe. The room felt clouded over despite the bright light streaming through the windows. The ghost of their relationship shrouded her like a cloak.

"It's good to see you, Cornelia," Rafe said.

It was also good to see him—in a purely visual sense. He was a sight that begged for painting. His dark hair was shot through with silver now, which brought out his blue eyes, and his face had more distinction—the sharp jaw and cheekbones of a man at the peak of his maturity. His white skin was tanned to honey gold, as it always had been from his life of riding horses. With his brawny build and thick thighs set off by fitted buckskins, he looked like some sort of equine god.

On any other man, she'd enjoy such a sight.

On Rafe, she could not afford to.

She knew where that path led.

"I can't say I expected to see you again," she said.

If he noticed the coldness in her tone, he didn't acknowledge it. Instead, he grinned, and produced a sheaf of papers from a leather case.

"I come bearing what I think might be welcome news," he said, smiling in a way that made his eyes a pool of light.

He handed the document to her. "Page thirty-nine."

She took care not to touch him as she took the pages from his hand.

The document was marked "The Last Will and Testament of Charles Ludgate, Duke of Rosemere"—her uncle. And on page thirty-nine her name was written out in bold.

15.9.2. TO MY NIECE, CORNELIA LUDGATE, I BEQUEATH:

1. The sum of five thousand pounds, contingent upon her being wed and situated in a domestic residence in a state of holy matrimony, verified to the satisfaction of my executor by the time of the settlement of my estate.

She put her hand on the windowsill to avoid falling to her death from shock.

She had not spoken to her uncle in twenty years, when she'd fled his home at the threat of coerced marriage, abandoning her dowry, her worldly possessions, and her good name.

Then, he'd wanted to control her. Now he was still at it, from beneath six feet of dirt.

Good to see you remain a bully, Uncle. Enjoy the fiery gates.

She shook her head at Rafe. "It's my punishment for defying him, to dangle a carrot that may as well be a stick. He must have known I needed money and could not resist his final chance to torment me."

Rafe smiled at her. "A pity for him you're already married."

Already married.

There it was. The secret that had echoed back and forth between them since he'd walked into the room.

She unfurled her clenched fingers, forcing herself to maintain an unaffected air. "A pity for me that neither myself nor the man I'm married to would admit it in a thousand years."

He looked directly into her eyes. "Would they not?"

Why was he looking at her like that? So soft and kind.

"You think I'd be so hard-hearted as to deprive you of your inheritance?" he asked quietly.

A pause—a very long pause—fell between them as his meaning hit her like a sack of flour to the chest.

"What are you suggesting?" she asked, her voice rising higher than she liked.

He gave her that easy smile, as though this conversation was not at all odd.

"That we publicly announce you are my duchess."

Duchess. His *duchess.*

She dug her thumbnail into her index finger, trying to prod herself into a cool response.

He didn't wait for her to answer him.

He took her hand in his and gave her that old, seductive, sidelong grin.

"One last marriage of convenience, darling? For old times' sake?"

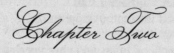

Chapter Two

Cornelia Ludgate stood gaping at Rafe with the erect posture of the fine lady she'd been raised to be. She'd always had the carriage of a duchess.

And now he was going to make her one.

It was only right.

He squeezed her fingers, urging her with his eyes to trust him. She pointedly removed her hand from his and waved it at him in dismissal.

"You can't be serious, Rafe."

Rafe. He got a little jolt of pleasure at the sound of his given name. So few people had called him Rafe in the several months since he'd become the heir apparent to a duchy. It was always *sir*, or *Mr. Goodwood*. Now it had become *Your Grace*.

It irked him. He'd rather be called "you rotten bastard" than assume a title at the top of an aristocracy he'd prefer to see abolished than ascend.

And then there was the fact that he was not only a duke, but the Duke of *Rosemere*.

The previous Rosemere's money came from labor he paid a pittance for as he lived in lavish luxury on an inherited estate he barely tended, while his tenants languished in near poverty. It was supplemented by investments in shipping firms that transported rum and sugar from the West Indies back to Britain—never mind that his niece, Cornelia, shared blood with chattel slaves on her mother's side.

Rafe loathed Rosemere and everything the man had stood for.

By a chance of birth he'd been given the man's name. But he would not take on his character.

And the first thing he wanted to do was right the egregious way Rosemere had treated Cornelia. Rafe's old friend. Rafe's *wife*.

He knew she'd hate to be thought of as "his" anything. But the sight of her—her brown eyes as bright and defiant as they'd ever been, her poise covering what he knew was shock at seeing him—brought back that old feeling that had always blossomed in his chest since he'd first met her: a desire to protect her. To make sure the world was safe for her to shine as brightly as she could.

"I'm proposing, Cornelia, that we get your uncle back for what he did to you," he said. "And all the other people the callous bastard has harmed."

She looked at him like he was a clot of phlegm he'd just coughed upon her shoe.

Not the answer he'd been hoping for.

"That callous bastard," she drawled with a tight smile, "has so amply buttered your bread for so many years I'm surprised you don't have gout. But then, I suppose you aren't famed for your loyalty, are you?"

Oh, that hurt—and she knew it, judging by the satisfied expression on her face.

Not that he was surprised by her scorn. She had every right to be suspicious of him. He'd made Rosemere stallions among the most sought-after sires in the nation, and been paid handsomely by the duke for the privilege.

He knew how this must look to her.

Still, her suspicion saddened him. "I know you must believe me to be your uncle's ally," he said. "And indeed, on the surface at least, I was. But things are not as they appear. I'd hope you know me well enough to allow I might have had—still have—good intentions."

He'd had sound reasons for getting close to the duke and his Tory friends. And they had nothing to do with money, or even horses. But he couldn't tell her that. Not yet.

"I don't know you at all," she retorted. She crossed her arms and drew her petite frame up to her full height. "And there is very little you could say that would make me wish to."

Another one that stung.

He wished he could tell her everything. Anything to wipe that disdainful expression from her face. But it was too dangerous to do so until he'd won her trust.

"Cornelia, I promise that I never meant to hurt anyone. Abandoning the cause was painful, but I had to do it for the sake of my work. It's complicated, and I can't account for twenty years in a single afternoon."

She shrugged. "In that case, you should leave."

God, her contempt was difficult to bear. He missed the way she used to look at him—like he was a favorite toy she couldn't wait to play with.

"I will leave if you desire it," he said. "But first, please let me explain my proposition. You don't have to like me to yield the benefits."

She raised a brow at him, skeptical. "I'm more curious what benefits *you* expect to yield. No man would invite such scandal without wishing for something in return."

She was right. He did want something, and it was not merely the privilege of her company—as much as he looked forward to enjoying it—if he could convince her of the wisdom of his plan.

"I want your expertise."

She gestured at her studio, hung with paintings. "In art?"

He scanned the room, which was paint splattered, vibrant, and disorganized in a way that contrasted with Cornelia's intense self-possession. There were sketchbooks scattered everywhere, the air smelled like turpentine, and the walls were lined with portraits.

Stirring, gorgeous portraits. Portraits he'd longed to see in person for so long he couldn't help but gaze at them.

There was a particularly striking one of a Black man in the regal gold-trimmed uniform of a general, begging in a dingy square. It must be from her series on enslaved men-turned-soldiers who'd been abandoned by the Crown in spite of their service to the British in the American revolt.

The gravity of the image contrasted with a lively, joyful painting in bright, cheerful pastel hues of Lady Elinor Bell, whose nudity was covered only by a buffet of artfully placed desserts.

Rafe's eyes lingered on a third portrait, a somber image of the radical printer Jack Willow, who'd disappeared six months ago, ceasing publication of his circular, *The Equalist Society*. In the painting Willow looked despairing and exhausted. The sadness it evoked made Rafe lose his train of thought.

"Well?" Cornelia prodded.

Focus. It's imperative that she agree to the plan.

"I'd like your advice on the running of Gardencourt Manor."

She looked as bemused as she might if he'd picked

up a glob of paint from one of her palettes and eaten it. Which was not exactly an unreasonable response, given that he knew she had not set foot on her uncle's estate in twenty years.

"Pardon?" she asked.

"You see, I'm planning to host a house party of several friends who can help me reform Gardencourt. And I'd like you to join us."

Her brow knit in obvious suspicion. "What do you mean by 'reform'?"

He smiled. He'd worked endlessly on his plan, and he was proud of it.

"Well, first I'm going to distribute the earnings of the duchy to the tenants in proportion to their labor."

Cornelia laughed, less a mirthful chuckle than a sputter of disbelief. "*You*, who abandoned the cause of justice years ago to set your lot with Tory nobs, would now like to turn the profits of a duchy to the *tenants*?"

He shrugged, for there was nothing else to do. "Yes. That is my hope."

She rolled her eyes. "Either you are lying or you have the steadfast values of a stick of mercury."

She'd always been frank, but her withering tone made him want to shrink away.

Even if, based on appearances at least, he deserved it.

It had weighed on him, what she must think of him, in the years since they'd lost touch. He'd only ever wanted her good opinion. Losing it was among the greatest of the sacrifices he'd made in committing his life to the cause that he believed in.

"I promise you, my intentions are sincere," he said.

She tossed back her head in frustration. "And why should I believe you?"

"If you come, I can prove to you my true loyalties

still lie with the radicals. You'll see the reforms I'm making. But to make them properly, I need a person with knowledge of the estate at my side. You were raised there. You were the mistress of the house. You know the place. And if you come to Gardencourt until the will is executed, and make known you are my wife, you will get five thousand pounds. So you see, we would both benefit."

Her mouth twisted in displeasure.

Even when she looked at him like that—like he'd just asked her to bite into a lemon—she was beautiful. Her eyes still darkened when she was annoyed—their flecks of gold flickering to umber. Her tawny brown skin was unmarred by age, her black curls pulled back in the upswept fashion she'd worn since girlhood. But she'd grown into herself, blossomed in a way that matched her character to her physical appearance.

He needed to stop admiring her. He was not here to repeat that mistake.

"You seem to forget that admitting we are married is the one thing you would never ask of me," she said.

He recalled. He recalled every single thing about his week with Cornelia twenty years ago. Every single thing.

"I know I promised. But just picture your uncle's world if you—the niece he cast aside—assumed its highest title. It would be just the kind of thing you're famous for—the kind of coup that would stir up the papers to no end."

She smiled at him like she pitied him. "A coup of *manners* is not the type I wish to be responsible for."

God, she was stubborn. She always had been, and he'd always admired her for it. But he did not enjoy having this quality turned against himself.

Whatever their past, he'd thought his offer would be too appealing to pass up. An aristocratic outcast revealed to be a duchess was a premise he could have pulled directly from Cornelia's portraits. Her fondness for restoring dignity to souls from whom society had stripped it was why her work was so coveted by some, and damned by others. And the more controversial her reputation, the more she seemed to sell.

"Cornelia," he said quietly, "you'll get *five thousand* pounds. You'd really turn that down?"

She sighed.

They both knew what her uncle had known: it would be very, very difficult for a woman of her means to reject that sum of money. It was a monumental, life-changing fortune.

And if anyone could do something important with a fortune, it was Cornelia.

She sucked on her bottom lip and rubbed the sleeve of her painting smock, clearly turning his proposition over in her mind.

"Let's say, for the sake of argument, I agree to attend your little party as your wife," she drew out slowly. "I would have demands of my own."

She regarded him with raised brows, like he would try to argue with her. Odd, since in his recollection, he'd never denied her anything she'd asked him for. He'd once agreed to *marry* her at an hour's notice, for Christ's sake.

"Certainly. Anything."

"I'll invite my own friends to Gardencourt."

That was manageable.

"Of course. Though I'd like to spend a few days with just the two of us before the group arrives, so you can become reacquainted with the place in privacy."

He suspected a return to Gardencourt would be emotional for her, given the circumstances in which she'd left it. And he happened to know she disliked being observed in states of high emotion.

She considered this, then nodded.

"Fine. But there is something else." She looked at him with challenge in her eyes. "I want to use Gardencourt for the debut of *The Jezebels*. My new exhibition."

It took him a few seconds to understand what she meant. "You mean you want to hold a painting exhibition at the house?"

"Correct."

"What an utterly unremarkable idea," he drawled. "Not shocking in the least."

She snorted, this time without scorn. He'd made her genuinely *laugh*. How refreshing. There was a time when he had done that frequently.

"You know I trade in irony," she said. "It is as much my art as my paintings are."

And a good test to see if he was lying about his politics, he reckoned.

Which he was not.

"I'm sure that can be arranged," he said.

She raised a brow, obviously pleasantly surprised he had agreed. Good. He liked eliciting any positive response, even if it was one predicated on the assumption he was a terrible man.

"Also," she went on, "I have no desire to be a duchess, and I despair at remaining married."

"Despair!" He grinned at her, attempting to use the charm for which he usually was known to his advantage. "That is rather unkind. I am not *so* bad."

He did not win another laugh. Instead, she wrinkled her nose.

"I certainly cannot be married to a *Tory*."

Obviously, it was going to take more than his word to prove himself to her.

"I promise you I'm not a Tory. I'm just a man with a passion for horses who worked for people who can afford to breed the best of them. If you come to Gardencourt, we can get to know each other once again, and I promise you that you will come to understand."

He loved the idea of getting to know who she was now that she was a mature woman of nearly forty years. He could see the self-possession she'd been known for in her girlhood had evolved into an intimidating confidence. He was certain it was hard-won, given what she must have faced in transforming herself from an aristocratic maiden into an infamous, radical artist.

He longed to know her.

"The past speaks for itself," she said. "Character is a question of one's actions, and yours bespeak a lack of integrity. You must promise me a divorce once the will is executed. Marriage is against my principles. *You* are against my principles."

"Fine," he said, for what else could he say? He could not force her to like him, only do his best to make her understand him. Besides, to end their marriage would not cost him a wife—he'd never had one anyway.

She sighed. "You're certain? It will be a terrible scandal."

"I do realize that. But no more than when we announce you are my duchess."

His duchess. The words gave him a thrill he knew better than to betray. Revealing he was proud of their connection—proud to be, in some way, hers—would do little to endear him to Cornelia.

"As to that," she said, "why are you so confident

anyone will believe we're married? Our only proof is a tattered witness paper from Gretna Green. Will it not raise alarm with the executor of the will, you suddenly having a wife when you have made no subtle thing of your desire never to marry?"

It would indeed stretch credulity. He was certain the few witnesses to their vows were scattered, forgetful, or dead. But he had a plan.

"If you come to Gardencourt, you will be in residence when the executor arrives to meet with me next week." He batted his lashes at her. "We'll pretend to be in love."

It would not be the first time.

Her face betrayed neither sentimentality for the past, nor humor.

"And what's to stop the executor from thinking it's a ruse?"

"I've thought of that," he said. "I will make it known to a few loose-lipped, high-placed souls that I was wed in secret as a young man, and intend to invite society into my home to meet my duchess in a fortnight. We shall have a masked ball where you will reveal your true identity. The solicitor will not be able to take exception to such a public display of wedded bliss."

She considered this. He saw it on her face as she worked through the possibilities and slowly, reluctantly, acknowledged the potential of the scheme.

It was very pleasing to watch.

"I suppose it could work," she mused. "I suppose for five thousand pounds, I could *see to it* that it works."

He suspected there was little in this world Cornelia Ludgate could not make work, if she put her mind to it.

"But I don't trust you," she said flatly. "And if you display even the slightest hint that you are lying or manipulating me, I will leave Gardencourt immediately."

The word *trust* brought back the last time they had seen each other. The way she had stared at him, looking beautiful and bereft at an inn in Gretna Green. How he'd fallen to his knees and wrapped his arms around her waist and begged her forgiveness. How she'd wrenched herself away.

This was his chance to redeem himself. To prove to her he was better than she thought he was. Better than he had been all those years ago. That he was a man she could trust.

He held out his hand. "We have an agreement?"

"For now." Tentatively, she reached out and touched his fingers. Her nails were speckled in paint. Her touch gave him a pang of longing so sharp he wanted to pull those fingers to his mouth and kiss them.

Instead, he dropped her hand and gave her a brisk nod.

"Then I'll send my carriage for you two days from tomorrow."

She laughed softly to herself. "Oh, I recall the duke's carriages. More luxurious than my bedchamber."

They were indeed. Everything at Gardencourt was comically indulgent. He was going to change that. But in the meantime, he was going to see that they both enjoyed it.

He grinned at her. "Do you know what, Cornelia? It's fun to be a duke."

She rolled her eyes at him. "Trust that I have never doubted that."

"And I think you may enjoy being a duchess. Just wait."

She shook her head.

"What I shall enjoy is leaving Gardencourt in a blaze of shame and ruin." She paused and gave him a long, satisfied look. *"Again."*

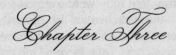

Cornelia made sure to seem cool tempered as she saw Rafe out. Having floundered more than she was accustomed to today, and in front of *him* no less, she wished to be perceived with her usual elegant composure as she said farewell.

She lasted until the door was shut behind him. At which time she promptly locked it, collapsed on a settee, and stared at the ceiling, shaking.

She felt as though the floor had turned to water, and she was struggling to float.

She and Rafe had promised to take their secret to their graves. As a matter of survival, she had pushed him from her mind, erecting a brick wall between her past and future—a task that had become easier over the years as Rafe's life had become tied to the sort of people that she loathed.

She'd shrunk him into a small, uneasy detail she rarely thought about. A slight pang in her side when she heard his name. A fleeting memory when she wore breeches, or smelled leather in the rain.

But it was a different matter entirely to be *near* him. For in person, he was no inconvenient detail. Nor was he the ogre she'd imagined when she heard his name in reference to Tory politicians.

She didn't know what he was at all, save for six feet, five inches of oddly friendly man with a wild scheme that could lead to wilder riches. Her instincts told her not to trust him, but they were overpowered by what she'd gain if the arrangement he proposed worked. For if she herself was shocked by the idea of revealing she was a duchess, imagine how the public would react. And she was in the business of inciting public reactions. It was the lifeblood of her art.

But first, she must elicit *private* reactions. A more unappealing task.

She locked the studio and climbed the stairs up to her jewel box of an apartment. It was half parlor and half bedchamber with a little hearth and table where one could cook, were one so inclined. Cornelia was rarely inclined.

"What was that about?" Sera asked immediately.

She and Elinor were sitting on the floor in their tunics, drinking tea and playing with Seraphina's daughter, Ella. They were a study in contrasts, Sera angular and tall with a mane of wild brown hair, Elinor short and plump, her perfect blond coiffure fading into white. Cornelia wanted to sketch them—were it not that she had to perform the odious chore of shocking them with her decades of a singular omission about her past.

"Something rather piquant, I'd gather, by the looks of you," Sera added.

Cornelia scratched the chin of her cat, Lucius, who was curled up on a sketchbook languorously licking a paw. She was not pleased they could see her discomfort on her face.

"There is something I need to tell you," she said quietly, with no earthly idea exactly how to phrase what she should say.

"Then you'd better wake our sleeping beauty," Elinor

said, smiling over at Cornelia's bed, where Thaïs was sprawled, wearing nothing but a sheet and her mermaid-length red hair, snoring.

Cornelia poked her foot. "You cannot possibly be asleep."

"I am, I am," Thaïs mumbled, throwing an arm against her eyes to block the light.

"Well then, wake up, slattern. There is something we must discuss."

Thaïs groaned so loud and long that Cornelia plucked a grape from the fruit basket on the window-sill and tossed it at her.

Thaïs, nimble in the art of erotic showmanship, caught it with her teeth.

"It is three in the afternoon, Thaïs," Cornelia said.

"Well, excuse me for needing rest, Miss Lady."

Thaïs enjoyed underlining the difference in their origins—Thaïs, an orphaned child of a brothel; Cornelia, an orphaned child of the fifth oldest family in England—when she was cross with her. Which was usually. They'd been bosom friends for fifteen years, and each year Thaïs had made a point to be ever more irascible.

Cornelia sat down at the edge of the bed, twisting her fingers as she gathered the courage to say the words.

"What is it, darling?" Elinor asked gently, her face evincing so much concern that it almost made Cornelia want to cry.

She had to brace herself to get it out. "I'm, erm— well, to start, I'm married."

Thaïs jolted up with such force the headboard of the bed slammed against the wall. "Wot! *To start?*"

As much as she found Thaïs's dramatics tiresome,

this was a fair reaction. Cornelia had long espoused the view that marriage was not compatible with her bone-deep zest for freedom. She might have yelled about it on multiple occasions, broken hearts based on the notion that the closer a relationship resembled marriage, the more it bore the chokehold of one.

She had done this without disclosing the technicalities of her matrimonial state.

Even if becoming shackled had been her idea, it was not one she had ever intended to publicly acknowledge.

Thaïs shot out of bed and marched to Cornelia, her pointer finger and her legendary breasts preceding her.

Cornelia slumped. "Oh, conserve your theatrics, Thaïs. I'm not finished."

"Can't do," Thaïs squawked. "You just told us something very, very wicked."

"Well, it gets worse, I'm afraid. It would seem I'm also—" she inhaled, smoothed her smock, gathered her resolve "—a duchess."

Thaïs froze.

Then she threw back her head and laughed.

And laughed.

She laughed until she had to hunch over, her hand pressed against her belly like she'd injured herself with her cackling.

It physically hurt to offer Thaïs such a mortifying morsel of gossip. Cornelia could feel it in her grinding teeth. She was usually a calm, even-tempered, even cheerful sort of person. Marriage was bad for her equanimity.

Meanwhile, Thaïs was galloping around, continuing to hoot even as she smacked her chest for air. Sera and Elinor only stared at Cornelia, their faces in matching expressions of disbelief.

"I'm still sore at you for ruining my nap," Thaïs said, "but to hear Miss Lady make her very first joke in all her days is worth it. Maybe by the time I'm old and dead you'll make another one."

She came and clapped Cornelia on the shoulder, her bosom bouncing so exuberantly the sight was likely against the law. "Oh, applause to you, my girl. Applause."

Baby Ella whimpered at all the noise.

Lucius hissed and ran beneath the bed.

Cornelia shrugged off Thaïs's hand. Her nails were long and sharp, and Cornelia didn't want them going errant and gouging out her eye.

"Very well, Thaïs, you've had your merry time of it. You are scaring the innocent child. And the poor cat. May I go on?"

Thaïs snatched a robe hanging from a peg—a damask chintz embroidered with nude figures frolicking *en flagrante* in hell that Cornelia was quite fond of—and shrugged it over her shoulders.

"Please, go on," Thaïs said. "I can't wait to hear your tale."

"Stop it, you two," Sera said. "Cornelia, tell us how it is you came to believe you are a duchess. I do hope the story does not begin with a blow to the head."

"I'm afraid not," Cornelia said quietly. "It's merely a convenient arrangement but legally speaking I'm married to . . ." She couldn't say it. Thaïs would burst the blood vessels in her eyes if she continued to quack on like this, and, as a legendary whore, Thaïs's income depended on her beauty.

Cornelia coughed, summoning her strength of will. "I'm married to the Duke of Rosemere."

"You can't mean you're married to Rafe Goodwood," Elinor uttered.

Her aunt searched Cornelia's eyes, waiting for her to reveal this to be another joke. The kind that no one found amusing.

Cornelia said nothing.

"You're serious?" Sera whispered. "You're *married* and you didn't tell us?"

They were used to her being close-lipped, she knew. But even she could see that this was different.

"It was years ago," she said, disliking the pleading in her voice. "*Decades* ago."

Thaïs grabbed the grapes and pelted one at Cornelia's forehead. "You rail against marriage every chance you get, and you never thought to say you've got a husband? Let alone a bloody Tory one?"

Cornelia thought back to that night. To her fear and desperation.

"You don't understand, Thaïs. I had no choice. Let me explain."

Chapter Four

Before

*I*t had been late, and pouring rain, and the knock—a staccato rap so deafening it drowned out the storm—had startled Rafe awake. He'd have thought someone was shooting a rifle in his parlor were it not that he'd recognized Miss Ludgate's voice calling out his name.

He barely knew Miss Ludgate, but he knew her voice.

He'd been mesmerized by it the few times they'd met. Miss Ludgate was every inch the dewy, well-bred maiden in her white frills and flowery bonnets—until that low alto came out of her mouth, a voice so cultured and sonorous that it made a melody of vowels and consonants.

At eighteen, she talked like most people recited poetry.

She pounded on the door again. "Mr. Goodwood? Ae you at home? 'Tis Miss Ludgate."

He found her standing on his paving stones looking as sodden as a sea sponge.

When she saw him, she closed her eyes. "You're home. Thank God."

"Miss Ludgate, what are you—"

"I'm unspeakably sorry for the intrusion at this hour. But may I please have a word with you? I'm desperate."

"Of course." He pulled open the door, though not without a moment's pause for what her guardian might think—or do—if he found out his ward was standing soaked in a horse trainer's parlor hours before dawn.

There was not time to worry over dreadful consequences, for as soon as Miss Ludgate stepped into the threshold of his home, she started sobbing.

He'd never seen her anything but poised to the point she was intimidating. He froze like she'd shot him dead.

Don't panic. They're just tears.

But tears were worse than bullets. He needed to make the crying stop. But how did one get a weeping, wet, young woman to collect herself when she appeared at one's door unannounced and without explanation in the middle of the night?

Same as anyone, he hoped.

Sit her by the fire, give her tea, and let her talk.

It must have been the right thing, for she surrendered to his care like an orphaned fawn who'd take mothering from a wolf.

He settled her in front of the fire with a steaming mug.

"Miss Ludgate," he said cautiously, sitting down across from her. "Has something happened to you?"

Poachers were known to prowl at night on the forest roads between his house and Gardencourt Manor. She could have been attacked, or worse. And if she had—

She shook her head. "No, I haven't been harmed." She paused, blew on her tea, and looked up into his eyes. "Yet."

Her voice broke on that final word. He wanted to gather her to his chest and stroke her back to soothe her.

"Tell me what's the matter," he said, keeping his voice gentle.

"I need a husband," she said. She drew a breath

and looked him directly in the eye. "And I hoped you might be him."

"I— Pardon?" He'd expected her to say something along the lines of "I've fallen off my horse."

"I'm sorry to ask. But I've gone through many calculations and you are the only person who can help me."

He felt guilty for doing it, but he laughed.

He couldn't help it. It was the strangest thing he'd ever heard.

He was a commoner. His closest claim to gentle birth was some old family Bible that proclaimed him the ninth-odd cousin of Miss Ludgate's uncle. He trained horses and sometimes bred them, when he could get the money for their keep.

She was the kind of girl who would marry the third son of a viscount. Maybe better, if her dowry was as hefty as the rumors held.

"I assure you, this is not a jest," she said.

"I'm sorry. I'm just imagining the likes of me as the only possible suitor for you. It's quite amusing."

"You don't know me very well, though, do you?" she asked evenly.

He shut up and let her talk.

Her explanation was halting, interrupted by many fortifying gulps of his bracingly hot tea. By the time she was done, she'd consumed the entire pot, told him a long story about painting lessons and a tutor from Vienna she'd been found with in the nude, and a list of dreadful suitors her uncle had threatened to make her choose among—or else.

"So you see," she concluded, "I must marry someone of my own choosing, before he marries me off against my will."

"What about your tutor?"

She snorted. "No, impossible. If I married him, he'd think I was his *wife*."

"That . . . is the resulting consequence of matrimony."

"Yes, and therefore you see why I have asked you."

"You are speaking in riddles," he said.

She smiled. "I love riddles."

So had her mother.

Her parents had died when she was an infant, but her composure reminded him distinctly of Demeter Ludgate, her mama. Cornelia's stubborn courage, however, was an inheritance from her papa. Even at his most well-mannered, Jamesy Ludgate had never held back the slightest impulse. It had made him brave. It had also gotten him killed.

And here was their daughter, a combination of the two of them in looks and temperament, staring at Rafe like he was the answer to a puzzle he couldn't see the pieces to.

"Please, explain, in a way my simple mind might grasp," he said.

"Mr. Goodwood, my aunt Elinor trusts you, and you knew my parents. So I thought you might understand the unfairness of my position and be willing to help."

"I'm still not sure why marrying me would help you."

"Because I'm not marrying to gain a husband. I'm marrying to avoid having one. To protect my freedom."

It was irritating to deal with an eighteen-year-old who was leagues smarter than you.

"You wish to marry me so that you cannot be forced to marry someone else by your uncle?" He hoped he was following her meaning.

"Yes." She paused. "I know it is a tremendous thing to ask, and that I am quite outrageous to ask it of you, given we are only so casually acquainted. I shall not prevail on you to accept my scheme if you are opposed to it. But I am desperate, and in going through the small list of men I know well enough to ask, your name came to mind. It's well-known among the girls in town that you are determined not to marry. Therefore, I hope I would not be depriving you of a chance for happiness by asking you this favor."

He had, in fact, sworn off matrimony repeatedly and publicly. He was not opposed to love—he welcomed it, fell into it constantly and with a fervor that often got him into trouble—but he was not the marrying kind.

"I won't prevail on you beyond a trip to Gretna Green," she said, not giving him a chance to talk. "I intend to go to Florence as soon as I'm certain my uncle can't capture me and make me marry someone else. I'm his ward, you see. And I'm eighteen. He has control of me for three more years."

Rosemere was more than Miss Ludgate's guardian— he was also Rafe's landlord and most coveted potential patron. Rafe was courting a prime role to help the duke establish a breeding stable to rival the top horse-flesh investors in Britain.

Winning Rosemere's ire would be most unwise.

Which made it odd that Rafe was entertaining this proposition.

But Jamesy and Demeter had been kind to him. They'd made introductions that had changed his life. Surely, were they aware their daughter was in danger, they would wish for him to help her.

Not that he was convinced he *could*.

"And how do you expect your uncle to react when you tell him you've married the horseman in the stable cottages?" he asked.

"I have no intention of telling him unless he captures

me. I have no intention of telling anyone. Were it not so difficult to procure an annulment, we could end the marriage when I come of age. But it's impractical and terribly expensive. So, if you give me your word, we'll simply go to our graves with the secret."

He worried she was being horribly impulsive. He hated the idea that tomorrow she might regret leaving her bed, let alone proposing marriage to a man she'd met three times who was nearly twice her age.

"You're aware that if anyone heard a whisper of this—even after you come of age—it would create a tremendous scandal. One that would be difficult to ever overcome."

She gave him a look that evoked bedrock. "I'm not afraid of scandal. I'm *afraid* of losing my freedom."

He loved her for that answer.

It was that answer that decided it.

He did not know why, for what she asked was mad.

Maybe he wanted to help her for her parents' sake.

Maybe he wanted to say yes because he knew what it felt like to have only options that did not fit the person that you were. To have to choose between concessions.

Maybe some part of him thought the gesture was romantic. Never mind that the romantic in him had always wreaked havoc on his life.

"Please, Mr. Goodwood," Miss Ludgate whispered. "Please help me."

By God, he would.

He extended his hand to her. "Well. If we're to be married, I suppose you should call me Rafe."

She clasped his hand, and her grip was hot and firm. "Cornelia."

Chapter Five

Seraphina, Elinor, and Thaïs stared at Cornelia, rapt, as she concluded the tale of her marriage. Even Seraphina's baby seemed fascinated.

"So you married Goodwood," Sera said. "And then what happened?"

Much.

But she would spare them that aspect of the story.

Spare them, and spare herself, for if she was going to spend a fortnight or more with Rafe, it would not do to linger in her memories of the past.

It was too tempting to focus on the good ones. And she'd never been much of one to deny herself temptations.

"I never saw him again," she said. "Until this afternoon."

"What was it like to see him?" Sera asked. Her voice was rather delicate, as if she gleaned that Cornelia was holding something back.

Confusing. Unnerving—

"Sexual, I reckon," Thaïs supplied, with a firm nod of the head and a wink at Cornelia.

"Pardon?" Cornelia and Elinor asked in unison.

Thaïs rolled her eyes. "Excuse me, dearlets, but I saw him in the flesh. If I'd been in a room alone with him, he'd not have kept his breeches on for long."

Cornelia was not going to discuss Rafe's breeches. It was not *good* for her to discuss Rafe's breeches.

"I am far too delicate for such coarse talk," she sniffed, in her best imitation of the drawing room damsels with whom she'd grown up.

"Oh, you're not," Thaïs crowed. "Not with him built like a stallion. You too, Sera. If you weren't pledged to Adam you'd climb him like a tree."

"I would never climb a Tory like a tree," Sera retorted.

"He claims his association with Tories is driven purely by pecuniary interest," Cornelia said. "He no longer needs their money, being a duke."

"And you believe him?" Sera asked.

Did she? She certainly did not trust his motivations. But she'd never known him to be an outright liar. His crimes were of betrayal, not dishonesty.

And there had been a time when he'd been reformist in his views. Was it possible he was being truthful when he said they hadn't changed? He was still a scoundrel for putting coin ahead of principle, but she did not need to admire his ethics to profit from the plan they had agreed upon.

"I don't know," she said. "But I have chosen to withhold judgment until I can get to Gardencourt and see for myself. He is having a house party, and I have agreed to join him in exchange for his agreement to host our exhibition."

Sera stared at Cornelia over her nose. "You talked Goodwood into hosting the most reviled portrait series of the century?" She glanced over at Thaïs. "Perhaps she did climb him like a tree."

"I did indeed. Talked him into it, that is, not climbed him. Can you imagine the scandal? A duke hosting a showing of my paintings? At my uncle's house? It's nearly too good."

Elinor looked unconvinced. "The irony is diabolical, to be sure. But I thought Goodwood had turned his back on the reformist cause. Why is it, do you think, he has agreed to this?"

She didn't know. She couldn't account for it herself.

But the claim piqued her curiosity. For all it had unsettled her, she'd never had a more intriguing afternoon.

She shrugged. "If it seems Rafe has some nefarious purpose, I'll simply leave."

She hoped she wouldn't have to. In part because she could nearly taste the revenge against her uncle. And in part because if Rafe *wasn't* lying—if he was not the scoundrel he had seemed—she might feel better about having chosen him to be her husband all those years ago.

She prided herself on her sound judgment and ability to read people. She'd always harbored a private shame that she'd been so wrong about him.

"I think it's worth the risk," Seraphina said. "If all goes to plan, it will be a vindication to use your uncle's bastion of supposed morality as the locale for your most scandalous exhibition."

"Rosemere deserves it," Elinor said with an uncharacteristic edge to her voice. "I only regret he could not be alive to squirm and seethe at the obscenity."

Elinor knew, more than anyone, how badly Rosemere had hurt Cornelia.

He had raised her from the time she was orphaned as a baby. Though he was childless, having lost three wives, he'd told her once that he considered her his own daughter.

And she'd believed him.

She'd enjoyed the role of pampered ducal ward, as any young girl would when made the princess of a charmed life. When her uncle's third and final wife had died in childbed, she'd assumed the role of the miniature lady of the house, and managed it with the ease of a girl raised to nobility.

Until, in the space of a single afternoon, Rosemere had turned on her as if she were no more to him than a maid who'd shattered an heirloom vase.

His love had been conditional.

Just like that of every man she'd ever known.

If they could not control you, shape you into what they desired you to be—you were not worth the ground on which you stood.

It was better to hold one's feelings in reserve than to risk that kind of pain.

Thaïs snapped her fingers in the air, thoroughly delighted. "Your rotten uncle will rot faster in his grave because of this."

"He will. And your revenge will be just the kind of thing you're famous for," Sera said. "The kind of statement that will stir up the papers to no end."

Cornelia laughed, picturing the scene. "When I imagine his precious ballroom filled with loose women and people of color and liberals and so-called seditionists . . ."

She had a thought. What if the ballroom were not *merely* filled with the types who made up her circle of friends and acquaintances?

What if the scandal were even bigger?

Rafe had said he was planning to reveal their marriage at a masked ball. Cornelia could hold a masked exhibition the same night, in the same place.

The events could be one and the same.

"Ladies. I think I have an idea," she said. "Rafe wishes to reveal our marriage at a masquerade ball before the ton. What if it were to be the same event as the exhibition?"

Everyone in the room looked at her quizzically. Not least Lucius, though he always looked somewhat quizzical.

"What do you mean, dear?" Elinor asked. "I'm not sure I understand."

"We could make the *Jezebels* exhibition a masquerade as well, and hold back the location until the day before, so the invited guests don't realize they're going to Gardencourt. Meanwhile, the ton could be invited for a masked ball at the same time. No one will have the opportunity to piece it together. The guests will all arrive in masks—half expecting a grand celebration, the other half expecting licentious art. And then, when Rafe reveals my identity, I'll reveal the portraits. The aristocrats will be horrified when they learn they are guests of my infamous exhibition, and my patrons will be so delighted by the scandal they'll pay double."

She watched the expressions on her friends' faces take on the singular sharpness that came with plotting wicked intrigue.

"Oh my," Elinor breathed. "That could just work."

"The portraits will sell for hundreds, for everyone will want a memento of the night of scandal," Seraphina said. "People all around the country will want a look. Collectors will be salivating."

It was true. Splendidly, gloriously true.

"And with that and my inheritance, we may just have enough money to begin construction on the Institute," Cornelia said.

"I can't believe it is happening so quickly," Elinor said. "Not a year ago it was only an idea."

"Such is the power of angry, clever women, Ella," Seraphina said to her baby, tapping the child on the nose.

"Not to mention brave ones," Thaïs added.

"Will you come to Gardencourt and help me with the preparations?" Cornelia asked them. "We won't have much time to make arrangements, and it will take some clever planning to achieve. Besides, I still must finish your portraits."

"I love a duke's house party," Thaïs cawed, fluffing out her hair. "One of my favorite ways to pass the time."

"I'd be curious to see Gardencourt again," Elinor said. "It's been decades since I last set foot there."

"I'll do anything you need, Cornelia," Sera said. "Always."

How she loved these women. Who else could she confess her deepest secret to after twenty years of lying, only to receive compassion, abiding loyalty, and a willingness to travel to the countryside?

"Then it's settled," Cornelia said. "We shall create all manner of mischief."

Sera raised her teacup. "To bacchanalia," she said.

"To bedlam," Thaïs echoed.

"To the power of the Society of Sirens," Elinor said.

They clinked their teacups.

As Cornelia sipped her tea, she smiled.

For perhaps Rafe Goodwood appearing in her painting studio was not the crisis she had thought it was.

Perhaps there were worse things than marriage after all.

Chapter Six

*R*afe was clenched with nerves.

There was, on the surface, no reason for it. He was doing nothing more daring than sitting in the library of Gardencourt Manor staring at the mountainous pile of estate books that needed to be analyzed. Though, to be fair, this was a highly unpleasant task.

He was a creature of the stables. Sitting still in a hot, overstuffed formal library with his every need catered to and nothing to do but pore over figures sucked the vigor from him. He hated this ancient manor, with its stiff grandeur and militia of servants trained to defer to his every whim.

What a difference a few weeks could make, when one, by no efforts of one's own, went from a common man to a noble lord.

It was despicable that this was the way the world worked. That he should be given a kingdom, while beneath his nose a hundred people scraped out fire grates and scrubbed the floors and cleaned the chamber pots for residents who didn't even notice their existence. And all for less money a year than it cost to keep a horse.

He couldn't wait to tear apart the place at the seams and sew it up anew.

But it was not the complexities of estate management that had him anxious.

It was Cornelia Ludgate.

Specifically, the fact that he had not been able to take his mind off her since they'd parted in London, when she'd made clear she was not happy to see him and did not trust him.

It was a reasonable stance, given his work for her uncle and the company he'd kept since their none-too-happy parting. Nevertheless, it bothered him like an itch deep beneath the skin he'd give anything to scratch.

At least one thing had not changed in twenty years: his inordinate desire to make her like him.

"Neglecting your work?" an amused voice drawled.

Rafe ceased gazing out the window and smiled at the welcome distraction of Rory Thompson leaning against the massive carved wood door with a lazy grin. Rory was a sight for sore eyes. But then, he was always some kind of sight. They had worked together in the stables for three years—Rafe leading the breeding operation, Rory overseeing its finances—and become friends and occasional lovers. Now Rafe had asked Rory to help him untangle the mystery that was the running of Gardencourt.

Rory came and propped himself against the unfashionably large desk, which must date back to the Tudors. "Your Grace."

"Stop," Rafe said. Meaning stop using that awful title on him, and stop giving him that *come hither* grin.

Rory winked, and Rafe laughed, grateful for the casual ease between them. Rory was the kind of man who made you fleetingly, exquisitely happy, and then disappeared as quickly as he'd come. He was all lust and charm and kindness and friendship, and made it abundantly clear he had a roving eye, many lovers, and didn't desire commitment.

Exactly what Rafe needed.

Exactly who Rafe needed to train himself to *be*.

Exactly the kind of man he wasn't.

Rafe was the kind of man who was always turning acquaintanceships into flirtations and flirtations into love affairs with nothing more than the power of his thoughts.

He got attached too quickly. He made impulsive declarations of emotion and planned sweepingly romantic gestures. He gave gifts. He professed love. He did it in the span of weeks.

And inevitably, when the object of his infatuation was taken aback by his ardor—even alienated by it—he got hurt.

He was tired—so bloody tired—of being heartbroken.

He'd made a vow after his last doomed enrapturement, a horse buyer named Susannah with flashing green eyes, left him the very night he told her how he felt about her: *no more devastating love affairs*.

His bed was open. His heart was closed.

"To what do I owe the pleasure of your company?" Rafe asked Rory.

Rory passed him a sheet of paper with a list of names and times. "I've set up meetings for you with the foreman of the quarries, the vicar, and the head forester tomorrow."

"Ah, excellent." Rory was nothing if not masterful at making order out of the estate's behemoth inner workings.

"Will you ride out with me?" Rafe asked.

"No time. I have to be back in London to meet with the executor of the estate on your behalf."

"Make mention of my marriage. The more he hears of it, the less suspicious he will be."

This morning Rafe had charged Canette, the housekeeper, with drafting out an invitation for the masquerade to Lady Lowell, a countess who considered herself the grand dame of society. The note included an explanation that the ball was in celebration of the Duke of Rosemere's marriage. He expected news of his secret wife would reach the papers soon after Lady Lowell received it. Once the news was out, all of London would hope for an invitation.

"I've also received word of an auction at Tatersall's next week," Rory said. "And rumor has it Lord Bell is looking for a racing horse."

Rory gave him a meaningful look. They'd been searching for an inconspicuous reason to make contact with Bell for months.

"Just what we have in abundance," Rafe said. "What a fine opportunity to make the man's acquaintance."

"I'll make the arrangements on the chance he shows," Rory said. "Now then, when is your wife due to arrive?"

Wife. He knew Cornelia would hate to be called such a thing. Almost as much as she would hate being called *duchess.* Still, he liked the word applied to her. For it meant he was her husband.

"Cornelia will be here any moment," he said.

"Is that why your reading remains unread?" Rory said, gesturing at Rafe's pile of reports and ledgers.

"Yes. I'm apprehensive."

"*You?* You're the calmest person I've ever met. What could possibly be troubling you?"

He debated telling Rory, for speaking his torment aloud would make it all more real. But in his misery, he could use a friend.

"I admire her and she despises me," he summarized.

Rory put a hand on his shoulder. "No one could despise *you*. You're far too handsome and affable to inspire more than faint dislike."

"Now's not the time for humor, pest," Rafe said, pulling Rory in by the cravat so he could kiss him.

"Rafe?" a husky, cultivated voice called from just outside the door.

Fuck. He'd forgotten to lock it. He and Rory mustn't be so casual in their affection, now that they were no longer in the privacy of the stable offices.

He released Rory and jumped away.

"Come in." His voice was only a little hoarse, thank God.

Cornelia sauntered in and flashed him and Rory a quick, appraising look. She wore a crisp blue dress cut to flatter her petite proportions. The simplicity of the gown showed off the sophisticated beauty of her features. She made him feel shabby in his riding clothes.

Of course, the way Cornelia was looking at Rory, it didn't seem she much cared about *Rafe*'s attire. Rory's though—he saw a flicker in her eyes as she regarded him.

Rory saw it, too. Being Rory—damned saucy Irishman—he sauntered over to make Cornelia's acquaintance, Rafe all but forgotten.

"I'm Rory Thompson, Your Grace," he said, with a deep and slightly impish bow. "Confidential secretary to the esteemed duke."

"Oh please, don't call me *that*." Cornelia gave an exaggerated shudder. "Cornelia is my name."

"Well, Cornelia, I knew of your great beauty from your fine self-portraits, but to see the model in the flesh is a pleasure all its own."

She cocked her head, an invitation to flirtation.

"Bold of you, to discuss flesh on our first meeting, Mr. Thompson."

"I hope it won't be the last we speak of it."

Great. Cornelia was going to steal his lover.

He couldn't blame Rory for trading him in. She was a far superior model of humanity.

"May I have a moment with my wife?" Rafe asked. He'd meant to use the word *wife* ironically, but it came out sounding far too sincere.

"Of course," Rory said, bowing graciously. "I'll leave you two to renew your nuptial bond."

He reached out for Cornelia's hand and kissed it. "Whatever you need, my lady, don't hesitate to ask. Publicly or privately."

Cornelia gave Rory an appreciative wink. She'd never been a woman who shied from innuendo. Even as a girl she'd exuded an arch, knowing manner when it came to flirtation. She was never bawdy in her banter. But she was so frank she could make a man sweat through his shirt.

How disappointing she was lavishing this quality on Rory, and not Rafe. It was difficult to look upon her gorgeous face and not remember a time when he'd felt that there was no one else on earth he'd rather be with. She, however, did not look awash in misty memories.

"How was the journey?" he asked briskly, to keep from dwelling on emotions. He could not stop himself from *feeling* things, but he could stop himself from acting on those feelings.

"Lovely," she said. "Quick."

The trip from London was little more than an hour in the fine carriage and six that numbered among the vehicles in the ducal equipage.

"The Rosemere horses are far superior to the nags that pull the London hacks," she added. "I suppose my uncle had you to credit for that."

There was an edge to her voice. He needed to explain his years in the duke's employ, and soon. He planned to do so at supper, once she was settled in the house.

"You must be tired," he said. "Canette has prepared a room for you. I'll ring for her."

He pulled a lever tucked discreetly beneath the desk. One that ensured the servants appeared silently, as if by magic.

"Canette is still here?" Cornelia asked, looking as pleased as a girl with a new doll.

"She is. She was promoted to housekeeper. She's looking forward to seeing you."

This was an understatement. When Rafe had informed Canette of Cornelia's forthcoming arrival, she'd begun to cry.

"I've arranged dinner for us tonight at seven. We can go over our plans and become reacquainted."

She smiled at him. "I can bring myself to endure a bit of your company in exchange for food, I suppose."

He chuckled, but her words were not without a light sting. He didn't want to trade barbs with her. He wanted to trade memories. To learn of her life. To make audacious plans.

"Gracious of you," he said.

She curtsied ironically and batted her eyelashes at him. "I don't suppose Mr. Thompson will be joining us?"

Rafe felt an unattractive flare of envy. "Absolutely not," he said.

She chuckled at the knowing tone in his response. God, he'd missed that infectious laugh.

"It's good to have you here," he said. "The house was never the same without you."

The words came out oddly stiff, and he looked down at his shoes. Before he could recover, the door flew open.

"Cornelia!" Canette cried, her voice heavy with emotion.

"I'll leave you," he murmured.

But Cornelia was not paying him any mind. She was running into Canette's arms.

Chapter Seven

Cornelia was grateful for a reason to tear her attention away from Rafe in all his unholy masculine splendor. It was bad enough she'd been preoccupied with him for days. But to see him in his riding clothes, hair loose and mussed, nearly twice her size—

Stop swooning, you amnesiac woman. He isn't good for you.

He'd proved it decades ago, in a way it would do her no favors to forget. Men like him—emotional, demonstrative, easily attached—were anathema to the way she lived: uncommitted to one person. Free of heart.

Cornelia bounded into her girlhood nursemaid's outstretched arms. "Canette, my God, it's really you," she murmured.

Behind Canette was Mr. Singh, the servant who'd been kindest to her when she was a child. She beamed at him over Canette's shoulder, tears beading in her eyes.

"And Mr. Singh. My heavens, I never thought I'd see either of you again."

"Miss Ludgate," Singh said, bowing to her deeply. "We are beyond pleased you have returned."

"Mr. Singh, you needn't bow to me," she said, still nestled in Canette's bosom. "God knows I'm not an esteemed guest of this establishment."

"You are an esteemed guest in our opinion, dear girl," Canette said, squeezing her so tight it hurt.

The hurt felt good. Normally she was not free with her embraces. But there were so few people in her life that had known her when she was young. Canette was like a piece of herself that she'd not realized she was missing until now.

They pulled apart and looked each other over. Canette was only a decade older than Cornelia. She'd been seventeen when she'd been hired, and at the time, she'd been the only Black servant in the house. Cornelia had instantly been taken with her, this pretty young woman with brown skin so like that of her mother's in the only portrait she had seen of her—a miniature painted by Cornelia's father. Canette was from Barbados, like Cornelia's mama's family, a link that made Cornelia feel less like an outsider inside her uncle's walls.

Canette meant so much to her—something between a parent and the closest friend Cornelia'd had in all of her strange childhood.

"We've had the duchess's bedchamber prepared for you," Singh said. "We heard the happy news. Imagine, our girl, a duchess." He beamed at her like a proud father.

"A duchess!" Canette sighed, before Cornelia could protest that she was no such thing.

"Mr. Goodwood always seemed so fond of you," Canette went on, taking Cornelia's hand and squeezing it. "When your uncle would rail against you, he would always say a few words in your defense. Now I see why. We were delighted to discover you were wed to him. He's a good man, I think."

That remained to be seen.

Still, she was touched by Rafe's loyalty. All these years, she'd assumed he loathed her after the bitter way they'd parted. But she should not dwell on rumors of his kindness. For then she'd be tempted to recall how he'd looked breathless when she'd walked into the library. How he'd sidled his eyes at her with envy when she flirted with his friend. How his shirtsleeves had been pulled up to reveal his forearms—

Don't you dare.

"Oh, it's not like that," Cornelia said quickly, waving away the idea that she and Rafe were *really* married. "Just a temporary situation."

Canette and Singh both inclined their heads at her, perplexed, for everyone knew marriage was a lifelong institution.

"Well, regardless of the situation, you would deserve the finest chamber even if you were married to a troll," Canette said.

"Can trolls marry?" Singh asked.

"They can if I can," Cornelia said with a laugh. "It would be no less unlikely."

"Shall I take you to your room?" Canette asked. "The footmen have brought up your things. And your . . . lovely cat."

"I hope Lucius was polite. He can be a difficult guest."

Canette laughed as they walked down the grand hallway to the vast, three-story staircase. "He is less than enthusiastic about his new dwelling."

Cornelia didn't blame him. The house was stifling in its luxury. Overheated, overstuffed, overfurnished. One could scarcely breathe for all the clutter. Not to mention all the memories.

The duchess's rooms were no different.

As a girl, Cornelia had coveted the chambers of the lady of the house—a sumptuous suite with a bed draped in ruffles and walls lined in pink silk embroidered in gold flowers.

Now that she was grown, she was not charmed by it. She wandered around, reacquainting herself with the wardrobing chamber, the powdering closet, and the bathing room with its massive, luxurious soaking tub. The bathing chamber that sat between their two suites, connected by doors. Where Rafe no doubt soaked after long rides.

In the nude.

Stop it, you incorrigible, amorous—

"Could you fix my hair before supper?" she asked Canette, to avoid thinking of how easily she could visit Rafe in the night if she chose to. "I'm afraid it went limp on the drive."

Canette had always had a gifted hand with Cornelia's hair. She'd taken one look at the frizzled state the hapless white maids had made of Cornelia's voluminous corkscrew curls when she'd arrived at Gardencourt and suggested she take on the seven-year-old child's coiffure. So had begun the elegant hairstyles Cornelia wore to this day—and her first memory of feeling truly beautiful and cared for.

"Oh, you couldn't stop me from fixing that hair," Canette said. "But first, let's get you dressed."

They turned to Cornelia's gowns, which had already been hung in the wardrobe. "I think I'll wear the red silk," Cornelia said.

Canette grinned. "I think I can hear old Rosemere groaning from the mausoleum at the very thought of it."

Cornelia laughed. "I think you mean screaming."

She'd never been allowed to wear bold colors when she lived here. She was told they were too brash, and she must be demure. She must behave with the utmost respectability. She must be better, even, than other gently reared daughters of lords. After all, her mother had been an artist's model and courtesan who'd moved to London after she'd been granted freedom by her father, who had owned the plantation where she'd been born enslaved. Cornelia's father had been notorious for marrying a woman of another race and lower class, for rejecting the aristocratic customs and values he'd been born to, for making art and taking risks.

Cornelia had been born marked—from the color of her skin to the reputation of her parents. She must, therefore, be perfect, she was told—tacitly, and aloud. And if she slipped, it was impressed upon her, she would be ruined in a heartbeat.

And they'd never stopped waiting for her to slip.

She'd been watched, scrutinized for any lapses in her comportment, manners, beauty, and most importantly, her morals.

For so many years, she had shaped herself around that pressure. She'd told herself her value was in her ability to perform the role so perfectly that she would be loved despite the strikes against her. But that vigilance had drained her until, at the age of sixteen, she'd found a cache of her late father's belongings tucked away in a long-forgotten wardrobe in his abandoned cottage on the far side of the grounds.

And what she saw in them was not dissipation, but joy, and life.

She began to question everything.

She wanted to talk freely of the ideas she'd found in her father's books, to see for herself the vivid world he'd painted. She wanted to live exuberantly and sensually, the way her mother had.

She'd begun by learning to paint. It had been the doorway to finding what moved her soul.

And the cost had been all *this*.

This manor, and its army of attendant servants clad head to toe in fuchsia livery. This luxury, supported by the labor of unseen thousands, who paid half their livelihoods, or more, in rents. The society of the proper guests inside, who found the very notion of her presence too threatening to countenance.

And she did not miss a lick of it.

There was not a moment of the old life she had sacrificed that she regretted.

Her days brimmed with adventure and friends and pleasure and laughter and tears and sex—joy and sadness that had nothing to do with propriety or caution; victories that had nothing to do with ballrooms or marriage.

She had chosen freedom.

And now, here she was: storming the castle keep from a position not of apology or desperation for acceptance, but power.

"There," Canette said, clasping the tiny buttons of her scarlet bodice tight around Cornelia's waist. "Now for your coiffure."

Canette fashioned her hair into a loose chignon, allowing tendrils to fall down from her temples. As a finishing touch, she pinned a few bright red roses behind Cornelia's ear.

Cornelia looked striking and sensual and not at all ladylike in her crimson gown and hothouse flowers.

She couldn't keep the smile from her face as she

thanked Canette and descended the many steps downstairs.

Menacing winged gargoyles leered down at her as she walked toward the doors of the dining room. As a girl, she had always thought of them as sentries. But maybe, with their outstretched wings expanding toward the sky, they'd also been trying to flee this place.

Maybe, despite the unsettling bitter memories mixed among the happy ones, this was Cornelia's chance to make Gardencourt more welcoming for everyone.

Perhaps she could take Rafe at his word when it came to his promises of reform.

She would find out, for he was waiting for her at a table that comfortably accommodated twenty people.

Alone.

Looking more edible than the food.

He wore a deep navy coat that set off his blue eyes, and a slim black vest that clung to the impressive musculature of his chest. His chestnut hair was swept back from his face, held in place by a ribbon, rather than tucked shaggily behind his ears. It brought out the gray at his temples. She'd always liked silvered hair on a man.

"Good evening," he said, rising from his chair. "Have a seat."

"Shall I sit at the opposite end of the table?"

He laughed. The table was approximately twenty-five feet long.

"Only if you want to shout at me."

She gave him her most enigmatic smile. "We'll have to see if you deserve it."

He looked at her levelly and gestured at the chair beside him. "Cornelia, before we eat, there's something

I'd like you to know about me. I think you'll find the meal more palatable if you listen."

Had he ever spoken to her so firmly? Could it be that he was even more attractive when the authority of his voice matched his intimidating physicality?

She sat.

"You certainly have captured my attention. What is it you wish to confess?"

He locked eyes with her. "When I told you I'm not a Tory, that wasn't the whole truth of it."

"I knew it!" she said. Disappointing, but it was no more than she'd expected. She picked up her wineglass. Being right deserved a toast.

"No, you didn't. You don't understand," he said firmly. "The truth is I'm a member of the Equalist Society."

She put her wineglass down without taking a sip and snorted. She'd sooner believe him if he said he was a turkey.

"You aren't," she said. "*I'm* a member of the Equalist Society. I would certainly know if you were one of us."

"You wouldn't, actually," he said flatly. "I'm a spy."

"Pardon?"

"I'm a spy. I've been gathering information about the Tories covertly for eighteen years, and passing it to Jack Willow."

Jack was the founder of the Equalist Society and the publisher of its circular. Not to mention a chief enemy of the Tories, who pegged him as a seditionist for his views. If what Rafe said was true, he'd been in a very dangerous position.

If what he said was true. She had no reason to believe him.

"Jack never mentioned you to me."

Rafe shrugged. "Why would he? He was not aware you and I were . . . connected."

Connected. The vagueness of the word almost made her laugh out loud.

"Tell me more," she said. "If what you say is true, how does it work, this so-called spying?"

He relaxed a bit, as though grateful to be given a chance to win her credulity.

"As you know, I've been acquainted with Jack since my youth. Your parents introduced us. It was his idea for me to secure a position with your uncle and ingratiate myself with him and his Tory friends."

"Why you? You're not exactly inconspicuous."

He was six feet five inches of broadly built horseman. Surely such a role would be better performed by a retiring clerkish type.

"I was uniquely situated to gather information. Horse trading is an expensive undertaking, and your uncle's customers and friends are among the most powerful men in the country. Successful breeders easily win the respect and camaraderie of horse enthusiasts. Meals are shared, rides are taken, and the conversation inevitably turns to politics. I made them my friends. And all the while I gathered information about their positions and plans and shared it with Jack."

She supposed it was plausible. She knew Jack had sources of information he did not share widely with the group, for reasons of safety and discretion.

"Who else knows about this?" she asked.

He shook his head, solemn.

"No one knew until last month. I've told a few associates who will be joining us for the house party."

"And they believe you?"

He looked taken aback. "Yes. They have no reason not to. What could I gain by lying?"

"You could be spying on the Equalists to help the Tories. Trying to gain our trust."

He nodded. "Ah. I suppose that's true. But in turn, inviting your allies here would make me vulnerable to their scrutiny."

She considered this. There was no right answer. She would simply have to remain on guard until she decided whether she could trust him.

A thought occurred to her.

"If you are so close to Jack and share secrets with him, do you know where he is?"

It had been six months since anyone had seen Jack, and no one had heard a word from him. He had a habit of disappearing for weeks here and there when the political winds turned against him. But he had never left without informing at least one member of their circle where he'd gone, and this time he'd left without a trace. The only thing to think, after months and months without word, was that he had not left willingly.

Jack had enemies. Powerful enemies. And the man chief among them was Elinor's estranged husband, Lord Bell, who had accused his wife and Jack of having an affair. Bell was suing Jack for criminal conversation in an attempt to ruin his good name and render him destitute. But he was capable of worse.

Rafe looked down at his fingers. "I don't know where Jack is," he said. "I've been keeping my ear to the ground for any word of him, but our usual channels have gone silent. I'm very concerned."

The way he said this—without meeting her eye— made her suspect he was keeping something back. Perhaps his story wasn't true at all.

Yet for some reason, despite everything, she wanted to believe it.

"You spin a very convenient tale," she said slowly. "But all I have is your word. And it's never meant much before."

This time he did meet her eyes, and oddly, there was pain in them.

"That's fair. But I want to show you who I am. It's important to me that you can trust me. That we can trust each other. Otherwise our scheme has no hope of working."

He was right.

And she wanted five thousand pounds.

She was willing to reserve final judgment until she could glean where his true loyalties lay.

She picked up her wineglass, and this time she did take a sip.

"Well, Rafe, my dear husband, you'd better have a plan for proving you're what you say."

He bit his lip, like he was holding back a grin. "Believe me. I do."

Chapter Eight

Cornelia was smiling at him.

Smiling.

He wanted to get up and skip around the room. It was such a relief to unburden himself, after all these years of knowing how harshly she must judge him. He knew she was still somewhat incredulous. But that smile gave him hope that she might come to know him.

To forgive him.

"I was hoping you might ride out with me tomorrow," he said. "Rory has arranged interviews with a number of people important to the inner workings of the estate, and I think when you see what we're trying to achieve, you might be more inclined to trust me. Besides, your insights on our plans for reform would be most welcome."

She hesitated.

He held his breath. If she said no, it would be much more difficult to win her over. And after that smile, winning her over was all he wanted on this earth.

"I'd be willing to come," she said slowly. "There's only one problem."

"What's that?"

"I barely remember how to ride."

He exhaled. *That* he could fix.

He grinned at her. "How lucky you have a horseman at your disposal."

"Indeed," she drawled. "A blessing."

"I'll teach you in the morning, if you don't mind an early start."

"I love an early morning rendezvous," she said. She held up a finger. "But I have a condition. If you wish for my help, I'd like yours. I have an idea for your ball. An idea only a true radical would accept."

She looked at him as though whatever she was about to propose was a test of character.

He would do just about anything to pass it.

"What is it?" he asked.

"I'd like to show my paintings at the masquerade. As a pleasant surprise for your guests."

It took him a moment to imagine this.

"But that would mean . . ."

She nodded, smiling serenely. "The ball and the exhibition would be one and the same."

He threw back his head and laughed.

"Cornelia Ludgate, you are a shocking woman."

It was one thing to hold her exhibition here. It was quite another to trick the better part of high society into attending.

She smiled at him more broadly. "You used to love my wild notions."

He most certainly had.

"I still do. But how would we carry it off? Not a single proper lord or lady will come to the ball if they know they'll be confronted with the devil's own art."

"We will see that they don't know until it's too late. I shall issue invitations to a masquerade exhibition for the same evening as your ball, but hold back the location until the day before. The aristocrats will be none the wiser, and if any of my patrons realize the trick, they'll likely be amused rather than scandalized."

It was utterly preposterous, this plan.

He loved it.

The audacity of it.

That fact that she was willing to conspire with him on it, just like in the old days.

He lifted up his wineglass. "To being incorrigible renegades."

She clinked her glass with his.

He tried not to luxuriate too much in her smile.

"Shall we eat?" he asked.

"Please. All this talk of covert radicalism has left me starving."

He lifted the lid from an ornately filigreed silver tray.

The pomp of the tray was at odds with the meal that rested on it, which bore little resemblance to the repasts he'd had here when Rosemere was alive. The duke's staff had prepared as many courses as there were people every night, and hovered to serve them out of dishes polished to such a shine you could see your own reflection as you were served a slice of candied ham. The food was prepared in the French style, doused in fresh butter, studded with currants and sweetmeats and caramel creams.

Rafe liked a lean, simple diet. The ducal table tasted like gout.

And the waste—he hated to think about the waste.

He'd asked the cook to simplify the dishes, and she'd acted like he'd asked her to commit treason.

"How refined," Cornelia said, eyeing the humble chicken and pile of buttered potatoes. "My uncle would be so proud of his heir."

"I'm sorry if you desire a more elaborate repast. I've been eating goose-fat-drenched veal puddings and the like, or whatever they serve in this damned house, for so many weeks that I won't be able to sit my horse if it goes on."

She groaned. "It's always been that way. Being here is like stepping back in time."

He knew what she meant. Her uncle had changed nothing in the forty years he'd held the title.

"You know, the moment I became the surprise heir, a few months before the old man's death, he called me in for a long lecture on the importance of the place's history, on being—"

"A mere custodian of the title, a mere servant of the crown," she interrupted, in a strikingly accurate imitation of the duke's clipped accent.

They both laughed. "Precisely. It struck me as quite apt from a man who distanced himself from his last remaining living family in the name of preserving a symbol he'd inherited as randomly as the color of his eyes."

He looked at his lap, wondering if he had overstepped in speaking of what Rosemere had done to Cornelia.

But she didn't seem upset. "Indeed," she said. "Indeed."

He decided to venture further.

"If it's any consolation, he was a miserable, lonely person at the end. It's sad, the things people will destroy their lives for."

"Let's not speak of him," she said. "I'll lose my appetite, and I'm very hungry."

She reached across the table, picked off a crispy piece of skin from the chicken, and popped it in her mouth. She closed her eyes, licking grease from her finger.

"Perfect."

She'd always liked humble, earthy pleasures. He remembered it from their time together—her satisfaction at a warm fire out of doors on a cold night, or a perfectly yeasted loaf of bread on the table between them at a tavern.

"Odd to eat a simple meal inside this room," Cornelia said. "I've always despised it in here. So cold and formal."

"It nearly obliterates one's appetite."

She smiled. "You know, you're right." She picked up the platter of chicken and potatoes and stood. "Let's eat somewhere else."

"Wherever you like."

She tapped her chin. "On the terrace, I think. The weather's so lovely."

"But there's no table," he said, thinking of her pretty dress.

"Then we shall picnic."

"How roguish."

She met his eye. "We always were, weren't we? Take the cutlery."

She was bantering with him. *Bantering!*

He gathered the forks and knives and followed her out of the dark room and through a hallway to the nearest sitting room. She balanced the tray on one hand and unlatched the glass door to the terrace with the other, pushing it open with her hip.

An artist's dexterity.

She tossed him a smile over her shoulder and marched outside into the evening air, plopping down on the terrace steps, never mind her fine red gown. She put the tray next to her and nodded at the space beside it, gesturing for him to sit.

He obeyed, even though the shallow steps were not exactly accommodating to a man of his height.

"That's better, isn't it?" she said, plucking a fork from his hand and using it to spear a potato.

It was. The night was cool and slightly humid in a pleasant way that made the air smell of the lush grass and trees and hedges that surrounded the stone terrace.

"Much better," he agreed.

She leaned back against a step, her profile lit up in the dimming, golden sunlight.

"So, Rafe, aside from your alleged espionage, what has occupied your life all these years?"

She popped the potato in her mouth and looked at him expectantly as she chewed. He was flattered by her interest. So flattered he could barely summon an answer.

"Horses, mainly," he attempted, racking his brain for something more interesting to say.

"Ah. Your greatest love."

Hardly. His life would have been far less complicated if horses were his only passion.

"One of them. Though, of course, there have been others."

"Are you trying to tell me you have not been faithful to me?" she asked lightly. "How heartbreaking."

He took a chicken leg with his bare fingers and munched on it. He wasn't sure why he'd said that. He'd not been thinking of others.

He'd been thinking of her.

"I meant good cheeses, chess, and woodworking, of course," he quipped. "But yes, there have been love affairs. One must warm one's bed."

She laughed. "I'm afraid I've been decidedly adulterous as well. It will be quite fertile grounds when we pursue our annulment, my legendary fleet of lovers."

Hearing her talk of her lovers was making his face grow hot. It was strange, this sudden intimacy. But Cornelia had always been the type to skip the usual courtesies. She was as blunt as they came.

"Have I scandalized you?" she asked, when he could not think of a reply.

"Yes," he admitted. "I'm a duke now, as you'll recall. We're a prim and proper lot."

She nodded with mock gravity. "I'll spare your delicate sensibilities the details."

"Thank you."

"Tell me," she said, before he could ask her a question. "How is your family?"

He was touched by her curiosity.

"My father passed away in '92."

She reached out and lightly touched his shoulder. "Oh, I'm sorry."

He shivered at the light pressure of her fingers. "Thank you. He went peacefully in his sleep."

She lifted her hand away. He missed it.

"And your brother?" she asked.

"He lives in Norfolk with his wife and children. Seven of them."

"Seven!"

"Indeed. They're quite adorable, if you like that sort of thing."

"And you?" she asked.

"Me what?"

"Did you have children?"

He grimaced at the thought of it. "Not to my knowledge. I never wanted them, as much as I like my brother's. I'm careful about that sort of thing."

She nodded. "As am I. And I've been fortunate."

She said this solemnly. He knew the unfair burden on women to avoid pregnancy—and how easily the battle was lost. Her friend Seraphina had written an entire treatise on it, published by Jack Willow. He devoured everything she wrote.

"And what of your life?" he asked. "How does a famed painter fill her days?"

She raked her fork along a chicken breast and tore off a hunk of meat. "She paints."

"I'm excited to see your portraits. I've always wanted to attend your exhibitions. I followed them in the papers."

"So why didn't you?"

"It would have been discordant with my supposed politics to be seen admiring your work. Raised suspicions." He paused. "And I assumed you wouldn't want me there."

She nodded. "Correct," she said softly. "You'd not have been welcome, given what I thought of you."

He took meager comfort in the fact that she said "thought" and not "still think."

"I know," he said. "I know."

He wanted badly to take her hand. He'd give anything to touch her. Instead, he turned his head a bit to look directly into her eyes.

"It hurt, all those years, knowing you believed the worst of me. I wish I could have been honest with you."

He wasn't sure how she'd react to this, given her skepticism about his story.

She searched his eyes, her face unreadable.

"That wasn't the only reason we didn't speak, Rafe," she finally said.

He couldn't help himself. He put a hand on her shoulder.

"I know," he said, squeezing it. "But I've missed you, Cornelia. I've missed you so much."

Her eyes widened and her mouth slackened, like she could not work out what to say in response. She shrugged off his hand.

"I'm sorry," she said, looking not at him but off in the distance, toward the mazed gardens. Her tone said that the feeling was not mutual, and she did not appreciate his sentimentality.

Fuck.

He'd overstepped. He should have known the weight of the past was too heavy to be dispensed with over a few pleasant words and bites of chicken.

They were not friends. Not yet.

She stood up abruptly and let out a yawn so long and loud it seemed like it was fake. "I'm tired. I think I'll retire. You can carry in the food?"

He nodded, his cheeks flaming like he was a man thirty years his junior. He was grateful it was nearly dark. He hoped she couldn't see.

"Sleep well," he said as lightly as he could. "And meet me in the stable yard at eight. We'll get you back on a horse."

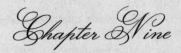

Chapter Nine

Cornelia walked quickly to her room, taking the shortcut up the servants' staircase as Rafe's words echoed in her mind.

I've missed you.

She could not account for why those words made her legs shake.

She had not missed Rafe. She'd taken great care not to think of him at all. But perhaps the effort she'd put into expelling him from her mind was itself a form of longing. For when he'd taken her hand, she'd felt a wave of regret so powerful it was all she could do to flee before she was overtaken by it.

And what a shame. For he was so kind. So easy to talk to. So seductive in his masculine beauty that were he another man, she'd have suggested they retire to the library for an intimate conversation, and would have not hesitated should the mood have led to even more intimate activities.

But with Rafe, she knew where that led.

Some men were free and easy. You could flirt with them, sleep with them—even care for them—without trepidation. Others were intense and passionate. The sort to want to embed you in their lives.

Rafe, unless he'd changed, was the latter. And she did not wish to be embedded in anyone's life save her own.

Better not to test whether Rafe's intensity had faded.

Better not to sit beside him beneath a rising moon remembering the past.

She entered the duchess's chamber and found Lucius on the frilly bed, his face planted in the counterpane so thoroughly she wondered how he breathed.

"You ridiculous creature," she said, scratching his spine. He looked up at her with an abundance of love that from any other male would send her dashing from the room.

She stripped off her clothes down to her chemise and snuggled up beside him.

Normally she stayed up late to draw, recording her memories of the day in quick sketches that served as a kind of diary. But her impressions of today were dominated by Rafe's face as he sat across the table and told her of his secret life. His blue eyes flickering as he asked her to trust him. The profile of his brow and jaw as he grinned, speaking of his family.

Safer to go to sleep.

She counted backward by sevens from one thousand to keep her thoughts from wandering to Rafe, and allowed exhaustion to wash over her until she drifted off.

She awoke to a gray, cloudy morning and her cat snoring against her neck.

"I think it's going to rain, Lu," she informed him, gently detaching him from her shoulder. "No fine garments for me."

Lucius, as he was wont, said nothing and went back to sleep.

She put on breeches—the paint-smeared ones she wore when she needed to stand on a ladder and paint the top of a canvas—and an old, scuffed pair of boots. She wrapped her hair in a scarf, put on a wide-brimmed hat, and left the house on foot to walk the trail to the stables.

Rafe looked hale and handsome in the morning light of the practice ring, where he was talking to a horse as though he and the animal were old friends. As a woman who spent much of her time speaking to an indifferent feline, she found this endearing.

She greeted Rafe from behind, tapping his shoulder.

He jumped, prompting her to laugh.

"I didn't mean to alarm you. Good morning."

"Breeches, eh?" he said, glancing at her legs. He quickly caught himself and looked away. The classic sign of a man who wanted to stare.

She was flattered. Now that she was approaching forty, she'd begun to feel the waning attention of men who'd once followed her every move with their eyes. She felt more beautiful now than she had at twenty, with her more curvaceous body and the sharper lines of her face. It was nice to be in the company of someone who appeared to agree.

Even if he was, somewhat dangerously, Rafe Goodwood.

"I take it you prefer not to ride sidesaddle?" he asked.

She shuddered. Sidesaddle made her fear for her life.

"I hate perching precariously on the back of a giant animal. I want you to remind me how to properly mount a horse." She paused. "Again."

He looked at her long and hard, no doubt remembering the last time he'd taught her that particular skill. It was unwise, perhaps, to prompt that recollection.

Unwise and decidedly delicious.

She rarely felt so sultry at eight in the morning.

"You're certain?" he asked.

She nodded, and she was not sure if she was affirming her wish for a lesson or giving him permission to look at her like that—like he was also overwhelmed by a memory that had far more to do with attraction than it did with horsemanship.

He winked at her. "Come into the stables. I have a horse for you. A gentle, sturdy mare."

"You don't think I can handle a stallion?" she asked, before she could think better of it.

Oh dear. Was she turning into Thaïs?

Rafe gave her a long look. "Oh, I think there's very little limit to what you can handle."

She laughed, then bit her lip, regretting the innuendo. It was she, after all, who had shied away from him last night. She shouldn't encourage flirtation.

Rafe led her inside, where his fleet of gorgeous horses idled in their stalls. He walked her past them to a tall, chestnut-colored mare near the back.

"This is Nelly. She'll be gentle with you."

"A pleasure to meet you, Nelly," she said, stroking the mare's head.

"When did you last ride?" Rafe asked.

"Oh, a decade ago, I'd think."

He nearly dropped the saddle. "A *decade* ago?"

She shrugged. "I live in London. I walk. And when I don't walk, I take hackneys."

"Well, luckily, riding's not a skill that's easily forgotten."

"I recall it's a question of balance, staying on the horse?"

She knew it was more complicated, but she did not want to betray the fact that she was nervous.

"It's a question of gripping with your seat and calves and keeping tension in the stirrups," he said.

"Gripping with the legs. Oh my. How redolent of . . . other pursuits."

She definitely *was* turning into Thaïs.

He ignored her comment, which must have taken a not inconsiderable amount of self-restraint. He finished tacking Nelly and led her out of her stall and toward a mounting block.

"There," he said. "You'll want to climb into the stirrup and swing your leg over her."

Cornelia hopped onto the block—no easy task, given her petite stature. She was annoyed at herself for the flash of fear she felt as she vaulted onto the horse. She didn't like riding. She'd avoided it as best she could her entire life, knowing her parents had died because of a spooked horse that overturned her father's speeding barouche.

Besides, Nelly was very tall, and Cornelia was quite short.

"It's all right," Rafe said. "She won't hurt you. She's gentle as a lamb. But you have to communicate your authority to her, so that she trusts you."

"I don't feel particularly authoritative toward an animal ten times my size."

"Cornelia," he said with a slight laugh, "few people I've ever met are as naturally authoritative as you. You missed your calling as a general."

The words made her smile. Not because she particularly wished to be thought of as suited to the military, but because Rafe's compliments gave her a rush of pleasure.

"You're good at this," she said. Meaning at flirtation.

He winked. "I know. I'm good at many things involving mounted ladies."

Before she could counter with a dirty witticism of

her own, his arm was around her waist, bracing her into place against his massive side. He was warm and smelled like leather.

"I'm sure you've had many willing students," she said. She was curious about his love life. She wondered if he had a lover now.

He chuckled. "I stay busy. Now steady your weight and take the reins," he said, placing them in her hands.

Cautiously, she did as he instructed. The saddle shifted a bit as she adjusted herself, and she yelped, pulling involuntarily on the reins. Nelly tossed her head at the sudden movement, and Cornelia yelped again.

"Steady there," Rafe murmured. "Be careful not to pull the reins unless you wish for her to stop or turn, otherwise she'll be confused." He drew closer and raised his arms up toward her. "May I help you?"

She nodded. He put his huge hands sturdily on her hips to balance her. Oh heavens, the feeling of him holding her. She relaxed into it, nearly enjoying herself despite her nerves.

"You're fine," he said in a soothing tone. "Now remember, it's your legs that support you, and your feet in the stirrups—not the reins."

She wobbled. She had never found riding to be an intuitive task.

"I don't remember much of anything, except that I do not enjoy sitting on beasts large enough to kill me."

"Nelly would sooner sprout wings and turn into a sparrow than kill you."

"I did not say she would mean to. But I shall fall if she moves."

She'd wanted to ride so she could roam about the estate while she was here, without relying on others to drive her. She had not expected to be so genuinely terrified.

Rafe put one of his large hands on the small of her back. She reached out and grabbed his shoulder, fearful she might fall.

"Cornelia," he said kindly, "we can take a barouche. Let's get you down."

But she was embarrassed to be having this reaction. She did not want him to think she was the kind of woman who gave up so easily. Not when he must remember her as the fearless girl with a will as immovable as a stone wall.

Besides, she wanted him to touch her again.

"Not a chance," she said. "I won't be defeated."

He looked at her with concern, but she ignored him. "How is my posture?"

"Not particularly good, I'm afraid." He came close again and tugged her left ankle backward. "Feel the difference? You must remember to keep the balls of your feet in the center of the stirrups to stay steady. Your toes should point up, your heels down. Use your weight to help you."

"Like this?" she asked cautiously, shifting forward.

He grimaced. "Not exactly. Here, steady yourself with your backside. You should feel it in your stomach and legs, if you're doing it properly. Do you remember the day I taught you?"

How could I forget?

"Oh, I remember."

She'd felt it in her stomach and legs indeed.

Chapter Ten

Before

"I have one condition," Rafe said, as he and Cornelia plotted out their predawn escape.

"Very well," she said. "Name your price."

"I don't want money," he protested, taken aback that she would think he would extort a desperate eighteen-year-old girl for funds.

"You needn't be offended. It's a reasonable request. And I do have money, though not much beyond what it will take to reach Florence."

"What I mean," Rafe said, "is that you must pretend to be a boy while we travel."

"How forward," she drawled, as if he'd suggested something naughty.

He ignored the implication. He was not flirting in the slightest. It was imperative that she be disguised.

"A woman in a fine gown in a carriage is exactly what Rosemere's men will be looking for if they pursue us," he said. "But two men on horseback can ride quickly, off the carriage roads. We'll have a better chance of remaining undetected if we alter your appearance."

"You'll have to style me as a young man, in that case," she said dryly. "I neglected to bring my valet."

"I'll find you something to wear," Rafe said, rising to go to his own wardrobe. "Friends have left things here before."

"I'd hope you don't intend for me to wear your clothing. I'm quite a bit more petite than you, sir," she said, looking him up and down. She was tiny, and he was very nearly a giant. He could lift her with one hand.

A fact he should *not* be thinking about, given her age. It was bad enough he was asking her to clad herself in breeches.

He went and collected a few stray items left behind by his last paramour. Luckily, Luke was small of stature and had liked to stay the night when he could get away.

"Here you are," he said, producing a pair of breeches, a leather jerkin, and a linen shirt.

Disguising Cornelia as a boy was easy. Her slim figure was well suited to men's clothing. In her breeches and coarse linen, with her hair tucked into a hat, she could have been a farmer's son.

"I feel quite spry in knee breeches," she said. "Perhaps I will dispense with gowns entirely."

"They suit you," he said, and then regretted it. He should not be commenting on her body any more than he should be noticing it at all.

"I believe we may have a bigger problem than my choice of garments. I only know how to ride side-saddle."

"Of course," he groaned. "I should have thought of that."

Ladies of Cornelia's class rarely rode astride, as a man would. He would have to teach her, and teach her well enough that she could ride quickly and efficiently on rough terrain.

"I believe a rain-soaked predawn lesson in equestrianism is in order," she said. "Our first adventure of the day."

Her cheer seemed to dissipate when she saw the horse he intended for her to ride. The broad, quiet mare was his gentlest horse, but also his tallest.

"Are you ready?" he asked Cornelia quietly, not wishing to be overheard in case his neighbor's servants were awake.

"Of course," she whispered, with what he suspected was false bravado.

"Up you go. A leg over her back, your rear square in the saddle."

He blushed at mentioning her rear, which he had taken pains not to stare at when she'd emerged from his bedchamber in Luke's old breeches.

She squeezed his hand and launched herself from the mounting block and into the stirrups.

"Very good," he encouraged her.

"I straddle like a natural," she affirmed.

Did she mean . . . ? No, he would ignore that. She may have had an *affaire de coeur* with her painting tutor, but he doubted she was so worldly as to make off-color jokes that crude.

(Though if she was, she was awfully clever.)

"Feet in the stirrups now. Press the horse's belly with your calves gently to urge her forward," he instructed.

Cornelia complied capably enough. But when she shifted her weight, the saddle moved on the mare's back in a way that unnerved the rider. Cornelia gasped.

Poor girl. He could see real fear on her face.

"If the saddle shifts, slightly adjust your weight," he instructed. "You want to sit up long and straight and balance on your rump."

She nodded, but each time the horse moved, she flinched and went clutching at the reins, turning the horse's head left and right in a way that could get her killed in the wrong circumstances.

If she could not find her grip, she would not be able to maintain so much as a trot on the rough forest roads without risking an injury. And trotting was not going to allow them to elude her uncle.

He led her slowly around the practice ring, holding the mare by its reins, but every time the saddle moved, Cornelia resisted—fighting it rather than balancing herself.

"It's hopeless," she said after half an hour. "I don't understand."

There was not much time to teach her. The first shimmer of dawn was gleaming behind the clouds, and it was imperative they leave at first light.

He thought for a moment, then offered her a hand.

"Here. Get down. We'll try something else."

She looked relieved when she stepped down onto solid ground.

Rafe took a saddle blanket and spread it on the wet earth. He lowered onto his hands and knees.

"Climb onto my back," he said.

"On your back?" she repeated slowly.

Her incredulity was merited. What he was asking would get him called out for a duel in most circumstances. But no one was here to shoot him, and they didn't have much time.

"You need to know the proper grip, and if you're frightened, we'll do it this way."

She raised a brow at him. "Some might argue that climbing *onto your back* is obscene."

She said this in an amused tone, not a shocked one.

He was beginning to see she *was* rather worldly, at least for a sheltered eighteen-year-old girl.

"Cornelia, if this is too difficult, we can try our luck in my carriage. But it will be riskier—"

"Hold still."

Before he could even brace himself, she swung her leg over him and attempted to find her seating on his back.

Luckily, she was a slight thing, nothing compared to his bulk. He liked the feeling of her weight on top of him. It made him feel strong.

"Put your rear on the small of my back," he told her, refocusing on the task at hand. His voice was oddly normal, failing to display any of the tension he felt with her seated on top of him.

She adjusted herself, moving backward as gingerly as she could. He chided himself for being a schoolboy about this, but he could not help but think of the parts of her intimately in contact with parts of him.

"Now sit up as straight as you can. Hold yourself up from your middle, like there's a string from the ceiling pulling up your head."

Cornelia adjusted herself, and he tried not to think of bedchamber acts.

He felt horrible for even *thinking* of thinking about such things, given this girl's innocence. Or, at least, her age.

"Now put your feet on the ground, with your weight on your heels, as though you're in stirrups," he said. "Your toes should point up to my ears."

"Like that?"

"Yes, good," he said. "Now grip the sides of my back with your legs to show me it's time to ride forward."

No. Bedchamber. Acts.

She gripped him with all her power.

"Tighter," Rafe instructed, keeping his voice as firm as he could manage with a beautiful woman gripping his midriff with her thighs.

She squeezed him until he groaned. She laughed.

"You did say as tight as I could."

"You don't want to suffocate your horse. Or me, in this case."

"No, my intention isn't to suffocate you. It's to ride you," she said in that wry tone that left him uncertain if she was stating a fact or making a bawdy joke.

Pondering that was inappropriate. Instead, he bucked. She yelped and fell off his back.

"Excuse me!" she cried.

"I'm sorry, but it had to be done. If you don't want to fall off, you have to be prepared to react. Climb back on."

She did, and this time without the slightest hint of suggestive humor. He was not sure if he was relieved or disappointed.

"Put your hands over your head, so you aren't relying on them for balance."

She did. He shifted his weight suddenly to the left.

In return, she shifted hers to the right.

"There you are," he said. "How does that feel?"

She patted him on the shoulder. "Sensational."

He willed himself not to dwell on her touch or the double meaning in her words. She had come here for protection. Not to be lusted after by a grown man who could easily violate her trust.

"I think you have the hang of it," he said briskly. "Let's try it on the horse."

She stepped off of him and he rose to his feet. He caught her looking at him.

"A fine piece of horseflesh," she said approvingly.

Fucking hell.

He clenched his teeth, offered her a hand, and jutted his chin at the horse. "Up you go."

She climbed up on the horse's back. This time, she looked more natural, and her feet found the proper angle in the stirrups.

"Your form is good," he said. "Looking stable. How does it feel?"

"Less desirable than your back. I've never liked riding horses. But I find I enjoy riding men."

She winked at him, confirming he had not imagined the tinge of flirtation in the way she spoke to him.

This, he realized, was going to be an excruciating trip.

Chapter Eleven

"Take a lap around the ring," Rafe instructed Cornelia, breaking his own reverie.

He'd been thinking back to the day he taught her to ride astride.

It was making him emotional.

Again.

Damn it.

He knew he had gone too far last night. He should not repeat the mistake this morning. He was trying to win her trust—not drive her away. Especially when she seemed relaxed around him, like she was willing to forgive the previous evening's awkwardness.

She pressed her feet into the horse's sides and trotted slowly around the ring.

He watched her as, seemingly all at once, she remembered how to ride.

"How does it feel?" he called to her.

She gave him a smile childlike in its pleasure.

"I forgot what a joy it is to ride this way," she said.

"Are you ready to try it outside the ring? We should leave while the weather holds."

The sky was the color of iron, though there was no sign of rain.

She nodded. "Where are we going?"

He told her of the meetings they had scheduled as

he mounted his horse and they set off across the lush green downs.

"Ah," she said. "You intend to prove to me your bona fides as a progressive landowner this morning."

"Yes. I think you'll like me better in a few hours."

She gave him a look that conveyed *we'll see*.

"Where are we headed first?" she asked.

"To the ragstone quarry. We've heard concerns about its safety."

She gestured at a turnoff to the carriage road that led through the woods. "Let's cut through the forest. It's faster than going over the downs."

"I knew your knowledge of this place would be of use."

Rafe had lived on the estate for years, but the intensity of his work—and double life—had kept his peregrinations around the place limited mostly to the stables, his cottage, and the village. The surrounding miles and miles of countryside were as foreign to him as if he'd been a stranger.

He rode slowly, setting a gentle pace that would not challenge Cornelia's skill. The woods were cooler than the meadow, and dark without the sun shining through the canopy.

"It's rather eerie in these woods," Cornelia said.

"I'll protect you should we encounter any malevolent spirits."

"Like that of my uncle?"

"Especially that of your uncle."

"Let's turn off here," Cornelia said, veering toward a cut-through in the path scarcely wide enough for the horses. Soon they were back on the downs, and the quarry master's building was in view. It was dilapidated, situated beside the entrance to a tunnel underground.

"Good day, sir," Rafe called as a man stepped outside to greet them. "I'm Rosemere, and this is my friend Miss Ludgate. You're expecting us?"

"It's an honor, Your Grace," the man said, ushering them inside.

As Rafe formulated a way to delicately discuss the state of operations without making the man fear criticism, Cornelia cut directly to the heart of the matter.

"We've heard the conditions here are not safe, through no fault of your own," she said. "Is that true?"

The foreman closed his eyes, as if in relief that someone was asking him this question. Bless Cornelia's candor.

"Unfortunately it's very true, ma'am. The caves are overtunneled. Have been for years. They're at risk of collapse and we've already had injuries from falling rock."

She grimaced. "The workers must be terrified."

"Aye. They're fearful of the danger. But just as scared we'll have to shut down the caves, and they'll be out of work."

"Is there a solution to improve their welfare?" Rafe asked.

The man hesitated, seeming nervous to speak openly.

"We'd be most grateful for your honest assessment," Cornelia said gently. "We're here because we want to make changes that will benefit your men."

He nodded, looking relieved once again. "I encouraged Lord Rosemere to close the caves and move to open quarrying. It's safer, and can give a larger yield. But the duke didn't want to mar the vistas. He preferred to mine underground for the sake of the pretty views."

Rafe and Cornelia exchanged a look of horror.

"The beauty of the grounds should not come before the safety of the workers," Rafe said. "We'll change that."

"I'm glad to hear you say it," the quarryman said.

"And with a potentially greater yield," Cornelia mused, "there will be more earnings to distribute among the men, for a similar amount of labor. Is that correct?"

"Nothing can guarantee it," the foreman said quickly. "But odds are that's right."

"Then the first step should be improving safety," Rafe said. "We'll close the caves and work out a plan to move to open quarrying. I'll personally ensure that there are no lost wages in the meantime."

"That's generous, Your Grace," the foreman said, looking shocked.

"No," Rafe said. "It's my duty. It should have been done long before conditions reached the point of danger."

Cornelia nodded. "Quite right."

Her approval made him happy. It was pleasant, being in league with her.

They bade the quarry master goodbye, promising to be in touch to help him plan and finance the open mine.

"What an absurd thing," Cornelia said as they rode off toward the vicar's, their next stop. "Imagine my uncle risking men's lives over the appearance of one patch of land on his miles of estate. You can't even see it from the house or gardens."

"Absurd," Rafe agreed. "Bastard."

Cornelia shot him a look of complete relish. "Execrable stinking bastard."

"Rotting, hell-bound bastard," he said.

She smiled at him again. "I must admit I did not expect you to be so sincere. Part of me did not believe you were truly making changes."

"Well, you did spend two decades thinking me a bloody Tory. I can forgive you a bit of suspicion."

He said this mildly, when in fact he wanted to jump off his horse and roll in the grass in victory. Ha! She was impressed with him.

"I wish I had known sooner," she said.

"I wish I could have told you."

They took the path to the village road, passing humble, pretty farms on the road leading to the market square. Despite the disrepair of some of the houses, the land was beautiful.

"Is that not your old cottage?" Cornelia asked, pointing to a house in the distance.

He was shocked she recognized the unremarkable old house after so many years. How inconvenient.

"It is," he said.

"When did you leave it?"

"A few months ago, just after I inherited."

"It looks like someone is living there now. Do you know them?"

"I do," he allowed, not willing to say more. There were certain things it was critical she not know. Not yet.

"Shall we go say good morning? I should love to see the place again." She looked over and smiled at him dryly. "It will remind me of my days as a blushing bride."

He hated to deny her anything when she was in a good humor with him, but he couldn't grant what she asked "No, let's not. They wouldn't wish to be disturbed."

"But certainly no one would turn away a duke," she teased. "Come, let's make a visit."

She began to turn her horse onto the dirt path toward the house.

"No!" he called sharply. "The occupant is elderly, and ill. We should not intrude."

She looked taken aback by his tone, but steered her horse back onto the path. "Very well, Rafe."

"I'm sorry," he said. "I just don't want to burden a sick man."

She nodded. "Of course. I understand."

He cursed himself for taking this route. He hated having to deny her something when they'd been having such a pleasant morning.

He didn't want to ruin it.

He was glad it was only a short ride over to the vicar's, where after a few brief pleasantries, the tension between them was lost in a discussion of how few children were attending school.

"The schoolhouse is small and worn down," the vicar said. "And it's often filled with just a few students, especially at harvest time."

"We can work on improving the schoolhouse," Rafe said. "But why do you reckon there is poor attendance?"

"Rents are so high that parents can barely afford to feed their children," the vicar said. "They need help in the fields, and it comes at the expense of education. And even if the children had the ability to come, the schoolhouse is in town, far from many of their homes."

"It's a desperate parent who would deny their child the opportunity to learn," Cornelia said. "That attendance is low means the parents need more money and more help."

"You're right, miss," the vicar agreed. "The problem comes down to keeping families fed."

"Miss Ludgate and I will muse on this," Rafe assured him. "Thank you for your time."

"I have an idea," Cornelia said as they rode off toward their appointment with the forester. "Families are large among the farmers. We could provide a stipend for each child, to help offset the cost of food and clothing. That would no doubt allow families to hire farm hands, and also remove some of the burden on mothers. They could better afford to send their children to school, and to bring in a cook or a maid to help with housework."

He loved the way her mind worked. It would not have occurred to him to think of the burden on mothers in particular.

They continued to share thoughts, most of which were feasible if the profits of the estate were turned away from enriching the duchy and toward providing wages and services to the tenants. It was inspiring to work with Cornelia. Where others might see obstacles, she found an interesting puzzle. Their brains were good together.

By the time they met with the forester and began to make the journey back to the manor, he felt confident that the reforms he had in mind would greatly improve the way of life at Gardencourt. And once they were underway, he could work with the tenants to govern the estate themselves, without his interference.

"Thank you for coming with me, Cornelia," Rafe said. "It was immensely helpful."

She smiled at him, looking genuinely pleased. "It

was a fruitful afternoon indeed." She paused. "You make for an excellent duke—if an unusual one."

"I'm not proven yet," he hedged.

"I'm looking forward to working together," she said. "It might be a bit like old times."

God, he wished it so. He knew that they would never be as close as they were those few days they spent on the road to Gretna Green. He knew he could not risk that kind of intimacy with her. But if they could only be friends, it would fill an empty space in his heart that had been vacant since she left him.

Chapter Twelve

Cornelia had never been so delighted to have been so wrong.

Rafe was a good man. One she could trust. After so many years of harboring scorn for him, it was soothing to simply like him.

Ahead of her, he glanced at the sky, which had darkened as they rode, moving from an iron gray to an ominous shade of dark purple.

"I'm afraid we may get caught in the rain," he said apologetically, as if he could control the weather.

"I think we have another half hour. If we're lucky, we'll just make it home—"

Before she could finish the thought, the sky burst open. Sharp, cold rain pelted down through the canopy of trees, soaking them in as much time as it took to shout out in surprise. Rivulets of water poured down the brim of her hat, splashing her nose and getting into her mouth.

"Are you all right?" Rafe called over his shoulder above the din of the droplets crashing onto the leaves above them.

"Just very wet," she called back.

Thunder boomed out long and low and a bolt of lightning crackled through the sky. Her horse whinnied.

"We need to take cover," Rafe called over the rain.

"Ride slowly, in case the horses spook at the sound of thunder."

"There's a summerhouse nearby, a mile up the path," Cornelia said, relieved he wanted to stop. She knew she was not an experienced enough horse-woman to sit a bucking animal if Nelly took off out of fear.

Terrifying.

Thankfully, the summerhouse was closer than she'd remembered. Rafe guided the horses to a lean-to against the house, where they'd be protected from the storm. He dismounted quickly and went to help Cornelia, as there was no mounting block.

"Take my hand and slide off," he said. "I'll catch you."

Her gloved hand was soaked, as was his, and water dripped as he squeezed her fingers. She put an arm around his shoulders and jumped. He caught her, staggering for balance on the muddy ground as she clung to him. Her weight sent his foot askew. He groaned, wobbling as he tried to steady himself. He staggered back as he set her down. As soon as she was safely on her feet he fell to one knee, cursing.

"What happened?" she asked. "Are you hurt?"

Slowly, looking pained, he rose to his feet. "I twisted my ankle," he grunted. "I'll be all right. Just a twinge of discomfort."

But when he stepped forward, he nearly buckled.

Cornelia rushed over and put her arm around his waist. "Here, lean on me. Let's get you inside."

He looked like he wanted to protest, no doubt unaccustomed to his physical strength failing him.

"Don't be shy. We can't risk you falling and causing a sprain, or worse."

Gingerly, he leaned into her touch, like he feared he would tip her over. She braced against him, unworried by his heft.

"Thank you," he murmured, letting her slowly lead him to the door. "You're surprisingly mighty, for such a little person."

She was pleased he noticed. "Painters must be spry."

She tried the door. Blessedly, it was unlocked.

Inside, the summerhouse seemed to be in regular use, which was a relief, as it was clean and stocked with firewood.

"Sit down," she said, gesturing at a sofa near the hearth. She dragged a chair in front of Rafe so he could put his leg up.

"Are you comfortable?" she asked, once he was situated.

"Aside from the throbbing in my ankle. But being taken care of by Cornelia Ludgate more than makes up for the pain." He tossed her a charming grin.

"Your injury must not be severe if you can flirt with me."

"I'll never be too injured to flirt with you. I'd do it on my deathbed."

"You would, wouldn't you." She was fairly certain he would flirt with anyone until his dying breath, but that was fine, as so would she. They were an incorrigible pair.

"I'll make us a fire so we can dry off," she said, kneeling before the pile of wood.

He watched her in silence as she worked. Outside, the rain pounded all around them. The glass windows of the summerhouse were designed to make the occupants feel surrounded by the forest. Everywhere one looked was the deep emerald of the trees. With the rain sliding down the glass and the rumble of thunder, it was cozy and a bit romantic.

Not romantic in the . . . loving sense, she clarified in her own head. Romantic in the sense of picturesque and atmospheric. Why she needed to make this note purely in her thoughts she did not know, except that it was important to draw a line where Rafe was concerned.

The fire flickered from sparks to a healthy blaze, and Cornelia sat down beside Rafe on the sofa.

"How's your ankle?" she asked.

"It hurts, but the pain is drowned out by your nearness."

"I'm serious."

"Getting better, I think," he said. "Twisted, but not sprained."

"Will you be able to ride back?"

"Hopefully by the time the storm breaks, the pain will have dulled."

She patted his shoulder and felt him shiver—either from being cold and wet, or from her touch. She wanted to pull closer to him and see if she could make it happen again.

She'd once exulted in her power to make him tremble.

"Today reminds me of our journey," she said. "All those years ago, but I remember it so vividly."

She remembered his unfailing kindness. How much he'd done for her. The way her whole body sparked when he was near her.

She took his hand.

She kept doing that—touching him before she could think better of it. He looked down at their entwined fingers, then up, searchingly, into her eyes. She considered taking her hand away, but would that not be more odd than clutching his in the first place?

Besides—she didn't want to.

Instead, she squeezed it.

"Rafe, I'm not sure I ever properly thanked you for what you did for me," she said.

She looked into his blue eyes, trying to convey the depth of her sincerity. It was appalling, really, that she'd never fully expressed her gratitude.

His eyes flashed darker, and he squeezed her hand back. It sent a little thrill through her, the strength of his big, warm paw against her delicate fingers. His size had always made her fluttery.

Do not flutter *for Rafe Goodwood.*

"It was the honor of my life, to be able to help you," he said softly. "I'd not take it back for anything."

He looked so sincere that her heart squeezed a little.

"That's kind of you to say."

"I mean it. I've thought about you often, Cornelia. I wanted to write, but I was doubtful that you'd welcome it."

"I wouldn't have," she said. "I wouldn't have wanted to remember that I once liked you."

Despite the awkwardness of her confession, he gave her a rueful grin. "And now?"

"And now what?"

"Does the lady like her husband?"

She smiled into his eyes.

"I'm afraid she might."

They were drawing closer together. She knew she should move away, break the tension, but it was so pleasant and warm beside him that she kept giving herself a moment longer to linger, and then another, and then another.

"How is your ankle?" she asked again, to distract herself from his nearness.

He grinned at her. "Stinking painful. But I'm quite pleased about it."

"Oh? And why is that?"

"Because being trapped alone in a deserted summerhouse with Cornelia Ludgate is a fantasy I didn't know I had."

His voice was low and gruff.

She ought to say something to change the subject, but before she could think of anything that wasn't him, he put another hand on top of hers.

"I'm truly glad you're back, Cornelia."

The words were similar to the ones he'd said last night, but now, tucked next to him after a day rekindling their friendship, she didn't want to flee.

"Thank you," she said in a voice that was a mere thread above a whisper. "So am I."

Slowly, the corner of his mouth twisted up into a smile.

"That makes me happy to hear. I was afraid I made you miserable."

She shook her head. She was very far from miserable. She was dangerously close to stroking his knuckle with her thumb. Perhaps not the universal gesture for "come hither," but as close as she came to an emotional display.

She should move away. She knew she had her reasons for upholding a safe distance between them.

But sometimes the body made the mind forget.

Shouldn't she get to have a little taste of him? She hadn't felt like this in twenty years. She'd never been so attracted to another man in all her life.

She wanted more.

She slid ever so slightly closer, so their hips touched. God, the pleasure of his nearness.

He sighed at the pressure of her body and made room for her in the hollow of his side. They were silent, their breath far too halting to pretend either one of them was unaware of what was happening.

He lifted his hand off of hers and brought it to her shoulder. He hesitated, like he was afraid she'd move away.

"I want to kiss you," he murmured. "Just one more time."

A terrible idea, she knew—

"Me too," she confessed.

And then—she did not know how or who or precisely when—she was kissing him, and he was kissing her.

Not hungrily, but lazily, almost like it was a dream.

The rain pounded on and the fire flickered away, and she did not object as his hands ran up and down her body. Slow, slow, slow, his kisses.

She felt like she was breaking open.

She put her hands in his hair and pulled his mouth down harder on hers, demanding more from him. He pressed her tight against him and dragged his lips off her mouth and down her neck. She tugged her shirt out of her breeches and his hands were close behind hers, tracing up her stomach to her breasts.

She threw her head back against the sofa as his thumbs caressed her nipples and writhed against him, her hands fumbling for the bulge between his thighs, which was as mighty as the rest of him.

He gasped and kissed her harder, sliding his hand down beneath her breeches. She opened up her legs and let his fingers find the slickness of her quim, feel how wet she was, feel just how wrecked he made her.

"Fuck," he whispered. She found his falls to free his cock.

She wanted him inside her.

A violent crack burst forth and the cottage shook. They both jumped as a tree branch broke through a window and sent a spray of freezing water at them. Rafe leapt up and stood over her, protecting her as the ceiling groaned as though it might give way.

But it didn't. Moments passed and the creaking stopped.

All she could hear was the rain and their twinned breath, panting.

Rafe collapsed back down beside her and pulled her close to him. She slid just beyond his grip.

"Rafe," she rasped out, "we must stop."

She leaned back against the sofa, breathing hard. He leaned forward, attempting to catch his breath.

"I know," he murmured. "I know we must."

And though it was true, though it was urgent— detaching her body from his was still like detaching an errant lace sleeve cuff from the rough bark of a tree.

His lips on hers, his body on hers, felt like coming home. Her body recalled the pull he'd had on her so many years ago—the effortless attraction that he'd fought valiantly, and she had relentlessly stoked.

She'd been eighteen then, and the stoking of passions had been new, and exciting. She'd wanted to be wanted past the point of reason. She'd wanted to want in a way that was heady and blind.

But she was no longer eighteen.

She'd long ago learned the price of diving headlong into lust. The more naturally it came, the more one became mired in it.

And once one was mired, one's heart was exposed.

To expose one's heart to someone one liked well enough, or was indifferent to, was one thing. But Cornelia did not merely like Rafe well enough. Now that she knew who he really was—that his politics matched her own, that he intended to use his inheritance in an unprecedented way—all the old attraction rushed back.

And not just physical attraction. The type of emotional connection Cornelia did not ever court, and severed as soon as she became aware of it. Not because she couldn't draw a boundary between herself and a man she liked—but because the *men* couldn't.

She had turned down three proposals in her lifetime, and each one had been painful, for she hated hurting other people. But they had wanted more of her than she was prepared to give, and causing distress in a lover was preferable to a lifetime of meeting that person's expectations.

She did not wish to commit herself to a single person, to close off the possibilities. And love—especially men's love—came at a cost. The pleasure of it was bought at the expense of one's capacity for self-determination and adventure.

Rafe had already proved to be the kind of man she could not trust not to get attached.

She moved farther away, out of reach, toward the flickering fire.

"May I speak frankly?" she asked.

"Please," he said, looking up. He seemed more collected, though his face was still flushed.

"I've always had a difficult time staying away from you, and now is no different. But we must. I am in no position to become entangled. My life is exactly as I want it. And we already know we are incompatible."

He blew out a breath. "Of course," he said in a low voice. He paused. "I'm sorry. This was my fault. It's been a while since I've been in such close quarters with a woman, and I let my base impulses get away from me."

She sucked her lip in disapproval. "Rafe, I am the last person who would call your impulses base. If anything, I share them."

It was not his sensuality but his sweetness that made her wary. She could feel it even now—Rafe wanting to embrace her with affection rather than pure ardor.

"I'd be very happy to make love under different circumstances," she said. "Like if you, for instance, were someone else."

He laughed ruefully. "Am I so bad?"

Oh, he wasn't bad. Not in the slightest.

"You are so good, and that is the problem."

He reached out and tweaked her chin. "Oh, Cornelia. There was a time when you liked that about me."

And where had that gotten her? Nowhere she wished to go again. Or rather, nowhere she could *permit* herself to go again.

"I'm older and wiser now. I like dalliances. You're not a dalliance."

He grinned at her—perhaps a little sadly. "Correct. I'm your husband."

She snorted. "Don't boast."

"Well, if I can't kiss you, I may as well console myself with our famously sanctified state of matrimony."

"A temporary state," she said. "And if you are capable of such humor, your ankle must be feeling better."

"It is," he agreed. He stood up and walked over to the broken window, stepping around the dangling

branch. His gait was a bit stilted, but there was no obvious limp. He peered outside.

"The rain's dying down. It will be wet, but it may
be wise to ride back now while there's a break in the
storm. Lest we be trapped in here all day with falling
trees."

She nearly sighed aloud at the thought of being
trapped in here all day, falling trees and all.

There was another world in which she and Rafe
would ride out the storm in the cozy warmth of the
fire. They would take off their wet clothes, and en-
twine their bodies, and whatever happened—and
surely something quite pleasurable would happen—
would be a chance gift of fate.

Her will nearly buckled, thinking of how easy it
would be to throw off her scruples and her clothing.
Maybe if she and Rafe agreed to limit their lust to a
single, rainy afternoon—

But she had never been good at limiting her lust
where Rafe was concerned.

And she could not allow her will to become subor-
dinate to another person's heartstrings.

If there was a single principle she held dear, it was
this one. She'd known it deep down in her bones since
she was eighteen years old.

And she'd made sure, even then, that Rafe knew it, too.

Chapter Thirteen

Before

It was still dark and rainy when they stopped for lunch at an inn. They sat in the parlor by the fire, drinking ale and eating sausages to fuel themselves for the coming journey.

Cornelia ate in silence, staring at the fire. She looked sad.

"It's time to tell me why I am the swain ferrying you to Scotland, and not your lover," Rafe said softly. "Rotten of him to abscond and leave you to face your uncle's wrath alone."

She puffed out a scornful breath.

"Oh, Osmond didn't abscond. He offered to marry me on the spot. Declining was the one thing my uncle and I agreed on."

She shrugged at Rafe and bit into a sausage. "Mmmm," she said. "Tasty."

He was surprised a girl of her age was so unperturbed by the dissolution of a love affair.

He wanted to know more.

"Osmond is his name?"

"Osmond von Kempt, esteemed Viennese painting tutor and less esteemed portraitist. Taught me everything I know." She paused and winked. "Except for my extravagant natural gifts."

"Ah," Rafe said.

"For lovemaking," she said dryly. "And to a lesser degree, painting."

Her manner was so deadpan it was sometimes hard to know if she was serious.

No doubt seeing his bemusement, she quirked her mouth at him. "That was a joke."

He buried his face in his mug of ale so she wouldn't see him smile. She was the most unusual young woman he'd ever had the pleasure of conversing with—though he felt ambivalent about taking such pleasure in ribald conversation with a girl so young.

He disapproved, after all, of the man who had caused her to be in this compromised position.

"And he is where? This Osmond."

She rolled her eyes. "Oh, I'd think in Rome, or perhaps Spain. He can no doubt afford to go wherever he wants with my uncle's money."

She continued on in the same dry tone, but this time, there was a slightly brittle note beneath her lazy cadence.

"Your uncle paid him off?" he asked, aghast at the entire situation. "And your lover accepted it?"

She shrugged. "He enjoys money very much, and rarely has enough of it. So yes, of course."

"Bastard," Rafe hissed.

"Perhaps. But had my uncle not paid, he would no doubt have finagled a way to marry me. Osmond's rather manipulative, you see. In his own charming way."

She sounded resigned, recounting this, which made his hackles rise.

"Manipulative how?"

She paused to take a dainty sip of ale. He sensed a reluctance in her to continue this conversation.

"He contrived for my uncle to come sit for me," she said finally. "To see the advancement of my skill. And contrived to be giving me . . . extra lessons just as my uncle was due. I was not aware he was expected. I suspect it was a trap."

Rafe's hands twitched with the desire to snap the man's neck. "Wretched swine."

"Indeed," she sighed. "He swore it was a coincidence, of course. That he had confused the time. But whatever it was, my uncle walked in on us to find Osmond posing for me in the nude."

Rafe almost felt bad for the old man.

"In fairness," he said, "that must surely have been horrifying for him."

"Oh, absolutely. Osmond was a bit *excited*, you see, and I had captured that in my portrait." She winced. "And in many drawings. Which I had rather indiscreetly left scattered about, as I was not expecting visitors."

She put a hand over her eyes and shook her head. "Quite a day, that was."

Rafe nodded, sympathizing. He couldn't imagine what he'd do in such a circumstance. Jump out a window, most likely.

"What happened when Rosemere discovered Osmond? I'm surprised he didn't shoot him."

"I'm sure he would have had he been armed. He chased him around the room, which was rather humorous since my dear tutor was naked. Osmond hid behind an armoire furiously trying to get dressed while pledging to marry me. My uncle and I were equally disturbed by that idea, I think."

Her tone was mordant, but it didn't quite match the expression in her eyes. He didn't believe she was unaffected by the way she had been treated. By her lover *or* her uncle.

He wondered if she had a broken heart.

"Did you love him?" he asked her softly. "This Osmond?"

She leaned back, smoothing her shirt over her thighs.

"I suppose I loved him a *bit*. Still do, I think. I'm grateful to him. Before him I knew nothing of passion. I knew I liked to draw and wanted to become a better painter. But he awakened me to the full potential of my possibilities. And the pleasures I might take in them."

"I see." He furrowed his brow, disapproving of this man. "But he hurt you."

She considered this, tearing apart a piece of bread.

"He did. I will admit I was wounded that he tried to entrap me in his scheme. But you see, I'm also grateful. Before him I'd not had so much as a kiss in all my life. I knew I had urges, desires—but they were vague . . . like a landscape through a haze of light, where you can see the horizon, and the clouds, but not the flowers in the foreground. And now I know. I know what my body is built for. I know what I love to do. And that is to paint, and to . . ."

She met his eyes and bit her lip, as if debating whether to go on.

He inclined his head, willing to hear whatever it was she wished to say.

"Make love," she finished.

"Cornelia!"

She allowed herself a laugh. "I'm sorry to shock you, poor innocent Rafe. But the truth is Osmond was a most excellent tutor. In bed."

She did not seem disturbed or regretful about this. She seemed genuinely . . . glad.

He didn't fully understand the complexity of her emotions. But he wanted to. It was clear she had not spoken of this before. He knew how lonesome it could be to be alone in complicated romantic situations. He knew what it felt like to want something as much as you wished to deny you wanted it.

"May I ask you a personal question?"

"Of course," she said, gesturing widely, as if nothing he asked could be too invasive.

"If Osmond was such a phenomenal lover, and you cared for him, why is it that you did not wish to marry him?"

She rolled her eyes.

"Because even before his scheme, I didn't trust him in the slightest. Osmond likes to have his way in everything, you see."

"Especially with young girls, apparently."

Rafe had nothing but contempt for a man who would abuse his position of trust to seduce an innocent maiden.

"Who eagerly welcome his advances," Cornelia countered firmly. "That's not what I mean. Osmond wanted me to paint what *he* wanted, how he wanted. He cared nothing at all for my opinion. He likes to *influence* me. To teach me his own ways. I have no doubt that if we married, he would wish to control me—to make me exactly into the image of the wife he desired. As his pupil, I could ignore him. But if he were my husband, he could force me to do whatever he wanted."

She paused thoughtfully. "And I cannot tell you, Mr. Goodwood, how much I loathe to be controlled."

"I understand," he said. "It would ruin your spark."

"Yes," she agreed. "And I am only just discovering it."

He was taken aback at her insight and wisdom. For a girl so young, she seemed to see far more than Rafe did, at least about human character.

"Besides," she said, "he only volunteered to marry me for money."

"He sounds like a manipulative, talentless fortune hunter."

She threw back her head and laughed. "Oh, he is, to be sure. But I told you—I'm grateful for him."

He raised a brow. "Remind me why?"

"Because he was also an excellent tutor of color mixing, perspective, technique—and he taught me all he knows. I have the gift, and I will forever be thankful he helped me to see it."

Rafe didn't quite believe her. She sounded as if she was trying to convince herself as much as him.

"And besides," she continued, "without him, and what he provoked in my uncle, I would still have a girlish, romantic, nonsense view of love."

She rolled her eyes, as if love were something worthy of contempt.

"What do you mean?"

She shrugged. "To be loved is to endure another person's idea of you. And to accept that love, you must accept their desires, at the expense of yours. Love means sacrificing freedom. I will always choose my independence over love."

She seemed so confident in this opinion. He did not agree that love was such a burden, but he thought he understood a little. Women were at a disadvantage in any relationship with men who had authority over them—be it a father, a guardian, or a husband.

But still, to eschew love at such a young age struck him as impossibly sad.

He hoped someday she'd change her mind. He hoped she'd be afforded circumstances to be loved by someone who would not wish to change her or control her.

"Perhaps that is a cynical perspective," he said gently. "We can see new aspects of ourselves in another person's love for us. It can be an opening, rather than a limitation."

She squinted at him, frowning. "You think I am lying to myself to safeguard my emotions?"

He did think that was part of it. Sometimes, he knew, we needed our evasions to protect us. Cornelia's spirit was not broken. That was what mattered in the moment.

He smiled at her. "I think that there is little that escapes you, Cornelia."

"Only my uncle's affection," she said with a trace of sadness he had not yet heard in her voice.

She looked down at her lap, as if she was gathering her thoughts. He was quiet, waiting to listen.

"He locked me away in my room once he'd dispensed with Osmond," she said finally. "My lady's maid, Canette, cozied to his secretary to determine what he was planning to do with me, and he told her about the letters in my uncle's correspondence between himself and a slew of loathsome men—old, gouty, mean, dull—on the subject of looking for a match for his 'ward.'"

She met his eye, her gaze filled with pain. "'Ward,' can you imagine? After all the years he'd called me daughter? It's just cruel."

"I'm so sorry," he said.

"You cannot imagine the indignity, Rafe. To think I was his perfect little lady for eighteen years. I doted on him, ran his home from the age of fifteen, served as his hostess. I did every single thing expected of me my entire life, and did it with more beauty, grace, and poise than even he could ask for. He professed to love me. And then, *one* infraction—and one borne of passion at that—and he wanted me entirely out of his life, with no care for my feelings or my future."

He could tell that this had been more painful than the rest of it. The way her transgression had robbed her of her guardian's affection in a single afternoon.

"He's a bastard for that, Cornelia," he said gruffly, not sure what else to say.

She let out a shaky sigh, tears beading in her lashes.

"I can't help but feel I have been judged doubly in all this—not just as a woman, but as a woman of mixed race. It's always been this way—that I am expected to be extra good, extra careful, and if I'm not, I'm punished extra harshly. I can't shake the feeling that if I were white, my uncle might have given me a second chance. Osmond might have been more cautious, might not have attempted his scheme. This whole nightmare might have been avoided."

She looked into his eyes, searching—awaiting his reaction.

He was furious on her behalf. And he could sympathize. Being a man who sometimes slept with other men, he was careful to be discreet, to keep that part of himself a secret, lest he face judgment, or even punishment by law. He always felt the weight of being different—of having to be cautious, to live with fear. It was not the same, of course, but he felt a kinship with her nonetheless.

"I'm embarrassed to say I'd never thought of that," he said. "I'm so sorry, Cornelia. I know I can't fully understand how that would feel, but I know this—you don't deserve it, and I'm glad that you explained it to me."

She smiled tightly. "Thank you."

"You deserve *real* love," he said, shaking with anger for her. "The kind of love that comes without conditions."

She shook her head. "Love without conditions doesn't exist—for anyone. That's just a fairy tale. But thank you for listening to me. I don't have many confidantes. Talking to you has made me feel much better. It helps me, discussing it, to know my own mind."

He felt such a surge of affection for her, this kindred spirit, this lonely girl.

"Of course. You may talk to me about anything you want."

He took her hand under the table, out of sight of the other patrons, and squeezed it.

She squeezed his back.

And though he was certain it was dangerous, he did not desire to let go.

Chapter Fourteen

$\mathcal{B}$eing good was torturous.

For three days, Cornelia worked alongside Rafe, going over account books, touring the estate, and interviewing Canette and Singh as to possible reforms in the running of the house itself.

For three days, she wanted nothing more than to touch him.

She ached with it.

From the bittersweet way he smiled at her whenever they parted ways, she suspected Rafe did, too.

Still, she dutifully kept her distance when they were not working together, which was not difficult to do in a house the size of a cathedral. She dutifully reminded herself some things were worth more than easy passion, that becoming entangled would be pleasant in the moment and disastrous soon after. She dutifully kept her hands to herself when he was near.

She was sick of being dutiful.

Thankfully, today the torture of being alone with Rafe would end. Their guests would be arriving for the house party any moment.

Cornelia waited anxiously by the window for a sign of her friends. Lucius sat beside her, eschewing his morning nap to help her keep watch. When a carriage finally passed through the gates, she rushed down the stairs and out the door to greet it.

"Welcome," Cornelia called as Elinor helped Seraphina out of the carriage with the baby, and Thaïs bounded up the manor stairs. "I've missed you so much."

"It's been right pleasant without you around," Thaïs said, wrapping her arms around Cornelia for a long, deep hug. "But I'll tolerate you in exchange for a week at the palace."

She shaded her eyes, taking in Gardencourt Manor's Palladian facade and the older wings that towered behind it, dating back centuries. "You'll have to drag me out of here by my hair."

Sera strode forward, holding her baby in one arm and wrapping Elinor's shoulders in the other.

"What an odd thing to be back here after so long," Elinor said. Her aunt had grown up at Gardencourt, but stopped calling on her brother, Rosemere, when he disowned Cornelia. She had not been to the house since.

"Are you happy to be back?" Cornelia asked.

"I've been happier," Elinor sighed.

Elinor looked ghostly. She had ever since Jack Willow's disappearance.

Cornelia knew her aunt had been struggling to keep a stoic temperament where Jack was concerned in the months that he'd been gone. But it was obvious whenever his name came up that his absence—more than any of the miseries her husband was bent on inflicting upon her—was what pained her most.

It made Cornelia's heart hurt just to look at her. She gave her aunt a kiss on the cheek, and a long, tight squeeze.

As soon as her hands were free, Sera plunked the baby into Cornelia's arms. "Ella missed you," she pronounced.

Cornelia nuzzled the little baby's soft head. "I'm shocked Adam isn't keeping you two at home under lock and key."

Seraphina's lover, Adam Anderson, was fiercely protective of her and their baby.

"Adam knows I would disembowel him if he attempted something so foolish," Sera said.

"Believe her," Thaïs said, shivering. "And he's too fine a man to be ripped open by the likes of her."

"You remember Marianne," Sera said, gesturing at a pretty young woman who was trailing behind them shyly. "Adam's sister."

"Of course," Cornelia said. "I'm so glad you could come."

"I'm so pleased to be here," she said in her soft Scottish lilt.

"Impossible to work with a baby on the breast," Sera said. "Marianne is a godsend as a nurse."

Marianne flushed. "You flatter me."

Sera barked out a laugh. "I certainly do not. I am too reticent about your skill if anything. If it were not for you, I would accomplish very little."

Cornelia ushered them all toward the house. "Come inside, come inside, I'm dying to populate the manor with figures from my uncle's nightmares!"

"It sounds like the manor is now *owned* by a figure from your uncle's nightmares," Sera said. Without sharing the details of his espionage, Cornelia had written to inform her friends of Rafe's "newfound" liberal politics. The rest she would share more discreetly now that they were here in person, before supper.

She introduced the ladies to Canette and Singh, who were waiting just inside to greet them and show them to their rooms. Cornelia had made sure that they would enjoy all the finest pleasures the grand house had to offer. She and Canette had prepared the best rooms and ordered meals that would have made a member of the Bourbon royal family blush.

"How is married life treating you?" Sera asked as they climbed the stairs up to the bedchambers.

Cornelia rolled her eyes. "Don't be irritating."

"Don't be withholding," Sera parried. "Have you and Rafe rekindled your romance?"

Sera was joking, having no knowledge of exactly what had transpired between Cornelia and Rafe all those years ago. And Cornelia had no intention of enlightening her. Her friends would immediately be on the watch for any sign of tension between them, and Cornelia did not need an audience observing her struggle to keep her distance.

"We'll be joined for dinner by several guests of Rafe's," she told them, pointedly changing the subject. "Let's get you to your rooms to freshen up."

CORNELIA WAS THE last to arrive in the salon outside the dining room for supper and found it was full of new faces. As soon as Rafe saw her, he raised his libation and cleared his throat.

"My distinguished guests," he said. "Shall we gather round for introductions?"

The guests ceased their chatter and looked at Rafe attentively.

"First, you have all met, or know by reputation, my wife, Cornelia."

The room went quiet at the word *wife*.

"You sly old devil," a man Cornelia recognized as Lord Eden said to Rafe, breaking the stunned silence. He raised his glass. "Well done, you."

The others followed suit, and before Cornelia could do anything to stop it, she was being lauded in a toast to her happy matrimony.

How dreadful.

"Uh, yes, thank you," she said, "but I'm afraid it isn't like *that*. It's simply an arrangement—"

Rafe threw an arm around her shoulders. "No need to be shy, my blushing bride," he teased.

She wanted to elbow him between the ribs. They did not need to make a spectacle of themselves when there would be enough speculation about what was between them just by nature of their surprise nuptials. She loathed making any kind of scene around her personal life. She would do it for her exhibition when the time came. But this setting, with new acquaintances around, made her squeamish.

"Rafe is my lawful spouse," Cornelia said in a firm tone. "No more."

Rafe's face lost its playfulness at the hardness in her voice. He shot her an apologetic glance. *Good.*

"In all seriousness," Rafe said, "Cornelia is absolutely correct. Our marriage is legal, but we have never observed the conditions of matrimony. It's simply a convenience to allow Cornelia to inherit in her uncle's will."

"Yes," Cornelia added, "and if you could all keep this information private—only to be known among us, for now—we would appreciate it. We're saving the news to announce at the ball."

"A secret!" the youngest guest, a beautifully dressed young lady, said. "Delightful."

Lord Eden gave the girl a stern look and shook his head.

"As for secrets," Rafe said, giving the girl a gentle

smile, "the work we've gathered here to do is very sensitive. No one must talk about it outside these walls. No letters. No chatter in front of servants."

They all nodded. Each had been forewarned of the need for complete discretion in advance of their arrival.

"We've invited only people we trust implicitly to help perform the work that we must do," Rafe said. "You may all speak freely among each other, and we hope you will become friends."

Tentative smiles were exchanged all around as the guests eyed each other with open curiosity. Cornelia had never seen Rafe in this mode before—as a leader. He wore his authority well.

"Cornelia, will you do us the honor of presenting your guests?" he asked.

"It would be my privilege," she said. She smiled at him—a tacit apology for her tone in dressing him down a few moments before.

She must find a middle way between coldness and flirtation. A way to be friends—no less, and no more.

She went round the circle, introducing all of her ladies to the other guests. When she was finished, Rafe began to introduce his own friends.

"Many of you know my secretary, Rory Thompson," he said, gesturing at the handsome Irishman Cornelia had flirted with intermittently since her arrival.

"And those of you in the Equalist Society will recognize Gilby Howe."

Cornelia did indeed—a slight, pale young man who represented liberal causes as an attorney, often donating his time to abolitionary cases.

"To my left is the distinguished Lord Peter Eden, an expert on estate management who has kindly agreed to help me understand how to modernize Gardencourt."

Cornelia had never met Eden, but had seen him at parties—an earl, and one of the most reform-minded figures in the House of Lords. He was about her age, with olive skin, dark silver-shot hair, and distinguished brows. He looked like he might be half-Turkish or Italian.

"Lord Eden's sister Lady Anna has also graced us with her presence," Rafe said, gesturing at the young lady who'd spoken before. Anna looked scarcely out of the nursery, decades younger than her brother. Cornelia suspected she was his ward, the product of a widowed parent's second marriage. The girl, blond and plump, curtsied with an enormous smile, looking not at all nonplussed to be, by far, the youngest person in the room.

"Well, now that everyone is acquainted, let's go in to eat," Cornelia said.

"There's one more guest who wished to greet us," Rafe said. "He's waiting in the dining room."

Cornelia looked at Rafe askance. When they'd discussed the party, he hadn't mentioned an extra person would be joining them.

He smiled at her mysteriously and offered her his arm.

She took it, lightly, not allowing herself to focus on its pleasing heft. "You're keeping secrets from me?" she murmured in his ear.

"It's a good one. I think you'll be happy."

They filed into the room in pairs, Cornelia and Rafe leading the way.

She froze when she saw who was at the center of the table.

Jack Willow.

"Jack!" Elinor cried, rushing forward.

"Holy hell," Thaïs yelped.

"You rat," Cornelia hissed at Rafe. She was *not* happy at this surprise—at least not with Rafe, the liar. She dropped his arm, its heft no longer pleasing.

Jack rose from his seat. "I hope I haven't startled you," he said in his broad London accent. He addressed them all, but his eyes were trained on Elinor.

"Rafe's been kind enough to hide me in his bachelor cottage while we work on my defense in court."

Cornelia elbowed Rafe in the ribs.

"Why didn't you tell me he was here when we passed the cottage?" she whispered in his ear. "I *knew* you were holding something back."

She had not asked the question quietly enough. Several heads turned to look at them. She took a deep breath and smoothed out her face. It would not do to make a show of her anger before their guests.

Jack stepped toward her. "It's my fault, Cornelia," he said. "I had to disappear in order to collect information for my defense without Bell sabotaging me, or worse. I didn't want anyone to know where I was until I could tell you myself, in person."

Everyone was quiet. No doubt, like Cornelia, they were cycling between relief at seeing Jack alive and safe, and frustration that they'd been kept ignorant of his whereabouts, fearing for his safety.

"Jack," Seraphina finally got out. "That's very sentimental. But you've been missing for *months*. Why in heaven's name did you not tell us you were safe?"

"Aye. We've been tearing out our hair," Thaïs said. "And my hair is far too delectable to be wasted on the floor."

Jack winced. "I'm so sorry I caused you pain. But

your fear for me made it obvious to anyone you didn't know where I was. After the threats to Seraphina last year, after Bell imprisoned you, Elinor—there's no telling what he would have done to you if he thought you knew where I was. The less you knew, the lower the chance of danger for all of us. He knows that I'd do anything to prevent you from being harmed."

He paused and took Elinor's hand. *"Anything."*

Elinor shook her head wearily. "You could have simply told us. Any of us. We would have kept your secrets."

The tension between them was so thick, so private, that Cornelia wanted to exit the room. She hated displays of emotion even when they were not directed at herself.

Elinor looked as if she could not decide whether to yell or weep. "We're not delicate," she finally said, her voice hard. "We don't need protection from the truth."

What a perfect example of the perils of love. Jack had taken it upon himself to withhold crucial information from Elinor, thereby stripping her of her right to make her own decisions. This was what men did, even enlightened ones. They limited your autonomy with their supposed superior knowledge and judgment.

They tried to control you, intentionally or not.

Jack came behind Elinor and put a soft kiss to her cheek.

"I'm sorry, love," he said in a raspy voice. "I was frightened for you. For us both."

Jack, who normally had the manner of a bulldog, seemed as vulnerable as a newborn kitten. He looked beseechingly into Elinor's eyes. "Forgive me?"

Elinor softened. "We'll talk later. I'm just so relieved you're safe."

He clutched her hand. Elinor closed her eyes at his touch, like she wanted to bathe in it.

Cornelia looked away. She hoped they could return to the more solid footing of their plans now that Jack and Rafe had indulged in their grand reveal.

"So let me piece this all together, if I may," Seraphina said brusquely. "Cornelia tells us Rafe is a radical who has been spying for Jack's paper for years. Now we learn Jack has been in hiding here with Rafe—doing what exactly?"

"Preparing for the trial," Jack said. "Bell is out to bring me down, and ruining my reputation will sabotage the Equalists and all we've built. Rafe and Rory have been focusing their efforts on finding a way to learn Bell's strategy."

"We're hoping to run into him at a horse auction soon. The plan, if we can pull it off, is to probe him for information under the guise of selling him a horse," Rafe said.

"Oh, I see," Eden drawled, as though this were a minor point. "Is that all you have been up to, Rafe, or have you also planned to lightly overthrow the government over tea."

"Well, there's more now that you mention it, actually," Jack said, glancing at Rafe, as though for permission.

Rafe nodded.

"It's about time you all know Rafe is King Crow," Jack said.

What? Cornelia whipped her head over to Seraphina, who shook her head in wonder. King Crow was among their heroes, and they did not have many. His column against monarchy, feudalism, and peerage in the *Equalist Society* circular expressed the most dangerous sentiments that the paper printed. Talk of ridding the country of its power structures flirted with sedition.

Cornelia couldn't hold back her amazement. She turned to Rafe. "No, you are not. Truly?"

He grinned at her. "I'm afraid I am. Which I think makes you . . . Queen Crow."

"You're telling us you are behind the antimonarchical screeds that have the Tories in fits?" she asked.

He laughed, clearly delighting in her disbelief. "I wouldn't call them *screeds*. Essays, perhaps."

"Oh, *demolish the aristocracy, institute a democracy*," she parroted, summarizing his views. "That, from the perspective of a Tory, is a screed, my good friend. A Jacobin screed at that."

He smiled, clearly pleased with her reaction. "I believe every person in this nation should have the right to the gains of their own work," he said. "They should have a hand in contributing to how it is governed."

She could not keep from smiling back at him. "Well, aren't you a fascinating character. I wish I had known this about you. I might have looked more fondly on our nuptials had I known I was married to a kind of hero."

She had not meant to say something so earnest. She was just so overcome with pride that the man she'd loathed for his politics all these years was so . . . *good*.

He blushed. In front of everyone.

"Thank you," he said. "I wish I could have told you." His eyes flickered with regret. The unspoken words were *but we were not in touch*.

She shared his sorrow. She wouldn't have welcomed communication from him. Not after the way they had parted. And so she hadn't known about his brave work, the same way he had not seen her paintings.

What a loss to think of how much they'd missed of each other's lives, when they might have been compatriots.

"I will look forward to reading your next column, now that I know your secret," she told him, in the spirit of being friends. She turned her gaze to Jack. "I hope there will be a new issue soon?"

Jack's lips drew into a grim line. "Not until after the trial, I'm afraid. It's too dangerous, with Bell trying to bring us down. But once he knows Rafe is among us, it will be more difficult for him to threaten the publication. They'll have a harder time crying sedition when the words are coming from a member of the House of Lords."

"In the meantime," Rafe said, "Jack will be returning to the cottage after the meal. A few of us will visit him there to help work on his legal defense. We were hoping that you might advise on it, Gilby."

"Of course," Gilby said. "It would be a privilege."

"There is much work to be done by all of us," Cornelia added. "Perhaps we should discuss what there is to do over supper."

They all took seats, and the conversation turned to the many things that needed to be accomplished in the next two weeks.

Mountains.

They agreed that Cornelia and her friends would put the finishing touches on the painting exhibition, while Canette and Anna would work on invitations for the masquerade. Meanwhile Rafe, Rory, Lord Eden, and Singh would design a plan for redistributing the assets to workers on the estate. Rafe, Gilby, Jack, and Elinor would assist with Jack's defense.

"And then," Seraphina said, "we will all collapse from exhaustion."

"Hopefully not from prison, in my case," Jack drawled.

"Not likely," Gilby said. "I'll see to it you're victorious."

Anna inclined her head with intrigue at the heretofore quiet young man. Noticing, he blushed, and shrank back in his seat.

"Enough of this solemnity," Rafe said, raising his glass of wine. "Let's drink and be merry."

They did. Heartily. By the time an hour passed, the meal was more like a rowdy assembly hall debate than the kind of dinner her uncle used to host in these rooms, with stiff talk of politics among the gentlemen and stiff talk of society among the ladies.

Cornelia loved the sense of purpose they all shared. It was the most pleasant meal she'd eaten in ages.

As dessert was served, Lady Anna spoke up for the first time.

"If it pleases the group, I should like to be in charge of our entertainment."

Eden smiled kindly but firmly at his sister. "We're here to work, my dear. Not to frolic."

Anna was not cowed. "But it's a *house party*, is it not? Surely we must have a bit of fun."

"I'm afraid this might be the least amusing house party in history," Cornelia said.

Normally a house party involved shooting expeditions, picnics, and endless games of whist. Their guests were going to be treated to such activities as chicanery, conspiracy, and espionage.

"I shall make it amusing," Anna insisted. "I specialize in the amusing."

"Let's not be *too* amusing, Anna," Eden said.

"I'll just arrange some pleasant diversions in the evenings, to refresh us."

"There's only one kind of pleasant diversion that refreshes me in the evening," Thaïs quipped in a low voice to Cornelia.

"Behave," Cornelia whispered back. "We are among the innocent."

"I hope you don't mean me," Anna said.

"She had better mean you," Eden retorted.

"Well, now that that is settled," Rafe said, "I thought we all might adjourn to the portrait gallery, where Cornelia has been hard at work. She has kindly offered to give us a preview of her paintings."

Cornelia smiled. "It would be my pleasure."

Not least, because she wanted Rafe to see her form of art, now that she knew of his.

Chapter Fifteen

God, the way Cornelia had looked at him when he said he was King Crow. He wanted her to look at him like that every moment of his waking life.

Which was *disastrous*.

It was classic Rafe—his heart always opening like a damned hothouse flower at the slightest encouragement.

He knew precisely where that path led. He had the past, and the wounds, to prove it—and the scars left by Cornelia were the deepest.

It was imperative he be more careful. To inure himself to the effect she had on him. To stop thinking of the bloody summerhouse, and her sighs of pleasure mingling with the pounding of the rain.

But how could he gird himself when confronted by the sight of her work in the gallery? He was shocked, as he led the others in, at the wizardry she'd wrought.

Throughout the epically long room, up and down the triple-height walls, an assortment of paintings of Rosemeres past had been unceremoniously removed. Some of them were on the floor propped against the wall, some of them had disappeared entirely, no doubt moved to the attic, where the parade of old, white men in wigs could rest in dusty obscurity.

In place of the portraits that had been removed, Cornelia had installed new works. The staid colors that made the previous collection so very dull had been replaced with Cornelia's saturated hues. Lords and ladies had been replaced by vivid portraits of whores of various races and degrees of wealth and class, all of them in sacred poses.

The effect was breathtaking. Her paintings alone made a point about the ways women were allowed to be perceived. But side by side with the hoary, gilt-framed aristocrats, they pointed to a different possibility of what made a human being worthy of enshrining in paint and hanging on a wall. They made equals of the proper duchesses and gaily painted harlots.

It gave him an idea.

He walked over to where Cornelia stood with Seraphina and Anna, who was wide-eyed at the shocking contents of the room.

"I think I might be compromised just from looking at this, were I the type to care about ruination," Anna said.

"A person cannot be ruined," Seraphina murmured. "Remember that."

Anna nodded solemnly.

"May I have a word with Miss Ludgate?" Rafe interjected.

Anna nodded and moved on with Seraphina to admire the next painting.

"These are extraordinary," he said to Cornelia. "Absolutely extraordinary. I knew they would be, of course, but the way you say so much with a simple image. By merely putting paintings side by side you make me see things differently. I am in awe of you, Cornelia. Truly. In awe."

She looked up into his eyes, and he saw that she was genuinely pleased with his compliment. "Thank you," she said. "I'm glad you like them."

"Like them" was not strong enough a sentiment. He wanted to take her hands—those brilliant hands that could create such marvels as hung on these walls—and kiss them.

Stop.

He needed to focus his appreciation on her art, not her beautiful, talented fingers.

How could he be so moved by *fingers*? He was coming untethered.

"Cornelia, I *love* your work," he said. "I cannot wait for the moment when we lead in the pillars of society to feast their eyes on it. We shall have to have a doctor on hand to see to their hearts. I'm sure there will be more than one person beset by palpitations."

"Murdered by art," she mused. "That would be perhaps a bit more controversy than even I am courting."

"That's true. I would hate to have to rescue you from gaol."

She widened her eyes and inclined her head. "Could you? I'm not sure even a powerful duke like yourself can pluck a murderess from prison."

"I'd break you out and abscond with you to the nearest desert island."

"Is that a promise?"

He grinned at her. "A most solemn vow, my lady."

"Hmm," she mused. "I suppose that wouldn't be so bad. I don't mind hot weather. Or you."

Her brown eyes sparkled, and there was flirtation in her voice.

Despite his vow not to nurture his affection for her, he was delighted.

In the past few days, he'd missed her.

He'd already gone twenty years in that state. He did not wish for a single moment more.

Surely a little harmless banter could not possibly send him reeling into heartbreak, or drive her to run away. They were adults after all. Adults could spend time together without falling headlong into romantic disaster. And he had an idea how to do it safely.

"I have a proposal for you," he said.

She inclined her head. "Oh? And what is that?"

"It's traditional for each new Duke of Rosemere to have a portrait painted. I was going to eschew tradition, given I plan to be a duke in name only. However, now that I have seen your work, I've had a notion. What if *you* painted my portrait?"

Her eyes flashed. He wondered if she remembered the way it had been between them the last time she'd captured his likeness.

She rearranged her face into a more playful expression. "You wish to request a commission?"

"Yes, but not in the usual style. Rather than the typical pompous attire, I could be dressed as a horseman. I was thinking we could unveil the work at the masquerade."

Her face changed; she seemed impressed he had suggested it. He exhaled to make certain he was not puffing out his chest in pride, as it would not do for her to see the profound effect her most minor positive emotions had on his mood.

"That's an intriguing idea," she said. "A comment that a duke is no more or less than any common man."

He nodded eagerly at the mischief that was blooming in her eyes. "Yes. But I'd like for it to be more than just a comment on dukes. You see, I want the painting to be called 'King Crow.'"

She cocked her head at him. "Do you mean you are willing to reveal your true identity at the ball?"

"There is no reason for it to remain a secret. By then we'll be days away from Jack's trial, and there will be no reason for me to continue as a spy. I can do more in Parliament as a radical duke than I can surveilling the nobility in secret. And it will drive up circulation and readership if people know a duke is writing for the *Equalist Society*. Even if they read it out of anger, they'll want to read it."

She nodded slowly. "I love it, Rafe," she said.

She was proud of him, he could see. *Proud*. It made him want to stalk around the room like a cock in a henhouse.

Instead, he merely nodded. "I'm glad."

"Come sit for me tomorrow, if you can. There isn't much time, and I'd like to make a study of you as soon as possible."

He could think of few activities more pleasurable than sitting for Cornelia. Being alone with her, with her attention trained on him minutely. He would exult in her company, even if it was only as a friend and collaborator. Even if he must take care not to let it become any more than that.

"Fine," he said. "Are you free after luncheon?"

"Perfect."

They stood nodding at each other, neither seemingly able to pull away. It was as if they were the only two people in the room.

In the world.

"I have an idea!" Anna called, jolting him back into reality. Cornelia turned to look at Anna—perhaps just in time, for if they had stared at each other any longer, Rafe might have forgotten himself and moved in to kiss her. He was only so strong.

"What is it, Anna?" Lord Eden asked.

"Let's all play a game of silent seeker."

Oh thank God. Something to take his mind off his desire to enjoy the presence of his wife.

Everyone seemed amenable to the idea.

"Yes!" Cornelia said, with a playful smile. "What a fine way to get acquainted."

Rafe waited for Eden to object, for the game involved feeling others' bodies with one's hands, but he merely shrugged with a long-suffering sigh as the others nodded enthusiastically.

Rafe was delighted. He loved games.

Especially when he was playing with Cornelia.

Chapter Sixteen

Before

The drive to Gretna Green was long and cold and rainy. The lush green of the forest might have been beautiful on a summer's day. Today, it was merely drippy.

But beside Cornelia Ludgate, it was far from miserable.

She was just about the most intriguing girl Rafe had ever met. Granted, Rafe was not one to spend his time with maidens. His preferred company was middle-aged radicals, well-bred horses, and the occasional mature and sultry woman or man in his bed.

But he would gladly spend as much time as he could with Cornelia.

"Escaping forced matrimony is duller than I expected," she said, yawning.

Obviously, she did not find him as enthralling as he found her. Not that the conversation of a thirty-four-year-old man was likely to be anything but boring to a girl her age.

"I hope it's not the company you're keeping," he said. "I can try to be more amusing."

"No, you're perfectly agreeable," she said. "It's the great distance between Gardencourt and Scotland. And the drizzle. Don't you find drizzle monotonous?"

"Not when it's falling on me. I find each drop quite unpleasant in its own unique way."

She laughed. She had a laugh as inviting as her voice—low and generous and long. It made him smile, though he didn't find what he had said terribly funny.

"I have an idea to pass the time," she said suddenly, sounding inspired.

"And what is that?"

"A game of Penalties." She looked at him playfully, brows raised.

"I'm not familiar," he admitted.

"It's easy. I will recite an enigma. If you know the answer, you receive a point, and you may ask me a riddle in return. If you do not know the answer, I extract a penalty."

This sounded harmless enough. "What kind of penalty?"

"You must answer a question of my choosing."

"Very well. And how do we decide the winner?"

She rolled her eyes, as though he were the slowest-witted man on earth. "Whoever has the most points before we get to the inn is victorious. Obviously."

"And does the victor get a prize?"

"What do you want?" She asked this in a tone that could only be described as flirtatious. The sadness she had evinced over their meal had dissipated as soon as they were outside. He was not sure if she was truly feeling better, or if flirtation was her way of distracting herself from her more painful emotions.

He tried to think of something that might cheer her up.

"A portrait," he said. "A sketch of myself, signed by the future famed artist Cornelia Ludgate."

She smiled. Clearly, she liked this penalty.

"And what do you want?" he asked her.

She glanced over at him, as if weighing her options. "A kiss, I think," she said.

He was quiet for a moment. "From, er, me?"

"No, from the horse. Of course from you."

All the questions he had about her tone over the past days resolved into an answer: yes, she *had* been flirting with him.

This was a problem. She was eighteen, and he was nearly double that. He couldn't possibly kiss her without feeling like a toad, however much he might want to if she were a few years older. Even flirting back made him feel like a lech.

"That would be entirely inappropriate," he said. "I'm an old man. I think you're forgetting."

She looked at him like *he* was the naïf between the two of them. "Oh, I haven't forgotten, ancient one. I happen to like a decrepit paramour. Especially a handsome one."

He blushed, damn him. He *blushed*. And worse, he was so embarrassed for blushing he could not think of a witty reply. An eighteen-year-old girl was robbing him of his most basic powers of banter.

"Besides," she said, "you don't get to choose what I demand. You shall have to martial all of your intellectual resources to preserve my chastity and honor."

She was right. If this was her penalty, he simply couldn't let her win.

"You go first," she said. "The first person has the advantage. It will help you protect my famed purity."

She was mocking him. His worry about the gap between their ages must irk her. He supposed if the tables were turned, the implication he was too young to know what he wanted would annoy him, too. Not that it was any inducement to change his mind.

"Go on," she prodded. "Stump me."

His mind went blank. The only thing he could think of was the most common, infantile riddle he knew.

"As I was going to St. Ives,
I met a man with seven wives,
Each wife had seven sacks,
Each sack had seven cats,
Each cat had seven kits:
Kits, cats, sacks, and wives,
How many were going to St. Ives?"

Cornelia snorted. "As anyone who has ever read a nursery book knows, in order to meet the man, the wives, and the profusion of cats, the teller must have crossed paths with them on the way to St. Ives. Therefore they were walking in the opposite direction. Ergo, the answer is one."

This was not helping his cause.

"Some of us are mere horse trainers and were not blessed with a milk-fed education in which there was time to learn the most complicated of Saxon riddles. Congratulations on being raised by a duke, with all the nursery books money can buy."

She laughed. "I happen to know you were raised by a prosperous horse breeder and educated in London, which certainly has its fair share of bookstores. So I think you mean congratulations on scoring the first point. Now then, since I have won, it is my turn to ask you a riddle. I shall take pity on you and begin with a simple one."

"I hope I am up to the challenge," he said, truthfully. Her presence was making him feel unusually dense. At least it was also distracting him from his damp clothing.

She cleared her throat.

> *"I view the world in little space,*
> *Am always restless, changing place.*
> *No food I eat but in my power*
> *Procure what millions do devour."*

It was a relatively easy enigma. He'd heard one like it before.

Perhaps she did not wish to be kissed after all.

"The sun," he said. "My turn."

She pouted. "I took pity on you due to your supposed intellectual infirmity, and look at you, knowing all the answers."

"Thank you for your mercy."

She grinned and rubbed a rivulet of rain off her face with the back of her hand. "Trust you won't receive it again. Now give me a difficult one. The point of this game is to amuse, not bore."

If she meant to goad him, it was working.

"Very well," he said. This one he'd read in a gentleman's magazine. She'd likely not heard it before.

> *"Black I am and much admired,*
> *Men seek me until they're tired;*
> *When they find me, break my head,*
> *And take me from my resting bed."*

Cornelia was quiet for a while, thinking. It was a relief that she did not immediately know the answer.

"Black," she mused. "So many things are black.

What sleeps? A cat, I suppose. But break my head—no. That doesn't make sense."

Good. He wanted his portrait.

"Poor dear. Stumped by the humble horseman," he drawled. "Do you forfeit?"

"Certainly not. I never quit at anything." She tapped her chin, thinking. "Oh! Of course. Men seek me and take me from a bed, but it tires them. Like miners. What is black and mined? Coal!"

She smiled at him, victorious, and wiped away another errant drop of rain that had landed on her nose.

He hadn't expected her to know the answer. She was intimidatingly intelligent.

"You are very clever," he said, genuinely.

"Aren't I?" she laughed. "Now I have one for you. Unless you would like to forfeit entirely, as I am clearly going to win and I would not want to exhaust you with so many miles left to cover."

Never. He was competitive enough to not wish to be bested.

"No, I'm energized by your wit. Please, go on."

She grinned at him slyly.

"I go in hard and dry
And come out soft and wet."

"What am I, Rafe?" She waggled her brows at him like a lecher ogling a barmaid in a revealing gown.

Which meant she was trying to trick him. He happened to know this one, too. It was meant to sound filthy, and the true answer was innocent.

"A sponge," he said triumphantly.

She shook her head and sighed as if in sympathy.

"Oh, Rafe. How *sad* you are. The answer is clearly a man's most private part. That's another win for me."

He nearly fell off his horse. Her combination of dignity, poise, and filthy-mindedness was going to undo him.

"Cornelia. Speak like that and you'll unseat me."

"I will stop when you beat me, which you most certainly have not. Now you owe me a penalty. One question of my choice."

"Fine. What is it you would like to know, you cheat?"

The victorious smile didn't leave her face. "Who was your first love?"

That had not been a question Rafe was expecting. Nor one that was easy, or simple, to discuss. And Cornelia clearly meant it as a challenge, for the smirk on her lips was proud indeed.

The smirk of a young woman delighting in her new-found powers over men.

It reminded him why the warm feelings he had for her could not lead to anything. He wished they were in a carriage instead of on horseback. He could have challenged her to a game of checkers instead of agreeing to this treacherous game of enigmas. He could beat her at checkers with his eyes closed.

"I had two, I think," he admitted.

"You *think*? Surely if you were in love twice over, you would know it."

"Love can be complicated."

She rolled her eyes. "I know."

"Do you?" he shot back, with more force than he meant to. She sat up straighter.

"If I do not, explain to the poor, naive child what you mean."

He closed his eyes, remembered he was on a horse, and opened them. The story still pained him.

"There was a girl when I was a very young man. A neighbor. We'd had a special connection since childhood."

"A special connection. I don't suppose you mean—"

"I mean affection for each other. Mutual understanding. Attraction to each other's bodies. She was sweet with me, and I was sweet with her."

"Very well, very well, I understand. Did you seduce her?"

"It wasn't like that. I didn't have to 'seduce' her. We wanted each other. I wanted to marry her."

"But you couldn't, because you were in love with someone else besides?"

"Yes."

"Well? Who was the other lady?"

He hesitated. He could easily avoid being honest— this was not her business, and it was delicate to share. Very few people knew about his attractions.

But the kind of girl who spoke of cocks, who asked distant acquaintances to marry them in the middle of the night, who knew the danger of your desires being used against you—something made him trust her.

He'd told so few people what had happened. In a way, it was a relief to talk about it.

"He was a trainer at my father's stable."

The teasing look fell from her face.

"You were in love with another man," she said softly. There was no judgment in her voice, and very little surprise. It made him like her more, that she would accept his secrets with such equanimity, the same way he accepted hers.

"We were both boys, really. But when we were

around each other, alone—it did not matter who or what we were. Friends, lovers, companions."

"And who did you choose?"

"Neither." He did not know how to put this in a way she would understand. Few people ever understood.

"Both. It's complicated. I don't wish you to think I was dishonest. They knew about each other. But ultimately, both of them wanted someone for just themselves. And so I ended up with neither."

They were both quiet. Perhaps because she could hear the sadness in his voice.

She looked over at him, compassion in her eyes. "Were they angry at you?"

"A little, I think. I could not explain how I felt—that I loved them both. That the one was not a threat to the other—that there was room in my heart for both of them."

That he fell in love so easily, so generously. That it did not mean it wasn't real.

"They couldn't share you," she surmised.

"Yes. And I understood that."

It was his first, harsh lesson that his feelings were excessive, overabundant. That his infatuations caused him to hurt people, and drove them away.

"What happened to them?" Cornelia asked.

"She courted with another man and married him. He became distant and ultimately left for another post. Never returned my letters."

"And what of you?" Her voice was soft, sad. There was no teasing tone to her voice or posture. Just sympathy.

"I was heartbroken," he admitted. He coughed. He felt vulnerable discussing this.

"This is why you won't marry." She said it as a statement, not a question.

"Only you," he said ruefully.

She smiled, but she didn't laugh. "I'm honored, Rafe. But I'm sorry."

He shook his head. "It was a long time ago. I've had many loves since."

She was quiet for a moment, and then her solemn expression went devilish.

"That's not why I'm sorry," she said, smiling at him as though to lift his spirits. "I'm sorry that you lost the game. Now I must demand my forfeit."

"But we haven't reached the inn," he protested.

She gave him a victorious smile and pointed ahead to a sign. "The Hare and Crow, 1 mile."

"We're nearly there, and I can't extract my victory prize in public." She inclined her head innocently. "You *do* remember my prize?"

As if he could forget it.

"Cornelia, you couldn't possibly want—"

She slowed her horse abruptly and pointed at a small clearing in the forest. "Stop your horse there."

He hesitated.

"Rafe, if you are, as you say, a man of honor, then you will do as I ask. It will only take a minute. Now get me off this horse."

He was a man of honor. He would kiss her to end this battle of the wills. On the cheek.

He helped her dismount and tied the horses to a tree.

"Come," Cornelia said in a low voice, beckoning him. He allowed her to lead him by the hand into a grove protected from the rain.

"Here," she murmured. "Perfect."

He leaned in to offer her a chastely buss on her cheekbone, prim and proper.

But Cornelia leaned up, took his head in her hands,

and rubbed her thumb over his lips. Her caress was soft and warm and welcoming. It did not demand, but beckoned.

He was stunned into stillness by the intimacy of the gesture.

He put an inch between their skin and expelled a breath. He wanted this, but he was not at all sure he would be a good man if he went on with it.

"Why do you want this?" he asked her.

"Because I like you," she said simply.

"And you kiss everyone you like?"

"No. Just the old reluctant ones."

He snorted, despite his nerves.

She glanced up into his eyes and traced her fingernails lightly down the back of his neck. "Please?" she asked.

He groaned. "Cornelia, you are too young."

"Experience and age are not the same thing," she said huskily. "And you can't tell me what I want. Only what you will give me." She exuded calm, as though she were the elder in the pair and wished to soothe his nerves.

It was her calm that made him nod in acquiescence. "One kiss."

Her eyes lit up.

She put her mouth to his gently, like he was a delicate thing she had to treat with utmost tenderness.

It was excruciatingly sweet and kind and it made him want her even more, for the sensitivity she showed him.

"You're sure," he whispered, finally believing her.

She laughed low in her throat. "Yes."

That was all he needed to abandon his last scruple.

He pressed her to him by the shoulders, bent down,

and offered her his tongue. She took it greedily, kissing him back expertly as her hands roamed the sides of his arms and down to his arse, which she pulled against her to draw him closer.

It was only when they heard the sound of a carriage approaching in the distance that they jumped apart.

He braced himself against a tree, worried he might stumble with the loss of her nearness and heat. But she stood straight and panting in the clearing, her eyes dancing with his and her swollen lips curved into a smile.

"Thank you," she said. "That was an excellent beginning."

Chapter Seventeen

Cornelia had always adored any game. Especially if that game took place late at night. Especially if it involved touching. She liked bedtime games best of all, but parlor games would do.

She was also charmed by Anna's enthusiasm for arranging diversions. When she'd been that age, she'd tried to finagle playmates out of anyone she could.

In particular, Rafe Goodwood.

The impulse hadn't changed.

"Who would like to be the seeker first?" Anna asked.

When no one immediately volunteered, Thaïs put up her hand. "Might as well be me. I have a skill for groping."

Cornelia groaned.

"You are quite predictable, my dear," Seraphina said.

Thaïs grinned at her. "I'm reliable, I am. And often lied upon."

Lord Eden stared at Thaïs from across the room, like he was not sure if she could possibly be real. Everyone else laughed.

"Excellent," Anna chirped. "We shall need a blindfold." She scanned around the room. "Ah, brother. Give me your cravat."

Lord Eden smiled pleasantly at his sister. "Absolutely not."

"Then I shall have to go up to my room to find a scarf. Unless some other kind gentleman would like to volunteer his neckcloth."

She said this looking directly at Gilby Howe. Poor Gilby turned the color of a beet. Seeing this, Rafe quickly stepped in. "As your host, I believe the duty should fall on me."

He put his hands to his cravat and began to unfurl the linen, revealing his strong, ropy neck. His naked throat brought into relief the tremendous definition of his jaw.

She tried not to stare, and tried harder not to think of tomorrow, when she intended to make him remove more than that. She could not dally with Rafe more than flirtation would allow, but it would be difficult not to gaze hungrily upon him while she painted him.

She wondered if he was thinking of that, too.

"Right then. Tie me up, Your Grace," Thaïs said, walking over to Rafe and presenting herself rump-side to be blindfolded.

Rafe chuckled as he did the honors. "There we are. Nice and tight."

"Just how you like it, I reckon," Thaïs said sweetly.

Cornelia glanced at Lord Eden, who, without a word, placed his hands over his sister's ears.

"I'm going to count to ten, and everyone should run about the room so Miss Magdalene has no inkling where we are," Anna instructed. "And then I shall say 'seek' and you must stand in place while she tries to find the nearest person. The first person she touches will be our seeker next."

Anna counted to ten as everyone scuttled about the room, leaving Thaïs near the gallery doors.

"And, seek!" she yelled.

Thaïs, being a ham, made quite a show of stumbling around with her arms outstretched. Perhaps intentionally, or perhaps owing to a poor sense of direction, she walked toward the doors that led away from her fellow players.

She fumbled in the air, grasping at nothing.

The doors opened, and Marianne came walking in. Anna gestured at her to be still, pointing at the blindfold, but Thaïs had canny hearing and reached out and tagged the girl directly on the bosom.

"Who've I captured?" she cried gleefully, palpating her prey's breast.

Thaïs ripped off her blindfold, her other hand still clutched in the vicinity of Marianne's chest.

Marianne breathed in sharply.

"It's me," Marianne said. "I came to get Seraphina. I wasn't aware you were playing. I'm sorry for ruining the game."

Thaïs looked oddly flustered, if pleased.

"Why, I've caught myself Miss Anderson," she said, giving Marianne a saucy wink. "Nice haul for the first try."

"Will you join us, Marianne?" Cornelia asked.

"I would love to. But Seraphina, the baby needs feeding. She's fussing."

Sera stood and bowed to the assembled guests.

"Maternal duty calls. I shall see you all in the morning."

"I'll go with you, dear. I'm exhausted from the journey," Elinor said.

The two of them left the room, arm in arm. After a brief hesitation, Jack followed them.

Cornelia wondered if he intended to sleep here tonight. And if so, whether Elinor might welcome him into her bed.

Marianne went next, fumbling about until she landed on Gilby Howe, who seemed mortified to be touched by an attractive woman.

Poor man. Anna was going to eat him alive.

And soon, for when Marianne yelled "seek," Anna ran *toward* Gilby, rather than away from him.

Noticing this too, Rafe caught Cornelia's eye and they exchanged an amused look. She wondered if he was comparing Anna to herself when she was young. And she wondered whether he liked her as much now as he had then, when she'd been so eager to make him her strong, sturdy, handsome paramour.

She could not be so forward with him now. But watching Anna made her wish she could be.

Anna's attempt to be caught was, sadly for her, unsuccessful. Gilby took a sharp right turn and ended up tapping Canette on the shoulder. Rafe glanced over at Cornelia again, checking if she saw the piqued look on Anna's face. She did, and snorted with laughter, which made Rafe laugh, too.

She loved how he threw his head back when he laughed—generous and open-mouthed. It reminded her of the eager, joyful way he kissed.

"Is something funny?" Anna asked, looking genuinely baffled by their mirth.

"Just enjoying the game, my dear," Cornelia assured her. Rafe bit his lip and nodded solemnly.

Canette proved good at the game, catching Singh within a minute. Singh looked like he enjoyed being caught. "You always catch me, don't you?" Cornelia thought she heard him say under his breath. Cornelia didn't hear the answer, but from the look on Canette's face, she suspected there was something between them.

Singh took his turn—and caught Cornelia. (She'd made the mistake of standing in the center of the gallery—never a clever choice.)

She glanced out at the positioning of the room before she put the blindfold over her eyes. By now, she'd noticed patterns. Eden always chose a corner at far remove, clearly horrified at the possibility of having to be seeker if he was caught, and likely not eager to be touched. Anna had a habit of standing near Gilby, who had a habit of standing near the rear doors of the room. Everyone else moved around freely, making every effort to be very far from where they started, except Rafe, who barely moved round after round.

This was good for Cornelia. She didn't want to catch him.

She enjoyed looking at him, laughing with him, joking with him—but the last thing she needed was physical temptation. If she put her hands on him, she would have the memory of that touch to taunt her all night. She'd be gripped by it while she prepared herself to be alone with him at tomorrow's sitting. She'd be so tempted.

They'd promised each other they would not be lovers. She wanted to honor that, not sabotage what they'd both agreed was the only acceptable way to move forward.

She aimed herself opposite to where she imagined Rafe was standing and began to walk forward blindly, fumbling in the air. It was surprisingly difficult to cast about without seeing anything. She wondered how anyone had succeeded without falling over or concussing themselves against a wall.

When a few disorienting minutes went by with no success, she tried a different strategy: jumping. Without warning, she leapt up in the air and twirled herself around.

The shock of it elicited noises from the group, and she heard a low man's laugh coming from her left. Eden, she reckoned.

She charged in his direction, hooked out her arm, and made contact with a pair of broad, firm shoulders.

Lord Eden did not have broad shoulders.

Rafe did, but this man didn't smell like Rafe. She pulled off her blindfold to find herself staring directly into the sparkling smile of Rory Thompson.

He gave her a low bow.

"Nice catch," he drawled.

"Indeed, you are," she parried.

He winked at her, and she winked back.

It was all good fun. But beneath the banter was something else: genuine desire in his eyes. He was a ludicrously attractive man, and the way he was looking at her made it obvious he appreciated her looks as well.

This was excellent. She wondered why she hadn't thought of him before as a serious candidate of amorous interest.

She could picture Rory all night, with his playful green eyes and his black hair falling over his face, instead of Rafe, and his clever hands, and his hard—*no! Mustn't think of his hard . . . anything.*

She would focus on Rory. Perhaps, if he seemed amenable, she could even invite him to join her in the most pleasant house party game of all: musical bedrooms.

If she did, it would be just the distraction she needed.

Because the thought of painting Rafe tomorrow threatened to overtake her with memories of when she'd sketched him before.

Memories she carried in her body.

Memories she hadn't been able to shake for twenty years.

Chapter Eighteen

Before

Cornelia rode ahead of Rafe the short distance to the inn, cheerful, seeming blithely unaffected by their kiss. He thought he heard her humming.

He, meanwhile, felt like he might tumble off his horse.

"You tack up the horses. I'll get us rooms," Cornelia said, when they reached their destination. It was not a pleasant inn, with polished wood and fragrant meals wafting from the warm-lit windows. It was the kind with ticking mattresses and travelers four to a bed, sharing lice.

They could not afford to be spotted at one of the nicer establishments. This would have to do.

Cornelia met Rafe at the door and held up a key. She looked rumpled, soaked through, and tired.

"Only one room available," she grumbled. "No fire. Shared bed."

"I'll take the floor," he said immediately.

"And leave me to freeze to death? I think not."

He didn't argue, but he would not be sleeping beside her. What had happened in the woods had to be the end of the intimacy between them. If he took advantage of Cornelia's youthful enthusiasm, he would be no better than her painting tutor.

They quickly ate the humble fare they were given—a stew, no meat, that cried for salt. They did not linger, for the less time spent in public the less risk of being seen by someone who might recognize them.

They took their one allotted tallow candle from the innkeeper and marched up the creaky stairs.

Their room was small, the bed barely large enough for one, let alone two.

"I'll have to use you for a blanket," Cornelia said, not bothered in the least.

The idea robbed him of breath.

"I'd rather you use me for a subject," he said, collecting his resolve. "I still want my portrait. Can you do it by this light?" The rain had stopped and dusk was falling, damp and purple, through the open window.

"I can draw in any light," she said, as though he were a fool or had insulted her.

"Would you do me the honor?"

She considered this, tapping her long fingernails against the windowsill.

"You did not win at enigmas. I cannot reward you. It would pollute the integrity of the game."

"I did not win because you cheated with your filthy double meanings."

"'Tis not my fault you were not clever enough to outwit my cheating. I never said I played an honest game."

"Then what must I do to get my portrait, Miss Cornelia?"

"Miss Cornelia," she uttered. "I do like it when you call me miss."

"Shall we try another enigma?" he suggested. Her flirtatious tone was making it urgent that they do something other than have heated conversation, lest he succumb to the temptation to kiss her again.

"No. I shall take pity on you and draw you on good faith. However, I shall extract a penalty for my great mercy."

"And what is that?"

"You must pose shirtless."

He choked.

"Absolutely not."

She shrugged, all exaggerated pity. "Then I'm afraid I can't immortalize you. How sad."

"Why is this your condition?"

She bit her lip. "Because I want . . ." She trailed off and looked at him with heated eyes.

You, they said.

God help him.

". . . to practice drawing the male form," she finished. "I've only had one male model, because ladies aren't allowed to do the normal course of study due to our supposed delicacy."

She grinned at him, all practicality. "Do we have a bargain?"

He should say no.

He should say no *and* leave the room. Linger over a nice flat cider belowstairs. Chat with fellow traveling men about the conditions of the road, the coming weather. Wait for her to fall asleep.

But he truly did want a portrait. After this trip, he'd likely never see her again. He wanted a memento of Cornelia Ludgate.

So he took off his coat.

And then his shirt.

He couldn't look at her. He felt too exposed, his nipples puckering in the chilled air, goose bumps prickling his forearms. He glanced down, self-conscious in a way he rarely was, as his body was healthy and hale and lean from his days outdoors on horses. But she would not be used to the form of a workingman. She'd likely be shocked by the coarseness of muscles that were used.

He felt her eyes lingering on him, tracing his dimensions. He flushed, staring at his lap.

"I thought you would be beautiful," she said softly. "But I was not expecting this."

He looked up and found her gazing at him, shaking her head, like she could not believe what she was seeing. He felt acutely that he was only the second man she'd seen in any state of nudity. For some reason, it made him feel even more bashful.

He blushed deeper and was glad for the dim light in the room.

She rose and rummaged in her small bag, producing charcoal and a sketchbook.

"Sit there, at the end of the bed," she said over her shoulder, "so I can catch the light against your profile."

He did as she instructed. She came and studied him closely. So close he could feel the heat of her body on his skin.

"I'm going to adjust you," she said. "May I?" She gestured at his bare arm.

He nodded in acquiescence, though he probably shouldn't have.

Her soft fingers gripped him by the bicep and adjusted his arm so that it stretched along the windowsill.

Her touch made him shiver. God, his attraction to her. It was greater than he could recall ever feeling for another soul. Instant and gravitational. Dangerous.

She tipped up his chin and lightly pointed it away from the light.

"Better," she murmured.

And then she reached up and smoothed his hair out of his eyes.

For some reason this—more than her touch on his bare skin or the kiss she'd given him earlier—lit him up with want. It was such a tender gesture. One of caring, of close attention. He could not recall a time in his life when it felt like someone looked upon him and *saw* him, caressed every detail of him with her gaze, wanted to see more.

He looked up into her eyes.

"Cornelia, I'm not sure this is a good idea. I feel—"

"Fearful?" she asked softly.

"Vulnerable," he admitted.

She took his hand and kissed it. "Don't worry. It will make the portrait more interesting."

He inclined his head at her, feeling as though she, not he, were the senior of the two of them.

"That's it!" she said, clapping with satisfaction. "Stay exactly there. Don't move."

She moved back, sketchbook poised, and observed him.

And then she began to draw. Her hand moved rapidly, her eyes flitting between the page and him. It felt like she was casting a net with her gaze, capturing him in it, raw. And with nothing to do, frozen in place by necessity, there was no hope of distracting himself. So he just watched her watching him.

He'd never indulged in staring at her straight on. She was so beautiful.

He loved her lips—the way the top one was fuller than the bottom, like it wanted to be kissed. Her eyes were rimmed in long lashes. Her nose was broad and ever so lightly freckled, like her cheeks. Every detail of her: darling.

Occasionally she bit her lower lip in concentration, and he had to bite his own to keep from smiling, because it was so adorable.

"Stop that," she murmured. "Stay so still I'll think you're dead."

He was anything but dead.

Eventually, he got used to staying still and silent, and his thoughts turned quiet, a rare, inward calm suffusing him.

He liked posing for her, oddly.

He liked to be the only thing she cared about, even for this small stretch of minutes. For surely it would be over soon. The last of the purplish light was dying out now, and she drew faster, trying to catch the dregs of it.

As the dim flickering of the candle became the only light in the room, she lifted up her head.

"There," she said. "All done."

"May I see it?"

He expected her to attempt to extract some wild penalty—to make a flirtatious game of it. But she only smiled and handed him her sketchbook.

Instantly, he realized she did not need a game to extract a penalty.

For looking upon the sketch was more than a flirtation.

It was a statement of the unspeakable fact between them: that he wanted her so badly it transformed him.

The portrait, however cleverly it mimicked his likeness, was not a portrait of a person. Its life was in the eyes of the sitter. Eyes that drank in the artist, looked upon her with pure hunger in them.

Every nerve of his body stood at attention, as she watched him taking in the drawing.

"Cornelia," he whispered. "This is obscene."

She moved closer to him, so she could study it over his shoulder.

"And you love it," she murmured. "I can see it in your face."

He had no doubt she could see every thought that had ever passed through his mind on his face, for her powers of observation—of translation—were so acute.

He looked deep into her eyes, shaken. "What else do you know about me, if you know all this?"

"I know you know how badly I want you," she said. "And I know you think badly of yourself for wanting me back. And I know that feeling badly makes you want me more."

He had nothing to add to that. He just nodded.

She took him by the shoulders and leaned him back, so his head touched the mattress.

"I want to do another drawing of you. A real nude. Just for me. To remember you."

His heart came to attention. She wanted to *remember* him. They shared that—a growing sense this time was precious.

She reached out and took his hand. "Would you let me?"

No, he knew he should say. But then, he'd wanted a token of this time for himself. Was it so wrong to grant her the same?

And if she wanted a nude form, was it so different from a shirtless one? For he already felt naked, with this intimacy between them.

Slowly, he nodded. "If you promise never to show it to another soul."

"I do promise," she said quietly. She raised his hand up to her lips and kissed it. "I do."

He shifted, about to sit and take off his boots, but she stopped him with a hand to his solar plexus.

"I'll undress you."

Oh holy God.

Was he a heathen to agree to this? Was he helping her artistic education, or furthering her earthly corruption in ways she might be too young for?

She started with his boots and went methodically, slowly, removing garters, stockings, working her way upward to his breeches, which were doing nothing to disguise his excitement.

He looked down at the bulge of his erection, miserable and excited and hopelessly confused.

Now it was his turn to take her hands. He grabbed them, holding them in the air before she could complete the task that she'd set before her.

"This isn't a game," he croaked. "Please, if you possess even a shred of doubt, or discomfort—"

She shook her head. "I don't, Rafe. Only excitement. Please let me."

Please let me.

Could he possibly say no to such a plea?

He couldn't. Not just because he was aroused. But because there was such honest pleading in her voice. He let go of her hands.

She unbuttoned the waistband and tugged down his breeches.

"Oh my," she said. There was an odd, warm tone to her voice. A flattering note of girlish wonder at his hardness. She did not touch him, which surprised him. His surprise flooded him with guilt, for he should not expect this young girl to handle his cock.

She slid his breeches down his legs. And there he was. Stark as the day he was born in a dim room with a woman he wanted more than life itself sweeping him with her eyes.

She adjusted the candle so it cast dim light over his body.

She perched on the small table in the corner, using it as a seat to get a better view.

And then she was back into the flurry of sketching.

This time, there was a slight smile on her lips.

He was so aroused, lying here vulnerable to her gaze. Nothing between them save air.

She snapped her sketchbook shut. "All done."

He held out a hand. "May I see?"

"No. I told you. This one is exclusively for me." She paused. "Besides, you know what it looks like, Rafe. Don't you?"

She crossed her arms and stared down at him. "You know."

He did. And it made him want to reach out and slowly strip off her boy's clothing. To undress her piece by piece, as she had done for him. To draw her to him on this bed. To feel her skin on his.

He couldn't.

She came toward him and sat on the edge of the bed. He clenched his hands. He would not touch her again.

"I changed my mind. I think perhaps *I* want to be the blanket," she said.

He reached for a sheet and drew it up over his waist. "I'm sorry," he said. "You mustn't. We mustn't."

Her brow knit, but she did as he asked, keeping her hands folded in her lap.

She was still and quiet for what felt like minutes. The silence made him tense, but he did not know what to say to free them from the tension.

"Rafe, you need to understand something. I know what I want. And I'm not new at this."

He believed her. But just because some other man had been indelicate with her age and lack of experience did not mean that Rafe felt comfortable following suit.

"I don't mean to insult you," he said. "I mean to protect you."

"From yourself?"

He considered this. "Yes. No. Yes—from regretting being with me."

She shook her head. "I'm very serious. I want you."

Not as much as I want you.

But he'd come to his senses at the reminder that another man had taken liberties with her—to grave consequence.

He gently lifted her away, stood, and wrestled his shirt back over his head, covering himself.

"I can't, Cornelia. I won't."

She let out a shaky sigh. "Truly?"

"Not for lack of desire, I assure you. But truly."

She sighed, moving away. "Very well. Condemn me to agonized frustration."

We shall share in it together.

"Good night, Cornelia," he said softly.

He prepared to lie down on the floor.

"What are you doing?" she asked, looking genuinely perplexed.

"Giving you the bed."

She snorted. "Rafe, don't be ridiculous. You won't

be able to ride tomorrow after sleeping on the hard, cold wood, and we only have one blanket. You can share the bed. I promise to be good."

The idea of sharing her warmth rather than tossing and turning on the dirty floor was too great a relief to pass up. She'd seen him naked and aroused. She'd kissed him, felt his body. Surely sleeping beside her would be no worse.

"You're certain you don't mind?"

"I'm a very certain creature in all matters," she said. "Soon enough you'll have to learn to take me at my word."

He was too exhausted to debate this. He sat back down, climbed beneath the sheets, faced the wall, and tried to fall asleep.

And he pretended not to rouse when she snuggled up beside him and put an arm around his waist.

The last thing he heard was her soft snores.

Chapter Nineteen

Cornelia's body felt tender and swollen, her thoughts of Rafe ripening her like fruit.

Despite her vow to think of Rory Thompson, she could only think of Rafe. She had gone to sleep with her hand between her legs, thinking about the last time she had drawn him. Wondering if he was remembering the same. Wondering if, perhaps, he had reconsidered the need to stay very far apart.

Wondering if *she* had.

Was it worse to pine for his body than it would be to simply allow herself to take it, and perhaps end this near illness of obsessing over what she couldn't have?

As she prepared the mise-en-scène for him to sit before, she wondered if he would actually come. It was one thing to request a portrait impulsively. It was quite another to commit to hours of sitting still in front of a woman you were trying not to want.

Assuming, of course, that was what he was doing. Or perhaps it was merely *she* who still felt the pull toward him—and was increasingly tempted to give in to it.

She was almost surprised to hear a knock at the door promptly at one o'clock.

She opened it to see Rafe standing there in riding clothes. With his tight breeches straining over his thick thighs, the sight of him was almost like a challenge.

He must have known the effect he had, for he smiled at her raffishly and breezed into the room.

How forward.

"Undress to the waist," she instructed briskly. "To paint you as a horseman, I'll need to make a study of your musculature."

Did she, though, really? Certainly it was her practice to be as detailed as she could, but in this case could she not puzzle out the specifics of his contours with his shirt and vest on? After all, she certainly would not be painting him in the nude.

But no, he sat his horse straight and imposing, and she wanted to do justice to the man he was. It suited the artistic statement to show King Crow in his full majesty.

Besides, he did not seem to mind. He smiled and began to unknot his cravat. "Anything for my wife."

She clucked her tongue, admonishing. "If you call me your wife, you will not like to see how I paint you."

He chuckled and widened his eyes. "And how is that, my duchess?"

"Buried in a tomb, with all the other dukes."

"Ah. How grim."

She nodded. "And the recently dead heirs. All eight of them."

He threw back his head and laughed. "Aren't you the charming one today."

Not as charming as you look.

Without his neckcloth, he more closely resembled the Rafe she remembered. The Rafe from their journey, armed with a gun and dressed like a highwayman.

The Rafe who'd shivered under her touch when she was eighteen years old.

Don't be sentimental.

She endeavored not to react to his naked throat and to ignore her strong desire to caress it with her tongue.

Don't get distracted.

"Much better," she said. "Now take off your coat."

He discarded it, and his lawn shirt winged out with the breadth of his massive shoulders and broad back.

Savoring it, she watched him lift the shirt over his head.

His body was a work of art. Hard, flat stomach, broad shoulders, and hair that rose in a trail from his groin and thickened around his chest. His small nipples puckered in the air. She had the strong desire to take them into her mouth and bite them.

She had long decried her male peers for treating female subjects as objects rather than people. But it was tempting, with such a subject as Rafe, not to join their ranks.

Don't you dare.

"How would you like me to pose?" he asked.

She pointed at a chair she'd positioned beside the window, in a shaft of excellent, bright light.

"Straddle that chair, with your legs apart, as though you are mounted on a horse."

The words were suggestive, but she refused to acknowledge it when he raised an eyebrow at her.

"Like this?" he asked, drawing his thighs over either edge of the seat. The position pulled his breeches so tight against his lap she could see the bulge of his cock. Which had not been her intention, but still made her weak in the knees.

She dragged her eyes away and nodded. "Yes. Perfect. Now then. Sit up straight and look over to the left. I'm going to start with your profile."

He obeyed. She decided to ask him questions to distract herself from lusting after him as she drew.

"What did you do this morning?"

"I met Rory at the stables just after breakfast. We've heard Bell's in the market for a Thoroughbred. We're auctioning our most promising yearling in hopes he'll hear word of it and want a viewing."

She sketched his shoulders as he talked—an activity that reminded her of how they felt beneath her hands.

"Have you met him?" she asked, to distract herself.

"Bell? No, though your uncle sold him one of my horses, and I'm told he's fond of the stallion. As a lowly breeder, I was never blessed with an audience."

"Not so lowly," she said. "You are quite tall."

"I am, aren't I," he agreed. "I hope you will do justice to my immense height in my portrait. It's my most striking feature."

His most striking feature was actually his beautiful blue eyes, but she didn't need to tell him that.

"In seriousness, your reputation as a horse breeder is so sterling that even I knew of it, and I can barely ride a horse," she said. "How is it that you went from horse trainer to prestigious breeder?"

"Well, my father was a breeder, so I grew up in the trade. Mind you, he was not an especially successful one, but he sold a few horses to the duke and some other local squires. I was in charge of training them from a young age. When the duke hired me to train his personal steeds, I was able to learn more about fine pedigrees. I asked his permission to try my hand at improving his equipage, using my father's knowledge as the basis. He granted me leave, and over the years, I proved to have a knack for it. Eventually, his stables developed a reputation—and so did I."

"You must have had his confidence, for him to trust you with his precious horses."

"It was my duty to earn it," he said. "I hope you don't despise me for it."

He glanced at her eyes, looking like he was already tender from the blow that he expected. It made her want to hug him.

"I don't despise you," she said quickly. "I never despised you, even when I thought that you'd betrayed me. I simply . . . scorned you."

She felt bad saying it, but she couldn't lie.

He smiled sadly. "Well, I suppose scorn is the lesser of two evils. And I understand. I always understood."

Of course he had. He'd had to shoulder so much for his sacrifice. Including the certainty of the ire of a woman he'd once cared about.

"I don't scorn you anymore, of course. I admire you. You must have given up so much, to allow your friends to think you'd changed so radically in a direction they had nothing but contempt for."

"Yes." He paused. "I won't pretend that it wasn't lonely. Nor that I regretted losing your good opinion."

The words moved her, so much that it wouldn't do to show it.

"Now look to the right," she said, gesturing for him to turn his head away from her.

He met her eye. "I'd rather look at you."

Oh God. His naked flirtation made her want to dispense with the pretense of painting and take off the rest of his clothes herself.

"I know," she admitted, for if she let the flirtation go on unacknowledged, something assuredly would happen. "I feel the same way. But we said we wouldn't do this."

His expression sobered. "You're right. I'll be good."
Must you be?

He must. She must. They'd been through the reasons
why: he would become emotional and unsteady, and
she would hurt him. The merits were sound.

"Square your shoulders," she said, returning to her
task. "You must assume the noble stature of the hard-
working man."

This was primarily for the drawing's benefit, not
hers, but it was pleasant to look at him with his fine
body fully on display. She focused on her lines, on
capturing his planes and angles, on the shading around
his hips, where they tapered to his—

"I thought you were going to paint me," he said.
"But you seem to be drawing. Why is that?"

Oh, a technical question. Thank the Lord.

"Yes. I'm starting with charcoal studies, to mark
down the shape of your anatomy," she said. "I'll paint
you later."

He chuckled. "Studying my anatomy, eh? Now who
is testing our agreement?"

She frowned at him, but she appreciated his return
to a light mood. Harmless banter punctured the taut
quality of the air between them.

"I assure you, I'm not," she parried. "And I'm starting
on your face, so you'll want to shut your mouth, lest I
make you gape-jawed."

He smothered a laugh. "Very well. I shall be most
serious and noble. But if I mustn't talk, entertain me
by telling me how is it that you went from runaway
young woman to famed portraitist."

She told him the story as she continued to sketch.
How she'd taken work as an artist's assistant in Italy,
which had led to commissions painting the children of

wealthy Florentines. How she'd met collectors, gone to Paris, met more. Begun to paint more adventurous subjects and developed a small following. Moved back to London. Held her first exhibition. And then a second, and then a third—each more daring than the last, until her paintings had become infamous and valuable.

Occasionally, she gave Rafe an instruction, and he obediently obliged her—adjusting his chin toward the ceiling, casting his eyes toward the floor, raising a lock of hair to afford her a better view of the shape of his brow.

It was luxurious to position him exactly how she wanted—and to make a record of that moment.

To make art was to wield a kind of power. Even kings must have a glimmer of fear, sitting before their portraitists. A painting could be thrown out if the canvas was unflattering. But one could not ever unsee the artist's view of oneself. One could not erase what the artist had discovered.

It was this realization that had made her see she had surpassed what her tutor could teach her, back in the early days when she had first learned to paint seriously, as an artist rather than a girl desperately searching for genteel activities to fill the time. She'd realized art was about insight, not possession. And its principal power was not in accuracy of form so much as accuracy of the intangible—a conversation between the artist and the sitter. The strange, intimate connection between them that revealed the soul of one in the brushstrokes of the other.

It was a bit like making love.

She finished the last line of Rafe's eyelashes and shaded around the lips.

There.

She looked down at what she'd drawn and nearly gasped.

It was a portrait of a man in all his masculine glory. A man who looked like he could throw you on a bed and ravish you. A man one could see would be masterful above you, or beneath you, or—

She snapped her sketchbook shut before he could see what the drawing revealed—not of him, but of her.

How much—how utterly much—she still wanted him.

Rafe was watching her closely. Like he'd seen what had passed over her face. Like the heat she'd captured was not merely her own, but one that ran between them.

"You are so beautiful, Cornelia," he said softly. "It stings me, the sight of you, every time I get to look."

Her breath caught in her throat. "That sounds painful."

He sighed. "It's *worth* it."

They locked eyes. He stood and ran a hand over his hip bone, scratching his bare skin in a way that brought attention to the deep vee between his abdomen and groin. The hairs on her arms stood up.

She bit her finger. It was a gesture she made when she was thinking, but with her body thrumming she found it utterly erotic. She wanted so badly to be touched.

Touched by *him*.

She walked toward him, scarcely breathing.

He met her in the middle of the studio, standing half a foot apart from her. She could feel the heat emanating from his naked chest. She wanted to put her palm to his flat belly and drag her hand down his breeches, where she could see that he was hard for her.

Instead, she took his hand. That instinctive gesture she kept making. The one that said, "I can't help myself."

He looked down at his hand in hers. And then he raised her knuckles to his mouth and kissed them. Slowly. Tenderly. Like her skin was a rose that might bruise at the pressure of his breath.

She gasped, and he heard it, and he looked into her eyes.

"You said you didn't want a dalliance," he said in an achingly low voice.

"I did say that," she agreed, not sure if she believed it anymore. She wanted to be friends with Rafe, but she had many friends she'd slept with, and they remained nothing more than friendly sometimes-lovers. It was not *impossible*. One could be *careful*, could one not?

"And now?" Rafe asked.

Fuck me.

She cleared her throat, drawing every last strand of self-possession in her body to attention.

"What if we promised each other it wouldn't mean anything at all? That it must be as playful as one of Anna's drawing room games."

He stepped two inches closer, looking deadly serious. "We both love games, don't we?"

She nodded, just as grave. "I'm afraid we always have."

He reached out and wrapped a stray tendril of her hair around his finger. "If we make a game of it, the rule must be this—I will be your plaything, and you will end the game if you tire of me." He looked at her intently, searching her face. "I can't always be trusted not to want to . . . play too much."

She knew what he meant. He was asking her to end the game if she felt overwhelmed by him. If he was becoming too attached.

It was a rule she could accept.

She nodded at him. "I agree. Let's kiss to seal the terms."

He grinned back. "Oh God, I'd love to. Come here, gorgeous girl." He pulled her toward him and lifted her up off her feet and sat them down on the chair where he'd been posing.

She wrapped her arms around his shoulders. She could feel his health and vigor through his skin.

He put his large, warm hand firmly behind her neck and tipped her face up to his. She sank into his lap and kissed him.

It was not a delicate type of kiss, the way it might have been between new lovers.

Rafe had always been like her: famished. And under the terms of the rules, he did not seem afraid to feast on what he wanted.

She climbed atop his knee to get more traction on him, and brushed her hand over his cock. She felt him throb.

"Ugh, you'll kill me," he whispered, leaning back to make his entire body a mount for her to play with.

But she wanted to attenuate the longing before she ravished him.

She stood up.

"Where'd you go?" he asked, smiling but sounding bereft.

"Let's play a game called 'take off my gown,'" she whispered.

"I love that game, as it happens," he said. "An old favorite."

He stood and ran his hands along her bodice, springing away the tiny hooks one by one. "How fun."

"Delightful," she said, breathlessly, losing the patience to prolong the satiation of desire. "Let's play faster."

He obliged. When she was finally free of her bodice, she pressed his face into her bosom, moaning as he took one breast and then the other out of her stays and into his mouth.

"Off, off," she panted, as his fingers shimmied the fabric off her skin.

When her breasts were free, she stood and untied her skirts, standing before him in only her shift. Why, for the love of God, were women expected to wear so many clothes? She fumbled off the chemise and finally stood nude before him.

He reached out to pull her back on his lap but she stepped out of his reach.

He groaned. "Come here."

She shook her head. "If I'm undressed, it's only fair that you are. Games must be equitable for all players."

"I am nothing if not an honest sportsman." He stood and removed his breeches gingerly, for his erection was full and he had a pleasingly thick cock.

She wanted it in her mouth.

"Now the game where we—"

"Hush," he said. "I think I know the rules of this one. Ladies first." He dropped to his knees before her and pressed his lips to her belly.

It was shockingly arousing. She threw back her head and took her breasts in her hands as he knelt before her. His mouth pressed down on her navel.

Her entire pelvis clenched at the feel of his lips on her skin. God, she wanted him.

She'd always wanted him. From the moment she'd

first seen him as a girl, she'd not been able to look away. It had been inappropriate. She'd been sixteen, and he'd been thirty-two. But the day Elinor had introduced them, she'd gone home and touched herself, imagining it was him.

She took his neck and drew it lower, toward her quim.

But this time Rafe resisted her.

"Don't *stop*," she whispered, confused by why he would turn his attention elsewhere.

"My apologies," a low voice said behind her. "I should have knocked. Louder."

She looked over her shoulder.

It was Rory Thompson, standing in the doorway.

*W*hat was *Rory* doing in here?

Rafe and Rory did not have an exclusive arrangement. In fact, Rory was greedily fucking a barmaid in the village, and had been before he and Rafe had discovered they enjoyed each other's company in more than a working capacity. But Rafe felt a pang of protectiveness for Cornelia.

He jumped away and quickly picked up Cornelia's chemise so she could cover herself.

She ignored it.

She wasn't looking at Rafe.

She was looking at Rory.

She turned to the other man, shimmering with sensuality.

"Oh, you aren't disturbing *me*," she said. "We were just playing a harmless little game. And I never mind a bit of an audience."

Rafe should have been shocked, but he wasn't. Because the way Rory looked between them put a tension in the room as palpable as a plangent note on a violin.

His face was the picture of lust itself. It made Rafe more aroused than he had already been—a miracle of excess.

Cornelia turned to Rafe. "Do you fancy another player?"

A pull thrummed low in his belly. "I would never object. The lady makes the rules." He paused and met Cornelia's eyes. "I'll do *anything* the lady wishes."

She licked her bottom lip, smiling. All at once, the mood was lighter.

Playful. And thank the holy heavens, because for all he'd promised Cornelia this was a game, up until this moment it had felt more like an all-or-nothing wager.

"In that case, Mr. Thompson," she said, "would you care to join us?"

Rory's face went from a rarely seen expression— tentative—to wicked. "What a pleasant invitation," he drawled. "I most enthusiastically accept."

Cornelia put her hand to the wet cleft between her legs. "I think we shall enjoy ourselves. Perhaps most especially me."

Rafe and Rory exchanged a look. They'd never shared a woman before, nor made love with a third. Rafe's cock was pulsing with the idea of it, and watching Cornelia touch herself in anticipation made him want to fall to his knees yet again.

Rory looked on, his face athirst. "Let me just prepare myself for you two, since you're ahead of me." He put his hand over his cock and began to rub it into hardness. Watching him, Rafe groaned.

"Rafe, why don't you lock the door," Cornelia said, eyes on Rory's bulge. "One guest is perhaps enough for today."

Rafe did as she suggested, while Rory shed his clothes. Rafe turned back, put his hand to Rory's back, and kissed his neck.

Cornelia leaned back on a settee and took in the sight of the two of them. She looked like a wealthy woman examining her finest jewels. "You two seem familiar with each other. I take it it's not your first time together?"

Rory turned to Rafe and slid his hand down Rafe's stomach, brushing his fingers against his erection. Rafe widened his stance, letting Rory stroke his balls. "No," he gasped out. "We occasionally . . . play games of our own."

"Aaah," Cornelia murmured. She continued to stroke herself as she watched them. "What a happy coincidence. Now, how shall I best make use of you two beauties?"

She paused. "First, I think you will have to kiss me. Come. Both of you."

"At your service, milady," Rory said.

"The pleasure is ours," Rafe agreed.

"No, I think it will be mine." She gave them an exaggerated leer, beckoning them forward.

The three of them burst into laughter. Rafe felt positively frolicsome. He took Rory's hand and led him to Cornelia, who welcomed them with open arms. Rafe bent to his knees and took her mouth while Rory sat beside her and feasted on her breasts.

She took their cocks and teased them against each other, grazing Rory's tip against Rafe's shaft. He pulsed with excitement at the sight of both their erections in her hands.

"I think," Cornelia said, running her thumbs on both their cockheads, "that I shall enjoy watching the two of you together. If you'd be so inclined."

Cornelia was magnetic in her role as mistress of the two of them, murmuring her wishes with as much hunger as warmth and care. He'd do anything she asked him to when she spoke to him like that.

But then, he'd do anything she asked him to in general.

"I share your inclination," Rory said, running his hand across the inside of Rafe's thigh. "If Rafe agrees, I'd particularly enjoy it if you helped us, duchess."

"Please," Rafe managed to get out.

"Very well, my boys." She put their cocks together and began to stroke them both rhythmically.

Rafe's stomach nearly buckled.

"Kiss him," she instructed Rafe, massaging them together. Rory let out a groan, pumping his hips to urge Cornelia on.

Rafe leaned in and took Rory's mouth.

"Oh, that's lovely," Cornelia whispered. "I love watching you enjoy it."

Rory, whose cock always leaked when he was gearing up to fuck, was dripping, and Cornelia used it to slicken them both. Rafe gasped at the sensation.

"Oh, that's a good lass," Rory murmured. "Rub all that slickness out of me."

"Shall I go faster?" Cornelia said.

"Oh yes, love. Make us explode," Rory got out, panting.

Rafe loved it when Rory talked like this. He loved it more to watch Cornelia loving it, too. Her breath was fast, her pupils fixed on the sight of their cocks.

She increased her speed, and Rafe bit down on Rory's lip.

"Ah, you thick piece," Rory rasped, taking Rafe's chin in his hand. "Lower, love, lower."

Rafe ran his nails down Rory's back like he knew he liked and landed on his rear. He massaged Rory deeply, putting his hands beside his cheeks and stretching him, his fingers achingly close to Rory's hole.

"That's nice, isn't it," Cornelia crooned, pumping them faster as she watched. "Tell him how nice it is."

"Ah, *nice* isn't the word. Inside a little, please, inside," Rory moaned.

Without oil, Rafe was as careful as he could stand to be, his brain half working from Cornelia's rubbing of their cocks together.

As soon as his finger gently toyed with Rory's channel, his lover came, exploding all over Rafe's cock. The hot, liquid burst of it nearly broke him, and he felt his body begin to quake. But Cornelia let go.

"Not yet," she rasped. "I need you."

He loved the raw arousal in her voice. He'd do anything to make her feel that way.

"What do you need, princess?" he whispered.

She opened up her legs to him. "Fuck me before you come. I'm so wet, I can't stand it."

He quaked again from her words alone, but he bit his lip, determined to hold back and do whatever pleased her.

She looked over at Rory. "And hold me while he fucks me."

Rory took her in his arms and lay back on the settee with Cornelia nestled between his thighs.

She spread her legs and braced her ankles against Rory's lovely calves, opening herself. Her beautiful sex glistened, and he wanted to put his mouth to her. But she reached out for his cock.

"Take me," she whispered. "Now. Hurry, please."

Rafe did not need more encouragement. He slid himself into her cunt. The heat of her nearly broke him.

Don't come. Not yet.

She cried out, rocking her hips to take him deeper. "Touch me while he fucks me," she gasped out to Rory.

"Oh fucking yes," Rory whispered, massaging her clit while Rafe pumped into her.

Her body was so beautiful, stretched between them. The way she bit her lip, the little sounds she made, took him to the edge.

"You like that, darling?" he managed to ask.

"Yes. Harder. Harder."

He gave her everything he had, this lovely, precious woman. He was determined to last until she came. But determination and ability were two different things.

"I'm going to come," he got out, barely managing to pull his cock out of her before he erupted on her breasts.

She moaned at the feeling.

"I want to taste you," Rory said, rubbing Cornelia's shoulders. "I want to taste him on you."

She opened her legs to him, took his hand, and placed it on her pussy.

"Please."

Rory slid down, kissing Cornelia's beautiful, limpid body as he went. As soon as his mouth pressed down on her quim, she whimpered in pleasure.

Rafe took her hand. She squeezed it so hard it hurt, thrashing about as Rory pleasured her. It was the most erotic thing Rafe had ever seen, her body undulating under Rory's mouth, her hips rising to urge more, her eyes fluttering as she bit her lip. He had never wanted a woman more. Until she screamed in pleasure.

The sight of her. My God, the sight of her.

She was glistening with sweat, sprawled out like they'd allowed her soul to briefly leave her body. It made him want to weep. Instead, he held her as the bliss washed over her. He held her as it ebbed. She snuggled into him, panting.

If this was a game, it was the most intense one he had ever played.

And he was not sure if he had just won, or lost.

The three of them lay there, entwined—Rafe holding Cornelia, and Cornelia's leg thrown over Rory's shoulder.

They remained that way, spent, for at least a quarter hour, recovering in silence.

Cornelia stretched and lifted up her leg to free Rory from her thighs.

"Thank you," she said. "What a lovely surprise." The edge of amusement returned to her voice. Reminding him: just a game.

"Convenient timing," Rafe drawled.

"Bespeaking the intuition of your confidential secretary. Though I did have a higher purpose than making their graces yell my name in pleasure."

"And what was that, you humble man?" Cornelia laughed.

"I wanted to tell you the executor of the estate has just sent word he will be coming for a visit with Rafe tomorrow morning."

Cornelia raised a brow at Rafe. "How lucky we have so recently been together as man and wife."

And it had been amazing. So amazing, that a little pang of anxiety went through him. Rory or no, play or no, they had just done what they'd sworn not to do. And now, with a day of feigning love ahead of them, he hoped he wouldn't be tempted to feel it.

He must remain detached—for the sake of his honor and his heart. The pretense would have to be another game. Playacting, like performing a vignette at a house party.

You like games, he reminded himself. *You're good at them.*

"Hopefully he will not sense our coupling was just

a friendly romp," he said quickly, to cover up his nerves.

"Utterly meaningless," Cornelia agreed. "And extremely diverting."

Rory looked back and forth between them, as if wondering at the meaning beneath their words. "Pure fun?" he echoed.

"An empty lark," she confirmed. "Though I would be open to having such fun again, Mr. Thompson. Don't be a stranger."

Rory was pulling on his clothing. "I am nothing if not accommodating, duchess."

Chapter Twenty-One

Had she ever been so thoroughly pleasured? Cornelia felt like she was made of moonlight as she lay still and spent, enfolded in Rafe's arms, and watched Rory dress. He was shorter and slimmer in build than Rafe, sinewy and muscular. His skin gleamed in the bright light of her studio—pale save for the pink marks where Rafe had scratched his back.

"I'll leave you to recover, my queen and her consort," he said as he redonned his coat. He kissed them both on the cheek and left the room, leaving her entwined with Rafe.

Without Rory here, the intimacy of his embrace felt less like a game.

She should get up.

But her disobedient body was heavy and relaxed, refusing to give up the comfort of his warmth just yet. Instead, she lay still as he held her, lightly stroking her arms and nuzzling her neck.

It made her nervous enough to stir.

"How very pleasant that was," she said brightly, shimmying away. It had been quite a bit more than pleasant, but she felt compelled to speak in an arch tone to keep the mood light.

"One of the better afternoons I have spent at Gardencourt," Rafe agreed, his tone equally affable. He let go of her and stretched.

Was he also deliberately affecting distance? Or was he genuinely unmoved by what they had just shared?

"Perhaps we'll play again," she said. If there was any mercy in this world, they would do so soon, before their time together ended.

He smiled at her, reached up, and tweaked her nose. "I hope so."

Tweaked her nose?

Was he better at this game than she was?

Well, if he was: good. How unexpected and welcome.

She'd promised not to let him get attached, and it would be far easier if he viewed her as an erotic play-fellow, rather than a romantic lover.

He shot her a lazy grin. "Are you ready to be my ardent ladylove tomorrow?"

She gestured down at her nude body. "It would appear so."

He chuckled. "How shall we handle Mr. Hugue?"

She considered this. "Honestly, I think. We'll tell him how we met. How I diverted you at parties."

"You *did* do that, didn't you?"

"Oh, every chance I got. You were very handsome, Rafe."

He gestured down at his well-built chest. "Still am."

"Still are," she laughed. "Though you've grown more vain."

He put his hands behind his head and arched his back, displaying himself for her benefit. "I deserve it."

She rolled her eyes at him. "Get dressed."

He sat up. "So we'll tell Hugue the tale of our elopement. Only we'll make it . . . romantic. Is that right?"

"Star-crossed lovers," she agreed. "Reunited, finally, after decades."

"Paramours whose passion cannot be denied."

"And finally, that rarest thing—happily married spouses."

He kissed her on the cheek. "The wildly in love duke and duchess."

The words made her shiver with nerves. She covered it up by picking her chemise up off the floor. "I'm cold."

He stood. "I would warm you, but I must go. I am due for a tour of the wheat farms with Eden."

She nodded at him, hoping she seemed casual, and looked beautiful. "I'll see you at supper."

She waited for him to leave, then she dressed.

She felt observed, and glanced at the study she had made of Rafe. It gazed back at her, full of longing. Longing she still felt, despite the way her body shook a bit from the depth of her satisfaction and the emotional turmoil it left.

Which was ridiculous, of course.

If Rafe was unbothered by what had happened, certainly *she* could be—though, despite her joking, it would be harder when they must pretend to be in love tomorrow.

Well, no matter. She simply needed something more physical to do, to channel her strange, ambivalent feelings into action.

And luckily, there was a task awaiting her: hauling heavy paintings.

She headed to the attic, which she had commandeered for storing the art she was rearranging for the masquerade. She took the shortcut through the service corridors that wound between the main rooms of the house, making the work it took to run the massive place invisible to the occupants until they required tending.

The attic spanned the entirety of the east wing. It was vast, quiet, and chilly—the weather inside ranged from autumn to winter, even when it was spring or summer outside. The damp was kept in check by old tapestries hung along the walls—some dating back to the Tudors, with the singe marks and wormholes to prove it. Hazy, filtered light floated in through the dormer windows, illuminating the dust in the air.

The majority of the space was taken up by old furniture draped in sheets, which lent an otherworldly quality to the room. It was almost like a church. A very, very dusty church.

Cornelia wandered around, inspecting this and that. She'd been up here many times in the past days, but only to stash paintings from downstairs—not to investigate the ones that had been stored for years under old sheets. She wondered if they might include any interesting works that would add irony or poignance if hung alongside portraits in her exhibition.

She began to lift up the sheets, looking through old canvases and frames.

It was mostly fruitless—portraits of previous dukes' dogs and babies that had not made it into the gallery for lack of interest or beauty. She found some middling landscapes, a picture or two of the village, but nothing that intrigued her.

A large canvas leaning alone against a wall in the far corner caught her eye. It was surrounded by old trunks marked JLL.

Her father's initials. But that was likely a coincidence. His things, as far as she knew, had been stored in his old cottage, which she'd gone through as a girl.

She stalked over to the corner, hopping over stray furnishings and crates, and dragged the canvas out into the strongest light. She lifted up the cobweb-covered sheet protecting it and gasped.

It was a portrait of her mother.

Demeter was seated in an artist's studio, bathed in golden light. The brushstrokes depicting her were gentle and precise, capturing the long coils of her hair, the shining umber of her eyes. She was posed with a hand on her belly, which was slightly rounded with a child. Her mouth turned up at the corners—perhaps with affection for the painter. Or perhaps the smile was maternal, full of love for her unborn girl—the one she would name Cornelia, and not live to see grow past the age of two years old.

The portrait was signed in the corner by her father—James Ludgate—and there was a brass plaque attached to its frame reading: *My Demeter.*

How, in all the years Cornelia had lived here, had her uncle never thought to tell her that her mother's portrait was sitting in the attic just above her head?

It was cruel, when Cornelia had so little of her mother. She teared up as she gently traced her father's brushstrokes, her mother's image.

She felt a fresh wave of fury at her uncle, a man so narrow in his ability to love that he had hidden this away—no doubt threatened by her mother's brown skin; by his brother's rebellious nature; perhaps by their relationship to Cornelia herself, the not-quite-daughter he'd sworn he loved as his own.

It was so unfair. Why should her mother be covered in sheets in an attic while portraits of distant cousins—all white, mostly male—so prominently lined the walls downstairs? No doubt for the same reason there had never been a portrait of Cornelia herself, even when she lived here.

Because they were considered lesser. Less worthy of enshrinement in the memory of the family, and less worthy still of their place in it.

She would change that.

She would hang her mother's portrait in a place of honor in her show.

And she would also hang a portrait of her mother's daughter.

She would paint herself in the style her father had painted Demeter: in a studio, bathed in light, wearing a yellow dress.

She rummaged through the trunks near her mother's portrait, which were filled with belongings of her parents that her rotten uncle had never given her. There was not time to savor them—she would have to do that later. Instead, she looked about until she found one that contained female clothing. She sorted through the contents, pulling out dress after dress until she found exactly the one she was looking for—the resplendent yellow gown from the painting.

It was a rich-hued saffron, nearly gold—no doubt chosen to bring out the warm tones in her mother's complexion and to set off her beautiful eyes.

It would have the same effect on Cornelia.

And she would wear it in a self-portrait. A portrait of Demeter Ludgate's only daughter—a duchess of the house that had scorned her.

She wondered what her mother would think of her having this title. Would she be proud of her daughter assuming the highest rank in the land, short of queen? Or would she be uneasy with Cornelia claiming ancestry from the family that had treated Demeter as the downfall of their son? Perhaps both, as Cornelia was of two minds herself. She scorned duchesses for what they represented. She also coveted their power to set the standard of feminine desirability and dignity, to shape the hierarchies of society. People wanted proximity to them, wanted their good favor. Journalists followed their lives. They set the fashion, swayed politics.

It presented a dilemma.

She wished she could ask her mother's counsel. There were so many things she would give anything to know—how her mother felt about this family, this country, living as a woman of color in a world that could be hostile. Navigating the white, wealthy society of the Rosemeres and their aristocratic circle. She'd been robbed of her mother's guidance, robbed of the chance to ask her questions, to grow up in the light of her example. She mourned the fact that her mother had left no diary or letters that Cornelia had ever come across. The only record of who she'd been was in the paintings of her by Cornelia's father.

And as much as the images were radiant with love, they could only convey so much of the subject's thoughts, views, passions.

Devastating, that she couldn't ask the mama she would never know what she should do. Divorce Rafe, as she planned, and rid herself of the title? Or was there merit in staying married and claiming the title for women like herself?

Demeter could not help her. She would have to decide for herself what the title meant to her. But she knew what her self-portrait would mean. It would stake a claim of belonging *and* defiance. For she *was* a duchess, wasn't she? The fact was incontrovertible, for now.

She would hang her own portrait beside Rafe's, at

the center of the ballroom, to smile down on all the guests—those who would love it and those who would find it a violation of all the rules of the world they were trying to uphold.

She lifted up the painting of her mother and carried it back downstairs to the parlor she was using as a painting studio. She would begin to paint herself this very afternoon.

It would be an honor to memorialize her mother this way.

And as an added benefit, it would take her mind off Rafe.

Chapter Twenty~Two

*R*afe was pleasantly, deliciously exhausted. There were few things he loved more than a vigorous session in the bedchamber or a vigorous ride out of doors, and today he'd been blessed with both.

He sat alone and content, sipping on a whiskey amidst the lively conversations of the guests gathered in the library. Occasionally he heard the vibrato of Cornelia's infectious laugh and tried not to gaze at her. She was sitting near the windows with Seraphina and Canette and did not seem to register his presence.

He wondered if that was by design—if she was ignoring him so as to remind him not to make this afternoon about anything other than sex. He wondered if, like him, she was determined not to let what they had experienced today, and the closeness they must feign tomorrow, become confused with real emotions.

He'd meant it when he vowed to make a game of the pursuit of pleasure.

But if he was truly honest with himself, he did not feel playful. He felt tender. About Cornelia. About the world.

She made him want to say things that he shouldn't. Sentiments that would push her away, and get him hurt.

It was terrifying. And yet he could not let her go.

Rory glanced at him inquisitively from across the room, as if to say, *Is all well with you?*

Rafe shrugged.

Rory pursed his lips in sympathy. Then he raised his glass and turned to the other guests.

"Our host looks like a man in need of a distraction," he said. "Miss Anna, why don't you lead us in a *game*."

Rafe tried not to groan at that loaded word. Wicked Rory. Always teasing him.

He glanced over at Cornelia. She met his eye and quirked her lips. "How I *adore* a game," she said. "Yes, do, Anna."

"Oh, please don't ask her," Lord Eden said grimly. "My sister doesn't need encouragement."

Anna clapped her hands together. "No, I certainly do not. I know just the game! It's quite diverting."

"Quite unnerving, I'd reckon," Eden said.

Rafe had to admire the man for the gentle way he had with his sister. A wry, long-suffering air that belied quiet affection and care.

"It's called Sculptor," Anna said.

"How does one play this game?" Lord Eden asked. "I've never heard of it."

"Yes, because you are *old* and *boring*," she chirped.

"Quite," he said with a nod.

"How do we play?" Seraphina asked.

"We start by choosing a sculptor," Anna said. "Their job is to pick two models and arrange them in a classical pose, choosing whatever scene they wish. Then, the models must stay in the pose—they cannot move or change expression. Whoever lasts the longest in the pose is the next sculptor and may choose two models of their own."

Eden looked pained by this explanation, but Anna did not wait for his approval and went right on talking. "I nominate Miss Ludgate as our first sculptor, of course, as she's the artist. Miss Ludgate, who do you pick for your models?"

Cornelia's eyes sparkled with mischief. "You, darling," she said. "And . . . hmm. I think Mr. Howe."

Anna went bright red. Rafe had noticed that the two youngest members of the party seemed to have an interest in each other. Clearly, Cornelia had noticed too—and was being either kind, or incorrigible, depending on one's point of view.

Howe—also much rosier than his usual pallid, scholarly complexion—shyly came and stood next to Anna.

"How would you like us to pose?" Anna asked.

Cornelia made a show of thinking this over. "Mr. Howe here is a man devoted to justice. Therefore, Anna, you shall be Themis, the goddess of justice, holding up your scales. And Gilby, you will be a mortal who worships at her feet."

Rafe bit his lip to avoid smiling. So did a number of others in the room—though notably not Thaïs, who laughed outright, and Eden, who looked like he was debating putting a stop to it.

Cornelia told Anna to take off her boots and instructed her to stand on a low table, holding a candlestick over her head in the place of the symbolic scales of justice. She posed Gilby on his knees beneath Anna, holding out a hand to just below the candlestick, as if in prayer—or simply lovestruck.

"Look desperate," Cornelia instructed Howe. "And whatever you do, don't break eye contact with her."

Everyone got up and made a circle around the two models.

"Remember," Cornelia said. "Our models must not

move an inch, not even to smile. The first one to crack loses. But of course, we may try to distract them, to hasten their losses."

Rafe enjoyed watching Cornelia's enthusiasm for the game. It reminded him of her love of enigmas. Which reminded him of his affection for her. Which reminded him of her quaking underneath his body.

Which he really shouldn't think about in the presence of a houseful of guests.

Instead, he moved closer to inspect the two models, deciding he would be the first to try to break them. "What a hideous sculpture," he said teasingly. "Miss Ludgate, I thought you were more talented than this."

The models did not laugh at his quip. Gilby, especially, had a talent for remaining completely still. He stared up at Anna with rapt adoration that looked decidedly genuine.

"Oh, it is no fault of mine," Cornelia replied. "My models are utterly stiff. Perhaps they should relax."

The models did not take the bait.

Suddenly, Elinor clapped her hands and stamped her feet. It was effective in startling Seraphina, who yelped in surprise, but neither Anna nor Gilby blinked.

"Anna, go to bed," Eden said in a brisk, loud voice.

Anna ignored him.

"Oh no. A bird has flown inside!" Seraphina yelled.

No reaction from the models.

"Gilby, stop looking up her skirt, lad," Thaïs screeched. "She's an innocent maiden."

Gilby reared back, his eyes crossing with pure horror. "I wasn't! Please—"

He stopped, realizing he'd been tricked.

They all burst into laughter—no one more heartily than Anna.

"She fooled you, Mr. Howe," Anna said. "We all know you would do nothing of the sort. You're far too good."

"Thank you," he said to his toes.

The boy looked so mortified Rafe wanted to give him a hug.

"Anna is the winner," Cornelia announced. "As we all expected she would be. Anna, who will you choose as your victims?"

"Certainly Mr. Thompson," Anna said immediately. "He is a classic Narcissus."

Rafe snorted. Rory did have a habit of stopping at mirrors to adjust his lustrous hair.

Rory laughed. "Not unfair, to be honest. But who shall be my gorgeous reflection?"

"Me!" Thaïs shouted, running her eyes up and down Rory's body.

"You are quite an enthusiast at this game, Thaïs." Seraphina said, chuckling. "And to think you said you only enjoy games that occur in bedchambers."

"Who said this won't lead to bedchamber games?" Thaïs asked, winking at Rory.

Rory winked right back. Rafe had little doubt he would be ready and willing to indulge Thaïs in whatever pastime she suggested.

"Very well," Anna said. "Mr. Thompson, you are to get on your knees and stare down at your reflection. And Miss Magdalene, you are to lie beneath him, mirroring his face."

Thaïs put a hand on her generous hip and waggled her eyebrows at Anna. "I'll gladly lie beneath *him*."

Anna put her hand over her mouth and laughed. Marianne laughed even louder.

The models assumed the pose, making faces of pure rapture at each other. They managed to stay unnervingly still, obviously relishing the intimacy of their gaze. So much so that Rory seemed startled when Seraphina called out, "Kiss her!"

Thaïs cracked a smile. "Aye, please do," she purred.

"Ah, she loses!" Eden shouted—clearly enjoying the game more now that his innocent young sister was not at the center of it.

"Oh, but I shall have my winnings," Thaïs said. She lifted up her head and smacked a kiss directly on Rory's mouth. It surprised him so much that he rolled back onto his haunches, laughing.

"Well, it seems I am the victor," he drawled, throwing an arm around Thaïs's shoulders. "But who shall be my victims?"

Thaïs lifted onto her toes and whispered something in his ear, a naughty smile on her face.

Rory rubbed his chin reflectively. "Yes, excellent suggestion. Cornelia is our artist, always insisting on making models of her friends. So it is only fair to make her pose, I think."

Cornelia smiled graciously. "Only fair indeed."

"But who shall I match with her?" he asked Thaïs.

Thaïs whispered in his ear again. Rory barked out a laugh.

"Yes!" he said, snapping his fingers. "Rafe here is our strapping Adonis. And Cornelia creates beauty in all things. Therefore, it is only natural she pose as his lover, Aphrodite."

Rafe nearly choked on his whiskey. Rory was undoubtedly trying to do him a favor by fanning the flames of the fire. But theirs was a fire that did not need stoking.

Especially not in front of an entire bawdy audience.

Cornelia feigned a tragic sigh. "It will be a great trial, but I will venture to touch him if I must."

Everyone laughed, looking at him expectantly.

"Come, stand in the center of the room in all your manly glory, Rafe," Rory prodded.

"Very well," Rafe said, matching Cornelia's tragic tone. "I shall endure it."

He put down his drink and walked toward Cornelia, hoping he did not appear too nervous. She turned to him with a smile. "How shall I pose?" she asked Rory.

"You must stand on your toes, clutch him, and look up into his eyes, admiring his beauty."

Cornelia shot Rory an amused look. "I shall try."

She turned to Rafe and threw an arm across his chest. There was such a differential in their height that she had to lean on him. He braced himself to support her and angled his head down.

"And Rafe," Rory instructed, "you must look upon her with rapture."

He didn't have to pretend to give her an adoring smile. The sight of her wrapped around his body made it impossible not to beam.

She mooned back at him, doing her best impression of a lovestruck goddess. He tried not to focus on her nearness. On the pressure of her hand over his nipple. On the way she smelled like sage.

He wondered if she felt as desperate as he did to be closer.

She wobbled on her toes and toppled down with a strangled laugh.

"I lose!" she cried gaily.

And she deserved to, for Rafe had felt her give up on the posture. And he suspected he knew why: she sensed the danger of touching him. The worry that the intensity between them would only continue to grow until it erupted into something neither of them could control.

"Pity," Seraphina said. "You were doing so well at *pretending* you couldn't keep your eyes off him."

Cornelia laughed. "Perhaps I should abandon art for acting."

But she avoided his eyes as she said it.

And in his gut, he knew she had not been acting at all.

Chapter Twenty-Three

Cornelia opened her eyes and let the morning light filtering through the windows complete the task of rousing her. She never closed the curtains before she fell asleep. She liked to wake up with the sunshine.

She felt well rested, owing to having fled the library—as subtly as one could—as soon as she sabotaged her turn at playing a statue. She'd gone to bed immediately, despite her habit of sketching late at night, to avoid thinking of what had just transpired.

With another man, posing as two adoring subjects of a sculpture would likely have been the beginning of a very pleasant evening. With Rafe, it made it difficult to parse what was pretense from whatever it was that had begun to twinge, unwanted, in her heart.

How inconvenient that her entire day would be devoted to a game of romantic make-believe. She needed to stifle the feeling. She needed not to get confused.

She picked up Lucius, who was tucked into her side, and gave him a kiss on his soft head.

"Good morning, cat."

He purred and bumped her cheek with his. It was nice, uncomplicated affection from a creature there was no danger in showering with love. Maybe she should get another cat. Perhaps if she acquired enough of them, there would be no more affection left for Rafe.

There was a brisk knock at the door and, at Cornelia's greeting, Canette swept in.

"I'm here to be your lady's maid again," she said, brandishing a fistful of hair ribbons.

"It's early yet, Canette."

She did not want this day to begin any earlier than it had to.

"Disguising you as a duchess will take time," her old friend said dryly.

Cornelia sat up in bed and scowled.

"How dare you, cruel one. I take pains with my appearance when I'm not painting, I swear to you."

"And when is that?" Canette said with a chortle, drawing the curtains farther apart to let in more light. "I've seen you in nothing but paint-spattered tunics since the day you arrived."

"Well, there's no one to dress up for, and I'm working."

Canette put the ribbons on the vanity table and drew out the low-backed chair, gesturing for Cornelia to come and sit.

"Miss Anna would say you are working too hard. Come and let me pamper you."

Cornelia dragged herself onto her feet, picked up a blanket, and wrapped it around her shoulders.

"Miss Anna is a lovely girl with very little seasoning. It affects her sense."

She plopped down in the chair and submitted to Canette, who began rubbing a sage-scented salve into Cornelia's face. It gave her the dewy appearance of a woman who'd recently exerted herself in the sheets. Which, of course, made her think of Rafe.

She looked away from her reflection.

"Let's get you dressed before we finish your coiffure, my beauty," Canette said.

Cornelia rose and Canette helped her don a gown—her finest, the one she wore to exhibitions where she charmed wealthy patrons. She dutifully sat still while Canette dressed her hair into a tall, ribboned arrangement that gave Cornelia a duchessly loft.

When Canette was finished, the image in the looking glass made them both laugh.

"You look royal. The solicitor will think you are a princess. Maybe I should take it down a bit."

"No," Cornelia said, inspecting herself. "It amuses me. Perhaps I will make you dress me like this every day. Imagine my hair scraping against the ceiling as I stand on a ladder to reach the top of a canvas."

Fully disguised as a duchess, Cornelia carefully walked down to the drawing room where she and Rafe were to await the arrival of the estate executor, going slowly so as to be sure not to trip on her hem in the high-heeled shoes she rarely wore.

"Well, good day, Your Majesty," Rafe said in greeting, bowing deeply in a way that reminded her of Thaïs's good-natured mockery.

She reached out and flicked him in the chest with her bejeweled fan. She hoped Mr. Hugue's eye for finery was not so good that he would notice the jewels were paste.

"You look no less august yourself," she said. Rafe was also in uncharacteristically fine dress clothes, with a powdered wig to boot. It was unjust that even dressed like a prerevolutionary French peacock, he was irresistibly rugged.

"I must dress to set off the beauty of my demure,

retiring duchess," he murmured, taking her hand and bussing it with a courtly kiss.

His mood was light, confirming he was unmoved by the previous day's activities.

She'd been unfair to think *he* was the one who would struggle to remain aloof.

She summoned her most flirtatious manner, to remind herself this was purely sexual—a game.

"Well done. You are just the picture of the virile and handsome Tory duke."

"Virile *and* handsome! Who are you, kind lady, and what have you done with my wife?"

"I hid her under this towering hair. No doubt she's suffocating."

"She looks beautiful as she gasps her final breaths."

She fluttered her eyelashes at him. "Not as beautiful as she looks *beneath* her gown, I assure you."

He made a sound something like a growl. "I'm aware, Cornelia. I'm aware."

Flirting, it seemed, required no pretense. The rawness of his words was genuine, she could tell. At least today there was a purpose for their flirtation. The more they appeared to want each other, the easier it would be to get her money.

"I have something for you," Rafe said. His eyes sparkled.

"And what is that?"

He reached into his pocket and took out a leather case gilded with the Rosemere crest.

"A belated wedding present."

Her heart caught in her throat.

"Those aren't . . ."

He flicked open the top of the case. "The Rosemere diamonds."

The jewels—two long earrings and a four-strand necklace—sparkled against their ivory satin pillows, enormous and glittering, so large they could be used as weapons. She knew these jewels. She'd seen them hanging from the ears and necks of her uncle's wives. As a little girl, she'd always wanted to touch them and rarely had been permitted, as her uncle's wives had never particularly warmed to the small child who occupied their husband's attention and affection.

She reached out and touched one, feeling small again, like her hand might be swatted away.

Seeing her hesitation, Rafe picked up the necklace.

"I thought you might want to wear it for the solicitor. More convincing than paste. May I put it on you?" he asked.

She wasn't sure. Draping herself in the duchess's marital jewels would indeed help the appearance of authenticity. But these jewels represented all the rejection she had faced from her uncle's family. The pain of being considered less than one of them. The exclusion. The judgment.

But they also represented her own heritage. She *was* a Rosemere. She'd been born one. And she was, for now, a duchess.

To wear the diamonds would be to defy all those who thought she did not deserve to be.

"Yes," she said, lifting up her neck to Rafe.

He clasped the heavy jewels around her neck, stood back, and smiled. It was the kind of smile that held so much appreciation she had to glance away.

He shouldn't be looking at her like that. It was too much.

Some things simply felt too real.

"Now the earrings," he said, holding them out to her. She carefully unscrewed the posts and clamped them to her ears. They were so heavy that her head felt encumbered, and they thumped her when she turned her neck.

"These are ridiculous," she said.

"They may be ridiculous, but you look beautiful in them. No previous duchess could have possibly out-shone you."

That gave her a thought. She would paint them into her self-portrait. She would wear her mother's finest dress and her father's family's most precious jewels. It would be a statement that the two sides of her heri-tage were not in opposition, but in harmony—creating something beautiful.

Rafe cleared his throat. "There's something else," he said. He reached into his pocket and produced a simple gold band.

"This one's from me."

He glanced into her eyes and held it out for her to take, like he was worried she might refuse. He looked shy as a boy.

She took it from him and held it in her palm. "A wedding ring?"

He nodded. "I thought it was the type of thing I'd have given you if we'd eloped as real lovers. I wouldn't have been able to afford anything more, but I'd have wanted to give you something."

He paused and swallowed. "You can tell the solicitor how precious it is to you. Sentimental value and all."

She stroked the smooth gold surface. Oddly, it *was* precious to her, this token of his thoughtfulness. It re-minded her of all the little things he'd done for her on the way to Scotland. The care he had taken with the young woman who'd arrived on his doorstep desperate in the middle of the night.

She held out her hand. "Will you do the honors?"

Rafe smiled, took the ring, and held it up. As it caught the light, she noticed it was engraved inside.

"Wait," she said, grabbing it. "I didn't see the inscription."

She angled it to catch the light. It said simply, *Yours.* Her breath caught in her throat.

"Yours?"

Rafe's cheeks flamed, but he looked into her eyes and smiled. "Yours, Cornelia. Yes. I would have given you my heart."

She knew he intended it as a prop in the play they were both performing. After all, he must have had it made in London, long before they'd renewed their affair.

She couldn't let herself think that it was *real.* But the light shining in his blue eyes as he watched her put it on her finger looked so real. The timbre of his voice sounded moved. Nothing about this ring, or its sentiment, felt like playacting.

Just then, Mr. Singh appeared in the doorway. "Mr. Hugue has arrived, Your Grace," he told Rafe. "Or, that is, Your *Graces,*" he said to Cornelia, grinning.

"Don't ever call me that, Singh," she warned with mock severity. "I shall have you dismissed. As a duchess, it is my prerogative to dismiss whomever I please with no cause whatsoever."

"Your notion of duchesses is quite cruel," Rafe said. He seemed to have recovered. He looked casual and confident standing in his finery. She did not care for wigs, but Rafe was so earthy that even the fussiness of the powdered curls could not diminish his masculine vitality.

The way he looked almost made her wish he *were* her husband. For imagine having access to his hale body every day.

But she was losing the direction of the conversation. "Well, I did live with three duchesses," she replied, a beat later than fit the natural flow of conversation. "They were not known for their tender characters. Although, being married to my uncle would try anyone's temper."

Rafe gave her a long look, his eyes lingering on the diamonds around her neck. "You did not deserve their ire. 'Tis a shame you are not planning on becoming the true duchess of this place. You could do quite a bit to expand the possibilities of what a duchess could be."

Well, of course she *could,* if she wished. That didn't mean she wanted the position.

Nor did it mean she shouldn't accept it.

Perhaps she owed it to womankind to valorize the beauty she saw and knew in her own world, rather than that governed by white skin, feminine respectability, and proximity to wealth and power. She could be a very effective duchess if she used the attention for her art and causes. She could demand respect for things that were dismissed, or considered unworthy of the attention of polite society.

But to keep the title would mean remaining bound to Rafe. A risk perilous to her own freedom.

Perhaps the trouble was that she did not want to be a duchess. Perhaps the trouble was that she could not afford to be so close to Rafe if she remained one.

She had no idea what she should do.

"Let's not speak of nonsense," she said briskly, dismissing the dilemma for now.

Rafe looked chastened. "I'm sorry. I meant to flatter you, not offend. Is that all right?"

He searched her eyes, taking care of her with only his gaze.

She nodded. God, he was so kind. So observant of her moods and sensitive to her feelings.

He always had been.

It was why she'd trusted him with her life when she'd been eighteen.

Chapter Twenty-Four

Before

Cornelia was uncharacteristically pensive on the final leg of the trip to Gretna Green.

Rafe wondered if she was having second thoughts.

"You know," he said, breaking the silence that had gone on for an hour. "We don't have to do this. If you like, I'll *say* we're married to protect you. I would say anything you want, do anything you want, to keep you out of Rosemere's grasp."

He could not imagine her forced into marriage with some man who didn't love her. Some man who would not admire her artistic talent and irrepressible spirit.

She shook her head, grimacing. "That won't work if I am caught and have no proof that I am married."

"You could say you lost the witness paper."

"That won't work either. My uncle would rather risk making me a bigamist than admit I'm the bride of a horse trainer."

He laughed sharply. "Farewell to my pride."

"It's true," she sighed. "You cannot weasel out of our agreement and leave me to the wolves."

Weasel!

He could tell, from her grumpy mood, that she was genuinely ill at ease. Her usual airy confidence was nowhere to be found.

He missed it.

He did not want her to enter this arrangement in a state of fear. But he did not know how to save her from it.

She was right to feel vulnerable. Women had few rights under marriage. They could not own property, sign contracts, possess accounts in their own names. Their person and that of their children were under their husband's sole control. He knew that in her position, he would be terrified wondering if he could be trusted. After all, once they married the only assurance she had that he would not use her as a pawn to extort the duke, or command she stay with him in Kent and bear him children, or any other deviant scheme he might invent was his word.

It was humbling to receive such trust from her. It made him feel so protective he wanted to scoop her off her horse and into his arms and kiss her hair. To promise he would never ask her for a thing.

But she did not look like she wanted physical affection. She sat ramrod straight on her horse, eyes trained ahead of her, mouth in a tight line.

"I'm not attempting to weasel out of marrying you," he said in his most soothing voice. "I just want to be sure you are utterly clear-eyed of the consequences."

"That's what I've been thinking about all morning," she admitted. "You must swear, *swear* that after we are married you will not make demands on me."

"I promise you, Cornelia."

"I must be free, Rafe." Her voice was filled with passion. "For my entire life, I have been confined to my uncle's wishes. And if I return to my old life, I'll never be able to live the way I wish to. He'll have me married off to some person of his choosing to live a sheltered, stultifying life. I must be able to set my own course, wherever it takes me. I want to cultivate my talents, take lovers, have adventures, see new countries, and meet new, fascinating people. If you cannot honor my wishes to allow me this freedom, please tell me now, and we will not go ahead."

He looked into her eyes and spoke with all the sincerity he possessed. "I would never wish to stand between you and what you want for yourself. It's my honor that you have asked me to play this role for you. You can trust me."

She nodded but did not look reassured.

"Yes. I suppose trust is all I have."

She mused on this so long he began to wonder if she really would change her mind. Oddly, the idea left him disappointed. He wanted to be the man to rescue her.

Finally she relaxed her shoulders and looked over at him, directly into his eyes. "Thank you, Rafe. I know what I have asked you isn't easy. Most men wouldn't do it."

"Most women wouldn't be brave enough to think it up. I admire you, Cornelia."

He more than admired her. What he felt for her—and how quickly he'd begun to feel it—was something so much deeper, more intimate and personal, than admiration that it made him frightened to consider it. A few days ago, she'd been a neighbor—an acquaintance—of a higher class and consequence. A girl who'd been kind to him at parties where he'd known few people. Little more than a stranger.

Now he couldn't think of a single person who was more important to him.

She was quiet again for a moment. "I have a request."

"Anything. What is it?"

She hesitated. "I don't know if you will loathe what I'm about to say or rejoice in it, but I expect it is the former. Please promise you will listen with an open mind."

He glanced over at her, trying to read her face. She was looking directly at him with so much grim, determined focus that he worried she would not properly steer her horse.

"You can ask me anything, Cornelia," he said gently.

"We must consummate the marriage."

This was *not* what he was expecting. Even in his most tempted moments, he had not considered *intercourse* with her.

He cleared his throat, worried his voice would be eaten up by the wave of nerves—or was it longing?— that had risen up at the idea of it. "That's not possible."

Her shoulders rose in exasperation. "It is necessary, Rafe," she said evenly. "Critical."

He understood why she might think this, but that didn't mean it was wise.

He sighed. It was time to clear the air.

"Cornelia, I am sixteen years your senior. Sixteen bloody years. You are scarcely out of the nursery, and I am a grown man. I knew your *parents*, for Christ's sake—"

She drew her horse to a full stop and held out a hand to stop him. He pulled at the reins. She crossed her arms and looked directly in his eyes. Her posture held as much defiance as it did pleading.

"Rafe, please *listen* to me. You seem to think you risk taking advantage of me. And yet here you are, on your way to Scotland at my behest, about to marry me purely because I asked it of you. So who is taking advantage of whom?"

He sighed. "I think you know my hesitation is not that I don't *want* to do it."

"Well, I want to do it, too." Her voice went softer, more fragile. "I want you. I would want you even if we were not in this situation."

He already knew she desired him. After their previous evening, there was not a question in his mind about her attraction to him, nor his to her. But he was still bestirred to hear her say the words aloud. Bestirred, and deeply nervous.

"And more than that," she went on, "I need you. I want to take every precaution with our scheme. There must not be suspicion that our marriage is a sham. In fact, we must be very amorous in public when we marry. We must be . . . loud when we make love. Leave witnesses."

He nearly choked at the idea—with shock or lust or dread he could not decide.

Could he do such a thing?

Well, certainly he *could*, but was it right? Or would doing so simply be a rationalization of a moral failing?

Cornelia reached out and put a hand to his shoulder. "Please, Rafe," she said. "Please do this for me."

Her voice shook. He hated the desperation in it. Cornelia Ludgate should not have to plead for anything.

He would do it. For her.

He would grant her the respect to treat her as a woman who knew her own mind and desires, and honor her request.

But first he had to marry her.

Chapter Twenty Five

Cornelia stared at Rafe over her nose, in the most duchessly expression he had ever seen her make. Her pique at the idea of holding the title was ironic, given how very much she resembled it today. She had looked the part in her silk gown, bejeweled shoes, and elaborately dressed hair, even before he'd given her the Rosemere diamonds.

But he knew the diamonds were not the problem.

The ring was the problem.

The ring had been too much.

Too sentimental.

He'd purchased it just after she'd agreed to the scheme, after he'd visited her in London. He'd been too excited at the prospect of renewing their acquaintance. If he had any sense he would have simply bought the band, foregone engraving it.

But he'd had his reasons. If they were to convince a solicitor their union was based in a love that had flourished in secret for twenty years, was it not best to act as he would were his heart unfettered by the need for distance?

For if Cornelia were his wife, he would wish to bedeck her in any luxury he possessed. He would want to cherish her in every way he knew how. Be it priceless diamonds or warm hugs or a plain gold band that proclaimed his feelings as simply as he could. *Yours.*

But this was not that world, and Cornelia did not look like a woman who wanted him any way at all.

He'd gone too far, even with his props.

"Would you like to slap my wrists with your fan as punishment for my undue exuberance?" he asked, hoping to lighten the mood once again. He proffered the underside of his arm to her in supplication.

She was quiet for a moment. Then she shook her head at him, and he let out a breath.

"I would never resort to physical violence against my beloved husband," she said, a slight hint of mirth returning to her eyes. "I would only withhold my favors. Or perhaps bestow them on others to make him jealous."

The idea made him want to growl—and not with envy.

"Oh, I doubt he'd be jealous. So long as you told him the details afterward."

It slipped out before he had time to reason that it was perhaps not the best time to evoke memories of their activities the day before.

The glint in Cornelia's eyes suggested she was remembering, too.

"Perhaps I wouldn't need to tell him," she murmured. "Perhaps he would already know."

Singh coughed. "Mr. Hugue?" he reminded them.

Rafe flinched. He'd forgotten Singh was standing there. Poor Singh, witnessing their repressed desire. *Barely* repressed.

"Ah, of course," Rafe said. "Show him in, please." He turned to Cornelia. "And you, Your Grace, are not to protest when he addresses you with the ostentation you deserve."

"Oh, I shall enjoy being heaped with respect by one

of my uncle's cronies, for once. After we give him the shock of his life."

The door opened and a tall man in an old-fashioned powdered periwig entered. His brow knit in bemusement at the sight of Cornelia. Knowing her uncle, he would know that she'd been banished from this house.

"Good morning, Mr. Hugue," Rafe said, rising. "Thank you for coming to visit me and my duchess."

Hugue looked from Rafe to Cornelia and back, as if to say: *Where is this duchess? Certainly not here!*

The solicitor covered his confusion with a bow. "It is my pleasure, Your Grace . . . Perhaps you might present me to her?"

Rafe put his arm around Cornelia. "Of course. I believe you are familiar with the previous duke's niece. Allow me to introduce my wife, Cornelia, Duchess of Rosemere."

The solicitor looked like he might topple sideways. "Oh, I see," he said faintly, though he clearly did not—or did not wish to. "I gather you were recently wed, then, Your Grace?"

"No. His Grace and I have been married for quite some time," Cornelia said.

"We were avowed at Gretna Green in 1777, to be exact," Rafe said, affecting a misty tone of voice. "It still moves me to think of it."

On second thought, the misty tone was not entirely affected.

The memory *did* move him. He'd never been able to think of that day without feeling like a love letter made flesh.

Hugue stared at Rafe in open confusion. "I was not aware you were married until I saw the reports in the papers, Your Grace. It did not come up at the reading of the will."

"Are dukes required to inform their solicitors of the matters of their bedchambers?" Rafe asked imperiously.

The man nearly choked.

Cornelia squeezed Rafe's arm, obviously loving this.

"Forgive my gorgeous, valiant husband," Cornelia said, in her most cultivated tone. "The truth is we have been forced to live apart, due to the ire of my uncle at our union. Rafe, being in his employ, could not risk him knowing of our matrimony."

"Rosemere would never have tolerated our love. And since my career depended on his patronage, we were forced to marry in secret."

"Star-cross'd lovers, like Romeo and Juliet," Cornelia sighed. "Though of course we visited one another when we could."

"They were very *pleasurable* visits," Rafe said, winking at Mr. Hugue. "You understand my meaning, don't you, you old devil?"

"So pleasurable," Cornelia sighed, smiling coyly at her husband.

"However, now that His Grace has inherited the dukedom," she went on, "we can finally proclaim our love and live in a blissful state of matrimony."

"Ah, to live as man and wife, the way the Lord intended," Rafe sighed, rubbing his belly as if in anticipation of a good meal. "How I rejoice in my marriage. And in my wife."

This time, it was Cornelia's turn to stifle laughter.

He put his arm around her and she leaned into him and kissed him on the side of the chin. She smelled so good, like sage and clean linen.

He took her hand and noisily kissed her palm.

"Oh, Your Grace," she laughed, pulling away her hand. "Not in front of poor Mr. Hugue. He'll be scandalized."

He snatched her hand back and clasped it in his larger one. "I cannot resist you, even in the presence of the law."

Cornelia giggled and squeezed his fingers back.

God, it was fun to playact with her.

Not that he was acting.

The solicitor seemed lost in confusion and oblivious to their mirth.

Rafe straightened his posture, without letting go of Cornelia's hand.

"Given our long marriage," he said loftily, "my wife will, of course, be entitled to the inheritance allocated to her in Rosemere's will."

Hugue looked vaguely nauseated. "Er, Your Grace, with all respect, I must verify her—your—married status, to confirm it meets the requirements of the codicil."

"You doubt my word, good sir?" Rafe asked. "How could you doubt a man would wish to be married to this *delicious* creature?"

He stood and moved behind her, placed his hands on her shoulders as possessively as if she really was his own. She leaned back into him and looked up adoringly.

"Just look at her, Hugue. Just look at her."

He savored every syllable. His words were as sincere as any oath he'd ever spoken.

This was the difficulty of feigning affection for Cornelia.

There was so very little to feign.

He bent down and kissed her neck. She reached up and caressed his face.

"You are too kind, my love," she said. "Isn't he, Mr. Hugue?"

Mr. Hugue's eyes darted from his own lap to Cornelia's face and back to his lap. He looked like a newborn lamb without a mother.

"Her Grace is a vision," he finally said. "But if Her Grace wishes to inherit, I must verify her marriage, per the terms of the will."

He said this to Rafe, as if Cornelia were not in the room. It made Rafe want to smack him. Cornelia, however, only laughed.

"I *do* wish to inherit," she said merrily. "Wouldn't *you*, Mr. Hugue?"

"Er, yes. Of course. I assume you have a witness paper?"

"Certainly," she said, producing the folded, nearly disintegrating paper Rafe knew she had kept safely locked away since the night it was signed.

"Be careful," she said, offering it gingerly to the lawyer. "It's very dear to me."

"And to me, my love," Rafe said, squeezing her shoulders. "I still tear up at the memory of the day we were wed."

And it was true. He did.

Chapter Twenty-Six

Before

The closer they got to Headless Cross, the famed road heading into Gretna Green, the more congested the route became. Rafe and Cornelia passed the time by guessing which of the carriages were filled with lovers, and which were toting fathers in hot pursuit.

They bypassed the infamous Gretna Green blacksmith's shop and its anvil for an inn with rooms a farther distance into town.

Cornelia took off her hat and let her hair out into a fetching nimbus of curls.

"Do I look the blushing bride?" she asked, fluttering her eyelashes.

"There's no one more beautiful," he said sincerely. "And you look most dashing in your breeches."

She laughed. "Thank you. They are quite practical. Perhaps I will trade in all my gowns. All two of them, since I abandoned the rest at Gardencourt."

He had not thought of that. How all she now possessed in the world was the contents of her satchel.

"How will you get by in Florence, with so few of your belongings?"

She smiled. "Oh, it will be wonderful to be so unencumbered. I've saved enough of my allowance for my passage to Italy, and to rent a room and buy paints and canvas. I won't need fancy gowns to paint. I can take portrait commissions or teach drawing lessons to support myself. It might be difficult at first, but I know that I can find my way."

Her bravery was admirable. Were he in her position, he would be terrified of destitution.

"I'll leave you with what little extra money I have with me," he said. "To help. Just in case."

"No need, Rafe. You're helping me enough by marrying me."

Marrying her. He was actually going to *marry* her. To elope with Cornelia Ludgate, singular human, gorgeous woman, brave soul, and aristocratic maiden.

He'd developed a dread of marriage in the years since his youthful affair with Lucy Collins. He'd sworn himself to bachelordom, fearing his heart was too open to allow himself to commit it to one person without inevitably hurting them. But Cornelia was not asking for the sole claim to his affections. She was asking only for his commitment.

And to give it to her felt like an honor, not a burden.

"Shall we stop here?" Cornelia asked, pointing at a pub that had a sign in front reading Rooms & Weddings.

"The Bride and Gun," Rafe said, reading the name painted on the pub. "Seems appropriate."

They stopped and put their horses in a stable. They were dusty and sweaty from the journey—so dirty they would not have been allowed to set foot in a church, were they marrying in the conventional fashion.

No one inside the inn appeared to notice their unkempt appearance nor Cornelia's masculine attire. The room was too raucous with similarly disheveled couples cheerfully swallowing back ale and toasting their newly minted spouses. A man in the front was serenading his bride—drunk, warbling, and off-key. At the chorus, others joined in, raising their glasses and sloshing their beer.

A small space in the back of the room boasted a line of couples waiting their turn to marry. A man Rafe assumed to be the innkeeper sat in a chair, administering quick ceremonies, while a woman beside him clutched a stack of paper on which to scrawl consecration of this blessed rite.

He'd known elopement was not a formal affair, but this melee was shocking.

"Don't look so appalled," Cornelia laughed. "Did you expect a hushed chapel?"

"I suppose I imagined there might be a bit of romance, even if the vows are said in an alehouse and not a church."

"I think it is romantic," Cornelia said. "All these couples stealing away, determined to love whomever they want and to live exactly as they please. And look how happy they all are."

She smiled at him, her eyes twinkling.

"Perhaps you're right," he said, reaching out to squeeze her hand.

She squeezed his back.

But when they reached their turn, and the woman greeted them with only the word "next," Cornelia met his eyes and swallowed back a laugh at the absurdity of such a solemn occasion being treated in so perfunctory a manner.

"You know how it's done?" the innkeeper asked, seeming indifferent to whether they did or not.

Rafe had no idea, but Cornelia smiled brightly.

"Yes," she said, taking Rafe's hand.

Despite the din in the room, the boredom of the man officiating their nuptials, the lack of future between them, and the smell of stale ale drifting from the floor, Rafe felt oddly moved by this strange ritual. Despite everything, they *were* bound in something—if only the memory of this experience.

Whatever happened, Cornelia was now a part of his life.

His past, at least.

But he ached for her to be part of his future as well.

"I don't know what to do," Rafe whispered to Cornelia. "Enlighten me."

"Just do as I do," Cornelia said. "I'll go first, since this was my idea." She winked at him.

She turned to the innkeeper. "I, Cornelia Ludgate, hereby pledge myself in marriage to Rafe Goodwood."

She smiled at Rafe, eyes shining. "Now your turn."

He swallowed. "I, Rafe Goodwood . . ." He stopped and cleared his throat over the lump that was forming. "Pledge myself in marriage to Cornelia Ludgate."

He waited for Cornelia to say something else, but apparently that was it.

They were married.

He was this precious woman's husband.

He wished he had something to give her, some small token that might make the marriage feel more real.

He wished he had a ring he could slide over her finger.

Instead, he squeezed Cornelia's hand.

"Thank you," she whispered in his ear, squeezing his hand back. "Thank you so much."

The woman scribbled her signature on a piece of paper with the place and the date and handed it to Rafe. "Sign yer names."

Rafe felt oddly proud watching Cornelia scrawl *Cornelia Goodwood* across the page. He signed his name in turn.

"On with you then," the innkeeper said, without warmth.

Cornelia took the paper, rolled it up, and stuffed it down her stays.

"Have any rooms available?" she asked jauntily. "A girl's needing to become a woman, if you know what I mean."

The innkeeper cracked a smile. "See Tommy there, at the bar."

Chapter Twenty~Seven

Cornelia had expected many things from the meeting with Mr. Hugue. Doubt. Discomfort. The tantrum of an old white man disbelieving a Black woman could be a duchess.

But she had not expected *fun*.

Yet with each question Mr. Hugue asked, with each clench of his jaw and tightening of the lines around his mouth, Rafe became more amorous and love-sick.

It was highly comical.

She reached up, took one of Rafe's hands from her shoulder, and kissed his knuckles, eliciting a pained wince from Hugue in response.

Dreadful man. She enjoyed torturing him.

"Will you join us for a light refreshment, Mr. Hugue?" Cornelia asked, gesturing at a tray of tea and cakes Singh had left for them.

The old man eyed the food like it might be poisoned.

Rafe raised a brow at him expectantly. A man such as Hugue would know that when a duchess offers you tea, you drink the tea.

"Yes, thank you, Your Grace," Hugue said miserably.

Rafe took a buttered cake and chewed merrily, beaming at Cornelia. "Excellent butter, my dove."

She put a hand over her heart, like he'd pledged his love. "All to the credit of your fine cows, my handsome lord."

Hugue coughed on a scone, then sputtered a bit in embarrassment at spewing crumbs before the duke and his alleged wife.

"Forgive me," he said.

"Your company is a credit to us. No forgiveness is required," Cornelia cooed.

"I do have several more questions, if you can spare the time," Hugue said. "I hate very much to pry, but in order to fulfill my duties to the estate it is necessary to understand more of the circumstances of your marriage, given they were unknown at the writing of the will."

"We are always overjoyed to speak of our love affair," Rafe said. "Ask anything you want."

"Well, let's start with your introductions to each other. How is it that you became acquainted?"

Cornelia remembered the first time she'd set eyes on Rafe. She wondered if he remembered that day, too.

"He was a guest of my aunt when I was visiting her in London," she said quickly, glancing in Rafe's eyes as if to say, *Follow my lead.* She intended to do as they'd discussed the day before: tell the truth, only with embellishment.

Rafe nodded in agreement, picking up where she'd left off. "I was friendly with Cornelia's parents—we'd traveled in similar circles, though they were older. They introduced me to Lady Elinor, who was kind enough to have me to a musical salon in her home."

Cornelia had been so excited to travel to her aunt's house for the event. Though it was another stately home, it had a different tone from her uncle's—the furnishings were newer, the atmosphere livelier, the company far more urbane.

"After the music," Cornelia continued, "the guests

mingled, and I noticed Mr. Goodwood alone at the refreshments table. I found him exceptionally handsome, and I was quite bold. I made it my mission to engage him in conversation."

Rafe grinned at her. "And here I thought you'd only been hungry."

"Not for *food*, my lord," she quipped.

Rafe tilted back his head and laughed. "Well, in any case," he said to Hugue, "I didn't know anyone except for Lady Elinor and the man I had come with, who was occupied in a game of chess. Cornelia took pity on me and led me about the room, explaining who was who."

"I may have spread a bit of gossip. I was very naughty when I was young."

"You're still very naughty, dear," Rafe growled, taking her hand.

He had touched her so many times in the last quarter hour that she was beginning to feel as if they really were married.

"One of my many charms, is it not?" she parried, stroking his thumb with hers.

She did not merely want to stroke it. She wanted to bite it.

"If I were to name your charms before Mr. Hugue here, he might fall dead," Rafe murmured, raising her thumb to his lips and sucking on it.

Her knees went weak.

Mr. Hugue's eyes bulged like he was having an aneurysm.

Rafe removed her thumb from his lips, kissed it, and then smiled at Hugue as though nothing out of the ordinary had happened.

"Cornelia knew everyone, despite her youth," he

continued. "She had a kind word to say to them all and a gift for making people comfortable, though she was only a girl of sixteen."

It touched her that he'd noticed this, remembered it. She'd been proud of this ability then, and it was one she still had—the social dexterity to move between different types of people, mix with all sorts, put people at ease. She suspected it was due to her feelings of being out of place in her own world growing up.

It had certainly been valuable with Rafe.

"I found Mr. Goodwood very kind and endearing," she remembered, speaking to Rafe rather than Mr. Hugue. After all, they'd never talked of this, and it was pleasant to share their first impressions of each other. "He told me a bit about my mother and father, who had taken a shine to him when he was my age, before they died. I always love stories about them, and I'm afraid I may have taken more than my share of his time."

In truth, he'd seemed relieved that he had someone to talk to. It made her like him more, his gratitude to her for entertaining him.

"Not that I minded her attention," Rafe said. "She was very fetching."

He winked at her. She winked back.

"I was very sad when he departed early," she said honestly.

He laughed sheepishly. "Forgive me, my love. The only reason I left is that I was afraid Lady Bell would be cross at me for detaining her niece for the duration of an entire evening."

"Well, I was briefly morose, for I did not expect to see the intriguing Mr. Goodwood again. But then I had an idea—I would make him come to me."

Hugue looked horrified. "You were sixteen, you say?"

"Nearly seventeen," Rafe said, as though defending her honor.

"And very clever for my age. You see, my uncle, the duke, asked me to put together a large dinner to entertain a number of equestrians and horse investors that came to Gardencourt for a private auction at his stables. As Mr. Goodwood lived in a cottage on the estate, and was known for training horses, I invited him."

"I had no idea Cornelia was behind the invitation," Rafe said. "But when I arrived and found her there, in her capacity as hostess, I was overjoyed to see her again."

He *had* seemed very pleased. And unlike the stiff gentlemen of her acquaintance, whose emotions were hidden behind perfect manners, he had not been afraid to greet her with genuine enthusiasm.

"I seated him beside myself at dinner, so he would have to talk to me," she said, laughing a bit at herself.

Rafe nodded. "I was exceedingly glad she did. She was splendid at talking. Far more entertaining than the horsemen."

"And far more carnally exciting," she said blandly.

"Yes," Rafe agreed. "Most erotic. It was all I could do not to grab her skirts under the table and—"

"I see," Mr. Hugue said in a strangled voice. "And how was it you decided to elope?"

Rafe looked at her blankly, caught off guard. They had, rather stupidly, not discussed the specific answer to this question.

She decided to tell the closest thing she could to the truth. She knew whatever she said, he'd play along. He was very good at this.

"It was my idea," she said. "I was running away to study art in Florence. I had to leave Rafe behind in England, as his work did not allow for him to come with me. But I could not stand for us to sever our connection. So I asked him to come with me to Gretna Green, so that we could pledge ourselves in love."

She wriggled the wedding band off her finger and handed it over to Mr. Hugue. "He gave me this, do you see? *Yours.* So that I'd always know I had his heart with me."

Rafe's Adam's apple bobbed, as with emotion. "It meant everything to me that she knew exactly how I felt about her."

He met her eye as he said this. As if he *meant* it. But he could not be talking of the past, as he'd only given her the ring this morning.

Did that mean—

Playing this game was becoming intellectually dizzying. All she knew was that she wanted to hold the ring to her heart.

Hugue looked despairing with the romance in the air.

"How did you stay in contact, knowing the marriage must be secret?" he asked miserably.

"Clandestine rendezvous," Rafe said.

If only *that* were true. She took the detail and expanded on it, imagining a different path they might have taken.

"He would send me notes written from a Mr. Crow on the first day of every spring and autumn, setting a place and time. We couldn't meet where anyone would know us, so we found a little inn near Devon. Each of us told our friends we were taking a holiday. And there, we were known as Mr. and Mrs. Goodwood."

Hugue took a pencil from his pocket and wrote

something on a slip of paper. "Could you put me in touch with the innkeeper?" he asked.

"No," Rafe said sadly. "He died last year."

"From the ocean draft," Cornelia added.

"Quite sudden and unexpected."

"No heirs."

"And then the inn burned down."

"A cursed place."

"Except on the exalted nights we graced it with our love."

They clasped hands and looked at Mr. Hugue beatifically. She could feel Rafe holding back laughter.

"Do you have any other questions?" Rafe inquired, no doubt hoping to end this interview before they both collapsed in giggles.

"Well, I suppose I must ask what you plan to do now. The will stipulates you must reside together in matrimony. Will you?"

"Of course," Cornelia said. "I can't be parted from my love."

"I plan to claim this woman and never let her out of my sight again," Rafe said. "Perhaps you have heard the rumors—I'm planning a masquerade ball so that I can finally unveil my wife's identity after all these years. It will be the proudest moment of my life."

"And the most romantic moment of mine," Cornelia said.

"We'd be honored to have you as our guest, Mr. Hugue," Rafe added.

The solicitor seemed flattered, despite his generally mournful air.

"It would be a privilege," he said.

Rafe inclined his head, signaling the meeting was

over. "Very good. We shall look forward to it. Thank you for your time today. Mr. Thompson will be in touch to discuss the other outstanding matters of the probate."

Hugue stood and bowed. Rafe saw him to the door, where Singh waited to show him out.

As soon as Hugue was gone, and the door was firmly shut behind him, Cornelia sank down onto the rug and stared up at the fresco on the ceiling, as pleasantly spent as after a rousing bout in bed.

Rafe sat down beside her on the floor. "Have you fainted?"

"Yes. Dead away at the shock of our brilliant performance."

It was the truth.

She had never been good at projecting earnest emotion. She was better skilled at sparkling conversation, serene self-assurance in her work, and poise in various social milieus than expressing heartfelt sentiments.

It was not that she did not have strong feelings— she was a rather passionate creature at heart. It was that her upbringing had required such a repression of sensibility—such elegant reserve—that she had never quite lost the impulse to remain stoic and keep her emotions private. After all, the one time she had revealed herself, she'd lost everything.

It was safer to express her feelings in her paintings, where she could control what to reveal.

She was surprised she'd been able to display such romanticism as the lovestruck bride and to take such obvious pleasure in her "husband."

Rafe smiled. "That was the most fun I've had in

ages," he said, removing his wig and shaking out his hair. He looked so good in his ducal regalia she almost missed it.

"Thrilling, to be so sentimental," she said.

But also, if she was honest, a bit unsettling. For to summon all the emotion she had shown for Rafe had required drawing from deep within herself.

And something must be there, lurking in her heart, if she'd been able to feel it in the moment.

She didn't know what to make of it.

She twisted the ring around her finger.

Yours.

Did she want him to be?

Chapter Twenty-Eight

Rafe lay back on the floor beside Cornelia, wishing they were in bed.

"We did well, wife," he said, rolling over to give her a kiss on her cheek.

She turned to smile at him. "We did. You were wonderful."

Her compliment made him bashful. "I was just following your example. But I enjoyed myself immensely."

In fact, he could not remember the last time he had been so pleased.

Their dexterity in weaving details of the past into a romantic tale of courtship proved to him how good they could be together—their brains merging and functioning nearly as one organism.

If they could be as good at *talking* as they were at sex, was there not some hope for them?

Was it possible exploring it was worth taking a risk?

Or would she be furious at him for once again getting lost in unwanted emotions and leave him devastated?

Probably the latter, sadly. He couldn't risk driving her away now, when they needed each other, and needed to remain convincing as devoted lovers to Mr. Hugue and the guests at the masquerade. He couldn't risk crumbling with despair.

He was honor-bound to do what he'd promised her he'd do: keep his heart in hand.

He sat up. "We should go. Luncheon is waiting."

He helped her up and offered her his arm. She took it, and together they made their way to the dining room, where the others were gathered for the midday meal.

As soon as he opened the door, the room erupted in cheers.

"To the newlyweds!" Anna shouted, throwing a handful of rose petals in the air above them.

Everyone clapped, laughing.

"Welcome to your wedding luncheon," Anna said. "A mere twenty years late."

Rafe glanced at Cornelia, worried she would be annoyed, but she seemed amused.

"What a touching surprise," she said.

Tacit permission to continue being her adoring husband. Delightful.

He fell into a courtly bow at her feet. "To my bride," he quipped. "So clearly in passionate love with me the solicitor was embarrassed to be in our presence."

She took his hand and pulled him up. "Oh, I think the true victory was a credit to my husband."

"'Tis a shame Rafe is so very old, or I would wish you a nice long life together," Lord Eden cracked.

"Oh, he's young enough yet for certain vigorous activities by the looks of him," Thaïs instantly shot back.

"Stop coveting my groom, you wicked girl," Cornelia said, brushing his fingers with her own. He loved her habit of touching his hands. It was like a secret sign between them: *we mean something to each other.* Or, at least, it felt that way.

He hoped he was not imagining it.

He picked up a glass and raised it. "On behalf of myself and my gorgeous bride, I thank you all for coming here and for joining us in celebrating our matrimony—not to mention all your work on the ball and the estate. Your presence makes our home a happy one, and your good wishes make us ever more deeply in love."

"Yes," Cornelia said, laughter in her voice. "Never am I more enamored with my husband than when we are surrounded by our dear friends. I'm so grateful for you all." She turned to Rafe and looked up into his eyes. "And, of course, for you, my love."

My love.

Those words.

They'd always done him in. But to hear Cornelia say them was as close to heaven as a man could walk on earth.

"My love," he echoed softly.

He swallowed the contents of his glass, took Cornelia's chin in one hand and the small of her back in the other.

Her eyes went wide, and he smiled into them, swept her backward off her feet, and placed his lips on hers.

He kissed her like this could be real. He kissed her like he didn't know the difference. He kissed her like they would never stop pretending.

Their friends whooped and whistled and she moved her hands between them, to his chest. Christ, she was going for his nipples in front of all these people. Her brazenness nearly undid him, and he growled into her mouth as he bent her back and kissed her still more deeply.

She twisted her neck and wrenched away, her eyes blazing with anger, her mouth swollen, her body stiff.

Oh, Christ.

She had not been caressing his chest but pushing him away.

He was a bloody, unthinking *animal*.

Immediately, he put her down. The room went silent.

She looked at the floor, like she couldn't meet his eyes—or anyone's.

"I'm so sorry," he stammered to her. "It was only in good fun."

But it wasn't, if he was honest with himself. He'd been moved by genuine passion. So much that he'd forgotten everything he'd promised her.

And it must have been obvious to her, for she looked like she wanted to take a fork off the table and stab him in the hand.

Her expression crushed him.

"I think I've had enough merriment," she said quietly. "Excuse me."

She did not wait for anyone to respond. She was out the door, her high heels clicking in the corridor as she stalked calmly toward the stairs.

Should he go after her?

But no—that would no doubt embarrass her more. He'd made one romantic gesture too many—he could not afford to make another. He felt too pitiful.

And clearly the guests could tell, for no one spoke. Even the usually irrepressible Anna was looking at her plate, pushing around some creamed potatoes.

Rory, bless him, cleared his throat, breaking the awkward silence.

"I'm sorry to interrupt the festivities," he said. "But I received a letter this morning with good news."

A change of subject. Not for the first time, he thanked the holy gods for Rory Thompson.

"Oh?" Rafe inquired, sitting down to his meal in an imitation of a man who did not wish to flee the room. "What is it?"

"Official confirmation that Lord Bell will be attending the horse auction at Tatersall's tomorrow. He's indeed in the market for a Thoroughbred. And we just so happen to have a promising foal that fits the bill."

"That's excellent news," Rafe replied. Not only because it meant their plan was working, but because it would put some welcome distance between himself and Cornelia.

"I'll introduce myself under the guise of selling him my horse and attempt to tease out details of his strategy," Rafe said. "I have every confidence we can extract something to help defend Jack. I'm quite the actor after all. You should have seen me with the executor. He thought I worshipped at Cornelia's feet."

There was an awkward silence.

"Don't you?" Seraphina asked.

Rafe laughed long and heartily, as though this were the greatest joke he'd ever heard.

"Of course," he said with an exaggerated bow. "I am her most devoted *temporary* husband."

And he would renew his efforts to prove to her—to *both* of them—that he could perform this role without becoming overwhelmed with true emotion.

He would apologize and show her he knew it was all just a game, and one he'd play by the rules.

Chapter Twenty-Nine

Cornelia had not imagined it was possible to be bothered and moved at once. The combination made her nervous. The nerves made her restless. The restlessness sent her dashing for her sketchbook.

She spent the afternoon alone, in front of a mirror, drawing studies of herself in Rafe's jewels and her mother's yellow dress.

The drawings were rough and lifeless—perhaps because she no longer wanted to resemble a duchess.

It was too dangerous. People got confused.

She got confused.

Rafe got confused.

She was galled he'd made such an emotional display, embarrassing her in front of all their friends. He'd kissed her with so much passion that no one could mistake his sincerity—least of all her. Yet what mystified her was that despite her vexation, despite her horror at being observed by her friends in a moment of genuine emotion, she'd *liked* the ardor in that kiss. She'd liked it so much that she'd been unable to move away until he stopped.

She wanted to be angry, but she couldn't.

Because if they were alone, he could kiss her like that until she fainted dead away. And she might, because the way he used his tongue—

Tongues are not pertinent to self-portraiture!

And anyway, it was time for supper.

She put down her charcoal, cleaned her hands, and changed out of the yellow gown and diamond jewels. That left only the ring.

Yours.

There was no reason to leave it on, and yet she was reluctant to remove it. It reminded her of the way Rafe's eyes had looked when he'd slipped it on her finger.

Like neither of them was pretending.

She didn't know what to do.

She worried the ring with her thumb as she went downstairs, repeating to herself the boundaries of the agreement that Rafe himself had set: *I will be your plaything, and you will end the game if you tire of me. I can't always be trusted not to want to play too much.*

Did he want to play too much?

Did she?

They needed to talk. Alone. Tonight.

She had to make sure this was still a game. And if it wasn't, she needed to end it.

She was quiet all through supper, scarcely listening to the others, who were intently discussing the strategic possibilities of Rafe's opportunity to meet Lord Bell. Rafe was absorbed in the conversation, explaining horse provenances, breeding charts, auction prices, methods for gathering intelligence, and other topics that she paid scant attention to, because it was more interesting to simply watch him from the corner of her eye, observing how attractive he was when he spoke with such authority.

He, meanwhile, barely spared Cornelia a glance.

Was that good?

She wondered what he'd done this afternoon, and

whether he'd been preoccupied with her, or if she was the only one whose powers of cognition had deteriorated under the influence of that disastrous, paralyzing kiss.

"This party has become entirely too serious," Anna proclaimed as the plates were taken away.

Lord Eden grimaced at his sister from across the table. "That is because we are planning to spy on a viscount, win a trial, reorganize a vast estate, and throw a masquerade ball that will scandalize the entire country."

"And it's all continuing apace," Anna said brightly. "Which is why we deserve a bit of levity."

"I concur," said Seraphina's lover, Adam Anderson, who'd arrived that evening. "As Sera tells it, you all have been working yourselves into exhaustion. A bit of merriment is well deserved."

Anna beamed at Adam. "Well said, Mr. Anderson. Finally, someone with some sense."

"Adam is not a whimsical man," Sera said, putting a hand on his shoulder. "If he believes we should amuse ourselves, I must resign myself to being amused."

"Then amuse ourselves we shall," Rafe decreed.

Cornelia tried not to despair that Rafe wanted to play a game, which would prolong her waiting until they could have a private conversation. But she did not wish to seem out of sorts and draw attention to herself. After her abrupt exit from lunch, and quiet performance at supper, she knew her friends must be speculating as to the reasons for her strange mood.

"What do you suggest we play, young Miss Anna?" she asked with as much enthusiasm as she could muster.

"I have been longing for a lesson in drawing from

you, Miss Ludgate," Anna said. "Perhaps you would teach us all? We can make it into a friendly competition of skill."

"Very well," Cornelia said. At least if she was to be a tutor, she would not spend the whole night thinking about Rafe.

"Oh, how grand!" Anna said, rising. "I'm going to gather some pencils and paper for us. I'll come find you when it's time to play."

"Shall we retire to the parlor while we wait?" Rafe asked, standing to guide the group across the hall.

She hung back as the others filed out in twos and threes, laughing about this and that. Rafe trailed behind, the last to leave.

This was her opportunity. She took a deep breath and walked toward him.

"Rafe," she said quietly.

He looked up, as if surprised that she was speaking to him.

She felt awkward and slightly worried that others in the room would notice and surmise things from it.

She hated feeling anything but self-possessed.

"Cornelia," he said in greeting. His expression was warm, but searching. Like he wasn't sure how he should act either.

He cleared his throat. "I wanted to say—"

"I wondered if we could—" she said at the same time.

They both paused, gesturing for the other to speak first. When neither did, they both laughed at their helpless attempt to communicate.

She felt a little better, laughing with him.

"You first," he said.

"I wondered if we could talk. In private. After the game."

His face went soft. "Ah. I was hoping for the same thing."

She was relieved that she was not the only one who felt there were things that needed to be undressed between them.

Undressed?

Addressed, Cornelia.

"I will come find you in your bedchamber as soon as everyone retires," she said.

His bedchamber? Why had she suggested his bedchamber?

"Or, er, in the library, rather, if you'd—"

His face broke into a sympathetic smile at her stuttering. "My bedchamber is more private," he assured her, as if there was nothing suggestive about the location. "I'll look forward to your visit."

"I'm ready," Anna called, bounding into the parlor. "Everyone, come with me."

They filed after her to the gallery, which Anna had not set up as Cornelia had expected—with a still life set in the front for each of them to sketch. Instead, the chairs were arranged in a circle, with nothing in the middle.

"But what are we drawing?" Marianne asked.

"Air, I hope," Thaïs grumbled. "It's all I'm capable of."

Anna ignored her. "Since Miss Ludgate's specialty is portraits, I thought we might all draw each other," she told the group. "Miss Ludgate will assign us pairs, and we will each sketch the person across from us. When we're finished, Miss Ludgate will go around, critique our work, and choose a winner."

Cornelia had to hand it to Anna. The girl had a flair for scenarios that were as revealing as they were amusing.

She took a minute to think of interesting pairings.

"Adam and Seraphina must draw each other, of course," she said. Forcing Seraphina to draw the man she loved would be intriguing, as Sera so rarely showed affection in public. Cornelia and Sera were alike in this way. Perhaps it was why they were such good friends.

Sera laughed. "How boring. Adam draws me all the time. I can barely stop him."

Adam, an architect by training, was also a skilled artist. He shot Sera a wry look. "No, darling. You can't."

"Adam will be our model of competency," Cornelia said. "And you, Miss Arden, will finally draw a loving portrait in return."

"And who shall I draw?" Anna asked, looking hopeful.

Cornelia knew exactly what answer she longed for, and decided to indulge the girl. It was a house party after all. What was a house party without encouraging a little romance among the guests?

Someone should have an uncomplicated love affair around here.

"You and Mr. Howe will draw each other," Cornelia answered. "Thaïs and Marianne will do the same. And Rafe—"

She surveyed the group. Elinor was upstairs with the baby, and Lord Eden had insisted on dealing with his correspondence rather than participating. Canette and Singh had both excused themselves to go to bed. That meant they were an odd number, short a match.

"And I will judge the winner," Rafe interrupted, before she could give him an assignment.

"I believe that is my role," Cornelia said.

"Dukes can do whatever they want," he retorted pleasantly.

"And what does the victor win?" Anna asked.

"A penalty from their subject," Rafe said immediately.

Cornelia flushed. For two decades, she had not been able to hear the word *penalty* without thinking of her time with Rafe.

Yours.

Bloody stop it.

"I thought we'd be drawing an orange in a flower basket, or the like," Thaïs grumbled. "Not a bloody person. I can barely sign my own name."

This was true. Thaïs had not learned to properly read and write until Elinor taught her in her twenties.

"Legible script has nothing to do with art," Cornelia said gently. "And I agree with Anna. Drawing people is more interesting than drawing objects."

"Well, at least give us some instruction," Sera said. "Those of us who've scarcely held a pencil haven't the slightest notion of what to do."

"That's quite all right," Cornelia said. "Think of your task not as drawing your model based strictly on what their body looks like, but how their soul comes through in the *way* their body looks. That is the difference between a good likeness and a true portrait. It's humanity—yours, and your subject's."

"But how do I draw the damned body?" Thaïs asked grumpily. "Goodly or badly."

Cornelia showed them how to divide their paper into a grid to see proportion, and to make rough shapes to sketch out their subject's face and anatomy.

Gilby looked concerned, and Cornelia patted his shoulder. "Don't worry. Skill comes with time, and no one expects a command performance from a beginner."

Anna smiled at him brightly from across the room. "Indeed. Tonight is for *enjoyment*."

"With that in mind," Cornelia said, "everyone, pick up your pencils and begin."

Cornelia walked around the perimeter of the circle, silently observing, while Rafe went round and round, encouraging the artists with such vocal enthusiasm that it became a matter of parody.

She loved how amusing he was.

She loved many things about him. His kindness. The joy he took in horses. His deference to women. His intelligence in speaking of his work. His commitment to their shared causes. His hair—

Stop. Stop. Stop.

"A stunning show, Miss Anderson," Rafe said to Marianne, continuing his round of compliments.

"What a poignant line, young Gilby!" he cawed to Howe.

"Look at the shadow there, Thaïs," he said, clapping her on the shoulder. "Are you sure that it's not you who's the famous painter of the house?"

It was so clear he knew nothing about art that it was humorous. Before long he had the room in near hysterics.

Between the laughter and the permission to stare intently at the subject across the circle, the guests were exhibiting telling behavior. Marianne seemed too shy to even look at Thaïs, whereas Anna stared at Gilby with such rapt care that she didn't even laugh at Rafe's jokes.

Sera stretched out her epically long legs and drew idly in slashing lines—her manner bespeaking someone who did not wish to draw her lover, but to climb him. Meanwhile Adam, the more romantic of the two, smiled sweetly as he sketched her, the picture of sincere affection.

Once half an hour had passed, Cornelia ordered the subjects to drop their pencils.

"Now each artist must come to the front of the room and display their portrait," she said. "I will critique the sketches, and then the duke here, in his infinite wisdom and taste, will crown the winner."

She glanced at Rafe, whose amusement in this activity was so obvious and boyish that she wanted to throw an arm around him and giggle like two children. But she would not deign to show amusement before her friends, who might consider it confirmation that there was more between the two of them than fake matrimony.

"My lord," she said airily. "Who shall we judge first?"

"Let's begin with Thaïs and Marianne," Rafe said. "Miss Anderson, please stand and display your masterpiece."

Marianne's picture was startlingly adept—though perhaps Cornelia should not be surprised, given she was Adam's sister.

"Excellent work. You've captured Thaïs's frustration in this game quite well," Cornelia said, looking at the faint lines around Thaïs's eyes and the expression of incorrigibility that so defined her friend. "Your choice to focus on an aspect of Thaïs's mood rather than mere replication of her features or pose is very sensitive. It shows you really *see* her."

And liked her more than perhaps Cornelia had been aware.

Marianne smiled at Cornelia sweetly. "Thank you."

"Well done, Miss Anderson," Rafe said. "Thaïs, I believe that makes it your turn."

Thaïs rose up proudly and with great ceremony brandished a pair of breasts covered in a modest bodice.

Rafe audibly choked back a laugh. "I see. That is—"

"Faces are too hard," Thaïs said, interrupting him. "I drew her bosom."

Cornelia had never noticed what a prodigious bosom it was. Trust Thaïs to focus on a woman's tits.

Anna gasped, while Gilby Howe descended into a coughing fit.

Marianne, seeing the drawing, clapped a hand to her mouth and laughed. It surprised Cornelia she was amused rather than scandalized.

"Well, you've done a fine job if the task were to pretend to be a bored farmhand drawing naughty pictures in the dirt," Cornelia said.

Thaïs cackled, pleased with the analogy.

"But I daresay, Thaïs, that the drawing is as much a reflection of the artist as the sitter. You've deflected the activity at hand, turned it into a joke to avoid showing us your true skill, or lack thereof." It was a surprisingly dull gesture from her usually brazen friend. Cornelia wondered at the reason she had attempted to shock rather than actually try.

Was she scared to draw Marianne, for what it might reveal? Or was she merely a clown with a bent for delighting in perversion?

Probably the latter.

"Who's next?" Cornelia asked Rafe.

"Mr. Howe and Anna, I think," he said. "Let's begin with Gilby."

Gilby bashfully stood up and turned his drawing out to face the crowd.

It was clear he had no training. He'd focused on Anna's face. The eyes were mushed together, the hair was a chaotic scribble of messy lines, but he'd done a rather good job of capturing her pillowy bottom lip and the joyful, upturned quality of her mouth.

"Very nice," Rafe said kindly. He was always so sensitive, so sweet. She loved that about him.

No. *Liked* that about him.

"No, it's crude," Gilby said, looking ashamed. "Miss Anna deserves far better than I am capable of producing."

"I rather like it," Cornelia said gently. "You've captured her spirit quite well."

"I love it," Anna said with fervor. "Will you sign it for me? I wish to keep it."

Gilby blushed so bright red Cornelia's cheeks hurt for him.

Rafe shot Cornelia a grin, as if proud of their silent conspiracy to unite the two young people.

She wondered if Gilby and Anna had yet discovered that their rooms were linked by the servants' passage—and if Gilby was bold enough to use it.

She had no doubt that Anna was.

"Now you, Anna," she said, though the girl was already on her feet.

She proudly held up an extremely proficient portrait of Gilby. She'd idealized him—made him more symmetrical, given him a slightly stronger chin. It was clear she cared for him enough to wish to flatter him. But there was not life behind his eyes. He could be a handsome doll.

"Your artistry is very good," Cornelia began.

"Oh, thank you! I do love to draw."

"If that is the case, may I give you some advice, as you work on your craft?"

"I'd be honored," Anna said.

"You've done a wonderful job capturing Mr. Gilby's likeness. But I can't see *you* in it."

Anna was puzzled. "What do you mean, me?"

"What matters more than skill—more than perspective or composition or tones or even the pencil strokes themselves—is the artist's eye. The point of view. One can technically execute a perfect likeness and it is still just that. A likeness."

Anna considered this. "My tutor discourages me from focusing on expressions. He says the skill is in representing detail, beautifully."

Cornelia laughed. "That is the mark of a tutor, not an artist. Some tutors are both. Yours, likely, is not."

"Thank you, Miss Ludgate," Anna said solemnly. "I shall strive for greater originality."

Cornelia realized, belatedly, that she had hurt the girl. She hated to see Anna chastened. She racked her brain for something to say to smooth her feelings, but before she could think of anything Gilby Howe stepped toward her.

"You're always original, Miss Anna," he said passionately. "I've never met anyone as original as you."

"Precisely," Cornelia said to the sweet boy. "And with skill like that, I want to see every ounce of Anna poured into the work. She has true potential."

Anna smiled, appeased—though Cornelia suspected it was more by Gilby's kind words than Cornelia's reassurance.

"Last but certainly not least," Rafe said, "let's see

the work of the blissful couple. Seraphina, would you please display your drawing?"

Seraphina yawned, smiled affectionately at Adam, and held up a childlike sketch of stick figures.

"I drew our family," she said. "Adam is the one holding the baby. I'm the tall one with wild hair, and the two small figures between us are Adam's children, Jasper and Adaline."

Cornelia rolled her eyes.

"I would not have expected you to be even more juvenile than Thaïs. You are so wicked I am tempted to make you do it again."

"How dare you, you literalist?" Sera said. "You yourself told us to capture the theme, not the likeness. The theme of mine is love."

"Sophistry, more like," Cornelia grumbled.

Sera gave Cornelia a smug smile, then handed the drawing to Adam.

"It's wonderful, isn't it, darling?"

He snorted. "Yes, my darling. How very moving."

But he wrapped an arm around her and kissed her cheek. Cornelia could not be truly irritated, for it was sweet in its meaning, if a bit belligerent in execution. Just like her dear Sera.

"And lastly, Mr. Anderson," Rafe said.

Adam flipped his drawing around. The room went quiet at the sight of it.

If the theme of Sera's drawing was love, the theme of Adam's was adoration—the intimate variety.

Cornelia took the drawing and examined it in more detail. The lines were bold and confident. The proportions were natural and well composed. But what was remarkable was the expression on Sera's face. Her lips were upturned at the corners—her smile almost sly.

Her eyes were downcast and she glanced at the artist sidelong, knowingly.

It was the expression of a lover. No, more than that: of a conspiracy between two lovers who'd been separated for a fortnight, sharing a wry look as they awaited the moment they could reunite in bed.

"Remarkable," Cornelia said, for it seemed almost inappropriate to say more. "Just remarkable."

Sera gave Adam a lingering kiss on the lips. "You truly are," she said softly.

Cornelia looked down at her feet, as it almost hurt to observe the tenderness between them, which Sera, despite her best efforts, couldn't hide. She felt a gaze on her, looked up, and found that Rafe was staring at her with a strange expression.

She looked away, but not before accidentally lingering on his eyes.

Remembering when he used to look at her exactly like Seraphina looked at Adam in the drawing.

She almost wished he would again.

Yours.

Please stop. Please please.

But she couldn't.

What was happening to her?

She cleared her throat. "Well then," she said brightly. "Who does His Grace deem the victor?"

The obvious answer was Adam, of course. His sketch was beautiful and insightful—if anyone made a sketch like that of Cornelia, she'd have it framed.

But Rafe smiled kindly across the room at Anna. "I think Miss Eden's work deserves the most acclaim. For someone of her tender age, it shows the most promise. And the likeness is most accurate. Which may mean nothing to an artist but means much to a duke."

Anna beamed.

"You are too kind to me, Mr. Goodwood. But I'm touched."

"And what will be the lady's penalty from Mr. Gilby?"

"I'd like to try drawing him again, another time. Taking Miss Ludgate's advice. Now that I have seen Mr. Anderson's sketch, I believe I know exactly what she means."

Hearing his name in reference to the sultry work of Adam's, Gilby looked at the floor. But then, the boy seemed to find his courage.

"I'd like that, Miss Anna. How about when we return to London?"

Cornelia could not hold back a smile at the two of them. They were adorable in Anna's enthusiasm and Gilby's shy admiration.

Rafe caught her eye over their heads and winked at her.

She looked down at her hands, lest she make an expression in front of their friends that might encourage speculation.

The light caught the gold band on her finger.

Yours.

Chapter Thirty

Forgive me.

It was all Rafe could think as he helped Anna and Cornelia clean up the drawing supplies, and walked the two of them upstairs to bed.

It had been a challenge, throughout the game, to keep his mind focused on the art and not his urgent desire to apologize. Now that the game was over, he was impatient to be alone with his wife.

His wife.

Strange, how that was the way he thought of her.

Inappropriate, no doubt.

If she knew, she'd probably leave the house screaming and never return. But he came to the word reflexively because deep down, whatever happened between them tonight or in the future, he was honored it was true.

In the corridor along the row of bedchambers they found Thaïs and Marianne deep in conversation. The pair of them seemed to be developing a close friendship—a surprising bond between the gentle Scottish nursemaid and the brazen, foul-mouthed courtesan.

"Marianne and I were about to have a cup of chocolate in my room," Thaïs said to the ladies, clearly not tired in the slightest. "Care to join us?"

"I'm too fatigued," Anna yawned. "Drawing is more vigorous than one thinks."

"Many activities that require wear on the wrists are exhausting," Thaïs said with an exaggerated wink at Rafe.

"I'm tired, too," Cornelia said, yawning. "I think I'll retire." She bade good night to them and slipped inside her room. He was glad that she'd demurred. He did not want to wait for her to visit with her friends when he was so alive with nerves.

No, not just nerves.

The deeper trouble was his heart ached. Adam's drawing had reminded him of what it felt like to be in love. To be intimate with a person you adored. To know them better than anyone on earth.

He knew that feeling was too easy for him to crave, and the path to it was too easy for him to sabotage. That he was usually at fault for seizing love too early, too loudly, too grandly—before it could take root in the object of his affection. That it was no longer worth the pain.

But he still longed for it.

He wished that fate had unspooled differently, and he could have had it with Cornelia.

But he couldn't. It was too late for that. And he'd rather have what little of her he was able to than ruin it by reaching for more than she'd allow.

He'd overstepped at lunch, breaking his word. He needed to apologize before she severed their relationship entirely.

He paced about his room, ruffling his hair, cracking his knuckles, dickering about with the stack of books beside his bed as he obsessed over what he needed to say to her.

Forgive me. Don't end the game just yet. I promise to follow the rules.

Finally, a knock sounded at the door of the bathing chamber that separated his room from Cornelia's.

"Come in," he said quietly, not wanting his voice to carry to the hall, where others might overhear. After her obvious discomfort with the kiss in front of their friends, he needed to be more careful to be discreet.

Cornelia walked in wearing a dressing gown.

He sat up straighter, startled that she was undressed.

"You look comfortable," he said. And beautiful. Her hair was wrapped up in a blue silk scarf the same color as her gown, which swept just so over her figure, emphasizing the swell of her breasts and the curve of her hips. He had to look away to avoid ogling in an ungentlemanly fashion.

He gestured at two chairs in front of the fireplace. "Please. Have a seat."

She did, crossing her legs so that the gown fell open at the knee.

Don't stare. Don't stare. Don't stare.

"I'm glad you're here," he said. "I wanted to apologize for kissing you at lunch. I was so taken up in the spirit of our ruse, and the merriment of our friends, that I forgot myself and acted outside the bounds of our game."

She let out a long breath. "Yes. That mustn't happen again."

He nodded. "It won't. The game will stay strictly private. That is, if you'll allow me another chance."

She leaned back in her chair and sighed. He sucked in his breath. This was the moment that would decide their future.

"I'm sorry, too," she said quietly. "I should not have run away. But I panicked. I despise being the subject of emotional displays. No matter what the nature of our relationship is, I would never want it to be a matter for the speculation or entertainment of others."

"I understand," he said. "And I'm sorry for putting you in that position. I became . . . overexercised in the moment."

She nodded. "Thank you." She paused, screwing up her mouth like she was debating something. "So where does that leave us?" she finally asked.

This was his chance to make sure he got it right.

"Here is the honest truth, Cornelia. I want to play our game. And if you'll have me, I promise to follow all the rules. I'll be discreet. And if I become too overwhelmed with feeling, or you feel that it's too much, we'll tell each other."

He looked closely at her face, trying to read what she was thinking. She nodded slowly, and a smile spread over her lips.

"I believe, since you broke the rules, I deserve a penalty."

Oh, sweet Mary, the relief.

He smiled at her with closed lips, not wanting to grin and scare her away with immoderate enthusiasm. "And what would you like?"

Her eyes locked on his.

"Well, you see, Adam's painting reminded me of us. Of that night in Gretna Green."

"I'll never forget that night," he said softly. "I'll remember it in the grave."

She reached out and stroked his hand. That lovely gesture of her affection and desire.

His hand was becoming a proxy for his cock. It throbbed every time she touched it.

"And what would you like me to do about that?" he whispered, hoping he already knew.

"Hold me, for a start," Cornelia whispered.

A request he'd never been able to deny, no matter how vulnerable his heart.

Chapter Thirty-One

Before

Rafe led Cornelia up the stairs to their room above the alehouse, nervous as a virgin bride on her wedding night over what Cornelia had suggested.

Sex.

Raucous sex.

"Hold me," she said, opening her arms to Rafe as soon as the door was closed.

Despite the small fire, their room did little to insulate them from the chill of the damp Scottish air.

"I'm cold," she said. "I want to wear you like a coat."

She held out her arms, and it was perhaps the most welcoming sight he'd ever seen.

"How dare you use me for my warmth?" he teased, as he stepped into her open arms and let her wrap herself around him. If this is what it felt like to be her coat, he'd like to be her stays, and shirt, and breeches.

She stepped away from him and sniffed her arm, wrinkling her nose. "I smell like horses."

He put his sleeve up to his nose and inhaled. "So do I," he replied. "But then, I love the smell of horses."

"Neigh you don't," she quipped.

He snorted with laughter. "What an excellent impression of a mare."

"This is very serious—how dare you laugh at me," she said with false indignation. "We are about to sanctify our holy matrimony and your bride has the odor of a stable."

"Oh, I wouldn't worry. I doubt our union is particularly holy, given it was ratified by a barman."

"How dare you. Barmen are very sacred figures."

He looked up at the ceiling pointedly.

"What are you looking at?" she inquired.

"The heavens. I'm waiting for God to strike you dead for blasphemy."

"God wouldn't dare." She moved closer to him. "After all, I'm one of his most singular creations."

"That, Cornelia, is true," he said.

And he meant it. Christ, how he meant it.

"Now, I believe you were undressing," she said, twirling her finger at him impatiently.

"Was I? I thought I was lost in prayer."

"I pray that you will stop stalling and allow me to look upon your blessed form, exactly as God made you."

She opened her hands out wide, inviting him to look.

She was so beautiful it was almost ghastly. Her skin shone in the firelight, luminous with a freshness that only her youth could explain. Her long neck tapered into strong, broad shoulders that curved into firm breasts, then nipped into her waist.

She was like a gift.

And she was offering herself to him.

He went to her and put his hand to the arched small of her back. He wanted to cradle her. Worship her.

"You are among the most gorgeous creatures I have ever had the pleasure of looking upon," he told her.

She laughed—clearly less moved by this experience than he was.

"You'd best not be numbering me among your prized horses," she said.

"Only a few," he said, trying to match her tone for lightness. "Here, let me help you undress."

He came behind her and lifted off her coat and shirt, folding them and setting them on the table. Beneath, she had laced her stays tight to disguise the curve of her breasts. He had to yank at them to get them loose.

"How animalistic," she said lightly, though she winced. She wore no shift beneath them, and the stiff fabric had dug into her skin, leaving angry indentations.

"Poor thing," he said, leaning down to gently kiss the mark it left around her ribs.

She clasped her hands over her breasts. They were just large enough to fit neatly into her own cupped palms. She opened her hands and offered them to him.

It was the greatest gift he'd ever known.

"Kiss me," she whispered. She looked up at him, more vulnerable than he'd ever seen her. Wanting to be wanted.

Wanting to be ravished.

This was it. The moment he must make his final choice.

He chose surrender.

He fell to his knees and put his mouth to her nipples.

"Yes," she whispered. "I've been imagining this for days, you stingy man. So withholding of your favors."

"I am at your service now, Cornelia," he said. "Whatever you wish."

"Take everything off," she commanded. "You know I like you nude."

He cocked his head at her. "Then you, my dear wife, will have to return the favor."

"Gladly."

She wasted no time shimmying off her breeches. She stood before him naked, her hands at her hips, proud and confident.

Her thighs were slender, her calves shapely, her buttocks high and taut. The cleft between her legs, with its swirl of curly hair, was slightly parted. She stood unabashed in her wanting.

He simply stared. He could have stared for an hour. A year.

She grinned at him. "Your turn," she said, gesturing at him to hurry.

He tore off his clothes. His breeches were the last thing to go. When he took them off, her eyes went wide with appreciation. Even though she'd seen him nude before, she looked upon him like he was a miracle.

"You're an absolutely beautiful man," she murmured.

He shook his head, bashful at her praise. But not bashful enough to diminish his arousal. Especially when she added: "Even your cock is pretty."

He could not believe she'd said the word *cock*. It made him shiver.

He went to her and placed a tender kiss on her cheek. "Cornelia, are you certain you want to do this?"

She nodded solemnly. "I'm certain if we don't do this I'll perish of frustration."

He stroked the back of her neck. "I promise to be gentle with you."

She dug her nails lightly into the flesh of his arse. "No need. Now, on the bed with you, please, sir."

He moved to the bed and sat down on the edge.

She put her hand flat to his chest, between his nipples. "Lie down," she said.

He obeyed her. He liked how she told him what to do. How she knew exactly what she wanted.

Propped up on his elbows, he could take in every exquisite inch of her as she crawled on top of him.

She mounted him, wedged her thighs tight around his and knelt with her pussy so close to his cock he could feel her heat.

He reached down to tease her with his fingers, but she batted away his hand and put his cock to her quim. "Are you ready?" she asked breathily.

Oh God, was he ready.

She was wet, and he was hard, and they had been circling this moment for days.

"Yes, Cornelia. Yes."

She put a hand to his shoulder and gently pushed him down, flat on his back. "I want to ride you."

"Please," he got out, flinching in aching pleasure as she put her hand around his cock and took him inside of her.

She was so hot and tight and slick and bloody *fast* and she had not been exaggerating her experience as a lover. He could tell by the way she took him, rhythmically and athletically, her back upright, her head thrown back in pleasure, her fingers on his nipples, squeezing them in a way that sent jolt after jolt of pleasure through him.

Somehow, she sensed how he liked to be made love to—to be ordered, taken, made a plaything of.

She leaned down and bit his neck. He whimpered in pleasure. "Oh God, Cornelia, more of that."

She bit him harder.

He reared up, pumping from beneath her. "Use me, darling," he urged, for he wanted to give her as much pleasure as she could possibly take.

She put a hand to her cunt and massaged herself, rocked her hips up and down over his cock, and he could feel her getting close to finishing. She tipped back her hips to take more of him and it took everything in his power to keep from coming before she did. As soon as he felt the spasms of her pleasure, he yanked away and out of her, spilling on the sheets.

She collapsed beside him, panting. He gathered her in his arms and did what he'd longed to do before they fucked—smothered her in tender kisses. Her nose. Her eyelids. The lobes of her small, perfect ears.

"How delightful you are," she said sleepily, nestling into him.

But *delight* was not the word for what he felt.

It did not feel like lust, or satiation.

It felt like passion, like magic.

It felt, in a word, like *love*.

Chapter Thirty Two

Hold me," Cornelia whispered again. She stood, untied her robe, shrugged it from her shoulders, and let it flutter to the floor. She liked the sensuous feeling as the silk fell down her body and pooled around her ankles.

"Of course," Rafe said in a low murmur as he stood up. He took her body in his arms. "I will always hold you if you wish, Cornelia."

And she knew that it was true. She knew that even if she disappeared for another twenty years, Rafe would always be there to open up his arms to her when she came back.

Yours.

Sometimes, the thought was terrifying. But in this moment, just for tonight, alone, in the safety of what he'd promised was still a game, she wanted it to be true.

She nestled closer to him.

"Mmm," he whispered. "That's better."

And it was. "Yes. Much better. But it would be perfect if you were not wearing clothes."

Without another word, he stripped them off.

She never got over her awe at him. He was huge and strong with shoulders so wide he practically made two of her in breadth. His skin was more weathered now, and there were grays threaded through the thick mane on his chest. She reached out and ran her fingers over the springy hairs. He closed his eyes and shivered.

She took his hand and led him to his bed. "You're cold. Let's get under the covers."

They nestled in his sheets and he squeezed her close to him, enfolding her body in his arms and thighs.

"I have a new rule," she whispered in his ear.

"Anything," he said, kissing her hair.

"We must be silent. I don't want being the subject of gossip in the morning."

"I promise I won't make a sound," he whispered. "Except in ecstasy. You do bring it out in me."

She put a hand over his mouth. "Don't make me smother you."

He laughed and nuzzled his nose against her hand. "You can do anything to me you want."

She knew that he was telling the truth. *Oh, Rafe*.

They nestled together with the blankets over their heads to muffle the sound of their voices. It was delicious to be hidden beneath the covers, in darkness save for the dim flickering light of the candles that floated through the fabric.

Every inch she drew nearer, she wanted another. She could never be close enough. She would never be satisfied. But she could savor this. She could make it last and last and last.

"You know," she said, "there's something I might do differently if we were to repeat that night at Gretna Green."

"And what is that?"

"Take my time," she said, dragging her fingers slowly—infinitely slowly—down his bare ribs.

"Show me," he whispered.

She laughed softly and placed a finger over his lips. "Shhh."

She replaced her fingers with her lips, kissing him as slowly as she could bear to. When he shuddered, she did not increase her pace.

She went slower.

And lower.

Every time his breath hitched, she traced an inch with her tongue, drawing near his abdomen so unhurriedly that his muscles trembled.

His hands rested loosely on her shoulders—not guiding them, merely caressing softly, submitting to her touch.

When she made it to his cock, she didn't touch it with her lips or fingers—only her breath, as she delicately nuzzled the skin of his thick thighs. He widened his legs, and she lightly traced his balls until he writhed.

He was hard and straining, and she wanted to say his name—to mount him and end this torture for them both—but she held strong until his hands gripped her shoulders. All at once he pulled her up and effortlessly flipped them over, so he was on top.

Were he allowed to speak, she knew what he would say. Something like "my turn." Because he began to do to her exactly what she'd done to him. He kissed his way across her nipples and down her belly and let her quake. He put his hand over her mouth when she moaned involuntarily.

"Hush, darling," he whispered. "You promised."

She loved it. She threw her head back, and his fingers entered her mouth. She sucked them as his head ventured over her hip bones. She felt his whiskers on her thighs and she widened her legs, wanting his mouth on her.

He spread her wider, as wide as her legs would go. The feeling of being stretched, of his knees pressing against the backs of her own, holding her apart, made her want to weep.

This was a side of Rafe she'd never known.

They'd only ever been together thunderously, quickly, in throes.

He'd never known her body this way. As though he was sketching her with his tongue, memorizing her, so that he could paint her later just from the memory of her skin.

It was terrifying.

And the terror heightened the pleasure so much she could barely keep from crying out his name.

She lifted her legs and raised them up around his shoulders, turning the sheets into a tent. He silently accepted her invitation, his mouth coming down on her quim as softly and gently as she could remember it ever being touched.

The prickly whiskers of his chin and cheeks were in contrast to the soft heat of his tongue.

She wanted to scream, but every time she so much as whimpered, he stopped and put a single finger to her lips.

Excruciating.

Lovely.

She took his head and nudged it downward, begging him not to hesitate any longer, to lave inside her.

He obliged, but when she began to thrash about beneath him, fighting for the crush of rapture so close to overtaking her, he stopped.

No one had ever made love to her like this—torturing her with this aching, slow assault of pleasure. Perhaps because her presence was commanding, perhaps because she liked to be on top, to say exactly what she wanted—no one had made her succumb entirely to their will the way that Rafe was doing.

Perhaps no one else had ever understood she wanted it. Not even her.

But he understood her body. He understood her mind.

It made her wonder if there was a world in which making Rafe her lover—in giving in to the affection that kept bubbling between them, the attraction that raged whenever they were near—would not be a threat, but a gift to be seized.

Seized the way she wanted to seize him.

Were she allowed to talk, she would have demanded that he fuck her.

Instead, he used his mouth to bring her to the precipice, over and over, each time to the point of shaking need, then stopped.

Finally it was too much. She unhooked her feet from around his shoulders, grabbed his face, and pulled him up to kiss his lips.

He kissed her back with the same fervor he had kissed her cunt, and she slid a hand between them, found his cock, and pulled it up between her legs.

He did not plunge inside, as she expected him to.

Instead, without moving his lips from hers, he reached down, replaced her hand with his own, and rubbed the head of himself against her clit.

This time, he did not pull back as she began to come.

He entered her with a shallow thrust that made her body erupt from inside. He froze, his arms and body shaking, letting the tremors take her over and over. She had to tear her mouth from his and jam her fingers between her teeth to keep herself from making any noise. The silence ripped her apart, and she kept coming as he held himself pulsing but still inside her.

And then, when she thought she might die from pleasure, he thrust deep and hard.

Just two strokes was all it took.

And as he came, she screamed his name.

And she didn't care who heard.

Because if this was possible—this ecstasy—what else was possible between them?

Chapter Thirty-Three

Rafe awoke to a warm presence nestled against his side.

Cornelia hadn't left his bed.

She hadn't left his *bed*.

She was entwined with him, her warm arm flung across his chest in sleep, sheets tangled between her beautiful, slim legs.

It was the posture of a lover.

They'd made *love*.

And it had been at her urging. Their entire coupling had been at her urging.

He wanted to weep with gratitude that she had broken down a wall between them. And that, for all their intimacy, she hadn't fled with the light of morning.

He looked at her, the slight smile on her sleeping face.

Maybe he did not need to try so hard to protect his heart.

Maybe she already had it. And maybe he could trust her not to break it.

After all, whatever they were calling this thing that was building between them—game, lark, affair— they'd been connected last night in a way that was more than bodily. And she hadn't shied from him or held him at remove. She'd met his passion with her own.

She'd said not to develop expectations. And he wouldn't. But he had promised only the night before to be honest about what he was feeling, even if it was not returned.

He wanted to be a man she could trust.

He had to tell her, to reckon with it. Otherwise, it was time to stop.

But how could he broach the subject?

Normally he would fill the room with roses or hire an orchestra and dance with her in the middle of the night. He would take her riding to some abandoned castle to make love. But she preferred directness. Any of the grand impulsive gestures he might have planned for other lovers would only raise her hackles and ruin this quiet, sincere sweetness.

So perhaps here, in the stillness of the morning, he should gather the nerve tell her how he felt without theater or pomp.

He would not ask anything of her. He would simply find the courage to lay bare his heart.

He was too far gone. He didn't care that she might break it.

"Oh, good morning," Cornelia said huskily.

He hadn't realized she'd awakened.

She moved her arm and slid a few inches away, so their skin did not touch. The cool air where her arm had been hit him like a lash.

She sat up and stretched.

"I must have fallen asleep. I'm sorry. You probably wanted your bed."

He tried not to be crushed that she hadn't meant to sleep here.

"Not without you in it," he said.

She smiled, bent down, and kissed him on the forehead.

The forehead?

"Last night was marvelous," she said, rising briskly and scanning the ground for her robe.

Marvelous? A far too casual description for the intensity they'd shared.

He'd thought it was more than that. Emotional. Cathartic.

Pure bliss.

If that was how she felt, he couldn't possibly tell her what it had meant to him. He'd be too emotional in his disappointment and push her into greater distance.

Unless . . .

He lifted up his arm and held the sheets out, patting the space next to him.

"Cornelia. Come back."

Her expression changed from a wry smile to a tentative frown, but she did as he asked.

He wrapped his arms around her and buried his face in her neck.

Perhaps if they made love again, it would put her in a better mood to have the conversation he so craved.

One more penalty wouldn't hurt.

"Rafe, you have the auction at Tattersall's to get to," she said with a laugh. "I have paintings to finish. There's no time to lie abed, as much as I would love to."

"It's not the bed I wish to lie on," he said. He leaned up and nibbled her ear. "It's you."

Her body tensed. "Quickly," she said, like a prayer.

He wanted to make love slowly and tenderly, as they had last night. But where Cornelia was concerned, any chance at lovemaking had always been impossible to resist.

And he was, inevitably, already hard.

She took his hand and put it on her quim. She was wet. Silky, hot, ready for a cock. But first—

He slid a finger on her swollen nub and made her shiver.

"I made you break your silence last night," he said, sliding her wetness over her flesh. "I owe you a penalty."

She gasped. "Yes, you do."

She was so gloriously erotic. So dear to him.

He massaged her with his thumb as he gently penetrated her with a finger, then two.

She came quickly, hard, with a sharp cry.

He kissed her on the lips. "I love that sound," he whispered.

"I need to be quieter. I think we may face some mocking from our friends. I'm sorry."

He remembered her roaring out his name last night as he had the single greatest orgasm of his life.

"Don't be sorry," he said raggedly. "It was worth it. Let them talk."

For if they talked, would it not confirm what he knew so deeply? That he and Cornelia had an intense connection? That if they were so right for each other in this way, it was worth pursuing?

Cornelia, he thought, *let me love you.*

But he didn't say it. Instead, he slid his fingers back down inside her. She throbbed beneath his touch. He softly put a finger to her clitoris and rubbed. She gripped his hand, gasped, reared up, and came again. This time it rolled over her more slowly. She moaned softly into her hand.

"Oh God, Rafe," she whispered. "Oh God. Another penalty."

She rolled over and climbed on top of him.

She took his cock, slid it inside her. He thrust upward into her tight heat and a growl burst from his throat.

She put a hand to his chest, gently, and shook her head. "Let me."

She locked her thighs outside his hips and slowly began to ride him. He leaned back, watched the bouncing of her teardrop breasts. He fought the urge to close his eyes so he could see the pleasure on her own face each time she bore down on him.

He could come—it would only take a moment to relax and let sensation claim him. But he wanted this to last forever. He wanted to enjoy her.

She put a hand to her clit and closed her eyes, rubbing herself as she gripped him with the muscles of her cunt. Her breath quickened, and she went still, then threw back her head with a gasp and came.

It took everything he had—every ounce of willpower—not to come with her. But he wanted to watch her succumb again and again. He wanted her to use his cock as long as she bloody wanted.

"God, Rafe," she said again. "I'm being selfish."

Be as selfish as you want. I love you.

"I could watch you come a thousand times and die a happy man," he said.

She leaned down and kissed him, sliding to take him deep. She moaned as he filled her up.

Slowly—as slowly as he could bear—he drew back. And then he thrust again, ripping another sound from the back of her throat. She went limp, and he took her hips and began to fuck her languorously and thoroughly.

He could not contain himself any longer. He fucked her like he wanted to, like he could make a single body of them. He gasped with pleasure with each thrust, loud, not caring who might hear—almost wanting others to hear, wanting them to know that Cornelia, at least for this one moment, this blissful morning, was all his.

She squeezed his forearms and came, shivering and limpid, and he thrust one last time. He lingered there for just a moment until he began to quake, then quickly extracted his cock and came onto the sheets with a racking sob.

She rolled off of him, panting.

Now was the time to talk to her. While she was limpid and receptive and . . .

"I love—" she panted, and he went absolutely still, straining for her to say the words he would die to hear "—fucking you," she finished.

And then, with a gorgeous, happy smile, she pecked his cheek, sprang out of bed, plucked her robe off the floor, and left the room before he could summon another word.

Chapter Thirty-Four

Cornelia closed the door of her room, locked it behind her, sank onto the bed, and rested her head between her knees. Her heart was surging—half joy, half terror. She gasped warm air, trying to slow her pulse.

Lucius, who was curled in a perfect little ball, grunted at the shifting mattress. She took a deep breath, picked him up, and exhaled into his fur.

"What have I done, cat?" she whispered.

He yowled in protest and jumped out of her arms.

She understood the impulse to run from a show of affection.

She, too, had fled.

Of course she had. What other response was there after a night that left her shaking?

Go back. Go back and let him hold you.

What? No, Cornelia Ludgate. Very, very bad idea.

If she returned, he would want to pick her up and carry her back to bed. He'd want to wrap his arms around her and whisper feelings in her ear.

He would want to hear that she returned them.

The idea of it made her sweat.

"Oh, Lucius," she said to the cat, who was now licking his paws, ignoring her. "What should I do?"

He didn't answer. That was the problem with asking a cat for counsel.

She would simply push it from her mind. There was a ball to plan after all.

She knew many of the most influential members of society had sent their intentions to attend, and the confirmed guests for the painting exhibition included luminaries of the art world, liberal politics, and Cornelia's patrons. The secrecy surrounding both events was adding to the clamor. There was little time left to get the details perfect.

She dressed quickly, went downstairs, and found the girls in the gallery putting the finishing touches on the staging of the paintings.

"Good morning," she said brightly, sailing into the room as if nothing in the world was wrong. "What is the latest on the preparations for the ball?"

The ladies stopped what they were doing. Were they observing her more closely than usual, or was she just imagining that?

"Chef is preparing the delicious foods Rafe has forbidden her from cooking for us," Canette said.

"That clever man Lord Eden arranged a fleet of hackneys to transport our less wealthy guests from London to the ball," Elinor said. "Guests will receive word of the transportation when they learn the ball's location."

"And we've ordered hundreds of flowers to decorate the ballroom and the portrait gallery," Anna said. "It will set off the art beautifully."

"And what *of* the art?" Sera asked Cornelia. "Do you have any portraits left to finish aside from your own?"

"Just Rafe's, this afternoon. But I have the sketches, so I won't need another sitting."

"Pity for you," Anna said sweetly.

The room went silent.

And then Thaïs, in imitation of a hoarse orgasmic moan, cried out, *"Rafe!"*

The ladies erupted into howls of laughter.

Seraphina yawned. "I must say, I'm exhausted from being kept up all night by *something* coming from the ducal suite."

"Not to mention awoken this morning," Anna said slyly.

"Quite bawdy this young one is, for a lady," Thaïs said, beaming at her.

"Oh, I don't wish to be a lady," Anna said, looking with admiration at Cornelia. "I wish to be a *siren*. Like Miss Ludgate was last night."

Cornelia threw up her hands and laughed, though she didn't find it very funny in her state of crisis. "Very well, you wenches. I slept with Rafe last night. And, all right, this morning."

"I knew it," Sera said. "I knew it when he walked into your studio in London."

"Knew what?" Cornelia asked.

"That he would be the best sex of your life."

He was. More than that, he was the most tender, intuitive—

"Oh please," Cornelia said, waving her hand dismissively, before her thoughts became so overwhelming her friends could see them on her face. "It's nothing. A little game we play."

Thaïs stopped fiddling with a painting and caught Cornelia's eye. "No," she said. "It isn't."

Oh God, they could see it anyway—

"Excuse you," Cornelia said, trying to keep her tone measured, "but unless you were hiding in the armoire last night—and I wouldn't put it past you—"

Thaïs held up her hand. "I know all about games. They're my bread. You and Rafe aren't playing one."

Thaïs held her gaze longer than was comfortable. She was not teasing, for once. She was declaring the truth as if it was as factual as her own name.

"And how would you know that?" Cornelia asked more sharply than she wished to. Nothing was as irritating as when Thaïs stopped joking for a minute and revealed she'd been staring into your soul the whole time.

Cornelia did not need anyone looking at her soul.

"From watching you," Thaïs said evenly. "And from watching *Rafe* watch you back. Even if we didn't see the truth, he does."

"Fuck," Cornelia whispered.

Anna, who was sitting in the corner of the room, let out a little yelp at the curse, then clapped a hand over her mouth.

"If you want to run about with this lot, get used to worse," Thaïs said gaily.

"Darling," Elinor said softly. "Are you all right? You look unsteady on your feet."

She wasn't. Her knees were shaking.

She sank down into a chair and hung her head, staring at her lap so she would not have to look at her friends. Which meant she was looking at Rafe's ring.

It glinted up at her as defiantly as Thaïs's voice telling her what she didn't want to hear.

It was not a prop. Even if it had been intended as one, the inscription was true.

Yours.

Rafe was giving himself to her.

But did she want that? Could she possibly accept the sentiment?

Did he need her to?

And did she return it?

Her friends gathered nearer, hovering over her like she needed their protection. She felt absurd for cowering like a little girl, but too frightened by her own thoughts to look up.

"It's true," she said to her hands. "I believe he cares for me."

"Oh, you care for him too, Duchess," Thaïs said softly. "Don't pretend you don't."

Is that what she was doing?

"Oh God, it's all too much," she cried, standing up abruptly. She had the sudden urge to pace.

"Caring for him is too much?" Elinor asked. "But why?"

Because she was Cornelia Ludgate. And she didn't do this.

Especially not with bloody Rafe.

"I don't permit attachments. I certainly do not reciprocate them. You know how I feel about anything that might limit the possibilities in my life."

"Is she talking about falling in love?" Anna asked Seraphina, sounding hopelessly confused.

"Yes, dear," Sera said. "Do pay attention."

Cornelia's stomach buckled. "I don't *love* Rafe, Sera," she snapped.

"How would you feel if he walked in right now and heard you say that?" Sera asked, in a gentler voice than Cornelia even knew that she was capable of.

I'd be devastated. He'd be devastated.

Sera nodded, not needing Cornelia to say the words to understand.

"I can't tell him how I feel," she whispered to her friend. "If I tell him, he'll want too much of me."

"What do you mean?" Anna asked.

Oh, curse the gods that put this child in the room to witness her unraveling. It was bad enough to come unglued, but to have to *explain* every nuance of one's disintegration was excruciating.

"He'll want me to be his," she said to the girl. "He won't understand that I must safeguard my own spirit above all else. For no one else on earth can do that for you, Anna."

Anna shook her head, looking desperate to understand. "But what does that *mean*?"

"Anna, I know love must seem romantic," she said, "but you must understand you lose something precious when you succumb to another person's love. To be treasured is also to be depended on. You sacrifice the ability to move freely in the world, because another person's heart hangs in the balance of your actions. You're no longer free."

Anna looked at her, considering this. "I think that's the loneliest thing I've ever heard."

Cornelia breathed in sharply. She felt like she'd been slapped.

Did it sting because Anna was so young? Or because she was right?

"Darling," Elinor said, "we all know your independence is precious to you. But what if Rafe didn't ask you to sacrifice it? What if he merely took you as you are, for whatever you're willing to give?"

"But how much is that?" she asked, not knowing the answer. "I've never committed myself to anyone before. I've never *wanted* to. I love Rafe—fine, I do— but I grew up without choices here in this bloody house. I had to light my life on fire to escape it. I've spent my whole life claiming more, damn the consequences. I can't simply turn my back on what I believe for the sake of—" she threw up the hand encumbered with Rafe's ring "—some man's notions of love."

That's it. That's bloody it. She finally knew why the ring made her stomach twist: because she did not want Rafe to be *hers* any more than she wanted to be *his*.

Love was not possession. And if he thought it was, she could not be with him in any incarnation.

"Love is not all or nothing," Sera said firmly. "You can be in love with Rafe and still claim whatever you want for yourself—you could simply imagine the arrangement you desire, and ask him if he might be happy with it, too."

She supposed she *was* being rigid in her ideas about what a relationship might look like. Rafe, after all, had never wished for marriage. He'd been in love with more than one person at once. He'd taken both her and Rory in his bed with nothing but enthusiasm.

Could that be the model for their lives? Not *yours*, but simply *them*, in all their possibilities?

"When I was considering whether to be with Adam, you encouraged me to be brave enough to accept what I deserved," Sera said. "Today, I might challenge you to do the same."

What if they were right? What if she didn't have to be certain?

What if she only needed to be brave?

The devil of it was, she wanted to.

She smiled. She couldn't help it.

"Perhaps you're right," she said. "Perhaps when the ball is over, once our work is done and I can think, I'll tell him how I feel."

Chapter Thirty-Five

The air at Hyde Park Corner smelled like sunshine and horseflesh, a perfume that was second in Rafe's heart only to Cornelia's scent of sage. Rafe and Rory passed the familiar sale ring at Tattersall's, where horses had not yet begun parading. It was early in the afternoon, the auction not due to start for several hours.

They went directly to the stables where their most promising yearling, Zeus, was munching on hay, oblivious to the buyers and bloodstock agents milling about the center aisle, inspecting horses. Zeus's brown coat was brushed to a gleam that emphasized the elegance of his build. He was a paragon of Thoroughbred stock—sired by the Rosemere Stable's most renowned stallion, King's Hand. The perfect bait for a buyer in the market for an animal with a shape and bloodlines meant for racing. A buyer, according to Rafe's sources, like Lord Bell.

Bell was known to be a perspicacious investor with an increasingly strong stable shaped by a buying agent with a discriminating knowledge of pedigree. Notably to Rafe, Bell was also known to like to inspect horses himself before bidding.

This was Rafe's last opportunity to meet Bell and see what could be gleaned from him before Rafe revealed his true political leanings at the ball. He didn't

know precisely what he might learn, only that now
was his last opportunity to probe.

He was grateful for his decades of experience putting aside his true feelings to play a part, because
otherwise it would be difficult to focus on anything
except Cornelia.

He had spent the carriage ride in silence, obsessing
over the significance of her sudden departure from his
rooms. He did not want to make the assumption that
their night had meant nothing to her. But it would be
equally foolish to assume that her feelings about him
went beyond the banal warmth of a like-minded lover.

He should have followed her into her rooms and declared himself, for it would have saved him from this
insufferable brooding. Brooding that was destined to
continue an oppressively long time, for the auction
would go late into the evening, forcing them to spend
the night in London.

Which meant he must get through today, and then
tomorrow's ball, before he bared his soul.

Luckily, their stall was too busy to let his mind wan-
der too far afield.

A stream of men came to look at Zeus, their interest
no doubt driven partly by curiosity about Rafe. He was
familiar in this milieu, having brought horses here to
sell for years. But he'd never attended as the Duke of
Rosemere. And dukes were not known to stand before
their yearlings inside the stables, answering questions
about pedigree and speed.

"That's him," Rory said in a low voice, nodding at
a portly man with a balding pate and a gold-tipped
walking staff examining a Thoroughbred near the
stable entrance. "Bell."

The rotund old man was accompanied by his agent.

They walked slowly from stall to stall, the agent making notes on his auction sheet as Bell peered at animals and asked questions of the men attending them. They were stopping exclusively at the stalls of yearlings—a good sign that Rafe's intelligence had been right.

Rafe made a point of engaging in conversation with a trader, so as to be occupied when Bell reached them. It would not help his cause to appear to be lying in wait. When Bell finally approached, Rory cleared his throat.

"Your Grace," he said. "We are fortunate to be visited by the Viscount Bell." Rafe turned around, a gracious smile already plastered on his face.

"How do you do, Lord Bell?" he asked.

Bell gave a little bow—a gesture that must have been painful, given Rafe had so recently been a lowly horseman, and was now higher in rank than Bell himself in the hierarchy of the aristocracy.

"It's a pleasure to finally meet you," Bell said tersely. "You know my man, Somers?"

"I'm afraid not," Rafe said. "But your reputation precedes you, Mr. Somers."

Somers, a man of about thirty, had been making a name in the world of racing on behalf of Bell's stables. He grinned at Rafe, dropping his head into a bow. "It's an honor to meet a breeder of your talents, Your Grace. And look at this fine animal."

Zeus had turned his head around to examine his latest visitors. His velvety brown eyes took in Bell and Somers. He snorted, as if in distaste, and returned to munching hay.

Good taste, Zeus.

"We'd like to have a closer look, if you don't mind," Somers said.

"Not at all," Rafe said, unlatching the stall so that the men had a full view of the horse. They conferred in low voices, Somers scribbling notes.

"He's a handsome one," Bell finally said.

"He is," Rafe said cheerfully. "First yearling by King's Hand in three years, you know." He lowered his voice conspiratorially. "We're expecting a good price."

Bell winced at the blatant discussion of money, but Somers nodded. "We were pleasantly surprised to see him added late to the auction."

Rafe laughed ruefully, seeing an opening to direct the conversation to a potentially fruitful topic. "Yes. I had intended to give him to my wife as a wedding gift. But it turns out she's afraid of horses. Jewels will have to do."

Bell leaned against the stall door, suddenly more interested. "I had heard tell of your marriage. All of town is speculating as to who the lady is. Not least me."

Rafe lifted up a brow in good-natured mystery. "I believe you are acquainted with her. A beauty. You'll no doubt wish me much felicity when I introduce her tomorrow." He paused. "That is, if you are able to join us at the masquerade."

Bell nodded. "I wouldn't miss it. I'm as curious to meet your duchess as the next man. And I certainly wish you more success in matrimony than I have enjoyed."

Here it was. The opening he'd hoped for.

He frowned at Bell sympathetically. "I've heard of your troubles. You'll be at trial soon, no? I wish you all the best."

Bell glowered. "I can't wait to be rid of the vile

woman. Nothing would make me happier than dispensing with her altogether."

The sentiment was so distasteful that it took everything Rafe had to pretend to agree with it.

He narrowed his eyes and nodded. "Indeed. There must be consequences for such behavior as your wife has shown. And that bastard Jack Willow lacks not only honor, but is a scourge politically. He's a danger to us all."

"Indeed," Bell said. "An embarrassment to me, my children, and the entire nation, what he and that harridan Elinor have done. Luckily I'm not the only one who wishes him to meet the end he deserves. I'm calling a legion of witnesses who will knock him on his arse. I'm going to ruin the bastard. He'll never publish again."

Rafe nodded with relish. "A boon to you and to the Crown. The man has gone too far. Arrest would be too good a punishment. You're a kind of hero."

Bell puffed up. "Giving the bastard what he merits."

Rafe nodded, then paused, as if a thought was just occurring to him. "I'm impressed at your skill in building a case. From what I've heard it's watertight. I'd have expected some hesitancy among witnesses to testify—risk of notoriety in the papers and all that. You must be persuasive."

He hoped he wasn't being too direct. The aristocracy was known to speak in code. But Bell only smiled again.

"You'd be surprised by what incentives can be offered in exchange for *honesty*," he said, pronouncing the final word like it was a mockery.

Was he implying *bribery*?

This was a better opportunity than Rafe could have

imagined. He gave Bell his most wicked grin and lowered his voice. "You know, I knew both Lady Elinor and Willow as a young man—growing up as I did on the grounds of Gardencourt. I wonder if I could be of use to you."

Bell leaned in. "Of use?"

"I always thought there was something strange about the closeness between them. If you think another witness would be helpful, I could testify as to what I saw."

Bell mused on this. "Your good word would mean much at trial. No one would contest the opinion of a duke. But I'm afraid 'strange behavior' won't win a case." He looked meaningfully at Rafe. "It's a shame you did not see something more damning."

Rafe lowered his voice to a whisper. "Well, I could perhaps speak with a, let's say, *higher degree of certainty* as to the obvious closeness of the relationship."

Bell raised a brow. There was no mistaking that by "closeness" Rafe meant "sexual nature."

"That's very generous," Bell said. "I'm surprised you would want to be involved."

Rafe laughed sharply. "Your wife, Lord Bell, is a stain on the Rosemere line. I'd like to expunge it." He screwed up his face in distaste, as if the mere thought of Elinor made him ill.

Bell's lips curved into a greedy smile. "Quite, my good man. Quite."

Rafe gestured for Bell to move deeper into the stall, away from any stray listeners. "There is one thing I might ask for as a favor in return."

Bell nodded. "'Tis always an honor to be of service to a duke. How can I help?"

"I mentioned we are expecting a good price for Zeus. Record-breaking bids."

Bell's eyes locked on his in understanding. He nodded. "Your Zeus is a fine, fine piece of horseflesh. I have no doubt you'll be richly rewarded at auction."

Rafe offered his hand, and Bell took it in a hearty shake. The two men grinned at each other with the satisfaction of an even bargain.

"Have your barrister get in touch with my man Thompson here," Rafe said. "It was a pleasure to finally meet you, Lord Bell."

Bell gave him another bow, and this one seemed sincere. "An unexpected pleasure, Your Grace. I look forward to your ball."

Chapter Thirty-Six

The last day and night had been an age. Cornelia felt ninety-six years old.

She'd never been so frantic in all her life as she had been putting the final touches on her exhibition. Neither she nor anyone else had had time to do much beyond run about the house hanging paintings, placing flowers, instructing servants and finishing off their own costumes.

But all she'd thought about was Rafe.

The memory of fleeing from his bed the previous morning was like a small dagger in her pocket that lightly stabbed her in the leg every time she took a step.

She felt terrible for hurting him.

She was terrified that she felt terrible.

Her emotions were like a tempest roiling up the ocean, and she got seasick easily. She wanted to smile. She wanted to retch.

She wanted, most of all, to see him.

And finally, it was time. She waited for him in an upstairs parlor, looking out the window at the line of carriages depositing costume-clad guests at the doors of the manor. She and Rafe had agreed to enter the ballroom together, so they could easily find each other when it was time to address the crowd.

She checked her costume in the mirror. Beneath her flowing silver wig, sparkling purple mask, and the iridescent gold scales of her mermaid-inspired gown, she was barely recognizable. She wondered what Rafe would think of her in this tight, scandalous ensemble.

She hoped he'd want her. More than he already did.

She wanted him to look at her with passion, like he'd done before she fled. She wanted to apologize for running, draw him close and tell him everything. She wanted to ask him if they could find a way to be something permanent to each other.

And she would.

She was resolved. She would do it tonight, immediately after the ball. She couldn't wait until tomorrow. She'd die of nerves.

There was a knock at the door. That would be Rafe.

She needed to collect herself or she would be a glob of quivering jelly at the ball, when she most needed to be confident and brave.

She inhaled, let out a long breath, and smiled. A breath and a smile were good for the nerves.

"Come in," she called brightly.

Rafe entered the room alone, wearing a jester's costume that made him look like the tallest fool Shakespeare could imagine.

Even beneath his belled hat, he was an intimidatingly handsome man.

"Rafe," she said in a warm tone that she hoped did not betray her nerves. "Welcome home. How was your trip?"

She had not yet heard what had transpired in London, and whether he had managed to make contact with Bell. She hoped he had, as it was his last chance before revealing his true identity.

He grinned at her. "Quite worthwhile. I am now the best of friends with Lord Bell." He paused, looking distinctly proud of himself. "He bought my horse for a positively lavish price. And in exchange, I have agreed to lie about Jack's relationship with Elinor at trial. Or so he *thinks*."

"Well, holy God, you are a spy," she said. She was so proud she could smother him in kisses.

Which, of course, you will not.

"I did tell you I had something of a skill for it," Rafe said.

"How did you arrange this dastardly scheme?" she asked, lest she lose her resolve to wait and draw Rafe into a conversation on their future fifteen minutes before a ball.

"Bell implied very strongly that some of his witnesses were bribed," Rafe said. "I mentioned I knew Elinor from my youth and offered to exaggerate my knowledge of her history with Jack in exchange for an excellent price. And I got one. Bell offered six hundred guineas over the highest bid."

"Six hundred guineas," she repeated, shocked. Bell was notoriously tightfisted. To pay such a premium would raise eyebrows. He must be willing to stop at nothing to beat Jack in court.

"The entire auction house was dumbfounded. Bell's usually a savvy bidder," Rafe said.

"That maggot is worse than I imagined," she murmured. "But how can you prove the scheme? A high bid is not direct evidence of bribery."

"Yes, but there's a good chance it will sway the judge. Jack will call me as a witness and I will testify as to what Bell and I agreed at Tattersall's," Rafe said. "And of course there's the fact that I'm a duke. I will simply have to act imperious, bored, and certain, and

I suspect the judge will believe me . . . dukes, after all, can get away with anything they want."

"Even marrying me," she said, smiling.

"Even marrying you."

Her fingers itched to take his hand—a sure sign that she needed to distract herself.

"It's nearly eight o'clock," she said, glancing at the clock. "Singh is preparing to open the doors any minute. Are you ready for your moment, my lord?"

"I'm looking forward to the revelation of your brilliant work," he told her.

"And I yours," she said.

"Oh, I have little to do with it. You're the architect of this scheme, and I admire you for it."

"You made this possible, Rafe," she said. "And it will be remembered for a lifetime. Not least by me."

A lifetime. Exactly what she wanted. Except not memories. She wanted *him*. She wanted to go to sleep next to him and wake up beside him. She wanted to share meals with him, to laugh with him, to make him pose for her paintings, to assist him in his plots.

She wanted to find a way for them to make a life together, one that would honor who both of them were. She only needed him to agree to freedoms that she could accept.

Oh God, how she wished she could see inside his heart.

She came up, took his hand, and kissed it—damn her own rules. A bit of sweetness would carry her through the ball.

"Did I mention how handsome you look?" she asked.

He smiled, looking touched. "Have I mentioned you're a stunning beauty?"

"Several times, I think. But not yet tonight."

She gave his hand a final squeeze.

"Let's go enjoy our grand moment," she said, slipping her mask down over her face.

He nodded and linked his arm with hers. It was time to formally commence the ball.

Downstairs, the ballroom and portrait gallery had been transformed into a moody wonderland of candles and white draping. Each wall was lined with curtains hiding paintings, which were only to be revealed after Rafe had given his performance.

They weaved through the crowd inconspicuously and waited beside the dais that had been erected at the center of the room.

Suddenly, the doors burst open, and the small orchestra at the back of the room began to play a slow, mysterious song that complemented the otherworldly aesthetic of the room.

Guests filed in, talking and laughing among themselves, wearing elaborate masks and costumes that disguised them as birds and gods and bandits. A few yards away she saw the other sirens, dressed as mermaids in sparkling costumes of different hues, assume their positions at the draw cords of the curtains, awaiting their cues to reveal the portraits to the guests.

When the lively swirl had filled the room, Rafe gave her a final smile, then ascended to the top of the dais. With a sharp flourish of arpeggios, the orchestra finished its song. He removed his mask and raised a glass of champagne. The crowd burst into applause.

He bowed, looking amused and gracious—every inch the dashing duke.

"Ladies and gentlemen, thank you for joining us tonight here at Gardencourt. For those of us who haven't had the pleasure of meeting, I am the Duke of Rose-mere. And as some of you might have gathered, I have taken it upon myself to celebrate my new position with an evening's entertainment."

There was a ripple in the crowd—no doubt surprise from Cornelia's guests, who may not have known that Gardencourt was the seat of a duke.

"As some of you have gathered, tonight we shall enjoy the added entertainment of an exhibition of paintings," he went on.

Half the crowd murmured, for a painting exhibition was an unusual addition to a masquerade. He cleared his throat to quiet them.

He was a natural at commanding the room, and she loved watching him conduct the crowd's attention like an orchestra. She was so proud of him she couldn't stop smiling.

"It is the tradition that every duke of Rosemere is honored at the beginning of his tenure with a portrait of himself. And I, immodestly perhaps, am no different. I have indulged in commissioning a likeness from one of the most illustrious artists in the nation, and a personal favorite, I'd suspect, of many of you gathered here."

He winked at the crowd, half of whom exchanged knowing looks.

"This artist, I am pleased to say, has also done me the honor of painting a portrait of my wife. I know you are eager to enjoy this evening's celebration, so I will present them to you without further ado."

Cornelia clasped her hands together, twisted the ring around her finger, and prepared to meet the world as the Duchess of Rosemere.

Chapter Thirty-Seven

Rafe felt like he was about to take off a set of dirty clothes he'd been wearing for decades and step into a searingly hot bath.

Tonight would be the crescendo of twenty years of covert work, of hiding his true political leanings away at the cost of his most meaningful relationships. In a few moments he would finally end the charade.

Bliss.

Unable to hide his glee, he pulled open the drapes behind him to reveal the first of the two portraits on the dais—that of himself.

The crowd gasped.

Rafe, who had not yet seen the painting, gasped, too.

Cornelia had captured him from the waist up on a horse wearing a muslin shirt, his hair askew, his skin shining with sweat. Behind him was a field of wheat, signifying he was a workingman.

The portrait looked like him, of course. Strapping shoulders, a strong jaw, skin tanned a bit from riding in the sun. But the most striking aspect was not his image, nor the symbolism of the background, but the radiant way Cornelia had portrayed him. He was surrounded by golden light, looking directly at the artist with a lopsided smile. His eyes held the warmth of shared affection, an implication that his smile was returned.

Staring at it, he could only think of her proviso that a portrait was a conversation between the artist and the sitter. That it must capture not just the image of the subject, but the artist's own feelings.

And the way that she had captured him was suffused with emotion.

It was a portrait of a man in love. A man who *was* loved. And one bathed in the happiness that his feelings were returned.

He looked down at Cornelia in her siren regalia standing near the dais, awaiting her cue to join him. She was beaming at him. Nothing about her was reserved or distant. Her eyes were like an embrace.

If painting was the way she spoke her feelings to the world—this was her way of telling him she loved him, too.

She *must*, to paint him in such a way.

He wanted to go down, take her in his arms, and hold her close to him. To tell her he was moved. That he understood her language and returned the sentiment. To tell her that if he had the skill of painting, he would capture her with the same care and adoration.

But he had more that he must say to the crowd before he told her he loved her, too.

"Some of you may be wondering about my attire in the painting," he said. "The work is entitled *King Crow*."

The crowd went very still. He watched faces screwing up in consternation as the guests wondered why a painting of a duke would be named after a radical.

"Isn't that the antimonarchist from Jack Willow's paper?" he heard a woman near the front whisper to her husband.

"What the devil?" a man's aristocratic voice said, louder, from the back.

Cornelia glanced up at Rafe with amusement in her eyes. He cracked a smile at her before returning his attention to the crowd.

"The portrait is called *King Crow* for that is the moniker under which I write for the *Equalist Society* circular," Rafe went on. "I am, and have always been, the author of the column."

Hoots and curses and scattered applause mingled with outraged whispers. He could sense a stirring in the crowd, an energy building as they realized something extraordinary was afoot.

"Therefore, I can't in good conscience abide the divisions in wealth and power created by the aristocracy I am now a part of. It is my intention," he said over the din, "to make this estate more democratic and fair and to fight for those same principles in Parliament."

In the back of the crowd he noticed Lord Bell pointing at him and whispering furiously to a group of noblemen. He almost laughed.

"I invite you to enjoy tonight," he said, "for it will be the last grand ball held at Gardencourt during my time as duke." He caught Cornelia's eye. "But it is my hope that it will not be the last exhibition of such fine paintings, for my portrait was painted by my wife. And I'd like for you to meet her."

The crowd went still again, all eyes trained on the dais.

Rafe threw back the curtain to reveal the second portrait.

"Holy ghost," someone near the front whispered.

"My God, it's Ludgate," someone else crowed.

And indeed, there was Cornelia, dressed in a saffron yellow gown and bedecked in diamonds, looking out imperiously from the canvas.

She stood before an easel bearing her own likeness

and held a paintbrush in one hand. And sparkling prominently on her finger was his ring.

Yours.

Another symbol that she returned his feelings.

It sent chills straight down his spine.

He met her eye. She was smiling as hard and wide as he had ever seen her. And he knew. He simply *knew*.

He took her hand and helped her onto the platform, as they'd planned.

"Ladies and gentlemen, may I present my wife of twenty years, the Duchess of Rosemere. Or as you may know her, Cornelia Ludgate."

The crowd erupted into shouts and gasps. Beside him, Cornelia laughed softly, enjoying the reaction.

"My duchess's work here this evening is called *The Jezebels*, and it is all for sale to the highest bidder. I hope you will bid handsomely and join me in applauding her gifts." He squeezed her hand and she smiled up at him, performing the role of his adoring wife so pitch-perfectly he could not doubt she meant it.

It made him feel like he could fly.

"And none shall celebrate my wife more fervently than me," he said. "For I am not merely a patron of her art. I love her fierce spirit. Her incredible compassion. Her insights into the world. Her bravery in the face of injustice. Her remarkable gift for revealing it."

He dropped Cornelia's hand and knelt before her, embracing her at the waist as he looked up into her eyes.

"And I am madly, totally in love with her."

He took her hand and kissed the ring he'd given her.

"It's true," he whispered. "I'm yours."

She looked down at him, silent and utterly still. Moved, he hoped, by his boldness in returning the message in her paintings with a confession of his own feelings.

The shock left her face and was replaced by a vacant smile as she gently, subtly extricated her hand from his grip.

"How *dare* you?" she asked through her teeth in a low, calm voice that chilled him.

The same shattering words she'd uttered so many years before.

Chapter Thirty-Eight

Before

Rafe lay in bed beside Cornelia, still slick with sweat from their coupling.

"I wish we could do that every day," she said.

"Every hour," he answered, imagining it and smiling.

"It would kill you," she pointed out.

"And I would die a blessed man."

"I'd miss you terribly," she said.

That chastened him. For soon that would be his fate. Missing her. Forever.

She did not seem to share his perturbation. She drew nearer to him, grinning, never mind their damp bodies. "Rafe, I feel so free. I've been so anxious about what might happen to me for weeks, and now the fear is gone."

He put his thoughts aside and kissed her brow. "I'm so glad, Cornelia."

She laughed softly to herself. "I have this sense of opportunity. Like I can do anything I imagine and achieve anything I wish."

He'd never had any doubt she could. But he felt proud that he'd had a part in making her feel this way herself.

"There is no doubt in my mind that you are correct," he said. "I've never met a person whose capacity for greatness I've believed in more than yours."

She reached out and took his face in her hands.

"I will always have such gratitude for you—*love* for you—for doing this for me."

His heart crunched together like a fist. *Love.* Words he had not realized he longed to hear. He wanted to return them but before he could her face fell.

"Oh, Rafe," she said. "I'm sad that we must part. I've so enjoyed our time together." She paused. "Do you understand what I mean?"

Her eyes were luminous with tears.

Tears. He had to stop them.

"Oh, Cornelia, I do," he said, pulling her as tightly against him as he could. He kissed the teardrops from her lashes. "I do."

"Don't worry," she said. "They're happy tears. I'm just so grateful."

They held each other in silence until she yawned and spread out, limp.

"I'm exhausted," she said. "Let's do this again in the morning. To say farewell. So I am not so sad to part from you."

We don't have to part in the morning.

The thought rushed into his head—and it was true.

They were married. She was safe. She did not need to flee.

She was his wife, and the tenderness he felt for her was as genuine as any feeling a groom might feel for his bride, regardless of their arrangement.

It was astonishing. A few days riding alongside a fugitive aristocratic maiden, and he had fallen in love with her.

And he didn't want to say goodbye.

He got up from bed, quickly dressed, and went downstairs to the innkeeper to ask for a piece of paper and a quill. After a brief negotiation, he paid the man and moved to a table in the corner where he could write.

He thought long and hard about what he wished to say. When he was done, he folded the letter, tucked it in his pocket, returned the quill to the innkeeper, and went upstairs.

Cornelia was still dozing peacefully, but it was not that late. Not too late to wake her for something so important.

"Cornelia," he said softly, gently tapping her shoulder. "Wake up, sweet girl."

Her eyes fluttered open and she smiled at him. He leaned down and kissed her. She kissed him back, pliant and sleepy.

"Oh, love," he said into her hair, "I don't want to part ways with you."

She pulled him down beside her. "Nor do I. But we have all night to say goodbye."

Goodbye. The word echoed through him like a cold wind in a long stone hallway.

She began to pull up his shirt. She wanted to make love. He grasped her hand to stop her. He needed to say this first.

"I feel as though there is something between us I've never felt before. Do you not feel it? This strange connection?"

She nodded, her expression soft, her eyes shining. "I feel everything. So much."

He gathered his nerve. He had to say this in a way that could not be misunderstood. "I think I'm falling in love with you," he whispered.

She stroked his face and kissed him. "I am, too. You know I am."

He wanted to weep with relief.

He lifted her up, put her on top of him, and smothered her with kisses.

His Cornelia. *His.* No goodbyes.

She laughed at his exuberance. He kissed her eyelids, her nose, her chin. He wanted to fuse himself to her.

"It's so sad I'm off to Florence," she murmured, running her fingers through his hair. "We could have had quite the love affair."

He paused mid kiss.

Could have? No, no, he needed to explain. She probably did not want to make presumptions on him. Sweet girl.

"Darling," he said urgently. "I need to read you something."

She stretched lazily, like a contented cat. "Is it a love sonnet to my radiant beauty?"

"Better, I think," he said.

He took the letter from his pocket and read aloud.

> *Your Grace,*
>
> *I write to you with news of my marriage to your ward, Cornelia. We have eloped to Gretna Green, and are pledged to each other. Cornelia has no plans to return to your home. We love each other and will not be parted.*
>
> *Yours sincerely,*
> *Rafe Goodwood*

She was very still. And then, suddenly, she sat straight up, pulling her entire body away from him. She looked overcome with emotion. It moved him that this self-possessed young woman was speechless over what he was offering her.

He put his hand to her back and stroked her. "Come here, my love," he murmured.

But she stood up, moving out of his reach, her back to him. She was as rigid as he had ever seen her.

"You have the wrong idea," she said. Her voice was low, quiet, icy cold. "You won't be writing to my uncle."

What?

He jumped out of bed and took her shoulder, spinning her to face him. She shrugged off his hand. Her face was blank.

His stomach went leaden.

Had he misunderstood her?

But no, he couldn't have. She'd just said she *loved* him.

He gave her his most reassuring smile. "Cornelia, if we simply tell him we are wed, you won't have to run. And there's no need for us to part. We can be together."

"But I'm off to Florence," she said tightly, "and you'll be returning to Gardencourt. We can't very well be together by correspondence."

She wasn't understanding. He had to be clearer.

"What if you didn't go to Florence?" he asked, taking her hand.

She made an expression that frightened him.

"Pardon?" she asked, in a deadly tone.

He wished he had not begun with that, for it was clearly alarming to her, so he stuttered out a different explanation, striving to say what he felt, but having trouble finding the precise words.

"What if you married me in earnest?"

Her lips screwed into a hard line, but he kept going.

"We could be open about it, so that your uncle can't pursue you in secret, and you could study painting in London rather than Italy—"

She looked at him like they'd never met.

"How dare you? How dare you ask me such a thing? How dare you presume to *write to my uncle*?"

No, no, no. This was going horribly bloody wrong.

He fell to his knees. "Please listen. I'm in love with you, Cornelia."

She stared down at him with blazing eyes.

"This very afternoon you swore to me that I could trust you," she said. "And now you ask me this? To abandon all my plans for you? To settle the matter man-to-man with my uncle, like you are exchanging goods?"

Oh God. Is that how it looked to her? He'd been trying to be sweet, to make a romantic gesture that would touch her. How had he botched it so acutely?

"I'm sorry. I thought— It was stupid, but darling, I'll be yours any way you want."

She shook her head fiercely. "I have enough men trying to control me and limit what I do." A tear streamed down her face. "You *promised* me you weren't going to be one of them."

His throat burned, sour with shame.

He could not think of a single thing to say in his defense.

"Rafe, if I had known that you were considering such a thing, I *never* would have married you." She paused, as though the fact of their matrimony was really, truly sinking in. "I *married* you. Don't you understand what that means to me? The risk I've taken?"

She was right. It had been cruel to ask her to abandon her dream.

He'd promised to protect her, and it turned out he was one of the things she needed protection from.

"I'm so sorry," he murmured. "It was a foolish thing to ask."

His passion was always his liability. It blinded him. Made him too impulsive. And now, he knew, there was no way to fix it.

There was no way to explain away what he'd done. It was too fundamental a misunderstanding of who she was and what she wanted.

In a few scrawled sentences, he'd lost her.

She threw on her shirt and smoothed it down tightly, as if protecting herself.

"How dare you?" she asked again.

He had no answer.

"You'll be sleeping on the floor," she said.

He did so.

He was awake for hours, trying to figure out a way to fix it. He racked his brain until, eventually, exhaustion claimed him.

And in the morning, he awoke to an empty room.

She was gone.

And she had not left a note.

Chapter Thirty-Nine

Cornelia was so embarrassed she couldn't feel her toes.

But worse than that. She was so, so very disappointed.

She'd spun a tale where she might forget their past and forge a future.

But Rafe hadn't changed.

He stared at her, wide-eyed, the words she'd hissed echoing between them.

How dare you?

She meant them. Whatever she might have felt for him these last two days—these last ten minutes—she meant them.

For to say what he had said to her in *public*, when she'd explained her horror at displays of affection, was inexcusable. Once again, he shocked her by failing to understand her at all just when she felt closest to him.

He might love her. But he didn't respect her enough to *listen* to her.

And if he could not respect this simple wish, how could he possibly respect the larger ones? Her need to remain fiercely herself. To stay free.

She'd let herself get carried away. She'd forgotten the past.

She'd forgotten that she couldn't *trust* him.

And it broke her bloody heart. She wanted to fall

to pieces at this thing she'd not yet gained crumbling before she had a chance to ask for it.

She felt her breath coming fast and urgent. But she could not react. Not yet. Not in front of all these people. She'd worked too hard. First, she must do justice to her paintings.

The only way to avoid distracting from her work was to pretend that she accepted Rafe's declaration of love.

She stood on her tiptoes and kissed his cheek.

"Thank you, my dear," she said loud enough for everyone in the room to hear her. She turned her back to him and gestured out at the walls lined with white curtains.

"And to you, our guests, I am honored to present to you my latest collection, *The Jezebels*." At that, she signaled to the ladies to pull back the drapes.

At intervals set up around the dance floor, huge canvases were revealed—most of them portraits of nude women with their heads and shoulders covered in sheer veils, sitting in sacred poses.

Several canvases depicted aristocratic women in scandalous attire—Lady Elinor among them—painted in the age-old fashion of whores. They were scattered among the staid portraits of past duchesses and innocent young aristocratic girls. Their humanity and liveliness were in stark contrast to the formality of the traditional works.

The murmuring in the crowd erupted into a deafening roar. Guests began throwing off their masks—revealing that the putative crowd of respectable aristocrats was mixed with artists, louche men of leisure, courtesans, and radical politicians. At every corner of the room, people looked at each other in a combination of amusement (the radicals) and horror (the rich).

Already, mamas were ushering their young daughters out of the room, holding hands over their eyes to spare their innocent young gazes from the sight of Cornelia's work.

"While no artist can hope to control the interpretation of her art, I would like to say a few words about the inspiration for these portraits," Cornelia said. "Too often, women are seen as one side of an impenetrable divide. They must be pure—mothers, ladies, virgins—or they are some shade of whore. But in truth, every woman, every girl, possesses the full range of humanity, whether society believes she deserves respect or not. There is no supposedly virtuous lady who does not contain a trace of the sensuous harlot. And there is no harlot who is estranged from her morality, nor one who does not deserve respect. We are all one and the same—just women, alive and valuable whatever our lot in life, and worthy of the same rights as men."

She paused and drew a long breath as the crowd became more unsteady—half of it outraged by her words.

"So too must I point out that so often women—especially the enslaved, servants, immigrants, the poor—do not have the luxury of being the subjects of paintings. We see their lives only in the background of so-called serious art. And when we do see them, they are caricatured—a whore lying prostrate for an artist with a coy expression, or a Black servant girl portrayed as her mistress's pet, as though she were a parrot rather than a child."

"Hear! Hear!" someone yelled.

"Get the radical bitch off the dais," someone else cried.

"Quiet," Rafe shouted. "My wife is speaking."

He looked at her pleadingly, conscious she was furious at him.

She was not fazed. She could not afford to be distracted by emotion.

And if there was one thing she'd learned in this house, it was to conceal her feelings, no matter how tumultuous. Stoicism was her birthright.

"All of my paintings sold at auction this evening will benefit the Institute for the Equality of Women," she continued. "Should you wish to look upon His Grace's permanent collection of forebears, I shall direct you to the open doors leading to the servants' corridors, where they have been rehung for the occasion." She paused. "And, of course, the toilets."

Cackles of laughter combined with loud rumbles of outrage.

The crowd seemed to pulse, vibrating with something unstable, a combustive mix of anger and excitement. Someone yelled a profanity, and then a glass Venetian mask went hurling through the air toward Cornelia and shattered on the dais.

She stepped over it and gestured to her friends, who had gathered beside her unmasked.

"You may discreetly place your bids with Miss Arden or Miss Magdalene. We will be so forward as to ask you to be generous in supporting the cause of justice for women," Cornelia said. "The winners of the auction will be announced at the evening's end."

"I expect you all to bid generously and often," Rafe said, wrapping his arm around her. "My wife's genius is worthy of a fortune."

The audience looked profoundly perplexed by his affection for her. As if even the liberals in the room were unable to fathom a person like him being married to a person like her.

It made her angry, that even her supposed friends could not see her as a duchess. Angry and defiant.

Perhaps she would keep the damned title after all.

She turned to Rafe, took his face firmly in her hands, and kissed him long and hard. His eyes met hers, searching, as if unsure whether this was a sign of forgiveness.

It wasn't.

This kiss was not for him. It was for *them*. The crowd who felt a woman of her sexuality, her radicalism, her skin color, her heritage could not—did not deserve to—be his wife.

She took Rafe's hand and lifted it up to the crowd.

"A toast to my husband!"

The room erupted into pandemonium.

Those who had not yet thrown their masks at the dais threw them up into the air, making a rainstorm of fabric and glittering paste jewels. Men overstuffed into hot wigs and tight breeches hurled curses, causing their wives to tug them toward the doors. A few began to throw things at the paintings, or attempt to carry them away, prompting others to pull them back. A tug-of-war erupted over a particularly scandalous portrait of the notorious madam Young Bets, kneeling with a crucifix pressed to her famously shapely lips.

Meanwhile, other guests laughed, threw back champagne, and began to perform merry, shambling dances more befitting of a country assembly hall than a grand ballroom—further enraging those who felt the exhibition was a moral scourge.

It was exactly the scene she'd hoped for.

But she could not enjoy it.

She hopped off the dais, sidestepped a stuffed tiger's head that came careening from near the orchestra, and stepped into a puddle of ratafia that someone had launched at her feet.

And as quickly as she could without appearing to run away, she went marching for the nearest door leading out of the room.

Away from Rafe.

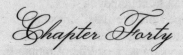

Chapter Forty

Cornelia was leaving.

This should have been her night, and instead of reveling in her accomplishment, she was slipping out a side door.

And it was his fault.

Why had he thought a painting would erase everything she'd told him? Even if the sentiment he'd seen in it was true, *of course* a ballroom was not the place to respond to it. Why hadn't he remembered her horror at the kiss before their friends?

It was his damned ever-melting heart, being grand and destructive. Losing him everything that was precious.

Fuck, he was an idiot.

He prayed that he could fix it.

"Cornelia, darling, may I have a word," he called gaily, to keep up the appearance of marital felicity as he bounded after her.

What he really wanted to do was plead for her to wait. To fall at her feet and apologize before everyone in this room. But he'd obviously sickened her with his first emotional display—God only knew what she would do if he risked a second.

She turned and paused, clearly also wishing to avoid seeming like she was running from him—though they both knew that she was.

Before he could draw closer to be near enough to speak privately, he felt a sharp tap between his shoulder blades.

"Rosemere, what is the meaning of this?" Lord Bell barked, his voice nearly hoarse with anger.

Rafe turned around to find the man snarling with rage.

Bell's lip curled. "Were you planning to humiliate us with this . . . this—" he waved his finger in Cornelia's face "—female *desecration*?"

Rafe snapped his wrist back and wrenched Bell's hand away from Cornelia's nose.

"How *dare* you call my wife a desecration?"

Cornelia stepped out from behind him and put a hand on his arm. "Don't dignify him with your anger, my love," she said pleasantly. "My uncle here flatters his own importance. The point of this exhibition is not to make a fool of you, Lord Bell. The point is to make a statement about what it means to be important in this world. To proclaim the value of those who are not given grand homes and titles. Whose portraits are not painted. Whose lives are forgotten or cast aside as less valuable. And if it scandalizes you, your outrage becomes part of the exhibition itself."

"Precisely," Rafe said, admiring her bravery in the face of the anger of this bully.

Bell looked beyond her, like she hadn't said a word.

"Damn you, Rosemere. You sold me that damned horse and—"

"And you exposed your character in asking me to lie for you to entrap Jack Willow," Rafe interrupted.

Bell paled, glancing around to see if anyone was listening. "I certainly did no such thing."

"We'll see about that at trial. You wanted a witness,

and you've gotten one. Just not the one you expected. Now if you'll excuse us, I need a word with my wife."

"Rosemere, goddamn you, don't you dare walk away," Bell yelled. "You are destroying any chance you have for influence among the people who rule this country."

Rafe glanced over his shoulder. "You forget I am among them now. And I believe you would be best advised not to tell a duke what to do in his own home."

Bell sputtered and the crowd around them tittered as Rafe took Cornelia's arm again.

"Where are you going?" he asked under his breath.

She discreetly pulled her arm out of his grip, smiling through clenched teeth at the guests. "Away from you."

Her distress gnawed at him. He hoped she knew that even if he'd blundered, he hadn't intended to hurt her.

"Cornelia, please. It was an impulse. An ill-considered one, but I—"

She darted through the entry to the service stairs, not bothering to respond. He veered off after her.

Despite his racing heart and growing sense of dread, he was filled with pride in Cornelia's work as he climbed the staircase. Formerly deserted except for maids with downcast eyes scurrying from room to room with heavy buckets of water or trays piled with refreshments, the servants' hidden corridors were teeming tonight with laughing guests inspecting the priceless array of art Cornelia had ordered hung sloppily here and there. Marchionesses from the age of Elizabeth and fourth sons of dukes of generations past commingled on the stone walls, hung as lopsidedly as sheets left out to dry by an indifferent laundress.

"King Crow," someone called out to Rafe, and a

group of guests burst into raucous laughter and began applauding. Rafe wanted to slow down, greet them, and enjoy the admiration in their eyes. He'd spent so long hiding his beliefs, deliberately distancing himself from those who agreed with him, reproduced his columns, built on his ideas. He'd hoped this would be a night of glory, of deliverance. He wanted to restore his friendships and to build alliances and affections with the people whose contempt he'd had to shoulder for so long.

But this—his heart, *Cornelia's heart*—was more important.

He would not give up. Not without apologizing and begging her forgiveness.

He found her in her bedchamber, her armoire open, throwing gowns onto the bed, as if she intended to flee this very instant. He would think it a childish gesture, were it not for the wildness in her eyes.

"Cornelia," he said quietly. "I'm so sorry."

"I'm leaving," she said just as quietly. "As soon as the guests depart."

He sat down on her bed beside the pile of gowns. "Because I said I loved you?"

She threw more on the bed, furious. "Because you made a *spectacle* out of what should be a private matter. You created expectations that I now must honor or deny. It was a public, embarrassing display in front of all my friends, all my acquaintances, all my bloody *enemies*. You know how I feel about these things because we've discussed them over and over. To behave that way means you neither understand nor respect me."

"It was a moment of passion," he said desperately. "Emotion I failed to hold back, when I should have said it privately. I got lost in my own feelings. I promise, you can trust it won't happen again."

She shook her head, looking past him.

It was as if they were back at that inn in Gretna Green, and her face was growing cold and blank once more.

"No, I can't. Because it isn't just about what the public saw. It's about *me*. If you truly cared about me, as you say you do, you would respect my decisions about my life and my own heart. And if you can't respect this one important thing, how can I trust you to honor anything I ask?"

She was right.

He was going to be sick.

He dropped to his knees before her.

"Cornelia, I'm more sorry than I can say. I thought I saw something in the paintings. They made me think you loved me, too. And in my hope—my joy—I . . . I blundered."

She stopped what she was doing and closed her eyes. He gingerly took her hands. She let him. He squeezed them in his own.

"I should not have spoken to you like that in public. But we promised we would tell each other if our feelings became more than a game. And mine have."

She began to cry.

This was not what he expected. Anger, perhaps, or forgiveness. But not tears.

It ate him up.

"Cornelia, what is it?"

"This is too much," she cried, throwing up her hands, panic in her eyes. "You are too much. And you swore to me you wouldn't do this."

He did not know if she meant profess his feelings or

speak them in public, but all he wanted was to give her what she wanted, whatever that might be.

He'd promised.

And this time he needed to uphold his word.

"Darling, tell me you want to end this, and I'll leave this room," he said, trying to keep his voice steady, and failing. "I will not go after you, or try to convince you to stay. You'll never hear from me again except through my solicitor. But if you feel what I feel about us, Cornelia, that we have a chance—even a little bit—forgive me. If you do, I'll ask nothing from you other than for your affection. Your touch. As much or as little as you wish to give."

He kissed the ring he'd given her. "I won't ever ask you to be mine. But I am yours."

Chapter Forty-One

God how she wanted to tell him she'd forgive him.

She wanted to stop this frantic packing, breathe, and soothe his conscience.

She wanted to kiss away the tears that were darkening his lashes.

She wanted to tell him that she loved him, too.

But the fact that she wanted to made it even more urgent that she not.

The part of her that controlled her rapid pulse, the sense of walls closing in around her—was reminded of that night so long ago when he'd ignored everything she'd told him. When he'd destroyed what she thought was a soul-deep connection by asking her for the very last thing she could ever give.

She could not be with a man who thought he knew her better than she knew herself. There were so many things about her life he would never fully understand. The fear she lived with. The sense of being watched, and judged, and threatened when she moved outside the carefully curated spaces she could trust were welcoming and safe. Her freedom was not a thing to take for granted.

This was why she guarded her heart so closely. To care so deeply for another person meant allowing them to sway you against your better judgment. To prioritize their feelings over your own. She did not wish to break Rafe's heart. She'd do almost anything to avoid hurting him.

But she knew that her desire not to hurt him was itself a limit to her independence. And she could never trust him not to ask too much.

"Tell me you don't feel anything for me," Rafe said again, raggedly. "Tell me, and I'll go."

She could not say that. It was too far from the truth.

The truth was that she adored his company. She flourished in his affection. She found few people more amusing. She loved making love to him.

She wanted him more than anything she had ever wanted in her life.

It was against her principles, and her better judgment, and it was utterly true, and it was so terrifying she nearly couldn't speak.

And so she had to end it. The sex. The tenderness. The marriage.

"Rafe, this was a mistake," she said as firmly as she could. "We knew it was a mistake from the moment that we kissed in the summerhouse. And it has only become a greater risk the more that we indulged in it."

He closed his eyes, his head downcast.

"I am going to go back to the party and entertain my guests," she said. "I'm going to ensure that my paintings make the greatest fortune possible. And in the morning, when I have triumphed, I am going to go home."

She expected him to look frustrated, or defiant.

Instead, he just looked broken.

Slowly, he rose to his feet. His knees cracked. For the first time in her recollection, he looked his age.

"That's probably for the best," he said quietly.

For the best?

Damn her if her heart did not shudder at those words. For some reason, she had expected him to fight.

He always fought for her.

But his posture was one of surrender. Defeat.

"You know how I feel about you, Cornelia. But I can't ask you to give up who you are, any more than I can change who I am."

She hated listening to the gravel in his voice as he tried to steady his emotions.

Why did she have the perverse desire to object to what he said? To take him in her arms and soothe him?

"We will remain married until you have inherited," he went on in a low voice. "I will encourage the executor to pay you quickly. And as soon as he does, I will go to Parliament with a bill petitioning for divorce. It's what you wish." He paused and looked at her with a sadness so deep it seemed infinite. "And I want you to have everything you want."

She felt like a bladder that had been pierced with a knitting needle. If she were to paint a self-portrait in this moment, she would depict herself in thousands of minuscule filaments—a swarm of emotions adding up to an inchoate woman.

She wriggled his ring off her finger and wordlessly gave it back to him.

He took it and slipped it in his pocket, his face like stone.

"Thank you," he said, clearing the emotion from his throat with a quiet cough. "Let's go downstairs."

They left the room in silence, walking slowly toward the sounds of raucous voices coming from the ballroom.

The crowd had thinned—no doubt the aristocrats

had left in droves as soon as they realized the nature of the gathering.

Bell, thankfully, was nowhere to be seen.

Those who remained were drinking champagne, dancing in a risqué fashion, and admiring the art.

Rafe murmured a farewell to her and walked off to join Rory, who appeared to be quarreling with two senior Tories in a corner.

She felt alone and cold. His absence felt final.

It made her want to weep.

Seraphina spotted Cornelia and beckoned her to join her near the dais. She walked over gratefully. It was all she could do not to collapse upon her friend in grief and topple them both over.

"Are you all right, love?" Sera asked. "You're moving like you're in a trance."

She was very, very far from all right.

"No," she admitted. "No, I'm not."

Sera's face tightened with concern. "What happened?"

"I'll tell you as soon as we clear out the crowds. Did Bell leave?"

"Yes, but not before screaming at Elinor that she's a whore and vowing to destroy her."

Her poor aunt.

"How is she?"

"She's shaken. I ordered her to go rest in her room, out of sight."

Thaïs galloped up to them, smiling from ear to ear. At least one of them was happy.

"The paintings are all sold," she sang, doing a little jig. "And we have made a mint."

Cornelia sighed with relief. "Then let's conclude the festivities."

The three of them climbed to the top of the dais. Seraphina chimed on a champagne flute with her fork.

"Ladies and gentlemen," she called out, "if you would gather around, we are pleased to announce the winners of the auction."

Cornelia pasted a smile on her face, determined not to show that tonight was one of the worst nights of her life. Thaïs handed her a paper with the list of paintings and the sale prices. The numbers were staggering.

Her smile grew more genuine.

Between the small fortune represented by these figures, and the sum she would inherit, they would have enough to begin construction.

Whatever the chaos and pain of this night, it had been worth it.

"First, for *The Virgin Moll McCann*," Seraphina called out, "we are pleased to congratulate Mr. Arthur Platt."

Moll bowed to the crowd so deeply that her bounteous bosom nearly fell from her low-cut angel costume. The crowd roared.

"Next, for *The Annunciation of Old Jess Fingers* . . ."

Cornelia and Seraphina alternated calling out the winners, until they reached the final painting.

"And lastly, for *The Portrait of a Duchess*—"

"It's not for sale," Rafe called out. "That portrait belongs to me."

The crowd seemed to slow. Guests looked from Rafe to Cornelia, fascinated by the idea that the notorious woman could truly be married to the Duke of Rosemere—the object of such ardent romantic love that he made speeches about her at balls.

He caught her eye, his entire body like a plea.

He wanted this. Despite everything, he wanted

this symbol of their connection. Perhaps because he could see in it the proof of her affection for him. The centrality he held over her heart, however much it scared her.

She reached out, took Seraphina's hand, and squeezed it for strength.

Rafe strode to the dais and stood as large as she had ever seen him, with his hands at his waist and his legs parted authoritatively.

"And it's time," he intoned, "for you all to go home."

Chapter Forty-Two

Usually, in Rafe's limited experience, the morning after a ball was the stuff of pleasant languor. One slept until noon, then lay in bed sipping tea while eating immoderate quantities of greasy food to mop up the previous night's excesses.

This morning was strikingly different.

He woke up at dawn feeling like his chest was filled with glass.

He rose from bed and, with a sickly kind of hope, knocked at Cornelia's door.

When there was no answer, he tentatively opened it.

She wasn't there.

There was no sign of her cat, nor her clothing, nor the sketchbooks she always left scattered about the room.

It was startlingly bare, like the bald pate of a man who'd lost his thick hair overnight.

She was gone. And she hadn't said goodbye.

He took her abandoned wedding band out of his pocket and rubbed his thumb along the inscription. *Yours.*

It was still true. But how do you give yourself to a person who does not want you? How do you endure the pain of holding so much love inside your heart, with nowhere for it to go?

He lay back on her unmade bed, put his head on her pillow, and hugged her blankets like he wished he could hug her.

The sweet, sagy smell of her perfume lingered on her pillow. He inhaled.

Tears he felt like he'd been holding back even in his sleep began, finally, to fall.

He lay in her sheets and cried.

He allowed himself an hour to wallow there. To recollect all the moments between them that had been sweet, and all the chances he'd had to act in such a way that he might not have lost her.

But perhaps he was always destined to lose her. He cared for her too much to pretend he held his heart in reserve. And it was the purest expression of his heart—its impulsiveness, its joy, its passion—that had driven her away.

He rose and lumbered back into his own room, rubbing salt from his eyes. He splashed his face with cold water and shaved away his morning beard. He slapped his cheeks for healthy color and practiced smiling in the mirror.

He'd already embarrassed Cornelia once by being too exultant in his love for her. He'd not do it again by being too open about his sadness that she'd rejected him.

By seven he looked more like himself and had gathered the strength to pretend to be, if not cheerful, solemn rather than devastated. He joined the occupants of the house, who were all assembled in the breakfast room.

The only person missing was Cornelia.

Her friends did not comment on her absence—no doubt knowing exactly what had happened, and wishing to keep the matter private between Cornelia and Rafe.

Clearly, they understood Cornelia's need for personal

discretion better than he did. Clearly, they knew that romantic love, to her, was a kind of betrayal.

Still, they looked at him tenderly, their expressions almost maternal in their gentleness. Their kindness was almost more than he could bear.

Eden cleared his throat. He surely sensed the unspoken emotion in the room, but, a good Englishman to his core, did not acknowledge it.

"Well, that was a memorable evening," he said.

"The best of my life," Anna sighed. She shot a grin at Gilby Howe, whom she had favored with quite a few dances at the ball. Gilby smiled down at his lap.

"We should all be so proud of Cornelia," Seraphina said. "Thanks to her devotion and her vision, we are so much closer to our goal. Her paintings will challenge notions of what a woman can be in this world, and her words will be written about in all the London papers, and help to call attention to the fight for female rights."

"She's a hero, our Miss Lady," Thaïs said with a grin. "Much as it pains me to admit it."

"And a wealthy one," Adam added. "Thanks to the funds she has earned, my firm will be able to begin construction on the Institute in the next few months, as soon as I can secure the labor and materials."

God, she was remarkable.

Rafe stood and raised his cup of coffee. "To Cornelia," he said quietly. "A true duchess."

Everyone jumped to their feet with their own cups in hand. "To Cornelia," they shouted.

He tried to smile, but he couldn't. He bloody wished that she was here to luxuriate in her accomplishment. To bask in her friends' pride. It shamed him to think that he was the reason that she wasn't.

He wondered if her victory would be tinged with sadness. If, like him, she had stayed up all night, tossing and turning, wondering if the scaffold of mistakes between them somehow might have been righted earlier on.

He hoped, for her sake, that she hadn't. He hoped she hadn't given him a second thought.

Perhaps sensing his sadness, Sera cleared her throat. "Now then. Shall we prepare to depart? There's much work to be done in London. We have a trial to win."

Elinor put a hand over her heart. "And I thank each one of you for helping Jack and I prepare to win it. We adore you all with every shred of love we have. We could not ask for better friends."

Seraphina and Thaïs got up and wrapped their arms around her.

The affection among all the women made Rafe's heart ache. He was grateful that Cornelia was blessed to be among them. For he wanted her bathed in love, even if she could not accept his.

"It's been a pleasure to have you here, and I'm enormously grateful to you all," Rafe said. "I'll see you in London." He gave them the biggest smile he could muster—a rather pitiful display—and left the room. He heard footsteps behind him.

"Rafe?"

It was Rory. Rafe stopped and waited for him to catch up. Rory put a hand on his shoulder and gave him a look so sympathetic that it nearly brought Rafe to tears. "You look like you could use some air. Care for company?"

He had not known he'd wanted air or company, but at the suggestion, he craved both. Thank the Lord for

Rory Thompson. He was an absolute bedrock as a friend.

"So she's gone, I noticed," Rory said as they stepped outside into the garden.

"She's furious with me," Rafe said. "She ended our affair."

"And you're devastated."

He exhaled slowly. "I am."

"Poor tenderhearted boy."

Rafe sighed. He and Rory had talked about Rafe's resolution not to fall in love many times since he'd made the promise to himself. Rory alone knew how exhausted he was of feeling broken.

"It's my fault," he sighed, "I broke my own vow. Acted too wildly, too soon. It's what I do."

Rory took his hand and kissed it. "Your affectionate nature is why we all adore you, Rafe—not least of all me."

Rory was kind. But it was Cornelia who deserved the kindness.

"I hurt her. I embarrassed her and made her vulnerable and I didn't even think about it. I'm sick over it."

"Rafe, she knows you acted out of love. Whether or not she comes back to you, she has that. And your love means something."

He hoped so. He hoped that no matter how he'd disappointed her, some part of her was comforted by his devotion.

"And," Rory added, "I have a sneaking suspicion that there is hope. Because I've seen the two of you together—it's like a lightning storm."

That was not necessarily a good thing.

"Lightning catches things on fire and burns them to the ground," Rafe pointed out.

Rory clucked his tongue.

"So grim. What you need is to go to London. Nothing like a trial to distract from a broken heart. Come, let's go inside and get packed for the journey."

Rafe stopped and put his hand on Rory's shoulder.

"Thank you," Rafe said. "You're the best friend I could hope to have."

Rory winked at him. "I really am the greatest. You're a very lucky man."

Chapter Forty-Three

Cornelia sat with her friends in the parlor of Seraphina's London town house, all of them nervously awaiting word of the verdict.

The fortnight-long criminal conversation trial had been a spectacle, drawing a multifarious crowd that treated the proceedings more like a play than a court of law. Rafe's surprise testimony against Lord Bell had caused a sensation in the papers. Journalists had swarmed him as he left the Inns of Court and followed his carriage to his town house, where a crowd awaited, yelling through the windows.

Or so she'd heard.

Despite her anxiety at the futures that hung in the balance of the trial, she'd stayed away.

She did not trust herself around Rafe, feeling as she did: alone rather than free. Adrift rather than empowered. Sad.

If she saw him, she might simply throw herself into his arms and weep.

But today, she had no choice. The verdict was being read, and she needed to be there for Elinor when the news came in—good or bad.

And so they sat idly in the brightly decorated room and waited for Rafe, Rory, and Jack to arrive with news.

And waited.

And waited.

"I shall die from worry," Anna moaned, as the hour chimed from three to four o'clock, and still they had no word. She turned a page in her sketchbook, where she had been drawing Gilby Howe, and began another sketch of Gilby Howe.

Cornelia suspected the entire book was filled with Gilby Howes.

"No," Elinor sighed, in an uncharacteristic show of dramatics. "*I* will die of worry."

"If only we liked sewing," Seraphina said. "Or playing dull chamber music to pass the time. If I read another word my vision will go blurry." Sera had spent the day poring over the morning's newssheets, analyzing the various columns predicting how the case would be decided. She had read them aloud until Elinor pleaded with her to stop narrating the specifics of the nation's opinions.

"I'm happy to perform an erotic dance," Thaïs provided from a sofa in the corner, where she had been intermittently napping for two hours.

"Don't corrupt Anna," Cornelia said.

"I am already corrupted. Did I not spend a week with the four of you? My brother despairs of my future."

"I believe your brother is quite sanguine about your prospects," Sera said. "Surprisingly tolerant fellow, if a bit stiff."

"Stiff indeed," Thaïs said. "In all the right ways."

Cornelia wondered if this was spoken from speculation or experience. She was not in the mood to ask.

Anna pretended to retch. "I beg you not to speak of my brother, Thaïs. I beg you."

Suddenly the door flew open and Jack walked in, grinning from ear to ear. He scanned the room for

Elinor, marched right toward her, picked her up, and twirled her around in his arms.

"We did it, dear girl," he said into her hair. "We bloody did it."

Rafe and Rory stood in the doorway, watching them. Rory looked elated. Rafe looked pleased but tired.

Cornelia hated seeing him look anything other than his usual hale self. It was all she could do not to stand up, fold him in her arms, and kiss away the worry lines around his eyes.

Instead, she remained seated and smiled at them in greeting. Rory gave her a courtly nod, but Rafe glanced down, either out of interest in the floorboards or a desire not to meet her eye.

It stung.

Was this what they had come to? An estrangement so deep they couldn't even share a glance?

Well, she wouldn't force it by addressing him directly. It had been her decision to flee Gardencourt, and him. And no matter her reasons, she knew that it had hurt him deeply.

Poor, sweet man who was foolish enough to love her.

And not just sweet. Brave and intelligent and selfless. A man who'd given up decades of his life to a fight for justice, who'd written powerfully for years in support of the causes closest to her heart. A man who'd done everything in his power to support her mission and her art.

A man who'd saved her life when she'd been at her most vulnerable.

A man who'd loved her, even if he made mistakes.

She forced her attention back on Jack and Elinor. They looked so happy in each other's arms that, paradoxically, it made her sad. It was not a generous emotion, nor one that she was proud of, but their obvious affection teased her with what she might have had with Rafe, if only . . .

If only what?

If you'd given him another chance?

If you'd given yourself one?

The reasons for her fear and anger had begun to feel murky. What she felt now was simple: pain.

Loneliness and pain.

"I'd like to say a sincere thank you to you all," Jack said, gesturing around the room with his free hand. "Without your support and hard work the verdict would undoubtedly have gone in Bell's favor. Now, with his claims of adultery disproven, he will have to find a different avenue to pursue his divorce from Elinor—one that does not vilify her character. It has turned public sentiment in her favor."

Elinor's eyes were filled with tears. "I don't mind ignominy for my own sake," she said. "But without this cloud over me, I'm hopeful it will make it harder for Bell to keep me from my children. The public is watching, and to do so would seem cruel. And Bell *does* care about his reputation."

Elinor had not seen her children since fleeing the asylum Bell had sent her to when she publicly revealed her politics the year before. As their father, he could keep them from her legally until they came of age. There was not a thing Elinor could do except plead for his mercy—and continue to be devastated every time he denied her even an hour's visit.

Bell took little interest in his children, except insofar as their usefulness as a cudgel that could be deployed against his wife.

It was disgusting.

Cornelia went up and hugged her aunt. "I'm so glad, Elinor. I've missed them, too."

Jack stroked Elinor's back. "It's going to be all right, love. We're in this together. We'll find a way for you to see them."

They turned to each other and held each other tight again. Jack wiped the tears from Elinor's eyes and kissed her forehead.

Cornelia could not stop watching them, thinking of the obstacles that they'd conquered. The things they'd had to endure, together and separately.

She suspected Elinor had loved Jack from afar for years before her marriage to Bell ended, and she suspected that love had been returned. But she knew that nothing had ever come of it—that both had lived with their feelings unrequited.

And despite that love, Jack had hidden himself from Elinor for months when he'd sheltered at Rafe's cottage. During that time she had thought he might be dead. He'd "protected" her in a way that robbed her of her own decisions and brought her pain.

He'd made mistakes.

And yet Elinor forgave him.

It was a form of bravery, to love that way.

It made her think about herself and Rafe.

What if she were brave enough to trust him like that?

To take the leap of viewing love as a joy, rather than an obstacle to freedom?

After all, seeing him today did not leave her invulnerable. It left her bereft. Independent, certainly, but unable to live the life she wanted: one with him in it.

She looked up and caught him glancing at her. She held his gaze. He gave her a sad, kind smile and turned his attention back to Jack.

That moment—that kindness—sliced through her.

God, she missed him. It had only been two weeks, but she missed him so much she felt like half of herself.

"Cornelia," Rafe said, "could I have a private word with you?"

She nearly staggered, shocked that he wanted to speak to her alone. Was the emotion of this moment affecting him the same way it was affecting her?

"Of course," she said. "Sera, may we speak in your study?"

Seraphina nodded and Cornelia led Rafe down the hall to a small, book-lined space that was as warm and snug as one of his hugs. He shut the door behind them, but did not move in for one of those massive, enveloping embraces.

Instead, he stood in a corner, as far away from her as the room allowed.

She should not be disappointed, but she was.

"How are you?" she asked him, hoping to draw him out with friendliness. "You must be very tired."

He nodded, looking uncharacteristically weary. "I was afraid it wouldn't be happy news today. I'm relieved."

"So am I," she said. "You've been quite heroic. I'm told you were a sensation as a witness. Convincing. Incisive. Deadly."

He shrugged. "It helps to be telling the truth. An advantage Bell and his minions did not have."

She wanted to ask more questions. Like *do you miss me?* Like *do you have regrets?* Like *would you kiss me?*

But he was distractedly rummaging through a sleeve of papers. He did not *look* like he missed her. He looked like he was performing an errand he could not wait to conclude.

"What is it you wanted to speak to me about?" she asked.

He looked up, a piece of paper in his hand.

"This," he said, handing it to her. "It won't be a long conversation, as you can see."

It was a banknote for five thousand pounds made out to "Cornelia Goodwood, Duchess of Rosemere."

"I was able to prevail on Mr. Hugue to carry out the bequest, now that our marriage is slapped across every paper in the country. It's addressed to your married name, of course. I can help you to draw on the funds when you need them, if you have any trouble."

"Why should I have trouble?" she asked, rubbing the banknote with her thumb.

"Well, after I petition for divorce, I mean."

She looked up sharply. She had never mentioned to him that she was ambivalent about whether to remain a duchess, but she was still surprised at the speed with which he intended to formally end their union.

His decisiveness was only sensible, she supposed. Why should he attenuate it? That she was awash in regrets and indecision did not mean he was.

"Oh, of course, how foolish of me," she said. "When are you going to petition?"

"Rory and I have been working with a solicitor all week. My plan is to submit the bill as soon as Parliament reopens Monday."

She pressed her lips together so she could not frown, and nodded silently.

He was studying his fingernails, which were blunt and short and clean as always. Something about them made her heart lurch. She knew his hands so well. She wanted to know all of him that way.

She'd had her chance to. And she'd declined the opportunity.

Or, more accurately, she'd run away from it.

And she'd lost him.

"Cornelia, you know this will be a spectacle," he said cautiously. "A huge story in the news. If there were anything, *anything* I could do to prevent the circus—"

She was touched by his concern.

"I know," she said quickly. "It's what has to be done. It's not your fault. And I can use it to my advantage. After all, most people cannot end a bad marriage. It's something to fight for."

She meant only that it would require a bill in Parliament to legalize divorce, but he winced at the words *bad marriage*. She felt terrible. She wondered if she should explain herself, but he tapped Sera's desk with his knuckle briskly.

"Well, I should be off. I'm exhausted." He walked to the door and paused. "Be well, Cornelia."

She tried to smile. "And you, Rafe."

As soon as he was gone, she fell back against the door and closed her eyes. She didn't know what else to do.

Minutes passed as she pressed herself against the cool wood, trying to slow her breath before she emerged to face her friends.

The door opened and she stumbled back against a pair of arms.

"Agh!" Thaïs cried, catching her.

"Are you trying to kill me at last?" Cornelia yelped, righting herself.

"I was trying to see if you were still alive," Thaïs parried. "If you were dead, I'd have no one to heckle."

"You'd have me," Sera called cheerfully, joining Thaïs in the corridor along with Elinor.

"We were worried about you," Elinor said. "Is everything all right?"

The three of them all looked at her with expressions of concern.

"Of course," Cornelia said. "Why wouldn't it be?"

"Because you're absolutely miserable," Sera said, not a shred of question in her voice.

"You and Rafe are both clearly beside yourselves," Elinor said. "You barely exchanged a word. Odd, for a man who publicly declared his love for you, and a woman who painted him as though he owned her very heart."

Cornelia threw herself down on a settee. She was being dramatic, but she didn't care. She *felt* dramatic.

"That's just it," she said. "I don't want anyone to possess my heart. Or, at least, I thought I didn't. I was *sure* I didn't."

"We know, darling," Sera said, for her friends were kind and patient, and had listened to her talk about it until even Cornelia was tired of hearing about her principles.

"It's only that for now, losing Rafe hurts," she admitted. "I liked him, you see."

Thaïs gave Elinor an ironical look. "Liked him," she drawled. "Our passionate creature."

Sera took Cornelia's hand. "I know what it's like to be terrified of the consequences of feeling too much. I've spent much of my life running from it, too. But, Cornelia, take it from an unlikely lovestruck fool. It's worth it."

Elinor came and propped herself up on the edge of the settee.

"If I've learned anything from my life, Cornelia, it's this," she said. "Love is a precious gift. A rare and precious gift. I spent years wasting it out of fear, denying how I felt. And I would give anything for those years back. I'd have lived so differently. Because if you are denying what's in your soul, you aren't better off. You have simply imposed limitations on your happiness."

Elinor was right. *She* was the one denying herself what she wanted—not Rafe. Rafe did not have that power unless she granted it to him.

She was in control of her own heart. It was hers to share as she wished. That, as an independent woman, was a choice no law could take away.

"Besides, have you *seen* Rafe?" Thaïs asked. "He is perhaps the most appealing sight in all of southern England. You'd be a fool to waste him."

Cornelia nodded, a sense of certainty flooding over her for the first time in weeks.

"Ladies," she said. "I need to see a jeweler."

Chapter Forty-Four

The Rosemere London town house was sumptuous, cold, and empty. After weeks amidst friends in the warm conviviality they had made of Gardencourt, Rafe had never felt more alone.

Despite the late hour, he was relieved when he heard pounding at the front door.

He dragged himself out of the study to answer it.

"Rafe? Are you decent?"

It was Jack.

"Decent, yes," Rafe sighed, opening the door. "Fit for company, well . . . that's debatable."

Jack walked in, looking rather ragged himself.

"You seemed wrecked when you left Sera's. I thought I'd come after you. Wasn't sure if it had to do with the trial. If so, I'm guilty of weighing on your happiness."

If only the hard work of the trial were responsible for his low mood.

"No," he said quickly. "It was my honor to assist you."

"Then it's Cornelia," Jack said. "I thought so."

Rafe met Jack's eye, surprised. "It's that obvious?"

"You have a habit of staring at her like you're arse-deep in bloody grief."

He snorted at this description. It was only amusing because it was so accurate.

"I hope she hasn't noticed."

Jack shook his head. "She's too busy trying not to cry."

Of course. Because every time she saw him, she was no doubt reminded of how he had ignored her deepest wishes. And of the love he felt, that to her was just a burden.

Rafe slumped deeper in his chair. "Tell me, Jack. How did you do it?"

"Do what?"

"Live without the person you loved for all those years."

Jack walked over to a decanter. "You, sir, need a whiskey."

Rafe accepted the glass but didn't take a sip. He did not want to drown his sorrows. He wanted to bathe in them. Wallowing in the pain of the loss of Cornelia was the only remaining thing that brought him close to her.

"The trick to it is hope," Jack said. "I knew I could not have Elinor. I knew it was dangerous to even consider it. But despite all that, I let myself hope that someday, somehow, there might be circumstances that would allow us to be together."

But allow himself to hope was the one thing he could not do. Cornelia had made her position abundantly clear, and out of respect for her, out of love for her, he had to make peace with the fact that what they'd had was over.

It was done. She had her money, and soon she would have her divorce.

He was resolved. He would give her what she wanted.

But he hated it.

Being married to Cornelia, despite everything, gave him comfort. It was the very last thread between them.

A symbol that they had once had something real, however briefly.

"I can't hope," he said to Jack. "To hope is to torture myself. What I need is solace."

"Then work," Jack said. "Throw yourself back into reforming the estate, writing your essays as King Crow. Work like the devil himself. It's what saved me, whenever I pined for Elinor."

Rafe nodded. He would soon return to Gardencourt. He and Rory were making progress on the list of needed improvements and, with Lord Eden's continued help, beginning to untangle the complex finances that married estate profits with the legal conditions of the entail. It was hard, fascinating work, and gave Rafe much to think about for his column. It was a means of putting to the test the theories he'd written about all these years.

Jack rose. "I won't keep you. But know that I'm here if you need an ear."

Rafe did not need an ear. He needed solitude.

He needed to think.

He said goodbye to Jack, went to bed, and like usual, barely slept.

He spent the next two days alternately holed up in the town house alone, and wandering the streets of London. His meanderings kept leading him back to Cornelia's studio. Twice in two days he stood outside, tempted to walk upstairs and knock at the big wooden door.

Twice, he lost his nerve.

She hated passionate gestures after all. She hated feeling pressured, feeling influenced. The more his instincts guided him back to her, the more he knew he could not follow them.

He couldn't break his word. Not again.

And then, finally, it was Monday.

He had not slept all night. He'd lain awake rehearsing in his mind what he would say in Parliament as he introduced his bill petitioning for the dissolution of his marriage. He wanted to declare he was at fault, but it was, legally, impossible to end a marriage without assigning female blame. He'd settled on accusing Cornelia of abandonment. He suspected she would welcome the charge—scandal, after all, was her lifeblood. Still, he intended to make clear that he deserved to be left, having betrayed her trust.

He finished writing his remarks, donned his robes and wig, and climbed into the fine Rosemere carriage bound for Westminster.

He'd never before sat in a Parliamentary session. The pomp of the chamber and the wigged, red-robed Lords who eyed him as he found his seat would have been amusing, were he not so depressed. He sat down beside Lord Eden, surrounded by a group of allies who Rafe had been assured would vote in favor of his bill. Eden gave him a tight, sympathetic smile—the closest the man came to acknowledging emotion.

"Welcome," he said. "Your petition will be heard after the first debate."

Rafe nodded. He didn't wish to speak, knowing his voice would come out hoarse.

He waited as the roll was called, the formalities of opening the session endured, the first debate conducted, until finally, hours later, it was his turn to introduce his petition.

A clerk read out the title of the proposed bill.

At the word *divorce*, the room went loud with murmurs. Hundreds of eyes locked on him—fascinated by what he was about to say.

Rafe stood. "My lords," he began. "I'm afraid I come to you today with deep regrets. Regrets that concern my marriage, and for which I am fully at fault."

"No," a voice called out from the back of the room. "I am."

He froze.

Even at a distance he recognized Cornelia's low, cultivated tones.

"Is that a *woman*?" someone asked, taking in her small, feminine form. She'd entered the building disguised as a male servant in breeches and a stiff livery coat.

"Eject her from these chambers at once," came another voice.

"I must speak to the duke," she said loudly, walking around a bailiff toward the center of the room where Rafe was standing. "I have an objection to this petition."

His heart began to beat so fast it felt like the flutter of a hummingbird. He walked through the sea of robe-clad aristocrats to get to her, ignoring their objections.

As soon as he was near enough to touch her, she grasped his hand and held on tight.

He looked down at it in wonder.

"I've made a profound mistake, Rafe," she said softly. "Profound."

His lungs flipped over in his chest. Could it be—

"Tell me your mistake," he said. "I'm sure it's nothing that can't be corrected."

She simply wrapped her arms around him and began to cry.

"There there, dove," he said, stroking her back. "Now, what's the problem, and how can I help?"

"I'm looking for a husband," she said. "And I hope you might be him."

He couldn't breathe. The way she was looking at him was so full of tenderness and affection. Emotions he had longed to receive from her, and to give to her in return.

And in *public*.

She was proclaiming her heart in front of the entire House of Lords.

"You're the only man I've ever been in love with," she whispered. "Twice."

Chapter Forty-Five

Every eye in the room was on them, and Cornelia didn't bloody care. All she cared about was Rafe's hand stroking her back. Rafe's jaw quivering with emotion.

Rafe. The love of her life.

"I'm sorry," she murmured in his ear. "I hope I haven't embarrassed you. I just want everyone to know how much I love you."

"I want to kiss you," he said raggedly. "Would you permit it if—"

She reached up, took him in her arms, and in front of the whole gaping room, put her lips to his.

And oh God, his mouth. Damn the eyes and damn the whispers. Sometimes being a spectacle was just what a girl needed.

Rafe put his hands—those enormous, strong hands—on her shoulders and pulled her closer, so close that they might have been one body were it not for the garments between them.

Her face flamed with the explosion of warmth she felt whenever Rafe was near. There was no place she'd rather be than here, in the House of Bloody Lords, with this man squeezing her like he'd never let her go again.

She coughed. "Rafe, I can't breathe."

He eased his grip, beaming at her. "Come," he said, taking her hand. "Let's speak in private."

They ran together through the sea of shouting Lords and out the chamber doors to a dark, wood-lined warren of ancient alcoves, until they found a private room.

Rafe shut the door behind them and moved in for another kiss. The faint stubble around his mouth burned into her skin and she welcomed it, dragged her lips over his to feel it chafe her cheeks. She wanted to be marked by him.

She wanted to kiss him with her whole body, her whole soul.

She wanted this kiss to last forever. She wanted *him* forever. She wanted—

Cornelia!

If she didn't stop soon, they'd be rutting on the floor and she could not lose herself to lust just yet.

There was too much she needed to say.

She tore her mouth away from Rafe's. They stood a few inches away from each other, eyes locked, panting.

"Rafe," she whispered in a trembling voice that possessed not a shred of the famed Cornelia Ludgate equanimity. "I'm so bloody sorry. I've been so unfair to you. Unfair to *us*."

He stroked her arm, soothing her. But he looked baffled by her words. "What could you possibly be sorry for, sweet girl?"

Was he so sweet he couldn't even blame her for the pain she'd caused him?

"For leaving like I did."

"Because I embarrassed you," he said flatly. "And I demanded something from you I knew you might not wish to give. I—"

She shook her head. "The truth is I was terrified because I felt the same way you did. I was terrified that if I let myself give in to it, I would lose my independence as a woman—as a being. Because love makes you vulnerable to other people's needs."

Her voice shook in a way she would have despised a month ago.

She didn't care.

Rafe looked at her gravely. "Love *does* make us vulnerable, Cornelia. I can't deny that. I would do anything for you, but I can't change it."

She took his face between her hands and gently stroked his cheeks.

"I don't expect you to. I don't *want* you to. Because loving you—accepting your love in return—is what I choose to give myself. I can make that choice freely. I can be brave enough to accept what makes me vulnerable in exchange for what brings me joy. And that, my love, is you."

His eyes went so soft she wanted to kiss his lashes.

"But how can you be sure when I've blundered at every turn?" he asked quietly. "For decades."

Oh, her sweet Rafe. He might have made mistakes. But he'd also been honest and gotten hurt for it.

"I've made mistakes, too," she said. "I've run away instead of confronting how I feel. Telling you—" Her voice broke. "Telling you how scared I am."

He closed his eyes. And then he wrapped his arms around her silently and simply murmured, "It's all right. I'll always be here."

He was so kind to simply forgive her. But she wanted him to know how deeply she admired the bravery of his emotions.

She pulled back and looked into his beautiful blue eyes. "I'm so grateful that you've been courageous enough to tell me how you feel. Because, Rafe, as much as you might act rashly, I am overcautious. And sometimes I need a little push from a man with a huge heart." She paused and gave him a rueful smile. "In private."

He looked at her like she was a fairy tale he wanted to believe in. "Are you saying you want to be together?"

"Yes. But—" She inhaled deeply, collecting her thoughts. This was important, and she needed to say it as clearly and earnestly as possible.

"But?" he prompted gently.

"But I would ask that we both think carefully about what it means to be together, and how we will live."

He gestured at a pair of chairs in front of the mullioned windows. "Let's sit down and talk."

She sank into the thick upholstery, grateful for the support of its plush steadiness. Trust the House of Lords to have well-made chairs.

Rafe took her hand. "Now tell me, Cornelia Ludgate. How do you want to live?"

She squeezed his hand. "I want us both to listen to each other—*really* listen," she began. "There are things about me—being Black, being a woman, being both—that you will never understand. So I need you to trust me when I tell you my experience. I must have your word that when I ask for what I need and what I want, you will honor my wishes. And I promise I will extend the same sensitivity to you."

He reached out and took her other hand. "I'm sorry, love," he said. "I've been an arse, and I can't say how much I regret it. But I give you my word I have learned from my loss of you. Your wishes will be the law of my heart."

She believed him. She believed in his intentions. She believed in his love for her and his desire to support her.

And it was enough.

But he went on.

"And there's something I must apologize for. I never should have asked you not to go to Florence. When I think of it, it makes me ill."

She laughed a bit, for it was so long ago, but she was relieved he'd said it. That he understood how he had hurt her.

"I agree—that was painful for me," she admitted. "But I forgive you. Because I know that you live in your heart, Rafe. And I love that about you."

He bent down and kissed her lips. For a moment, they were lost to it. But he pulled away.

"I also have a request, while we're discussing our future."

"Of course." She was pleased he was reflective— looking after his own needs the way she looked after hers.

"I would ask that if you ever have the impulse to run away—be it from a conversation or a house— you *tell* me first. We can talk about if you're scared. Please trust me that even if I seem exuberant, I would never, ever wish to ask you for more than you can give me."

She recognized this flaw in herself. And she was determined to outgrow it. For him, and for her. Because when you ran away from what you wanted, you had to live without it.

And she did not want to live without Rafe ever again.

"I know that now," she said. "I know it. And I

promise you, I'll talk to you if I'm uncomfortable. I'll trust you."

He grinned. "Is there anything else, before I ravish you?"

"There's one more thing. And it's important to me. But I'm not sure how you'll feel about it."

He looked into her eyes. "You can ask me anything."

"You gave me that lovely wedding ring," she said slowly, wanting to be delicate with his feelings. "And the sentiment was so pure and sweet. But I don't want you to think of yourself as mine. Or to see me as yours. I don't want us to possess each other. I want us to stay free."

He inclined his head, brow furrowed. "What do you mean?" he asked.

"I love you so much. But I don't want to move to Gardencourt, or force you to spend all your time in London. I want the ability to, say, run off to Florence, or for you to take a lover, as long as we discuss it first. I want us both to have the independence to be who we truly are, so long as we do it together."

He looked stunned. She braced herself. She could understand if what she proposed was a disappointment to him.

"Well, well, Miss Ludgate," he said slowly, his expression transforming from bemused to intrigued. "You *want* me to take other lovers?"

She laughed at the gleam dawning in his eyes. "Especially if I can watch."

"Oh, that can be arranged, my wicked girl."

They both grinned at the idea of it.

"I want both of us to have the option to be with other people," she said more seriously. "Together or separately, so long as we are honest and don't hurt each other."

He nodded solemnly. "That sounds like an arrangement I can live with. Especially if we share."

The idea of another ménage made her feel a little weak at the knees. "We will definitely share."

He laughed, but his face turned serious.

"Lovers aside, I want to make *certain* you know that you have independence. Would you like me to continue with my petition for divorce, so that you can have peace of mind? You will finally have your legal freedom."

She had already considered this question. She suspected her answer might surprise him.

"But, Rafe," she said with a wink, "if we divorce, I will no longer be a duchess."

He looked at her oddly. "You *want* to be a duchess?"

"Not *that* kind of duchess," she laughed. "*Our* kind of duchess."

"You're certain?" he asked.

She nodded. "When I saw my portrait in the ballroom at Gardencourt, I realized the power of it. Just imagine. A duchess has always been a symbol of exclusion. Of the power of the privileged over the masses. The importance of female respectability and purity. The symbol changes radically if *I* can be a duchess. In a way—" she took his hand "—it's as meaningful an artistic statement as I can make."

She put her hand in her pocket and fished out the parcel she'd collected that morning. From it she shook out two gold rings—simple wedding bands, like the one he'd given to her.

She held them out to him. "They're engraved," she said.

He took them and read the word that was inscribed on both of them. *"Us."*

She stood up, pulled him from his chair, and wrapped her arms around him. "One final marriage of convenience, darling?"

He took the smaller of the rings, grabbed her hand, and slipped it around her finger.

"It would be the honor of my life."

Chapter Forty-Six

Rafe went back into the Lords alone. Lord Andover was giving a speech on budgets, but he stopped abruptly when Rafe walked into the room.

"Are you quite done disturbing the proceedings, or do you have another scene to make?" Andover asked.

"One last scene, I'm afraid," Rafe said. He knew that the Lords did not accept him, being a commoner and a radical. He also knew that, given that he was a duke, they had no choice but to hear him out.

He felt a touch smug about it.

"My lords, I shall withdraw the petition I submitted," he said. "It seems my wife has not abandoned me after all. Now if you'll excuse me, that concludes my business for today."

With that, he turned on his heel and went out to the corridor where Cornelia was waiting.

He opened his arms to her, and she burrowed into them.

"I want to be alone with you immediately," he said.

"Let's go to my studio. I've had enough pomp for one day."

They went on foot, clutching hands. It was a beautiful, breezy, sunny day.

The walk, while less than an hour's time, seemed to last for half a day, for all Rafe wanted to do was kiss

Cornelia. And kiss her he did. In a mews tucked behind a building. In a leafy square under the shade of a tree. In front of a milliner's shop, with people dodging all around them. In the stairwell of Cornelia's studio, while pulling off their clothes.

"Come here," Rafe said, reaching for his half-dressed wife. He lifted her over his shoulder and carried her up the flight of stairs to her room.

He'd never been inside her apartment. It was small and pretty and full of light. The sketchbooks she left scattered everywhere were in piles all around. Lucius was sitting in a chair in a shaft of sunlight, his paws stretched out luxuriously in front of him.

"Look," Cornelia said to the cat. "It's your new father."

The cat licked one paw, jumped down, and strolled under the bed.

"I don't think he likes me," Rafe said.

"Don't worry. He doesn't like anyone until he gets to know them."

"I am hopeful he will get to know me very well."

"Oh, he will," Cornelia said. "He has no choice. I am quite attached to you. Come."

She took Rafe's hand and pulled him toward her bed. A sketchbook was lying on top of it. She began to clear it away, but he stopped her when he saw the picture on the open page.

It was him. She'd drawn him at the ball, on the dais, making his speech to her. In the drawing, she was standing beside him, holding his hand, and smiling at him.

"You revised history," he commented.

"If I could do it again, I would tell the world I love you, too."

She smiled at him apologetically. But he wasn't looking for apologies.

"You don't need to tell anyone but me."

He took her in his arms and they leaned back against the headboard.

The remainder of their clothes came off so quickly it was nearly impossible to tell who undressed who.

They were quick, but passionate.

"I love you, I love you, I love you," Cornelia gasped as she came.

It made him happier than he'd been in years.

"I love you, I love you, I love you," he murmured back.

They were quick but passionate again.

And once more for good measure.

When they were exhausted in each other's arms, sweating on damp sheets, Rafe scooped her up and put her on top of him.

"Have I mentioned I've been in love with you for twenty years?" he asked, idly stroking her back.

"Have I mentioned there is no person on earth I have ever felt this way about except for you?" she replied. She nestled into his arms. "I missed you so much these last weeks I could scarcely get out of bed. I cried so hard I scared Lucius."

"We can't have that."

"I know. His emotions are important. If you love me, you must love my cat."

He nodded gravely. "I do. Passionately. Perhaps more than I love you."

She laughed, and then got up.

"I need to draw us."

He watched as she gathered a pencil and one of her sketchbooks and became absorbed in her work.

A tendril of her hair fell from her loose chignon into her eyes. He loved how she transformed when she was making art. It was as though she bonded with her work, becoming a single organism with the pencil and the page.

"Here," she said when she was done.

He took the paper.

It was the two of them, nude, their legs entwined. Each of them had an arm flung out to the side. And each was grasping the hand of some other person, off the page.

"It's beautiful," he said, rubbing a finger over it.

"Let's make it true," she said.

He was hard again at the idea of a foursome.

He gripped her hand and kissed her cheek. "To us," he said.

She leaned in and whispered in his ear: "To us."

Epilogue

It was a crisp fall day in London, and the air smelled like wet earth. Cornelia enjoyed the feeling of mud beneath her mucky boots as she walked hand in hand with Rafe to the front of the construction site.

Today was the groundbreaking for the Institute for the Equality of Women.

It was also a reunion of sorts. Seraphina and Thaïs were huddled with Cornelia, looking over the plans. Rafe was deep in conversation with Rory, Lord Eden, and Mark Swanson, Adam's foreman, whom Rory had recently taken as his lover. Anna and Gilby Howe, newly engaged, were looking with excitement at the workers assembled with Adam under a canopy filled with tools. And Canette and Singh—also newly engaged—were chatting with Elinor, Jack, and Marianne, who held baby Ella.

It felt like a family back together for a holiday.

Adam approached with Mark Swanson, who was holding a large stake and an even larger mallet. He jammed the stake into the grass.

"Who would like to do the honors?" Adam asked, gesturing at the mallet.

"Cornelia should," Seraphina said. "She is, after all, paying for it."

Adam held the mallet out to Cornelia.

She looked at it skeptically. She had never held an instrument of such brute force.

"I'm not sure I am up to the task," she said with a laugh. "It looks quite heavy."

"There is nothing you can't do if you put your mind to it," Rafe said. "I should know."

She went up and accepted the tool, which weighed nearly as much as she did.

She began to gather the strength to lift it up when Thaïs cleared her throat. "Ahem, lady madam. Speech!"

Cornelia smiled. Talk she could do.

"Thank you all for gathering here today—especially to Canette and Singh for making the trip from Gardencourt."

The two of them were leading the effort to make the manor a space for the entire community. The downstairs parlors had been converted to schoolrooms for the tenants' children, the kitchens turned over to local bakers and cooks to use for their businesses, the gardens opened up as a public park, and the ballroom put to use as an events hall. While the space was quickly filled with country dances and local charity auctions, the most sought-after use was for weddings.

Anna and Gilby planned to use it for theirs in two months' time.

"I'm so beyond overjoyed to break ground on the Institute for the Equality of Women," Cornelia continued. "While there is much work to be done, and still more money to be raised, this is the next step in achieving the goal we all have worked so hard for."

"Hear! Hear!" everyone yelled.

She strained to lift the mallet up over her shoulder. "With that, I shall try to wrangle this enormous thing."

"You'd think she'd be used to enormous things from wrangling Rafe," Thaïs said.

They all groaned.

Using all her strength, she brought the mallet down on the stake and drove it deep into the ground.

Everyone cheered.

Rafe came up and lifted her into the air. "And another round of applause, please, for my wife, for her skill, vision, and bravery in securing the funding for this momentous day."

Cornelia grabbed Rafe's head and brought it down for a kiss.

"Look at her, displaying affection in public," Seraphina said.

"Imagine what she does in private," Thaïs said.

Everyone groaned again.

Rafe set her down.

"It is true, I have done my duty with aplomb," Cornelia said. "But our work is not yet finished. We will still need several thousand pounds to complete the project. And now it is Thaïs's turn to raise the money."

Thaïs ran her hands up and down her body.

"That won't be a problem. Any man would pay that for a month with me."

Marianne and Eden both went pale.

"You don't mean . . ." Marianne said.

"Is that, er, do you mean to say . . ." Eden said at the same time.

"Yes, indeed. I'm going to auction myself off to the highest bidder. The winner will get me as their mistress for one month."

This would be the first time Thaïs would sell herself to any man for longer than one night, for she was famously discriminating in her favors.

Lord Eden blushed so red he looked like he might suddenly perish of fever. Marianne merely shook her head and laughed.

Cornelia and Sera wrapped their arms around Thaïs's shoulders.

"Ah, our beloved harlot," Cornelia said.

Sera raised up a fist. "May she fornicate her way along the path toward justice."

The three of them laughed together and turned toward the patch of land their work had purchased. "To the power of sirens," Sera said.

"And the power of these hips," Thaïs said, wiggling between the two of them.

EXCERPT FROM THE
CATALOGUE RAISONNÉ
OF CORNELIA LUDGATE

WORK 4092:
THE HARLOT
Ink on paper
1797

Description: A curvaceous, freckled white woman lies flat on a bed of roses, her nudity shrouded only by curly red hair falling to her thighs. A banner ripples over her, reading "A Month with the Notorious Miss Magdalene."

Commentary: The work depicts the courtesan-for-hire Thaïs Magdalene, a dear friend of the artist and frequent subject of her portraiture. It served as the basis for a woodblock poster advertising Magdalene's efforts to raise money for The Institute for Equality of Women by auctioning a month of her services as a mistress to the highest bidder.

This poster, and the series that followed, were quickly reproduced around England, building a frenzy of interest in the auction—and the past of the woman at the center of it.

Acknowledgments

Thank you to Nicole Fischer for your incredible care and patience in editing this book. Thank you to Sarah Younger for your timely infusion of romance to the manuscript. Thank you to Peter Sentfleben, Dee Hudson, Jon Reyes, Johanie Martinez-Cools, and Tricia Tobias for your candid and insightful sensitivity reads. Thank you to the Rebelles for being the support system that every writer dreams of—couldn't slog without you. Thank you to my husband and cat for dealing with me when I'm trying to write.

And thank you to my readers—sorry it took so long, you guys!

*D*on't miss the stunning conclusion to
the **SOCIETY OF SIRENS** series . . .

**THAÏS'S STORY IS COMING
IN 2024!**